Resurrecting Langston Blue

Other books by Robert Greer

The Devil's Hatband

The Devil's Red Nickel

The Devil's Backbone

Limited Time

Isolation and Other Stories

Heat Shock

The Fourth Perspective

The Mongoose Deception

Resurrecting Langston Blue

Robert Greer

Frog, Ltd.
Berkeley, California

Published by Frog, Ltd.
Frog, Ltd. books are distributed
by North Atlantic Books
P.O. Box 12327
Berkeley, California 94712

Cover design by Brad Greene
Printed in the United States of America

North Atlantic Books' publications are available through most bookstores. For further information, call 800-337-2665 or visit our website at www.northatlanticbooks.com.

Substantial discounts on bulk quantities are available to corporations, professional associations, and other organizations. For details and discount information, contact our special sales department.

Library of Congress Cataloging-in-Publication Data
Greer, Robert O.
    Resurrecting Langston Blue / by Robert Greer.
        p. cm.
    Summary: "A political thriller featuring streetwise, Denver-based bail bondsman CJ Floyd, a host of other engaging and intriguing characters, non-stop action, and fast-paced dialogue"—Provided by publisher.
    ISBN-13: 978-1-58394-182-9
    ISBN-10: 1-58394-182-7
    1. Floyd, C. J. (Fictitious character)—Fiction. 2. Vietnam War, 1961-1975—Veterans—Fiction. 3. African American men—Fiction. 4. Bail bond agents—Fiction. 5. Missing persons—Fiction. 6. Denver (Colo.)—Fiction. 7. Political fiction. I. Title.
    PS3557.R3997R47 2007
    813'.54—dc22
                                                    2007009593
                                                    CIP
        2 3 4 5 6 7 8 9 DATA 11 10 09 08 07

Dedication

For who else but God's sweet angel,
my darling Phyllis

Acknowledgments

No novel finds life without support from a host of individuals other than the author, and *Resurrecting Langston Blue* is no exception. I would like to thank Tom Vandermee, a cop's cop, for his insights into police procedure. Any errors in depicting procedural matters accurately are clearly the author's. Likewise, I owe a debt of gratitude to Judge John Kane for offering legal instruction and a view from the bench. Thanks to John Dunning for his keen newspaperman's eye and a newshound's historical perspective. To Edward Greer, U.S. Army, Major General, Retired, I offer a nephew's thanks for details about U.S. Army protocol, and of course, Vietnam.

As always, I thank Connie Oehring for her astute professional copy editor's eye and I am grateful to my secretary of eighteen years, Kathleen Hoernig. No one else could possibly deal with a literary throwback who still believes that novels are to be written long hand, or have the skill and patience to decipher my writing.

Finally, I would like to thank my publisher, North Atlantic Books, who gives life to my imagination.

Author's Note

The characters, events, and places that are depicted in *Resurrecting Langston Blue* are spawned from the author's imagination. Certain Denver and western locales are used fictitiously, and any resemblance between the novel's fictional inhabitants and actual persons living or dead is purely coincidental.

"If it's love that you're running from,
there's no hiding place . . ."

—*The Temptations*

Chapter

1

THE MAN WALKED WITH A HESITANT, changing-gears kind of limp that mirrored more than twenty years of painful osteoarthritis. Flipping up his collar to ward off the wind and chilling 38-degree West Virginia coal-country mist, he slowly paced the final half mile of the more than two-mile trek to his cabin. It would be warm there, and safe, and above all familiar. His bed with the sagging thirty-year-old mattress. The potbellied stove. The well-worn Navajo rugs—even the creaky heart-pine floors and the smoky, dull gray, coal-dust-laden windows. The cabin had been his safety net for thirty-four years, tucked invisibly into the side of a West Virginia mountain, yards away from a petered-out coal mine.

He had walked the path that snaked its way up to his cabin more times than he cared to count. Over the years he had jogged, run, trotted, and even skipped his way home, until now, after half a lifetime, he knew the outline of every blackberry and gooseberry bush, every tree and rock, every hump in the earth that lined the narrow trail. It was almost as if they were well-placed stage props, there to add stability to his life.

Slowing his pace, he scooped a handful of gooseberries from a convenient bush, popped several of them into his mouth, and crunched down, marveling at their eye-watering tartness. He noticed a fresh half-dollar-sized impression in the dirt at the trail's edge and dropped the remaining berries onto the trail as he knelt to examine it. Chalking the imprint up to the partial hoofprint of a deer, he rose and continued walking, rolling the bitter skin of the gooseberries around in his mouth. When he spotted a second small imprint in the dirt, he stopped abruptly, realizing with sudden urgency that the two perfectly curved notches in the soil were far too close together to be the tracks of a deer and too deeply stamped into the moist loam to be the imprint left by a darting animal.

Painfully taking a knee again, he studied the second imprint, examining it closely for more than a minute before realizing that a third and then a fourth imprint dropped off the trail, disappearing into the thick grass at the margin. Rising slowly, the man forced back a cough as he methodically eyed the surrounding terrain. His cabin was fifty yards uphill and a slight dogleg to the west. Behind the cabin, Rosebush Mountain jutted up four thousand feet into the foggy, cloud-covered West Virginia sky. Attentive now to the familiar sounds of the backwoods, he froze and listened to the rustling of sycamores in the brisk northwesterly wind, the intermittent cawing of the pesky birds he knew as camp robbers, and the rush of Willow Buck Creek gaining speed as it charged downhill through a rocky mountain corridor in the distance. All seemed perfectly normal. Even so, there was something unusual about the sounds enveloping him—

something strange and unnerving. Something he couldn't quite put his finger on. A sound—no, perhaps it was a smell, or a tiny mutation in the sunlight as it faded for the day. There was something! For a moment he had the uneasy feeling that finally, after thirty-four years of self-imposed isolation, he might actually be going stir-crazy. Maybe the two-week-long high-country rains had finally thrown everything in his head completely out of kilter.

Perhaps he'd been thinking too much about the letter he had received the day the rains began. It had come in an oversized business envelope with a barely legible Denver postmark and return address and a two-inch-wide masking-tape seal. Now, three weeks shy of his fifty-eighth birthday, he was sensing and seeing things that shouldn't be in his woods. Maybe it was time for a meltdown. Maybe the letter stuffed securely in his shirt pocket was meant to keep him confused.

From the depths of the woodsy quietness he heard a chirp, then another and another, and finally the muted rustle of something in the dead wet leaves fifty yards ahead. The sounds were both disturbing and familiar, the trademark warning chirps of squirrels and chipmunks as they scurried from danger for holes in the dirt and hollows in the trees. Perhaps they were attempting to avoid a fox or a badger on the prowl. It didn't much matter—something ahead had the army of animals that served as his warning beacon clearly agitated.

Now, as intent on avoiding danger as he'd been during his days as a platoon leader during the Vietnam War, Langston Blue decided to circle his cabin's perimeter. He had no reason to suspect anything was seriously wrong, but after years of hiding he'd learned to play it smart as well as safe. His thoughts returned to the letter in his shirt pocket as he started working his way around the cabin. He had stepped close to twenty yards away from the trail when he heard what sounded like a snapping twig and then a lengthy, vacuum-like *whoosh*. Seconds later his cabin imploded before erupting into a ball of flames.

During his two tours in Vietnam he'd watched jungle shacks, thatched huts, and even substantial buildings go up the same way, the air sucked out of them by a well-placed incendiary device before fire exploded inside their bellies. But this time things were different; now he was the outsider looking in, like the ghost of a Vietnamese peasant watching his life erode before his eyes.

As the flames danced up to lick the sky, he dropped and hugged the ground spread-eagle, trying to breathe. Shivering as the musty smell of the damp West Virginia soil crept up his nostrils, he listened to the crackling of the fire.

Fifteen minutes later, still kissing the earth, breathing cautiously, and hoping that whoever had torched his cabin was gone, Langston Blue crawled back to the spot where he'd first spotted the strange imprints in the soil. Patting the ground, he fingered the edges of one shallow depression and cursed himself for missing a telltale clue. In hindsight, he recognized the notch for what it was: the imprint of the rubber tip guard of a cane. "Cortez," he mouthed in a whisper. "Son of a bitch." The words came out in a stream of spittle.

Rising to a crouch, he painfully duck-walked his way back

into the woods before finally slumping against a fallen branch. The aromatic smell of burning oak and cherry wood permeated the woods, punctuating the fact that after so many years of dodging it, the truth had finally caught up with him. Sighing and leaning back against the fallen limb, he slipped the letter he'd been carrying around out of his shirt pocket and began rereading it for what he suspected was the hundredth time. He fumbled with the dog-eared sheet of paper, inhaling the pungent charcoal smell of what was now left of his life as his eyes slowly adjusted to the letter's bold black handwriting.

The paper suddenly felt moist and heavy in his hands. He understood how Cortez had finally been able to find him. After all, tracking, searching, and destroying the enemy had once been Cortez's principal job. But he couldn't fathom how the letter writer had also been able to track him down. Reading slowly, he followed each perfectly aligned sentence to the bottom of the page until his finger came to a painful arthritic halt just below a boldly scripted closing: *Love, Your Daughter, Carmen Nguyen.*

Chapter 2

THERE WAS NO WAY OUT of the blind Denver alley, CJ Floyd told himself as he choked in an effort to block the smell from the mounds of garbage filling the dumpster that shielded him from the calculating approach of Newab Sha. Sha, a bond-skipping Haitian and a wife and child beater whom CJ had been chasing for over a week, caught a whiff of the garbage, smiled, clucked his tongue, and continued slowly closing in on the four-foot-high dumpster.

CJ gulped a quick breath of air, wondering as he strained to remain still how he'd ever been stupid enough to leave Mavis Sundee's house barefoot, without his gun, in hot pursuit of a masochistic Haitian with four diamond-studded, gold-jacketed front teeth and a head the size of a watermelon. Maybe his un-characteristically juvenile response had been a protective offer-ing to Mavis, the one sweet drop of feminine softness in his otherwise hard-edged life, served up to let her know that he still harbored an inner toughness.

Twenty minutes earlier, Sha had riddled Mavis's house with a barrage from a semiautomatic just as CJ and Flora Jean Benson, CJ's street-smart bail-bonding partner, had arrived at the front door for dinner. Sha had then sent a Molotov cocktail crashing onto Mavis's porch, catching CJ, as Flora Jean liked to say, with his drawers on the floor.

After beating back flames with a couple of cushions from a lounge chair and kicking off the thongs he'd been wearing in preparation for washing Mavis's car, CJ had taken off after Sha. He had chased Sha for more than three blocks through the alleys of Mavis's Curtis Park neighborhood without seeing a soul. The chase had then wound through the very heart of Denver's once jazz-rich, predominantly black Five Points community without so much as causing a head to turn. Most of the people were gone, hostages to the Fourth of July holiday, scores of free baseball tickets, and the promise of free food and postgame fireworks at Denver's Coors Field.

Now, as he crouched barefoot and winded, hugging the back side of the foul-smelling dumpster and looking for an escape, CJ could only kick himself for taking Sha's now very obvious bait.

"Bail bondmon, I gonna cut your nuts. Feed 'em to the dogs! Ha!" Sha's words reverberated off the dumpster's shell. "Den gon' go back and hump that girl a yours—squeeze her tits till she scream to da sky. Gon' split her wide open from hip to hip. But what da you care, bail bondmon? You gon' be dead."

CJ swallowed hard and clenched his teeth, aware that Sha's singsong mockery was meant to tease him out of hiding. Scanning the alley, he searched in vain for a rock, a broken bottle, a stick—anything to serve as a weapon.

"Come on out, bail bondmon. Got somethin' for ya, my

friend. Gon' skin ya like a rabbit. Gon' tan your hide. Whoop, whoop, whoop."

CJ glanced behind him toward the crumbling three-story-high brick wall of a former creamery that blocked his escape. He nervously eyed the two body lengths of space between the wall and the dumpster as he ran his hand along the dumpster's rusted frame, feeling for a protective fragment of loose metal to use as a knife. Nothing. The only possible weapon was a porous, baseball-sized rock that felt like a lump of Silly Putty in his right hand.

"Gon' skin ya and leave ya for the dogs! Ha! Den gon' kill your woman, ha!" Sha sucked a loud stream of air between his front teeth, so close now that CJ could hear his labored breathing. Clutching the rock tightly as he peered around the back corner of the dumpster and telling himself his aim had better be major-league perfect, CJ rose from his crouch to find that Sha was now less than five feet away.

"I know where you at, bail bondmon. Gon' skin ya, den toss you in da dumpster wit' da rest of da trash. Ha!"

CJ duck-walked his way along the back of the dumpster, inching toward the creamery wall.

"You gotta come outta one side a dat dumpster, bail bond-mon. De left or de right. Gotta pop out one way or da other, like a baby or a turd. Ha!"

Homing in on the sound of Sha's voice, CJ rose until he could see over the lip of the dumpster. He eyed the side of Sha's half-turned head, prepared to throw a temple-crushing strike.

"Ha!" screamed Sha, hearing the rustle of clothing as CJ's

arm shot forward. Grinning, he peppered the dumpster with bullets as the rock careened off his neck, then screamed, "Gon' kill ya now, gon' snip off your nuts!" as he raced toward CJ.

CJ suddenly thought about his days as a nineteen-year-old machine gunner on a navy riverboat during the final turbulent days of the Vietnam War. As he dove toward Sha, one arm draped protectively over his head, the unmistakable sound of a 30.06 rang out, and a hollow-point bullet dropped Sha like a 250-pound sack of sand just as CJ slammed into him.

Anticipating more shots as he rose from Sha's lifeless body in confusion, CJ raced for cover behind the dumpster. Within seconds, Flora Jean Benson ran into view. CJ let out a relieved sigh, stepped from behind the dumpster, and walked back to Sha's body. Glancing down at the pool of blood that cushioned the dead man's head and then up at Flora Jean, he said, "That was one hell of a shot."

"What?" Flora Jean looked dismayed.

"Dropping Sha like that." CJ quizzically eyed his six-foot-one-inch, Las Vegas showgirl-sized partner, looking for her vintage Winchester before realizing that she wasn't carrying a rifle.

Flora Jean shrugged and patted the 9-mm in her pocket. "Wasn't me."

The startled look on CJ's face caused Flora Jean to pull her gun, drop to one knee, and nervously scan the alley before repeating, this time in a near whisper, "Wasn't me."

♦♦♦

Blocking any exit from the alley, two police cars, their roof-mounted lights flashing in unison, blared police-band static into the hazy dusk. Newab Sha's body remained where it had fallen. A man sporting a coroner's ID and a red-white-and-blue-striped tie with a crescent of stars just below the knot knelt over the body with a plainclothes Denver detective by his side.

A few feet away a large, rumpled man in a cheap, ill-fitting khaki suit stood quietly asking CJ questions. "Seems like you're forever dodging bullets or the law, Floyd. Now it's Molotov cocktails. And on my beat, no less. Guess I'm just blessed."

CJ shrugged, glanced down at his bare feet, and curled up his toes.

The man followed CJ's eyes. "Times so hard you can't afford shoes?" His tone was mocking.

"It's a long story, Lieutenant." The word *lieutenant* lingered as CJ forced himself to say it. "But I'm guessing a big-time African American law enforcement officer like you probably doesn't have time for it."

"Surprise yourself and try me." Wendall Newburn tugged at the sleeves of his wrinkled suit coat and adjusted his stance. "Don't mind being quoted, do you?" he asked, slipping a small spiral-bound notebook from the coat's inside pocket.

"Nope. Not as long as it's what I actually said."

Newburn smiled. "Don't flatter yourself, Floyd. No need to edit the likes of you. Go ahead, sing your song."

CJ stole a quick glance toward Flora Jean, who was standing just beyond the draped remains of Newab Sha, knowing that he had one supportive witness. Catching CJ's gaze, Flora Jean, a former intelligence sergeant who'd done a tour with the Fifth Marine Division during Desert Storm, nodded at Newburn, eyeing him as if he were a target to be taken out, then reached into her pocket, popped a stick of Juicy Fruit into her mouth, and smiled as if to say, *I'm listening to this conversation too, asshole.*

"You lie and sweetie girl here swears to it," said Newburn, spotting the communication.

"Don't push me, Newburn. I'm not feelin' as giving as CJ today, and unlike him, I didn't go to grade school with you. We got no ties that bind, my friend."

Aware that Flora Jean hated being called either sweetie or a liar, CJ nudged her away from Newburn, who'd dropped a hand onto the butt of his service revolver. Staring defiantly at Newburn and smacking her gum, Flora Jean took the hint and walked away as CJ began recounting what had occurred, from the time he'd arrived at Mavis's house for dinner until Newab Sha crashed face first into the blacktop. Fifteen minutes later, his notebook crammed with notes, Newburn stood shaking his head. "Hell of a story, Floyd. Good enough for the silver screen. Maybe you should get yourself a Hollywood agent." Newburn glanced casually in Flora Jean's direction. His glance was met with a cold, hard stare.

CJ eyed the ground and gritted his teeth, aware that he'd just fired the opening salvo in a new conflict with Newburn. Their battles spanned twenty-five years, stretching back to the days when he'd first taken over his uncle's bail-bonding business and Newburn had been a wet-behind-the-ears patrolman. During that time they had clashed on the streets, outside courtrooms, at athletic events, and even in the sanctity of Denver's largest black church, and although the bad blood between them appeared at first blush to be linked to the natural friction between a bail bondsman and a cop, the real reason for their animosity boiled down to Mavis Sundee, who had long ago chosen CJ over Newburn.

CJ looked up as a pixieish crime-scene technician walked up to Newburn. "Coroner needs to see you, Lieutenant."

"Can't you see I'm in the middle of something?"

The technician took a dutiful step back. "He says it's important."

Newburn shook his head. "You'd think a deputy coroner could do his job without somebody holding his hand." Giving the technician a dismissive nod, he said, "I'll be there in a second," before turning his attention back to CJ. "This whole thing smells, Floyd. Like a sack of dripping sewer shit." He looked down at CJ's bare feet again before locking eyes with Flora Jean. "A suspicious person might even say that the whole thing smells like a hit."

Flora Jean spat out her gum and watched it dribble across the asphalt before wedging into a crack inches from Newburn's right foot.

CJ mouthed, *Cool it.*

Newburn eyed the gum wad and smiled. "Everybody knows you're an ex-marine, sweetie. Hear tell you've even got a few intelligence connections. But try taking a hint from your boss. This is my jurisdiction, not the Iraqi desert. Homicide's the operative word here, not Desert Storm. Don't push your luck."

"Are we free to go?" asked CJ, locking an arm in Flora Jean's and giving her a half turn before she could respond.

"Yeah."

CJ quickly began walking Flora Jean down the alley.

"Take the hint, Ms. Benson," Newburn shouted. "And Floyd, keep your ass close to home. I'll come calling."

CJ didn't answer. He was too busy nudging Flora Jean toward the black SUV that had been idling fifteen yards beyond the police cruisers, air conditioner blasting, at the mouth of the blind alley for the last five minutes. The right front and rear doors of the vehicle swung open in unison as CJ and Flora Jean approached. "Hell, I thought you and Newburn was gonna stand there and spar forever," said the man behind the wheel, shaking his head as CJ slipped into the front seat.

"I was beginning to wonder too," Mavis called out from the back as Flora Jean, in full huff, slid in next to her.

Roosevelt Weeks, CJ's best friend since kindergarten, snapped on his seatbelt and adjusted both hands on the steering wheel as CJ stared back to where Newburn and the deputy coroner knelt over Newab Sha's partially uncovered body. "Wonder what that coroner found that's so interesting?"

"Think about it later," Rosie barked. "Air conditioning costs money, my man. Shut your door."

CJ pulled the door shut and adjusted his rear in the seat before turning toward Mavis and Flora Jean. "Either I've got a vigilante guardian angel out there or Sha took a bullet for me," he said, sounding puzzled. Mavis leaned forward and hugged him tightly around the neck. "I'm betting Sha's bullet was meant for me." A haunted look spread across CJ's face. It was a familiar look that still frightened Mavis after more than thirty years, a look that CJ had worn night and day for close to two years after coming home from Vietnam. "Like my old patrol boat captain used to say after we docked up safe from a mission, 'They missed us this time, boys, but there's always more ammunition.'"

Mavis relaxed her grip, and tears welled up in her eyes as CJ turned his head to kiss her on the cheek. "It's okay," he said, stroking her cheek reassuringly as the big black SUV picked up speed and he began to think about just who might want to see him dead.

Chapter

3

THE SMELL OF SPICY HOT Southern fried chicken, candied yams, collard greens, and buttermilk biscuits hung in the air of CJ's apartment. The food that had filled the bellies and soothed the fears of black America for countless generations had been delivered moments earlier by a coal-black near midget of a man wearing a baseball cap, bib overalls, and a grease-stained white apron. At Mavis's request, the hastily delivered bounty had come from Mae's Louisiana Kitchen, the landmark soul food restaurant that her family had owned for more than seventy-five years. The man quickly disappeared into the night before Flora Jean had the chance to offer him a tip.

CJ had lived in the second-floor apartment above the bay-windowed downstairs wing of the ninety-year-old Victorian that housed his bail-bonding business since the day he'd returned home from Vietnam. Over the years, he had refurbished the once near derelict of a building to its original painted-lady splendor so that it now sparkled as the lone jewel among seven decaying downtown Delaware Street Victorians that sat across the street from the Denver police administration building. The assemblage of painted ladies had become known as Bail Bondsman's Row, and CJ's gold-colored gem with its purple filigree trim stood out as the queen. Only his vintage 1957 drop-top Chevrolet Bel Air engendered the same kind of pride in his heart.

It was close to 10 p.m. when CJ, Mavis, and Flora Jean huddled around the antique inlaid walnut table that occupied most of CJ's tiny dining room. Aside from the building, the table represented the only tangible piece of real property left by CJ's uncle, the man who had raised him, when he had died twelve years earlier.

Watching CJ and Flora Jean devour their meals, Mavis shook her head. "You'd think the two of you had never seen food before."

"They say it soothes the savage beast," Flora Jean mumbled between bites.

"It's not food that does that, Flora Jean. It's music. And it's 'breast,'" said Mavis.

Flora Jean scooped up a forkful of collards, eyed Mavis, and shrugged. "Whatever."

"At least it's stopped the two of you from rambling on about Newab Sha," said Mavis, who'd been forced to listen to CJ and Flora Jean dissect the evening's events nonstop for nearly an hour.

CJ reached across the table toward a platter filled with fried chicken. "For the moment," he said, picking out a thigh.

Mavis set aside the partially eaten biscuit she was toying with and frowned, knowing that the meal was only a brief respite from the treacherous world CJ and Flora Jean negotiated every day—a world filled with what her seventy-eight-year-old father called pond scum.

Realizing he'd said the wrong thing, CJ inched his chair back from the table and smiled at Mavis. "Good thing my main squeeze owns a restaurant."

"Cut the con, CJ."

"Significant other, then."

"Main squeeze, significant other, love of your life, whatever." Mavis slammed the biscuit down in frustration. "In case you missed it, a few hours ago a man tried to kill us."

"He's dead," said CJ, hoping to lower the flame under the waters he could see about to come to a boil.

"But whoever killed him isn't, and the bullet he took may have been meant for you. Both you and Flora Jean as much as said so."

"So somebody's pissed at me." CJ clasped Mavis's right hand reassuringly. "That's nothing new."

"And that's the problem. There'll always be someone after you. Second-rate thugs, wife beaters, scam artists—the drunks you spend half your days bonding out of jail. They're leeches, CJ, and they're sucking you dry."

"It's what I do," CJ said defensively, aware that he was getting older and slower, more callous, and clearly, in Mavis's eyes, less charming. He turned to Flora Jean for support.

"I'll get dessert," Flora Jean said, heading for the kitchen, in no mood to become a lightning rod.

Looking defeated, CJ watched the swinging kitchen doors close behind her.

"And what you do is turning you into something I don't like."
Mavis slipped her hand out of CJ's and began nervously biting
her lower lip.

"I'll slow down. Promise."

"No, you won't, CJ. Your job's your elixir. Has been since the
day you came home from Vietnam. It's your postadolescent
phase, midlife crisis, old-age jitters, and adrenaline fix all rolled
into one. The bungee cord that connects you to life."

"I'll try."

"You've said that before."

Looking frustrated, CJ said, "Then what do you want me to
do, Mavis?"

"I don't know."

Watching tears well up in her eyes, CJ lowered an elbow onto
the table and rested his chin in his palm. "Damn! Mavis. I'm
way too old a dog to learn new tricks. But I'll work on cutting
back—let Flora Jean carry a bigger part of the load."

"Promise?"

CJ clasped her hand again and nodded, watching as Mavis
forced a reluctant half smile.

"Heard my name," said Flora Jean, reentering the room with
three plates, each one top heavy with a wedge of sweet-potato
pie. Aware from the looks on their faces that the stormy seas
had at least momentarily settled, she said, "Got pie?" failing
miserably to sound like a celebrity from a *got milk* commercial.

"None for me," said CJ, forcing himself to pass on his favorite
dessert. "Had too much chicken."

"Mavis?"

"No."

"Suit yourselves." Flora Jean placed the plates in the center of the table. "Guess that means more for me."

"Guess so," CJ and Mavis said in near unison.

Flora Jean inched one of the plates her way, hoping there'd be no more need to play referee that evening. On the heels of the temporary truce, the room turned silent until she picked up a fork, tapped the plate in front of her lightly, and started on her first slice of sweet-potato pie.

◆ ◆ ◆

The light rapping on the metal door that led to the fire-escape landing and the turn-of-the-century wrought-iron staircase that wound its way from CJ's apartment to the driveway below was halting and barely audible. Mavis had said her good-byes forty-five minutes earlier, leaving CJ and Flora Jean puzzling over how best to deal with the police investigation that was certain to follow the death of Newab Sha. Mavis had given CJ a departing *I expect you to do better* kind of kiss and said, "See you both tomorrow." She had left without another word being spoken.

"Someone's at the door, CJ," said Flora Jean, interrupting CJ's calculation of how long they had before Newburn resurfaced.

When CJ didn't answer, she nudged the toe of his boot. "Didn't you hear me? You got a visitor."

"Oh!" CJ rose from his chair, moved slowly to the door, still crunching numbers in his head, slid back the deadbolt, and swung the door open without his customary glance through the peephole. He found himself facing an exotic-looking woman. Her face was illuminated by a dim yellow, insect-caked, sixty-watt bulb that jutted from a globeless fixture above the door. Even in the unflattering light, the woman was stunning. Her skin was smooth, the color of butter caramel, and her deep-set eyes were an intriguing shade of aquamarine. In contrast to his six-foot-three, 240-pound girth, she seemed very small. Taking a step back, he noticed that she was dressed in a loose-fitting, eggshell-white blouse, stylish designer shorts, and the kind of casual seaside wedges that added a few inches of height.

"Pardon me, but I was told that I could find Flora Jean Benson here."

CJ looked the woman up and down, concluding that she was Asian or Polynesian and noticing that she wore her closely cropped jet-black hair much the same way as Mavis.

"It's past midnight."

"I'm sorry, but this is important."

"Hope so." CJ called back into the house, "Flora Jean, got a visitor."

Flora Jean came to the door, looking perplexed. Eyeing the woman with a hint of suspicion, she asked, "What can I do for you, sugar?"

The woman flashed a look of relief at hearing Flora Jean's signature greeting. "I'm Carmen Nguyen. I'm in Denver doing a sabbatical at the University of Colorado Cancer Center."

Flora Jean's lower jaw relaxed momentarily before dropping open. "Damn!" She edged past CJ and wrapped her arms around Carmen, smothering her in a hug. Turning to CJ, she said, "Don't just stand there, let the sista in. And that's *doctor* sista," Flora Jean boomed.

CJ stepped aside to let Carmen in, surprised that Flora Jean would refer to someone so exotically Asian looking as a "sista." But as Carmen walked into the room's light, he recognized the subtle facial features of a person who was also African American.

"The man in the doorway looking totally befuddled is none other than the elusive boss I've told you about, CJ Floyd." Flora Jean shot CJ a broad *gotcha* kind of grin.

"Pleasure," said CJ, nodding as Carmen extended her hand.

"Believe it or not, this is the first time Carmen and I have met. We've talked to each other a lot, but always by phone. She's the one I told you about who got her butt in a sling over in Grand Junction a year or so ago behind some nutcase mad scientist type tryin' to develop a uranium-based potion capable of creatin' supermen. Carmen blew the whistle on him."

Recognition spread across CJ's face. "Yeah." He remembered Flora Jean telling him about saving the bacon of a former marine buddy of hers and some Amerasian doctor, but he'd always thought the woman was some white-bread GI's war baby, not a brother's. Aware that children fathered by GIs during the Vietnam War were called *my den* and were treated in Vietnamese society as half-breeds who were no more than trash, most ending up as street thugs, hookers, drug dealers, or lost souls, he was curious as to how Carmen had been able to escape that cycle. "You're the lady whose boyfriend served with Flora Jean during Desert Storm."

Flora Jean answered before Carmen had a chance. "Right on

the money, sugar. By the way, how is our lover boy, Rios? Still runnin' that river-raftin' business of his?"

"Sure is," said Carmen, blushing. "Right now he's on a white-water shoot down in South America with his brother."

"Men!" Flora Jean pivoted to face CJ. "Sometimes I think they're nuts."

Carmen hesitated before responding, as if hoping not to offend CJ. "But before he left he gave me this." She extended her left hand to show Flora Jean the two-carat diamond engagement ring on her finger.

"Hot damn! Diamonds on the soles of my shoes. Go on, sugar." Looking directly at CJ, she mouthed the word *Mavis.* "Maybe someone around here should take a hint."

"What?" said Carmen, looking confused.

"Nothin'." Flora Jean examined the ring, making certain CJ took notice, until Carmen slipped her hand out of Flora Jean's and smiled self-consciously. There was a brief moment of silence before Flora Jean said, "Now, sugar, sabbatical or not, I know you didn't come all the way over here from Grand Junction just to show off that ring. What's up?"

Carmen flushed.

"Ain't no problem with your aunt, is there?" asked Flora Jean, aware that Carmen's overly protective sixty-one-year-old aunt had been the one to end Carmen's troubles with the rogue scientist by taking out the hit man he'd sent after Carmen and Walker Rios with a point-blank blast from her shotgun.

"No, Ket's fine. It's . . . it's my father."

"What? Thought you told me he got killed during Vietnam."

"No. Just forgotten." Carmen's face was awash in guilt. "And now I'm afraid he's headed for trouble. Serious trouble. The kind that could get him killed."

Flora Jean had heard snippets of the details surrounding Carmen's father's Vietnam military stint, including his reported desertion from the army, from Walker Rios. Rios, a Persian Gulf veteran and a former marine intelligence officer, had done some homework concerning his disappearance, and he'd told Flora Jean that he had serious doubts that the highly decorated first sergeant had deserted. But Carmen had accepted the fact that her father had deserted not only the army but her and her mother as well. He'd always been an erased memory for her.

"Always thought the two of you were, what's the word I'm lookin' for," Flora Jean said before finally blurting out, "estranged."

Carmen's response was terse. "You can't be estranged from someone you've never known. But you're right. Until recently I had no use for him."

"What changed your mind?" asked CJ, walking to a nearby coffee pot and pouring himself a cup of thick, syrupy brew well past its prime.

Carmen eyed Flora Jean sheepishly, hesitant to respond.

"Spit it out, sugar. Talkin' to CJ's the same as talkin' to me."

"Ket," said Carmen in a barely audible tone. Looking at CJ, she anxiously asked, "May I have a cup of coffee?"

"Stuff might kill you. It's just this short of tar," Flora Jean responded, snapping her fingers.

"I'll chance it."

Smiling defiantly, CJ took a cup out of an overhead cabinet and filled it to the brim with bitter-smelling coffee.

"Thanks. I'm a little nervous." Carmen took the cup and clasped it thoughtfully with both hands before taking a couple of sips, setting the cup aside, and slipping a worn newspaper clipping from her pocket. "It all began with this about four months ago." She handed the *Denver Post* clipping to Flora Jean.

The headline at the top of the well-worn clipping read, "Margolin Well Positioned for Senate Bid." The two columns of newsprint that followed read more like an editorial endorsement than news copy as the article touted the fact that Peter Margolin, currently a third-term congressman from Colorado's First Congressional District, was poised to capture one of Colorado's U.S. Senate seats.

"What's Margolin's runnin' for the Senate got to do with your father?" asked Flora Jean.

"Ket claims that Margolin knows why my father deserted." The way the word *deserted* lingered on Carmen's lips told Flora Jean that it clearly wasn't her father's military desertion that Carmen was most concerned about. "Ket as much told me so. Ten days ago she broke down—said my father might still be alive and that if he was, I might be able to get in touch with him."

"Did you?" asked CJ, attentively leaning forward in his seat.

"I sent him a letter," said Carmen, surprised that the question had come from CJ instead of Flora Jean. "All Ket had was an old general delivery address. She wasn't sure if it was any good. I sent it there."

"Where's there?" asked Flora Jean.

"To a backwoods P.O. box in West Virginia. Ket told me that the address came to her scrawled on a postcard two days before Christmas twenty-five years ago." Carmen took another sip of the bitter coffee and forced back a frown. "She'd kept the card all these years."

"Any response to your letter?"

"Not a word. That's why I came to see you. I want you and CJ to find him."

"In West Virginia? That's a bit east of our normal beat," said CJ.

"I'll pay you. Double your normal rates, triple if necessary."

"Damn, sugar. Sounds like you wanna hook up with your daddy real bad. Why not just wait for a response to your letter?"

Carmen swallowed hard. "I can't."

Flora Jean looked puzzled. "Why not?"

"Because Ket's beside herself over giving me that West Virginia address. She's spent years claiming to hate the man who deserted her sister. Now I think she's having second thoughts, even feeling guilty. I have the feeling that Margolin's run for the Senate has opened up a whole set of old wounds for her—scratched her conscience—and made her wonder if she's been wrong about my father all these years. She even told me that if he's still alive, my letter to him could end up getting him killed."

"By who?" asked Flora Jean, eyebrows arching.

Carmen reached across the table and slipped the newspaper clipping out of Flora Jean's hand. "By him," she said, thumping Margolin's name with her index finger several times before looking at Flora Jean pleadingly. "Can you help?"

"Ain't up to me, sugar." Flora Jean looked over at CJ.

After a lengthy silence, punctuated by Carmen's penetrating gaze, CJ nodded and said, "Yes," uncertain why he'd done so, especially in light of his earlier promise to Mavis. "What's your father's name?"

"Langston. Langston Blue." Carmen realized only after she'd said it that for the first time ever, she'd said the name proudly.

Chapter

4

LANGSTON BLUE HADN'T PUSHED his gear-grinding, rusted-out '62 Ford pickup past 40 in years. Now he was cruising along at more than 60, and he felt an overwhelming sense of trepidation as he knifed his way west along the narrow switchbacks that followed Willow Buck Creek, the rising sun at his back. The asphalt pavement, damp with dew, had recently been replaced for the first time in fifteen years. The unaccustomed smoothness was unnerving and unfamiliar.

No one had gotten around to painting a center line down the road, so the strip of highway seemed to be all his as he breezed past the gnarled, road-hugging trunks of eighty-year-old creek-bottom oaks. After three and a half decades he was leaving West Virginia, racing along the same route he'd taken when he came home from Vietnam, following the outline of a creek that had choked to death on coal dust bleeding from a strip-mining slag heap twenty miles upstream.

Prior to joining the army he'd spent his early teenaged years bouncing around the West Virginia hills with his life stuck on idle, trying to figure out how to become a man, and for most

of his childhood he had been what people around his home-
town of Bluefield liked to refer to as "slow." But during high
school he'd become a basketball star, and in the wake of his
athletic success his marginal slowness had been conveniently
ignored by family, neighbors, and friends. He and Rufus Hawkes,
the only other black student at the then recently integrated Bluefield High, had taken their team all the way to the state basketball championship during their senior year, turning themselves
into West Virginia playground legends. They had both signed
letters of intent to go to Penn State, fully expecting that one day
they'd make it to the pros, where they would spend their lives
raining down jump shots and living like kings. But the summer after graduation, Rufus had been killed—gunned down in
a bar in the middle of the day by a thick-necked lumberjack
during an argument that had started over Rufus dating a white
girl from nearby Bexley, Ohio.

That killing had done something to Langston, more or less
slipping him into neutral out of drive. While lots of people around
Bluefield claimed that the murder had only eliminated the nigger whose job had been to feed Langston the ball, Langston knew
better. His mother hustled him off to college on a train in September, but when he came home for Christmas he didn't go back.
Two months into the new year he joined the army. Six months
later he was trudging through the jungles of Vietnam.

The army transformed him from a sometimes slow-to-get-it
athletic wonder into a precision killing machine, and while
many of his fellow soldiers were potheads, lost souls, street
hustlers, and horse-stall-mucking country loads, the worst pos-

sible candidates for members of a team, Blue's tenacity and need to fit in made him the perfect foot soldier. Early into his second tour he'd become a sergeant and sharpshooter who'd earned himself a spot on an elite eight-man assault team charged with carrying out clandestine missions behind enemy lines— no-accountability missions that included the green light to kill at will.

Langston Blue's palms were sweating as he nosed his pickup out of a final series of switchbacks and into a ten-mile straight-away that led to Route 119. Nursing the truck past 70 and into the shade of a half-mile-long stretch of cottonwoods, he thought about what he was leaving behind: thirty-four years of playing a role, close to four decades of self-imposed exile in an isolated back hollow lost to the world. During all those years his only trips outside his ten-acre retreat had been his monthly treks to Princeton, the nearest town, for groceries, snippets of news, and auto and building supplies, along with the occasional clandestine trek across the border into Ohio to satisfy his manly needs. Only during the past decade had he made an annual trip to Maryland to pick up twenty thousand dollars in crisp twenty-dollar bills. Before then, the money he'd been guaranteed when he had agreed to go underground had been delivered to him. During it all he had stayed busy, first building his cabin and clearing the acreage, then reading books, painting watercolors, fishing, hunting, and exploring the thousands of acres of surrounding woods. He had played the good soldier and now, in the blink of an eye, just like when his friend Rufus Hawkes had died in that bar, everything had changed.

His cabin was gone along with his cherished paintings, his books, his guns, his gear, and his twenty-thousand-dollar-a-year safety net—all replaced by someone who wanted him dead and a mysterious letter from a woman named Carmen Nguyen, who claimed to be his daughter. He nudged the accelerator and patted the letter in his shirt pocket as he slipped out of the shade of the overhanging cottonwoods and tried to think things through.

It made sense that the woman claiming to be his daughter would use his wife's maiden name, Nguyen. Who'd want to be saddled with the name of a man who'd been a deserter? Whoever she was, she understood the need to be detached from the past, and that meant she had to be smart. Blue suddenly smiled at the thought of having a daughter, a piece of his beloved Mimm.

He'd mapped out the trip across country, diagramming it in his head like a winning jump shot or an assault on a Vietcong stronghold. He'd take the West Virginia turnpike north to Charleston. From there, just to be on the safe side, he'd take a series of back roads to I-70. Then, traveling only at night, he'd take a shot at making it halfway across the country to Denver to find Carmen without getting killed.

A suitcase he'd bought for a dollar at a flea market the day after his cabin had burned sat on the floor, wedged against the transmission hump. A 24-by-12-inch metal strongbox filled with all that remained precious in his life—Mimm's wedding veil, her diary, and her wedding ring—rested on top of the suit-case. Their letters to one another, photographs of the good times they'd had even in the midst of war, his two Bronze Stars, and an official-looking government document with an army seal and a barely legible signature were also locked safely inside the box that he had stashed for years in the soft dirt below a tree a few yards from his cabin. The fact that his precious mementos had survived the fire had been the omen he'd needed to move ahead, a powerful signal along with the letter from his daughter that it was time to come up for air.

The truck's out-of-alignment front end began shaking as he banked into a series of curves, and his thoughts turned from Carmen and Mimm to Cortez. If worse came to worst, he'd handle Cortez. He had done it before, and he knew he could do it again. It wasn't Cortez he was worried about anyway. When you came right down to it, Cortez was probably still the same irrational, miscalculating, loud-mouthed, pot-smoking Jersey City Puerto Rican he'd always been. The man he had to worry about was their captain and kill-squad leader, Peter Margolin, a much darker, softer-spoken, thoughtful, and more treacherous man. Blue would be thinking about that incisive man of privilege all the way to Denver.

Eyeing a buckshot-riddled road sign that read *119 East,* Blue eased off the accelerator and rubbed his eyes in a final attempt to clear his thoughts. As he nosed his truck onto the much wider state highway, the engine sputtered. He tapped the accelerator to a chorus of engine backfires, then floored it. As if responding to some preprogrammed order, the engine slipped into a smooth rumble. Within moments the truck disappeared into the West Virginia hills.

◆◆◆

Peter Margolin looked up from his iced coffee, gritted his teeth, and eyed three briefcase-toting, downtown-Denver, 16th Street pedestrian mall white-collar types queued up heel to toe, champing at the bit to order their late-morning Starbucks caffeine fix.

"What the hell do you mean the SOB's still alive?" Margolin said to the man across the table from him.

Lincoln Cortez raised an index finger to his lips. "Lower your voice, Captain. This joint ain't soundproof."

"I thought I told you to solve the problem. And can that *Captain* shit. We're not on patrol, and this isn't the Mekong Delta."

Cortez nodded and smiled, flashing a set of perfectly aligned white teeth that seemed just a bit too large for his thin-lipped mouth and protrusive lower jaw. Aware that Margolin preferred that everyone, including his closest associates, call him Congressman, Cortez reveled in bringing his former commanding officer down a notch, all the way to just plain captain.

"Sure thing." Cortez eyed a nearby bleached-blond teenybopper who was wearing a pair of faded cutoffs that outlined her bulging cheeks. "Bet she ain't wearing undies." Letting out a lecherous sigh, he gave Margolin a wink. Margolin glanced in the girl's direction with an uninterested grunt.

"Don't be so dismissive, Captain. It's me, Lincoln C. Remember? I used to bring you fresh Vietnamese catches like that two, three times a week."

Margolin shot Cortez a death-trap stare that said, *Shut the fuck up, Sergeant, or else.* When he was certain the silent order had been understood, he smiled. "Now, what about Blue?"

Cortez shrugged and glared down into his coffee as if he expected the steaming brew to provide him with the answer. "He just up and vanished."

"Into the West Virginia mist? Just like a ghost? Bullshit! I've got a derringer aimed at your dick, Sergeant. You can do better than that." His tone was edgy and rising.

Cortez looked around the room, his eyes bloodshot from a two-day, 1,450-mile drive across country. Cupping his crotch and lowering his voice to a near whisper, he said, "I torched that rathole of his and ran a half-dozen perimeter sweeps right afterward. Even spent two hours the next day digging through the ashes. Nothing."

"And you're sure Blue was inside the cabin when you torched it?" Margolin looked unconvinced, recalling how adept Cortez had been with a flame thrower thirty-four years earlier. And how effortlessly Cortez used to pick off the Vietcong, and even innocent villagers when he felt like it, as they fled from their burning huts.

"Pretty sure," Cortez said hesitantly, eyes glued to the table-top.

"Then why didn't you wait for Blue to run for cover and pop him then?"

When Cortez didn't answer, Margolin leaned across the table until he was eye to eye with his former sergeant. Swinging one foot forward, he kicked Cortez in his grenade-mangled, surgically repaired right leg. The painful toothpick, three inches shorter than his left, had forced Cortez to use a cane for more than thirty years. When Cortez let out a yelp, the teenybopper in the cutoffs looked their way. Margolin flashed her a stern look that said, *Don't interfere,* and she turned away.

"I think the son of a bitch mighta made me," Cortez said, massaging his leg.

Margolin's nose remained just inches from Cortez's. "Why's that?"

Cortez looked up and swallowed hard before returning his gaze to the tabletop, aware that Margolin probably had the connections to shoot off his testicles and get away with it. "During one of my perimeter sweeps the next day, about thirty yards downhill from the cabin, I found a couple of footprints and a partial handprint right next to an imprint of the tip of my cane."

Margolin shook his head and sat back in his chair. "Then he wasn't in the cabin when you torched it."

"I'm not sure."

Margolin's face turned pensive. Turning away from Cortez, he gazed out at the mass of workaday people moving up and down the 16th Street pedestrian mall. "See those people out there, scurrying to their cubicles?"

"Yeah." Cortez twisted in his seat and moved his bad leg out of kicking range.

"I need them, every one of them, and so do you."

There was no response as Cortez looked puzzled. Smiling at the other man's befuddlement, Margolin continued, "They're the people who'll punch the ballots and pull the levers that'll send me to the Senate. And, my good First Sergeant, they're the people who'll keep you breathing. I'd dust your crippled ass right now if it weren't for them."

Aware that Margolin meant every word, Cortez took a deep breath. "I'll get him next time."

"No need. I'll handle it myself."

Margolin took a sip of coffee and continued watching the pedestrian flow outside, leering as the long-legged teenybopper's buttocks jiggled toward the exit. He shook his head knowingly as the look on Cortez's face quickly changed to fear. "You're a real Einstein, Lincoln. A real magna brain of a spic. I'm busy building a seventy-five-million-dollar high-rise, talking with heads of state, breezing into a U.S. Senate seat, and you're worried about me pulling the trigger on an over-the-hill, slow-thinking hermit of a nigger."

"Just recalling how intuitive Blue used to be."

Margolin broke into a Cheshire cat grin and slipped the derringer he'd been holding on Cortez's jewels into his pocket. "I don't think he's like that anymore. After nearly thirty-five years of living like a back-hollow coon, my guess is he's more like a stroked-out pussycat." Margolin broke into a snicker that quickly rose to a booming laugh.

Chapter

5

THERE WAS NO NEED TO RUSH THINGS, Celeste Deepstream told herself as she slowly strolled down a musty back aisle of Peterson's Guns and Pawn, a seedy East Denver, Colfax Avenue gun enthusiast's mecca, under the watchful gaze of an aging rodeo cowboy of a clerk, a man who, she'd been told by a prison snitch, would ignore the law and outfit her with anything she needed for a hundred bucks and a piece of ass. She had gained forty pounds during the last year of her five-year prison stay, transforming her trim, athletic frame into a sagging mass of loose muscle and increasing flab. Her once flawless skin, formerly the essence of Colorado ski-slope tan, was now mottled and lifeless, a tepid, washed-out, paper-sack shade of brown.

Eyeing bank after bank of floor-to-ceiling shelves stocked with every imaginable accessory for a firearm, she was at peace for the first time in years, knowing she had the rest of her life to kill CJ Floyd.

Gazing along a neatly aligned row of Ithaca double-barreled over-and-unders, she thought about the world-class swimming champion she'd once been and how, seven years earlier,

Floyd had destroyed her life. She had been a newly selected Rhodes Scholar poised to study anthropology at the University of London when a collision between her drug-addicted brother, Bobby, and CJ Floyd had derailed her plans. Because of Floyd, her dreams had been swamped. Because of Floyd, Bobby was dead.

She and Bobby had been more than brother and sister; they were fraternal twins born six minutes apart on the kitchen table in a crumbling two-room Acoma Indian reservation adobe. All her life Celeste had been stronger, smarter, and wiser than Bobby, miles ahead of her brother in all the things that mattered as if the couplet of DNA she had sprung from had harbored all of life's richest components, while Bobby's had been stripped to the bone. Until the day he died, Bobby's one claim to fame was that he was the oldest.

She had turned down the Rhodes Scholarship to spend time detoxifying Bobby, who had been strung out on Ritalin, Percocet, alcohol, and model-airplane glue. In time Bobby won his war with drugs, but her painstaking sisterly intervention transformed her into Bobby's permanent crutch, and the bond between them, no less tenacious, degenerated into an unhealthy codependent union fueled by Bobby's instability and her own deep sense of guilt.

And then came Floyd, an unrelenting bounty-hunting bear of a black man hired to track down her now dried-out, bond-skipping brother, who had been a small-time fence. Floyd had tracked Bobby across two states before hog-tying him in chains, dumping him in the back of a pickup, and hauling him from

Santa Fe to Denver to face charges of transporting stolen weapons and illegal fireworks across state lines.

While awaiting trial, Bobby had tried to kill himself in the Denver county jail. Guilt-ridden and enraged, she had unmercifully beaten the skinflint bail bondsman who had originally hired Floyd to track down Bobby, blaming him for her brother's plight. When the man died from injuries sustained during that beating, Celeste received a plea-bargained manslaughter conviction that earned her a twelve-year prison sentence. She never again saw Bobby alive.

With five years of model-prisoner check marks next to her name, chits that included saving a prison guard's life, teaching college-credit courses to inmates, and founding a Native American prisoners' prerelease job opportunity program, she masterminded an early release, dumping buckets of remorse around the room at two critical parole hearings and playing the role of a long-suffering sister forced all her life to shoulder responsibility for her bad-seed twin. She was paroled after serving just under half of her original sentence.

"Help you there, ma'am?" called out the pudgy, gruff-voiced clerk, sporting a silver-dollar-sized turquoise bolo and a broken-brimmed cowboy hat. The man had been watching her intently since she'd first walked into the store.

"Sure can. Need ammo for my thirty-ought."

The man flashed a half smile, showing several badly stained teeth. "Any particular brand?"

"I'm partial to Remington." Celeste flashed a brief come-hither smile.

"Good as any. Got 'em up front."

"And a scope," Celeste added, her tone suddenly expectant.

"They're three aisles over." The man eyed Celeste from head to toe, thinking that if she were thirty pounds lighter, she'd be a real knockout. "Got a brand in mind for the scope?"

"Nope," said Celeste, disappointment apparent in her tone. If her rifle had been outfitted with a scope the previous evening, she would have had the time to sight in properly on Floyd. Instead, she had mistakenly killed Floyd's bald-headed assailant, and although she felt no remorse over that killing, the missed opportunity had upset her.

Moving in a slow, arthritic horseman's hobble across the width of the store, the clerk said, "Follow me."

Her agitation mounted as she followed the man. She was glad she'd brought down the man who'd been after Floyd. Now, if Floyd analyzed that killing the way she suspected he would, he'd have time to think about the fact that someone was out to kill him. He'd have time to contemplate dying the same way Bobby had—cooped up in a prison cell for two years for no more than driving a truckload of illegal fireworks and stolen guns across state lines, then tossed out on the Denver streets, a helpless, nervous wreck without her there to protect or fend for him. When the drugs came calling for Bobby again, tempting and torturing him, there was nothing she could do from a prison cell to save him. Six months before her release, Bobby had died from an overdose of heroin in a squalid, rat-infested Airstream trailer on the outskirts of Denver. "You hear what I said?" grunted the man in the bolo.

"What?"

"Said, I got a darn good generic scope on sale. Fits any 30.06 made. Heck of a deal at ninety-nine bucks."

"Got anything better?" asked Celeste, trying to erase the image of Bobby's Airstream deathtrap from her mind.

"Got a high-end Remington. It'll match that rifle of yours. But it sells for one ninety-five."

Celeste frowned, wondering why the man was so intent on saving her money. She knew she looked dumpy and used up, and she also knew that six years earlier the man would very likely have looked at her, licked his lips, and asked to sniff her panties. "Is there much difference in the image accuracy?" she asked, her voice suddenly sultry.

"Yep. With the Remington you can practically double the distance from your target and still take Roosevelt's head off a dime."

"That accurate?" Celeste arched her back, showing off the outline of her still firm breasts before reaching for the scope. "I'll take it." She scanned the print on the side of the scope's box, eyelashes fluttering, before looking up at the man to see if he'd taken the bait.

"Anything else?" the man said matter-of-factly.

"No."

"I'll ring you out up front."

"Sure thing," Celeste said dejectedly as he turned away.

As the man packaged her purchases, she thought about all she'd lost in the past six years: her future, her brother, her beauty, and her youth, and all because of CJ Floyd. There'd be a reckoning, she told herself, hefting her purchases.

"You going after elk or deer?" asked the man, surprising her as she turned to leave.

"Deer."

"I hear they're thick as rabbits this year. Easy money with that scope," said the clerk, lowering his gaze and trying his best not to get caught in the act of ogling Celeste's breasts.

Aware that he was staring, Celeste squeezed her package tightly to one breast before seductively rolling it across the opposite breast and into her right arm. "Thanks."

"Sure thing," said the man, smiling as he took in the maneuver.

Halfway across the store's parking lot, a few feet from her pickup, Celeste looked back to see the man still watching her from the front of the store. Maybe she hadn't lost everything, she thought as she licked her lips sensuously, slipped into the truck, and flipped down the sun visor. Eyeing her reflection in the visor's mirror, she slipped the key into the ignition, glanced out into the noonday sun, and smiled, thinking maybe one day she'd be a knockout again.

◆ ◆ ◆

Lincoln Cortez, his withered leg still tingling from Margolin's earlier assault, stood outside a west Denver 7-11 talking on his cell phone to a contact that Peter Margolin had no idea about. Rubbing his leg, he growled, "Margolin's still an asshole."

"Nothing new under the sun," came the static-riddled reply.

"Whatta you want me to do?" asked Cortez.

"Lay low and read the obituaries. You never know when Margolin's name might turn up."

"If I don't beat you to it," said Cortez. He wiggled his foot, hoping to get some feeling in his toes. "And what about Blue?"

"It's handled. Get yourself a place to stay. You'll hear from me."

The phone went dead. Cortez rubbed his leg, thought about the risk associated with playing both ends against the middle, and figured that his chances of a big payday were a hundred percent either way. Grimacing, he flipped off his cell phone and limped toward his car.

Chapter

6

EXCEPT FOR NEW FLATWARE, recently purchased waxed checkerboard tablecloths still creased from packing, and central air conditioning, Mae's Louisiana Kitchen, Denver's premiere soul food restaurant, looked much as it had for more than sixty years. Only the Rossonian Club, half a block down the street, famous for its jazz and night life during the 1930s, '40s, and '50s, rivaled Mae's, originally established by Willis Sundee, as the most recognizable landmark in Denver's historic Five Points neighborhood.

The Points, the core of Denver's black community since early in the twentieth century, was a neighborhood in transition. Urban gentrification and increasing ethnic diversity were becoming more obvious every day. Longtime shades of black were making way for every color in the rainbow.

Catty-corner from the now empty Rossonian, a Bank One had set up shop in a meticulously restored building complete with a sandblasted brick facade that made it look more appropriate for Williamsburg than the Points. With a satchel of black patronage votes in their back pockets and white establishment votes in their front ones, Queen City pols pushing an Up with People–style new business agenda had managed to stamp a "times are a-changing" footprint on Five Points that included a light-rail system that served to cut the community in half, several apartment and condo complexes that longtime Five Points residents would never be able to afford, and a city government annex that included a rarely used driver's license bureau that most Five Points natives, including Willis Sundee, claimed had been opened to house community-destroying back-stabbers and political spies.

The best thing to land in Five Points in the last ten years had been the Five Points Media Center, home to three local radio stations, including the city's nationally acclaimed jazz oasis, KUVO. The nondescript, block-like, three-story media center rose above the neighborhood's aging Victorians and squat little bungalows like an overprotective sentry guarding Five Points's eastern edge. But Mae's Louisiana Kitchen remained the long, narrow, New Orleans–style shotgun house it had always been, still tucked in the center of the community between Ajack Prillerman's Trophy and Badge, and Rufus Benson's House of Musical Soul.

CJ, who had arrived at Mae's twenty-five minutes earlier in a failed attempt to beat the noon-hour rush, was seated at the closest table to the kitchen in the far back corner of the restaurant, flanked by Mavis, Carmen Nguyen, and Ket Tran, Carmen's aunt, who was talking. Ket had hastily flown into Denver that morning from her home on Colorado's Western Slope.

Next to Carmen and Ket, Mavis stood out. Her sharp facial features, flawless deep, rich cocoa-brown skin, and naturally curly, closely cropped jet-black hair screamed Ethiopian queen. Carmen was fairer, her skin closer to a cinnamon tone. Her hair, straight black and silky, accented exotic Asian features that mirrored those of her aunt. But her bold, pouty lips and noticeably larger facial features and frame told the more than casual onlooker that something in her lineage reached far beyond the borders of Vietnam.

The women were all fashionably dressed, in sharp contrast to CJ's wrinkled jeans, faded chambray shirt, and oiled work boots with run-over heels. Sensing that he looked out of place, CJ cleared his throat and looked at Ket. "So what you're saying is that Langston Blue wasn't quite as quick upstairs as everyone else."

Ket paused momentarily before answering. "Yes and no. He wasn't slow when it came to understanding mechanical things or tuning in on someone else's feelings, but when it came down to everyday things like counting out change or remembering a phone number or a street address, Langston sometimes had trouble. And more times than he should have, he let other people do his thinking for him."

"And that's why you think he deserted? Other people told him to?"

"Now that I've had all these years to think about it, I'm sure of it. He never would've left his unit or my sister unless someone either forced or tricked him into it. And I'd place my money on that someone being his captain, Peter Margolin."

"The guy running for the U.S. Senate?"

"The very same one."

CJ glanced at Carmen. "Sounds like somewhere along the way, whether he knew it or not, your father was connected." CJ stroked his chin thoughtfully, anticipating a response from Ket that never came. "He never knew your sister was pregnant?" he asked finally.

"Never. If he had, he wouldn't have taken off like he did." Ket reached over and patted Carmen's hand. "About a month ago, I found a letter Mimm never sent to him. She told Langston she was pregnant. I always thought he knew. But the letter was dated the day before he disappeared."

"What happened to your sister?" CJ asked softly.

"She was killed by a sniper during the war," said Ket, her voice laden with sorrow.

The words and their tone dredged up a rush of memories from a dark corner of CJ's mind—horrific memories of personal loss, violence, and pain. He had been a machine gunner on a 125-foot navy patrol boat during Vietnam, a swabbie instead of a grunt, and a much younger man than Langston Blue. But in a sense, like everyone who'd served there, they'd been the very same man. Sometimes when the mental shadows in his mind were bent just right, he still cursed the navy for stealing that part of his life. But deep down he knew that Vietnam had also transformed him from a naive, smart-talking Denver street tough into a man.

Aware that the conversation was headed for places that could turn CJ into a shell of himself for the rest of the week, Mavis spoke up. "And if your father's still alive, how do you expect CJ to find him?"

"By first talking to Congressman Margolin," said Carmen. "He was in charge of the eight-man killing unit my father belonged to. He has to know something."

CJ's eyes widened and the muscles in his face stiffened as if suddenly he'd recalled something long forgotten. "Go on," he said, his eyes darting expectantly around the room.

"During the war Margolin was in charge of a special team whose mission was to disrupt the North Vietnamese and Vietcong organizational structure through low-level grassroots infiltration, assassination, and even fraternization."

"Fraternization? Come on."

Ket nodded in agreement. "Carmen's right, Mr. Floyd. Langston's team was designed to be both politically and militarily effective."

"CIA, then?" said CJ, as if coaching Ket with the correct answer.

"No. They were all regular U.S. Army soldiers."

"You're sure?"

"Positive. My sister Mimm said Langston told her so himself."

CJ eased back in his chair and frowned, aware that the rules of engagement had prohibited grunts like Langston Blue or even his commanders from carrying out political assignments or fraternizing with the enemy. "Sounds far-fetched."

"Maybe, but it's the truth, and it's the reason Langston deserted the army, his wife, and an unborn child." Ket looked reassuringly at Carmen. "I've never told anyone this before, not even Carmen, but the day before Langston deserted he told Mimm that he had orders for a mission. Langston wasn't the kind of man who scared easily, but Mimm told me he sounded uncharacteristically nervous. He also told Mimm that none of the men in his team wanted to go except their captain."

"Did they go?"

"Yes. And as far as I know, only two of the eight came back: Margolin and a sergeant named Cortez who was badly wounded. Mimm had to beg for months to learn even that much. Margolin claimed the rest of his men were killed in a firefight and that Langston deserted. There was one strange thing, though. A few hours after they returned to their base camp outside our village, a medevac helicopter appeared out of nowhere, and within minutes Margolin and Cortez were gone. The next time I saw Peter Margolin's face was on a political poster announcing his first bid for Congress."

"When was that?"

"Nineteen ninety-two," said Ket.

CJ eased forward in his chair and stroked his chin again. "Guess twelve years of swimming with minnows in the House gave Margolin a taste for the big fish in the Senate."

Ket nodded. "And it looks like he'll make it. All the polls say he is way out in front."

"Anything else I should know about Margolin?"

Ket's tone turned steely. "Only that he's charming, conniving, and ruthless. Once I saw him shoot a motorcycle out from under an old man in our village. When the man, a petty black marketeer who specialized in fencing stolen U.S. contraband, got up to run, Margolin shot him in the back of the neck and watched him bleed to death next to a ditch along the side of the road. When he was sure the man was dead, he rolled his body down into a rice paddy and set fire to the motorcycle and the cache of cigarettes the man had been smuggling."

"Sounds like a prince. What about the conniving part?"

"He convinced everyone but my sister, including me and the U.S. Army, that Langston was a deserter. And he's on his way to becoming a U.S. senator. Need any more proof than that?"

CJ smiled. He liked Ket Tran's straightforwardness. "Guess not. He's the place to start." CJ glanced at Mavis for a hint of approval. Her face was expressionless. Turning to Carmen, he said, "Can I get that West Virginia address you had for your father?"

Carmen handed CJ a yellowed half sheet of paper with a general delivery address printed across the top in pencil. CJ recognized the paper as the kind of delicate rice paper he'd once purchased during R&R in Saigon and sent home to a long-forgotten girlfriend. The aging paper triggered memories of a week of drunken camaraderie and sex, a seven-day respite from hell. Looking at the address as if it were a coded secret message, CJ said, "Bluefield. Wonder what part of West Virginia that's in?"

"The southern part, near the Virginia border. I've done a little homework."

"Can I keep it?" asked CJ, fingering the limp piece of paper. "Sure."

CJ folded the paper in half and slipped it into his shirt pocket before looking again at Mavis. Realizing finally that no support would be forthcoming, he said, "I charge two fifty a day plus expenses, one week's charges up front. Flora Jean gets the same.

We'll stay on the case until we find out what happened to your father."

"Or find him," said Carmen.

"Yeah." CJ's tone was noticeably hollow.

The table turned silent until a tubby, mahogany-skinned waitress balancing a serving tray stacked high with food suddenly appeared. "Jambalaya, biscuits, a side of rice, iced tea, and honey for the two ladies," said the waitress, placing identical entrees and sides on the table in front of Ket and Carmen.

In near perfect unison, Ket and Carmen said, "Thanks."

The waitress nodded, smiled, and looked at CJ. "Your usual," she said, placing a plate of fried catfish, coleslaw, piping-hot biscuits, and red beans and rice in front of him. CJ eyed the steaming meal. "Looks great," he said halfheartedly, glancing at Mavis.

Sensing that something was out of kilter, the waitress asked, "Anything wrong?"

"Nope."

The waitress shrugged and turned her attention to Mavis. "Sure you don't want nothin', Ms. M.?"

"No."

"Okay." The waitress headed back toward the kitchen, leaving Ket and Carmen smiling and Mavis and CJ looking somber.

◆◆◆

Except for CJ and Mavis, the lunch crowd at Mae's had dwindled to just one other table with two people. Carmen and Ket had been gone for close to twenty minutes when CJ finally eased his chair back from the table to leave. He and Mavis had spent most of that time talking quietly as they skirted the same issue that always strained their often rocky relationship: CJ's always dangerous, too often life-threatening line of work. Work that included not simply the relatively mundane paperwork dance of bonding society's bottom-feeders and lowlifes out of jail but also mandated hunting down the 10 percent or so who routinely skipped their bond, refused to pay, threatened her, her father, or their business, or, like Newab Sha, tried to kill CJ.

"This isn't a bounty-hunting job, Mavis," said CJ, defending his decision to find out what had happened to Langston Blue. "I'm just gonna find out what happened to Carmen's father."

"Just like you were going to drag that dead Haitian back to justice. And like you were going to track down that lunatic Pinkie Duncan three months back, and like you were going to find that bond-skipping, whacked-out Indian kid, Bobby Two Shirts, a few years back. Face it, you're getting too old for the kind of life you insist on living."

"That's why I have Flora Jean. She's a lot younger, and don't forget, she's an ex-marine."

"Don't start that song and dance again, CJ. Flora Jean does what you tell her to. We both know that. I didn't see Newab Sha chasing her across Five Points trying to blow her head off."

"Mavis, you're exaggerating."

"Sure I am, CJ. Just like I'm exaggerating about Wendall Newburn coming in here first thing this morning flashing his badge and peppering me with a half hour's worth of questions."

CJ's eyebrows arched a split second before his face froze into a chiseled frown. "Why would that prima donna with a pistol be in here bothering you?"

"I'm not sure, but he had plenty of questions."

"Like what?"

"Like, were you after that Sha character for some reason other than him skipping his bond? And did you have some kind of relationship with his wife? And finally, did you have somebody kill him?"

"That high-yellow, half-witted dipshit's crazy!"

When the waitress who'd served them earlier looked up from clearing a nearby table, Mavis motioned for CJ to keep it down. "Maybe so, but people around here appreciate what he stands for. You might have missed it, CJ, but Wendall's carved out a respectable professional niche for himself. And, like it or not, he is Denver's highest-ranking black homicide detective."

"And I'm just a backwater bail bondsman."

"I didn't say that."

CJ stared down at the tabletop in silence before looking sadly at Mavis. "Sorry, Mavis, but it's what I do."

"I know what you do, CJ. I also know you're good at it. And believe it or not, I understand it's part of what makes you tick. But someday you're going to have to make a choice." Reaching across the table, she clasped CJ's hand tightly in hers. "I love you and care about you, baby. But over the years I've grown to hate what you do. Hate wondering if you're all right or dead in some alleyway." Rising from her seat, she slipped her hand out of CJ's and flashed him a hauntingly strange, hollow look. He'd seen the look before. It was a look that Mavis reserved for people she disconnected from her life.

"I'll work at doing better, babe."

"You've said that before, CJ."

"I mean it this time, Mavis."

"Hope so," said Mavis, heading toward the kitchen, the look on her face unchanged. "Because time's not on your side."

Chapter 7

IT WAS 4 O'CLOCK AND BREEZY when CJ pulled his immaculately restored '57 drop-top Bel Air into the driveway of the sagging old garage that flanked his Delaware Street office. Storm clouds were building to the west over the Rockies, and a hint of much-needed moisture was in the air.

Still off balance from Mavis's demand that he clean up his act, he'd stopped for gas at Rosie's Garage, the vintage Five Points 1950s-style gas station and auto repair shop owned by Roosevelt Weeks, to soothe his nerves. After an avalanche of prodding, he'd told his tale to Rosie, Morgan Williams, and Dittier Atkins, two down-on-their-luck former rodeo cowboys who did odd jobs for him and occasionally helped him with bond-skipping cases, ending with the fact that Sha had more than likely taken a bullet meant for him. Sipping beer and chasing it with salted pork rinds, the four of them had run through a list of thugs, drifters, muggers, con men, and murderers CJ had either crossed or brought to justice over the course of his twenty-nine-year bail-bonding and bounty-hunting career. The final culled list included a woman and three men.

Calvin Leigh, the son of a prominent black Denver doctor, who three years earlier had changed his name to Mohammad Rashaan and became a black Muslim, topped their list. CJ had helped put Rashaan behind bars for being the brains behind a Five Points chop shop and the point man for an "I'll blow up your building if you don't cooperate" shakedown scheme that had had Five Points and lower downtown businesses forking over seven grand a month.

Maurice "Pancho" Madrid, the abusive ex-husband of CJ's former secretary, Julie Madrid, made the number-two spot. CJ had once beaten him to within millimeters of his life for stalking and threatening Julie. He'd lived in Arizona for the three years Julie had attended law school, and word on the street was that now that she was a lawyer he was back in Denver looking to patch things up.

Bobby Two Shirts Deepstream and his twin sister, Celeste, who were both thought to still be in prison, or at least far away in parts unknown, rounded out the list. The four cracked jewels, as Rosie called them, had one thing in common: they had all threatened more than once to kill CJ.

CJ wasn't putting his money on any of them being Newab Sha's killer until he found out more about where they all were, but Rosie had his money on one of the Deepstreams, while Morgan and Dittier favored Rashaan.

CJ stepped from his driveway across the grass toward his office, spotting a couple of wooden slats missing from the fence that rimmed the yard and three large brown dead spots in the lawn. Reminding himself to get in touch with Morgan and Dittier about replanting the grass and repairing the fence, he bounded up the steps to his office and through the front door to find Flora Jean at her desk in her tiny converted entryway alcove of an office, hard at work.

Flora Jean had moved up from a job that had started six years earlier as a secretarial temp to become a licensed bail bondsman, and although CJ sometimes hated to admit it, she had become his right hand. Her move up the ladder meant that she performed fewer and fewer secretarial duties, so now they shared the responsibility for maintaining records, jockeying with computers, paying bills, and answering the phones, all tasks that CJ loathed. So he was happy to see Flora Jean busy at her computer. It meant that he'd likely have one less disagreeable thing to do.

Flora Jean continued typing, tapping her right foot and bouncing in her seat to the sounds of B. B. King belting out a blues tune from the gigantic boom box on a shelf above her desk. Over the years CJ had been able to expand her taste in music from a single focus on hardcore rap to his own musical passion, the blues. As B. B. sank into a bluesy lament, Flora Jean looked up at CJ and shook her head. "The brother needs to learn to stay at home a little more if he wants to keep his woman happy."

"It's the blues, Flora Jean. No one's ever happy with the blues."

Flora Jean shrugged, reached up, and turned off the music. "Whatever. We got work?" she added, aware that CJ had been at Mae's to discuss a job prospect.

CJ pulled Carmen Nguyen's $1,750 check out of his shirt pocket, smiled, and handed it to Flora Jean. "A week's worth. Delivered and signed."

Flora Jean beamed. For the past two months, business had been slow. Her car note and rent were a week past due. "In the nick of time, like the white folks say." She slipped a bank deposit slip from her top desk drawer, hastily filled it out, paper-clipped it to the check, and set the check face down on her desk. When she looked back up, CJ had taken a seat in one of the two small pressed-back wooden chairs that hugged the alcove's street-side wall. At six foot three and 240 pounds, CJ dwarfed the chair. He removed his sweat-stained Stetson, set it aside, and fumbled in his vest pocket for a cheroot, looking pensively at Flora Jean before lighting up. "Mavis is at her breaking point. I think the Newab Sha thing pushed her to the brink. She wants me to cut back."

Flora Jean shook her head. "Sugar, sugar, sugar. And you claim to be a man who knows about the blues? What Mavis wants ain't really got nothin' to do with the work comin' outta this office. Or any kinda cuttin' back. All the girl really wants is you. Look at you, CJ. Hate to say it, sugar, but you're a mess. Still the same street cowboy you were twenty years ago. And a black one at that. Shit, it's a wonder after all these years some white cop anglin' for a promotion or some thug lookin' for a way to build his rep ain't busted a cap in your butt. Mavis is right. You need to slow down your pace. Enjoy a few sunsets. Do somethin' other than bring Mavis the blues. That's all Mavis is after, a little bit of good times for the two of you before you're both too old to know what they mean."

"And just what would I do if I quit?"

"Hell, I don't know. Take a trip around the world. Write your memoirs, sell some of them antiques you got stashed in the basement, part with some of that Western memorabilia you been collectin' all these years. Then, if you gotta, buy yourself some more. Turn your collectin' jones into a business, the way white folks always seem to be able to do. Shit, if you can't do it, can't nobody in the world. You know the Western Americana game inside and out."

CJ looked around the alcove, eyeing every nook and cranny, and thought about how his uncle, the man who'd raised him and started him in the bail-bonding business, would sum up the last thirty years if he were still alive. His eyes drifted toward his upstairs apartment, where there were four rooms crammed with coffee cans full of cat's-eye marbles, jumbos in mint condition and eighty-year-old steelies worth their weight in gold. In the basement of the building he had stacks of mint-condition 45-rpm records—jazz, big band, and R&B—stored in tomato crates gathering dust, and plastic bins full of tobacco tins and inkwells from all around the world. He had spent a lonely childhood and all the years since Vietnam collecting old maps and movie posters, cattle-brand books—only the rarest of the rare—Tiffany lamps, saddle blankets, cowboy hats, spurs, bits, shaving mugs, and thousands of other folksy artifacts, folk art pieces, antiques, and even Western wear.

But it was his collection of antique license plates that made him the envy of antique aficionados and memorabilia enthusiasts across the United States. It was an assemblage that represented a collector's equivalent of the Nobel Prize, and it said more about him than any other collection he had. He'd started the collection during his teenaged years, when his uncle's drinking had reached its peak and street rods and low riders had taken the place of family in his life. He now owned more than six hundred license plates, a third of them rare early-twentieth-century gems fabricated using the long-abandoned process of overlaying porcelain onto iron. He had recently driven from Denver to Las Vegas to Minnesota, unsuccessfully chasing a rare 1917 New York City tag, laughing to himself all the way home, knowing deep down that the joy of the quest would buffer the disappointment of the failure.

"And if I don't?" said CJ, refocusing his attention on Flora Jean.

Flora Jean hesitated before choking out an answer. "Then Mavis will more than likely move on."

CJ swallowed hard and slipped the half-smoked cheroot out of his mouth. "And this business, the one that keeps the two of us clothed and fed, what happens to it?"

"Simple. I do more. You do less. And eventually, I buy you out."

CJ shook his head. He couldn't imagine selling a business that his uncle had started during the depths of the Depression, and a black-owned business at that. A business that had succeeded when you could count the number of African American families in Denver on just your fingers and toes. Blowing a smoke ring into the air, he said, "And who'll help you?"

"You, 'til you make your first million peddlin' antiques. After that, who knows?"

CJ leaned forward in his seat and tapped a cap of ash from the end of his cheroot into an ashtray inscribed with the insignia and colors of the First Marine Division, a reminder from Flora Jean to anyone who walked into her space that she was first and foremost always a marine. CJ took several long drags on his cheroot and watched the smoke trail up into the dust-covered wings of the room's ancient ceiling fan. His silence let Flora Jean know that he was at least thinking about what she had said. When he finally spoke up, his tone of voice told her the issue needed more consideration. "Now that we've mapped out my retirement plan, let's get back to earning our fourteen hundred bucks. For starters, we're gonna have to take an unpleasant trip down memory lane."

"To where?" said Flora Jean, wary of CJ's tone.

"Vietnam."

Flora Jean's stomach looped into knots whenever CJ mentioned Vietnam. Unlike her own war experience in the Persian Gulf, where casualties had been light and victory swift, Vietnam had been a horror-story disaster for half a million fighting men and women. Whenever CJ talked about Vietnam, the muscles in his face tightened and his eyes turned foggy.

"Carmen Nguyen's aunt told me something surprising today, something that I'd never heard during either of my two tours. I figured that with your marine intelligence background you might be able to shed some light on what she said."

"Shoot," said Flora Jean, wondering how two wars separated by almost two decades could be connected.

"Ever heard of either the army or the marines having uniformed eight-man teams designed to go behind enemy lines and, get this, fraternize with the enemy, carry out political assignments, and stomp the shit out of unsuspecting villagers?"

The muscles in Flora Jean's face began twitching. "Where'd you hear about that?"

"From Ket Tran. Sounded strange. But after I thought about it for a while, I remembered that once during my second tour in country, we ferried a group of special forces types down the Mekong River and dropped them off two miles behind enemy lines. The whole thing seemed bizarre. Especially since the navy didn't make a habit of slipping a slow-as-molasses hundred-and-twenty-five footer behind enemy lines without air cover or a high-speed escort. But we were blacked out communications wise, with orders to stay in the dark. Anyway, after we ran this bunch of bozos down to their drop point, I had the feeling that if the NVA or Vietcong had capped our asses, the navy woulda said they never heard of us."

"Did Carmen's aunt say whether the teams had a name?"

"Nope. But the number of men in the team was kinda strange. Eight, right between the numbers in a squad and a platoon. Somehow the term *rogue* came to mind."

"Did she happen to mention whether the officer in charge was a lieutenant or a captain?"

"She did, as a matter of fact. The guy in charge was a captain. Turns out, in fact, that he's that guy Carmen mentioned who's running for the Senate. Margolin."

"Shit!" This time the muscles in Flora Jean's face froze.

"You're starting to get that Sergeant Benson look, Flora Jean. Always means you know something I don't. Spit it out."

Flora Jean's response was slow and halting. "Sounds like Carmen's father was assigned to a unit that no one in the government, military or otherwise, likes to admit ever existed. A Star 1 team. An eight-man killer unit made up of everyday military grunts who were assigned the task of assassinating political leaders and taking out key North Vietnamese civilians during the Vietnam War. Army regulars who ended up doing what should have been 'the Company's' job."

"The CIA?"

"You got it."

"You're sure?"

"As sure as I am that I did a four-year tour in marine intelligence."

"So where does that leave us?"

"Not quite high and dry, but damn close to it. You can bet there's an official cap on whatever happened to Langston Blue and his buddies that's tighter than the lid on a coffin."

After a thoughtful pause, CJ broke into a half smile. "Maybe not. Could be good ol' Congressman Margolin can help."

"It's *one* place to start," said Flora Jean.

"You got another?"

It was Flora Jean's turn to smile. "I've still got a few contacts in the intelligence community, sugar. But it'll cost you."

Puzzled, CJ asked, "How much?"

"Not money, sugar."

"Then what?"

"Let me worry about that. Give me a day or two. I'll have some answers about Congressman Margolin, Langston Blue, and that Star 1 team of theirs. And you can count on the info bein' straight-up solid." Breaking into a broad *gotcha* kind of grin, Flora Jean reached up, turned up the volume on her boom box, and winked at a now totally befuddled CJ.

◆ ◆ ◆

Peter Margolin loved the view from the sixth floor of the twenty-story office building he was building in the Golden Triangle just north of Cherry Creek, as much as he loved the mildly acidic smell that still wafted up from the floor's curing concrete. Both served to arouse his senses, and for Margolin, titillation of the senses took a backseat to only two other things: power and money. He had used his political savvy, his social connections, and money he'd squirreled away for years to wangle his way into becoming managing partner in the $75 million project. After the fourth floor had been laid, with its panoramic view of the Denver skyline and the Front Range of the Rockies, he began making it a habit to visit the construction site once a week, just before sunset. As he watched the sun make its trek west and partially disappear behind Mount Evans, he knew that he was at the top of his game.

He'd worked his way through college doing summer construction—not that he had had to, given his family's wealth— and he'd always loved watching a project, no matter the size, rise out of the ground. For him it was akin to tending a garden. On big projects he loved to count each and every red clay-colored I-beam, inhale the woodsy smell of banks of two-by-fours, admire the stout geometry of intersecting struts. In many ways, watching a building rise from a hole in the earth gave him a sense of power. Not the kind of manipulative power he'd become used to as a congressman but the kind of raw physical power he'd known as a soldier during Vietnam.

The polls showed him six to seven points ahead of his opponent in the Senate race, and barring something catastrophic he knew he was less than four months away from striking financial and career high notes. The only possible fly in the ointment was Langston Blue, and he could deal with Blue. Even so, a puzzling problem kept gnawing at his subconscious. Just before he'd left his office for the day, his secretary had gotten a call from a bail bondsman asking about Blue. He'd shrugged the call off, saying that he was unavailable, certain that if it came down to it, he could also handle the bail bondsman. Now as he stood gazing into the orange glow of sunset, that phone call had him thinking.

The sky turned from orange to magenta as Margolin stood there thinking about success and failure, power and money, and the generational strength of his family's 150-year ties to Colorado. Glancing at his watch, he realized that he'd spent almost half an hour soaking in the grandeur. As he turned to head across the broad expanse of concrete and down a recently set stairwell to have dinner with his press secretary, Ginny Kearnes, the woman of the moment in his life, he had the sudden urge to shout, "Top of the world, Mom, top of the world!"

Starting his trek down the six flights of stairs, savoring the descent and enjoying the sound of his footsteps echoing off the metal, he remembered it was week's end and time to leave a twenty-dollar bill in the tool-shed lockbox behind the construction superintendent's trailer. The twenty dollars gave him access to the normally padlocked construction site, and the way he saw it, eighty dollars a month was a cheap price to pay for a weekly dose of pure exhilaration.

By the time he reached ground level, he was breathing heavily. In the thirty years since his military stint, he'd added twenty pounds to what had once been a lean, 185-pound frame. Closets full of tailor-made suits, custom-made shirts, and hand-crafted silk ties managed to camouflage the extra weight, and with just the right touch of silver at his temples and a pair of European-style glasses that he diplomatically inched up on his nose when the situation called for it, he had become the media's incarnation of a U.S. senator. As he walked along the narrow graveled pathway that led to his car, he paused to glance toward a newly excavated thirty-foot dropoff and the recently poured concrete stem wall that was the base for what would eventually be the northwest wall of the building's underground garage. The stem wall hadn't been there during his last visit, and something about it struck him as strangely out of place. He stopped momentarily, hoping to put his finger on what was so unusual. Unable to identify it, he turned away from the twenty-foot-long row of perfectly aligned rebar that spiked a foot above the top of the concrete and continued walking along the edge of the excavation. After a few yards he realized what had struck him about the wall. The plastic safety caps that should have topped off the rebar were missing.

Before he had a chance to ponder why such an important safety item was missing, he felt a shove from behind. Shouting, "What the fuck?" he turned to catch a glimpse of someone dressed in black from head to toe, wielding the hod carrier that was shoving him toward the thirty-foot dropoff. A second powerful shove sent him spiraling off balance over the edge of the pathway. He screamed, "Goddamn it!" as he grabbed the hod carrier's weathered four-foot-long handle, filling both palms with splinters. Then he slipped away, dropping toward the lethal bed of rebar below. Falling spread-eagled, he thought, *Top of the world, Mom, top of the world!* But the only word that escaped his mouth before his body slammed into the unprotected rebar was "Shit!"

Chapter

8

THE ADAMS COUNTY MOTEL on the outskirts of Denver just off I-70 looked as if it had been purposely constructed to look run down. Langston Blue had pulled into the dilapidated gem about 11:30 the night before, exhausted from driving halfway across the country in a truck with a bad cylinder and a front end badly in need of realignment. He had checked into a first-floor room that reeked of Lysol, plopped down across the room's sagging bed, and dropped off to sleep fully clothed.

The early-morning shower he jumped into turned cold after less than a minute, but he felt a hundred percent better than when he'd crashed nine hours earlier. After rereading Carmen's letter, he laid it aside on a rickety card table, the room's only other furnishing besides the bed and a wall-mounted black-and-white TV. He slipped on a pair of threadbare boxer shorts and flipped on the TV to see a pixieish, owl-eyed lady with a pageboy hairdo repeating the 8 a.m. news story lead. "Again, recapping our top story. Fifty-seven-year-old Congressman Peter Margolin was found dead at a Denver construction site late last night. Details surrounding his death are incomplete at this time, and the Denver police have not released a statement. A press conference has been scheduled at the State Capitol at 10:30. Be sure to stay tuned to Channel 9 for up-to-the-minute details."

Langston Blue found himself holding his breath as an inset photo of Peter Margolin that had flashed on the screen to the right of the news commentator finally disappeared. Margolin's hair was gray, he wore glasses, and he was jowlier, but other than that, he looked pretty much the same as he had thirty-five years earlier. Blue took a breath, stood, and turned down the sound on the television. He was nervous, and he didn't function well when he was nervous. When he was nervous he always reverted to the slow kind of thinking that had marked his youth. A jumble of disjointed thoughts raced through his mind. Taking a deep breath to calm himself, he tried to assess his situation. Someone had tried to kill him—that was a fact. And now someone had probably killed Margolin. He felt trapped, squeezed somehow between light and darkness. Maybe he should have stayed in West Virginia, started over from scratch, tried to make a go of it, the same way he had thirty-five years earlier.

Grabbing his pants from the bed, he shook them out for bugs, just as he had since early childhood. One more blow to his regimented normality and he knew he'd lose it. The way he had when Rufus Hawkes had died. The way he always did when he couldn't bear the pressure. The way he had thirty-five years earlier in the Vietnam jungle at Song Ve. What he needed was a plan, something he could think through and follow. A plan that would put him in touch with his daughter and keep them both out of harm's way if whoever had tried to kill him resurfaced.

It wasn't until he slipped on his shirt that he realized he was sweating. *To hell with a plan,* he told himself; after all, planning wasn't really his thing. He was a doer, good at carrying stuff out. Planning was for thinkers, not really for him. He glanced at the TV as he buttoned his shirt, wondering whether the press conference would be televised nationally. One thing for certain: he wouldn't be sticking around to see. He didn't need that kind of exposure, and he didn't need a bunch of talking heads, news commentators, prickly-faced cops, and phony sad-faced politicians to tell him what he already knew: Peter Margolin's death was no accident. Someone had murdered his former captain. More than likely the same person who'd tried to kill him, and he didn't need a plan to figure out that the someone was probably Lincoln Cortez.

◆◆◆

When it came to politics, a seven-mike press conference always meant serious business. Distraught and teary-eyed, Ginny Kearnes, Peter Margolin's press secretary and latest love interest, adjusted her skirt and told herself that she was as prepared as she possibly could be to duel with the media. It wasn't every day that a congressman and a shoo-in for the Senate with connections all the way to the White House was murdered.

Aware that what she needed right now more than anything was to maintain her composure, Ginny watched a wiry, rat-faced little man in a mustard-colored Colorado Rockies baseball cap that had once been white as he adjusted the center mike. The man tapped the microphone with his middle finger, listened to the hollow echo, grinned up at her as if he'd just won the lottery, and said, "Everything's kosher. Two minutes to showtime."

Fighting back tears, she tried to ignore the statement's irony. Everything wasn't kosher. Her world had been shredded. Peter was dead, her promising staircase to political stardom had collapsed, and two hours earlier an insipid black cop named Newburn had peppered her with fifteen minutes' worth of the most inane questions she'd ever heard, until she was shaking and bleary-eyed with tears. Now she had to stand tall, put on her press secretary's face, and pretend to be in control.

The only thing that had saved her from dropping into a despondent pit was the fact that Owen Brashears, editor of the *Boulder Daily Camera,* Peter's longtime adviser and one of their closest friends, had been at her side almost from the instant she had learned about Peter's death.

Hearing the words, "You'll do fine," from somewhere behind her, she spun around to find Owen a few feet away. Forcing a smile, he flashed her a thumbs-up sign. "Just be calm. Let Colorado and the rest of the country know what they've lost."

"I'll do my best."

"Do better."

Owen's words were stern yet comforting. It was the way he worked. As tears rolled down his cheeks, he offered a warning. "Watch out for that reporter, Grimes. He's an ass. And he had no love for Peter."

Certain that Owen was hurting as much as she was, she considered leaving the podium to comfort the man who had helped Peter with his girlfriend problems during college and his financial upheavals during a messy divorce and walked him through a minefield of grief when he'd lost both of his parents in the space of a year. When a squeaky-voiced man walked up behind the first camera and announced, "Thirty seconds, Ms. Kearnes," she knew that stepping away from the podium wasn't an option. Showtime was at hand.

Ginny ran one hand through her thick blond hair, pursed her lips, sighed, and eyed the News Link director. After her prepared statement, she'd take four questions: one from Owen, one from *Rocky Mountain News* investigative reporter Paul Grimes, then one each from reporters from the *Westword* and the *Denver Post*. If time allowed, she'd take a question from a national pool reporter, and then she could go to the newshound scrubs. She doubted whether viewers out in TV land understood how much any press conference was staged. She remembered watching Pentagon and White House press conferences during Operation Desert Storm. Pure fantasy, she thought as the on-air cue light atop the camera flashed green. When the assistant director said, "Cue the music," five seconds of News Link breaking-news music blared before the director barked "Voiceover," and in a prerecorded spot the 5 p.m. anchor announced, "This is News Link 4 coming to you live from the Colorado State Capitol with breaking news."

"Cue the podium," said the director.

Ginny cleared her throat as she watched the director's skinny index finger shoot point-blank at her nose. "I'm Ginny Kearnes, Congressman Peter Margolin's press secretary. I am here under the most tragic of circumstances on behalf of the congressman and the citizens of our state to answer questions concerning what can only be termed a Colorado tragedy and to recognize Congressman Margolin's immense contributions to our great state and the West." After another minute of platitudes, laced liberally with the Democratic Party line, she looked out into the press corps audience and said, "First question, please."

The questions rained down on her for what felt like an hour but in truth was less than ten minutes. She fielded the most obvious question first: "Was the congressman murdered?"

Her answer, "The matter's in the capable hands of the Denver Police Department," came easy.

Answering Grimes's question: "Can you describe more specifically for us exactly how the congressman died?" was the worst.

She suppressed her anger and handled the question deftly, aware that Grimes probably already knew the gruesome details and that the question had been asked in an attempt to unnerve her and create a little television theater. Her answer was brief and to the point. "The congressman died from injuries sustained in a fall at a construction site." The answer triggered a thumbs-up sign from Owen and stopped Grimes in his tracks. The rest of the predictable questions ranged from "Who does the Democratic Party have in mind to fill the congressman's seat?" to "Do you think Congressman Margolin's Republican opponent, Alfred Reed, is now a Senate shoo-in?" *Have you no decency?* she thought before giving the same answer to both questions. "I'm afraid you'll have to address that question to the parties' leadership."

After skirting delicate questions about her own relationship with Margolin and responding to a query as to whether Margolin's political leanings had shifted from the far right to the left over the years, she felt that she had been professional, gracious, and instructive and above all had held her own. She left the podium in a state of reflective remorse and stumbled into Owen Brashears's comforting arms.

"You were great," Brashears said reassuringly.

"Better than great—fantastic," a voice erupted just behind them. They looked back to see Elliott Cole, chairman of the state Republican Party, grinning. "And pointing to the parties on those two questions about succession. First-rate. Damn sure."

Brashears's temples throbbed as he stared down the party chairman. "Go blow smoke somewhere else, Elliott. This isn't the place."

Ignoring Brashears, the still athletic-looking seventy-one-year-old Cole doffed his trademark cowboy hat, bowed graciously, and eyed Ginny Kearnes. "No disrespect, Ms. Kearnes, but in politics you have to start where you start, and unfortunately, the starting line begins right here."

"Even vultures respect the dead," Owen countered.

"Horse shit, Owen." Cole flashed Ginny an apologetic smile. "Go peddle that sentiment in the left-wing newspaper you run. In case you missed it, Mr. Editor, honey drippings always fall to those who seek them. Peter's death just afforded us Republicans and Alfred Reed front-runner's status. My job is to make certain he stays out front."

Ginny's eyes welled up as she tried to think of something to say that was clever, biting, or hateful—but she couldn't. It was Owen who found the words that sent Cole scurrying. "Hope your budding front-runner can account for his time over the last twenty-four hours. I'd hate to have to dig into his where-abouts."

"You don't have the balls."

"Maybe not. But those overzealous reporters that I'm forced to overpay damn sure do. Don't push me, Elliott. Trust me. I'd enjoy unleashing my hounds on you."

"I'll remember that the next time I wrap my fish guts up in your newspaper." Nodding and smiling at Ginny, Cole reposi-tioned his Montana-blocked, wide-brim hat on a head of thin-ning silver-gray hair and turned to leave. "Remember this, though, my friend. Hound-lettin' works both ways." Cole flashed Owen a final broad, toothy grin before walking off into the still crowded room.

"*No mas,*" said Ginny, puffy-eyed and no longer a match for another TV camera, politician, or reporter, or even her own bathroom mirror. "Let's get out of here."

Weaving their way through the crowd and refusing questions, they rushed down a flight of stairs, scurried past a bank of leg-islative offices, and escaped onto the rolling grassy western expanse of the State Capitol grounds. They were on their way down the lengthy set of flagstone steps that led to 14th Avenue, where Ginny had disorientedly parked her car an hour and a half earlier, when a large black man, smoking a cheroot and wearing a sweat-stained Stetson, approached them.

"Excuse me, Ms. Kearnes. Can I speak with you a second?"

"Sorry, we're in a hurry," said Brashears, contemplating whether or not to shove his way past the man.

"I understand. Been on the move before myself." The man tipped his hat in introduction before slipping a business card out of his shirt pocket and handing it to Ginny. "CJ Floyd." He extended his hand. When Ginny didn't reciprocate, he said, "Congressman Margolin's secretary said that in order to get my questions answered I'd have to speak to you."

Owen grabbed Ginny by the hand without responding and they both stepped around CJ.

"It's about Langston Blue," CJ said, taking three quick steps backward and once again blocking their path.

"Never heard of him," said Ginny.

"You heard her. Now would you please get out of our way?" said Brashears.

"I'll call you to follow up," said CJ, stepping aside. "It's important."

Ginny glanced at the business card in her hand before tossing it aside. "No need, Mr. Floyd." Arm in arm with Owen, she followed his lead, taking the steps two at a time, leaving CJ standing alone, taking a long, thoughtful drag on his cheroot.

They didn't speak again until they were seatbelted securely in Ginny's BMW. Owen spoke first. "Who in the shit was the black guy?"

"Never seen him before. His card said he's a bail bondsman."

"What would a bail bondsman want with Peter?"

"You heard him. Something to do with somebody named Langston Blue."

"Strange-sounding name."

Ginny nodded, started the car, and eased into traffic, wondering why her day had now been bookended by two large black men asking about a man named Langston Blue. Wendall Newburn, the Denver homicide cop she'd met with earlier, had claimed Peter had scribbled a note on his home office day planner that read, "Ask Cortez about Langston Blue." She'd told Newburn the truth: she'd never heard of the man. But she had lied to the bail bondsman, Floyd. Sometimes her job required her to put a slight bend in the truth. Sometimes it called for flat-out fabrication. She had been in love with Peter Margolin, and if finding out why he had died meant being untruthful, she was prepared for that. She was savvy and well schooled in the world of politics, and painfully aware that when a political figure with as high a profile as Peter Margolin's had a bail bondsman sniffing up his shorts, things weren't entirely kosher.

"You okay?" asked Owen. "You're weaving in and out of your lane."

"Yes. Just exhausted and tired of bending the truth."

"It'll be okay." Owen patted her hand reassuringly.

Ginny didn't answer. She was too busy thinking about the mystery man Langston Blue and trying to erase the memory that no matter how much she altered the truth in a press conference, Wendall Newburn had told her earlier that morning that the man she loved had been murdered. If Langston Blue was the secret to why he'd been killed, that was the trail she'd follow, and if the bail bondsman, Floyd, held the key, that was where she'd start.

Chapter
9

CJ SPENT MOST OF THE AFTERNOON in his office trying to get a fix on who had tried to kill him and pinpoint the whereabouts of Mohammad Rashaan, but he'd come up with nothing but dead ends. A numbers runner he knew claimed that Rashaan was living outside Albuquerque, and a half-coherent retired mailman who had been a longtime drinking buddy of CJ's late Uncle Ike said that Rashaan had moved to Colorado Springs. The fact that Rashaan was nowhere to be found bothered CJ more than if he'd been forced to turn over every rock the self-proclaimed little anarchist might be hiding under.

The only solid information he'd come up with concerning who might be out to kill him had come courtesy of phone and computer work initiated by Flora Jean, who'd dug up the fact that Bobby Two Shirts, Celeste Deepstream's pathetic little worm of a twin, had died from a heroin overdose two years earlier. And although CJ and Flora Jean were reasonably certain that Celeste was still doing time in the Cañon City Women's Correctional Institution, CJ asked Flora Jean to follow up with a prisoner-release record search to make certain that they were right.

The fact that someone had tried to kill CJ had thrown Mavis off stride, and after an in-office lunch of fried catfish and butter beans, she'd hovered over him protectively for the rest of the afternoon. He tried to downplay the threat by telling her, "I'll worry about somebody trying to off me the next time I'm in a war," which had only added fuel to the fire.

Flora Jean had calmed the waters, reassuring Mavis that they would peg who the shooter was soon enough and that, as always, she had CJ's back. When Mavis went upstairs to CJ's apartment for a bag of coffee, Flora Jean stepped in to tone down CJ's bravado. "Are you crazy, CJ? Or just turnin' old-age stupid? You think Mavis wants to hear your half-baked macho bluster? She's worried to death about you. You blind?"

"What do you want me to say? That I'm scared of some half-wit with a back-to-Africa agenda or some woman who's doing time?"

"No, I want you to quit spoutin' off like a black-folks version of Rambo and take the time to see things through Mavis's eyes. How'd you feel if the shoe was on the other foot and it was Mavis bein' dogged by some shooter?"

Caught off guard by the question, CJ turned pensive.

"Cat got your tongue?" asked Flora Jean, aware that since the time of CJ's late Uncle Ike she was the only one who could get away with such a question.

"No," said CJ, still pondering the original question.

"Makes you think, don't it? It's a little different when you the one gotta do the lion's share of the worryin'. You don't never wanna lose somebody who loves you like Mavis, CJ. She ain't replaceable. So quit pushin' her buttons. Try a little tenderness. Might do wonders."

CJ stared past Flora Jean without answering, through the hand-blown divided glass panes of the old Victorian building's bay window into the twilight.

"Sure is quiet down here," said Mavis, returning with a pound of freshly ground coffee. Her trip upstairs had given her time to calm down. Walking around in the place where CJ slept, a space where they'd quarreled, shared the best and worst of times, and made love, seemed to have somehow suppressed her overwrought feelings. It was almost as if it had enabled her to get closer to him than he sometimes allowed.

"We're thinkin'," said Flora Jean watching CJ nod in agreement.

"Well, don't think too much," said Mavis, walking over and squeezing CJ's right hand. "It might hurt your brain."

CJ squeezed back and eyed Flora Jean. "Don't worry," CJ said, smiling. It was a broad, easy smile, the kind that let everyone know the earlier tension was behind them.

"Everyone up for coffee?" asked Mavis, heading for a battered coffee maker that was well past its prime.

The front doorbell rang as CJ and Flora Jean nodded in unison. "I've got it," said Flora Jean, heading for the door. "And Mavis, don't make the coffee too weak. Ain't got no use for weak-ass coffee or spineless men."

The woman standing face-to-face with Flora Jean was dressed in $150 Nikes and designer sweats. Her hair was perfectly styled. Her face expressionless, except for her eyes, which were puffy and red.

"I'd like to speak with Mr. Floyd," said the woman in a husky, gentrified voice.

"He expectin' you?"

"No," the woman said authoritatively.

"Come on in," Flora Jean said guardedly, leading the woman through her own cramped office. She squinted at the confining walls and thought once again about asking CJ to remodel the place. The thought had passed by the time they reached the dining room. "CJ, you got a visitor."

CJ looked up from the coffee creamer he was holding directly into the eyes of Ginny Kearnes. Ginny eyed CJ squarely and smiled at Mavis. "Virginia Kearnes. Everyone calls me Ginny."

She'd barely gotten the words out when CJ added, "The late Congressman Margolin's press secretary." Nodding toward Mavis, he said, "The java specialist over there is Mavis Sundee."

"And I'm Flora Jean Benson."

"My pleasure."

"Care for coffee?" asked Mavis. "Just freshly brewed."

"Yes. Black," said Ginny.

"Surprised you decided to look me up after our encounter this morning," said CJ.

"I was still reeling from the press conference. You threw me for a loop. I needed time to think."

"Fair enough. What can I do for you?"

"Well . . . I guess the best place to start is with being honest. I was more than Peter Margolin's press secretary, Mr. Floyd. We were in love. We were planning to get married as soon as he won his bid for the Senate."

"I'm sorry."

"Thank you." Ginny accepted a steaming mug of coffee from Mavis.

"I'll get mine," Flora Jean said, waving Mavis off and stepping between CJ and Ginny, noting that the lean Kearnes was just a couple of inches shorter than she.

"I've lost everything, Mr. Floyd. I need some answers, and I need your help."

"I'm afraid I operate in a world that might be a little outside your bounds. You might do better with a lawyer or the cops."

"Maybe so, but I'm here because we have a connection."

"Which is?"

"Langston Blue. The man you asked me about this morning."

"What do you know about him?" asked Flora Jean, as her intelligence-operative instincts kicked in.

"Nothing really," said Ginny, surprised that Flora Jean had responded. "Except that I started my day in a confessional with a homicide detective named Wendall Newburn who said that Peter had jotted Blue's name in his day planner. Some note to ask someone named Cortez about Langston Blue."

Flora Jean frowned. "That's it?"

"Yes," Ginny said.

"Not much there to sink our teeth into," said Flora Jean.

"But it's something," Kearnes pointed out. "So now that I've told you my story about Blue, how about sharing yours?"

"Might be difficult," said CJ, wondering how to best keep a line open to Kearnes in case she learned more, either from Margolin's records or from the police.

Ginny's face stiffened as she flashed CJ and Flora Jean a cold, hard stare. Her next words were measured and lacquered with authority. "That cop, Newburn, said Peter was murdered. And with or without your help, I plan to find out who killed him. I can pay you if that's the problem."

"I've already been retained," said CJ.

"I see." Ginny's face turned a faint shade of pink. "Well, you said it best, Mr. Floyd. We're more than likely from different worlds. Newburn's probably closer to mine. Same goes for the man who was with me this morning when we met, Owen Brashears. He's the editor of the *Boulder Daily Camera*. You see, Mr. Floyd, my world is filled with people like that."

Incensed, Flora Jean said, "So's ours."

CJ shot Flora Jean a look that said, *Pull in your reins*, before responding to Kearnes. "This isn't a pissin' contest, Ms. Kearnes, and I'd help you if I could, but I'm already obligated."

"We may end up at odds," said Ginny. "Remember that when you're out there in your world's orbit, Mr. Floyd."

"I will," said CJ.

"Thanks for the coffee," said Ginny, smiling at Mavis before placing her cup on a nearby table. "I'll see myself out."

Ignoring the offer, Flora Jean followed Ginny to the front door. Moments later Ginny Kearnes had slipped away as quickly and mysteriously as she had come. When Flora Jean returned, CJ and Mavis were staring at each other blankly.

"Wasn't that heavy duty?" Flora Jean asked.

"Different," CJ acknowledged with a nod.

"Think she really has any clout?" asked Mavis.

"A lot more than we do," said CJ.

"No matter," said Flora Jean. "We got ourselves a nugget or two we didn't have before. The cops are sayin' Margolin was definitely murdered, and we know he was set to have a meetin' with somebody named Cortez about Langston Blue."

"You learned something else, too," said Mavis, surprising CJ and Flora Jean with her uncharacteristic interest. "You're into it with somebody from a different league."

Winking at Mavis and then at CJ, Flora Jean said, "Can't speak for the two of you, but I know a heavy hitter or two."

Mavis looked befuddled, but CJ smiled, knowing exactly the kind of heavy hitters Flora Jean had in mind.

◆ ◆ ◆

Aided by the brightness of a nearby streetlamp, Celeste Deepstream watched CJ walk Mavis down his driveway, give her a lingering good-night kiss, tuck her safely into her vehicle, and wave good-bye. A lone cottonwood blocked any view he might have had of Celeste. Her left calf muscles ached, cramped from two hours of being scrunched behind the wheel of a subcompact rental car. But the surveillance and her patience had paid off. She'd gotten what she'd come for: an unfiltered view of Floyd and the soft spot in his life.

In college, she had once had someone besides her brother who cared about her. Back when she'd been a world-class athlete with a swimmer's sculptured body, a book full of NCAA records, and a national reputation. But Bobby, ever dependent, hampered by poor judgment, weak, and addicted, had destroyed the relationship.

Easing from behind the cottonwood, she turned on her headlights and latched on to Mavis's SUV. Before the night was out, she'd know where Mavis Sundee lived. In the end, she would make Floyd pay the same way she had paid when she'd lost Bobby. She'd make the Sundee woman suffer before she died, just as Bobby had. Then she'd kill them both.

Chapter

10

THE ONLY TANGIBLE THING Langston Blue had to point him toward his daughter was the return address on an envelope and a now dog-eared letter. It was as if whoever had written the letter was testing him, trying to see if he'd respond to the bait. As he crawled along in Denver's morning rush-hour traffic after spending the night in a Wal-Mart parking lot, he was hopeful. Seeing Margolin's face on a TV screen had thrown him for a loop, made him run, turned him into a jackrabbit. But driving around Adams County back roads for two predawn hours, through cow pastures and farm land, he'd had time to think. Following a map he'd bought in the Wal-Mart, he was now headed for the 1600 block of Wazee Street.

After threading his way down jam-packed Colorado Boulevard, he moved quickly down 17th Avenue, past City Park and the midtown hospital district into downtown. According to his map, 1664 Wazee, the address he was looking for, was on the western edge of downtown in a neighborhood called LoDo, a twenty-square-block area buttressed on its northern edge by a baseball park called Coors Field.

Gawking at the stadium's size as he passed it, he turned onto the 1700 block of Wazee and started checking addresses on the buildings lining the even-numbered side of the street. Ranging from three to eight stories tall, most were constructed of brick, marble, or limestone, and they all looked pretty close to new. Thinking that Carmen Nguyen must be doing pretty well for herself, he cruised past 1664, a red-brick building trimmed in ivy. The building's jutting balconies framed in hand-forged wrought iron and a solid brass front door fourteen feet high screamed *high end.* Right, wrong, or otherwise, this woman calling herself *daughter* was living in high cotton.

When he realized the horn blares behind him were meant for him, he eyed the building's entrance one last time and eased off the brake, driving two blocks south and a couple of blocks east past two parking lots jammed with cars and sporting signs that read "Parking, $10 an hour" before he found a parking-metered street.

He considered ignoring the meter but thought better of it when he realized that a parking ticket might be all Cortez would need to trace him. He fed two quarters into the meter before realizing that fifty cents purchased only thirty minutes of time, shook his head, popped in two more quarters, and headed back toward Carmen's building.

The concierge sitting behind the polished mahogany desk in the building's lobby was dressed in a dark gray sport coat and light gray slacks that made him look more like a stockbroker than what he was: front-line building security and a greeter. Realizing that there was no way to reach the building's inner sanctum without engaging the man, Blue cleared his throat and hitched up his pants. His washed-out jeans and sweat-stained T-shirt might violate the building's dress code, for all he knew, but he'd come 1,450 miles to find a daughter he'd never known, and with the journey's end clearly in sight, he forged ahead.

"I'd like to see Carmen Nguyen," he said, boldly stepping up to the desk.

The concierge flashed an insipid greeter's smile. "Is she expecting you?"

"No."

"And your name is?"

Blue thought about giving the man a fictitious name but said, "Langston Blue" instead.

The greeter eyed him from head to toe, checked a computer printout lying on his desk, cleared his throat, and said, "I'll ring Dr. Nguyen for you, Mr. Blue. You can have a seat if you'd like."

Blue almost said *shit* in response to the news that his daughter was a doctor. He had no idea if she was a philosopher, a veterinarian, or a baby doc, but she was a doctor. Suddenly he was full of questions, and his mind was awash with images of Mimm and the lush countryside of rural Vietnam. He wondered whether Carmen looked like her, petite, olive-skinned, and soft. Or maybe she was big-boned and dark-skinned like him. How had she gotten to America and escaped the war? And what about Mimm's sister, Ket? He knew that Mimm was dead; he'd gotten the word decades ago from another deserter—but was Ket dead, too?

His mind still racing, Blue stepped back from the desk to calm himself as he surveyed the spacious, granite-floored lobby.

Two posh leather chairs and a table occupied the wall to his left. He thought about taking a seat in order to gather his thoughts, but as he hesitated, a woman carrying a grocery bag brushed past him and plopped down in one of the chairs. He eyed the woman, who was now staring at him as if she was afraid he might any second ask her for money, and moved back toward the concierge.

Glancing down at a computer screen mounted in the desktop, the concierge reached to his left and tapped a red button. "I didn't get an answer the first time I buzzed her. I'll try her again."

"Thanks," said Blue, watching the woman with the grocery bags pack up her things. The instant she moved off, he walked over to the chair she'd vacated and sat down. The wall behind him had the look of Old World plaster. He studied its uneven texture and thought about why, after all these years, Cortez and a daughter he'd never known he had had come calling. He didn't know if the reasons were tied to Peter Margolin's murder, but he knew he had to be wary and not let his heart get in the way of his head the way it had with Mimm. For all he knew, the woman calling herself Carmen Nguyen could be working for Cortez or Margolin.

As his thoughts descended to a place that always made him mistake prone and nervous, the concierge called out, "Excuse me, Mr. Blue."

"Yeah?" said Blue, startled, one eye darting.

"Dr. Nguyen doesn't seem to be in. Would you like to leave a message for her?"

Blue paused, trying to gain control of his thoughts, uncertain whether most other people in the world, people who'd never been called *slow,* ever had to face the same problem. "Yeah."

"And the message would be?" said the concierge, his tone taking on an air of impatience.

"Just tell her Langston Blue came by and that I'll try to catch up with her later."

"Is there a phone number where you can be reached? I can leave it for her."

"Nope."

Noting the look of disappointment on Blue's face, the concierge said, "Sorry you missed her."

"It's okay. We'll connect."

"Enjoy your day," the concierge said perfunctorily as Blue turned to leave.

"You too," said Blue, suddenly thinking of Mimm and the amazing light of the Vietnamese landscape, the alternating bustle and serenity of the Can Tho canal district, and the vivid colors and enticing, exotic smells of the Vietnamese boat market.

◆◆◆

The morning sunlight streaming through the big bay window of CJ's office always caused the room to seem larger than it was. The aroma of coffee hung in the air as CJ, Flora Jean, Ket Tran, and Carmen crowded around CJ's battle-scarred conference table, mapping out a strategy they hoped would help him locate Langston Blue.

"Sounds like the Kearnes woman might end up being a pain,"

said Carmen, doodling a picture of a river-rafting boat on a notepad as she responded to CJ's comments about Ginny Kearnes's visit.

"We can handle her," said CJ. "Let's get back to Blue. Think he's still back in West Virginia?" he asked Ket.

"That's the only address I've ever had for him, and it's more than a quarter century old. I got it from a man who brokered safe passage to the U.S. for Vietnamese war refugees."

"Then we just might have to go lookin'," said Flora Jean. "I called a couple of active-duty MI contacts of mine back east first thing this mornin', hopin' to get some info on exactly what the army's Star 1 units did during Vietnam. Even asked them if they could pinpoint the unit Blue had been in. Hell, practically before I could get the words 'Star 1' outta my mouth, they both clammed up. And these are two boys that owe me big." Flora Jean glanced at Carmen. "Trust me, sugar, whatever your daddy was mixed up in over in Vietnam must still have one heck of a smell to it."

"And you can bet it's linked to Peter Margolin dying at that construction site," said CJ. "With Flora Jean's military intelligence people running for the exits, this whole thing could waft its way all the way up to the Pentagon or the halls of Congress."

"Another My Lai?" asked Flora Jean.

CJ pondered the question and shook his head. "Don't think so. That would've been too hard to cover up. No, whatever Blue was involved in was something more clandestine, something that was planned. Not the result of a platoon of unschooled army grunts melting down and going apeshit on civilians. I'm guessing Blue never knew what he was involved in until the very last minute."

"He had to know something," countered Ket. "I told you, the day before he deserted he told Mimm that no one in his unit wanted to go on that mission but that captain of theirs, Margolin."

"Well, Margolin's dead, and Blue's still missing. Looks like we may really have to head back to West Virginia."

"Hold on," said Flora Jean. "Before we head off on some wild-goose chase sprinting halfway across the country and droppin' in on a state where folks ain't had a job for the last half a century, I'm gonna try one last MI contact."

"Thought you exhausted your intelligence sources this morning?" said CJ.

"You know better than that, sugar," Flora Jean said with a smile. "I always keep one hole card for special occasions. I've got a source real high up. A two-star general. Served with him during Desert Storm. He was a military intelligence major during Vietnam. Best of all, he lives just down the road in Colorado Springs."

"What makes you think he'll 'fess up any more than those two aces in the hole you talked to this morning?"

"Oh, he'll talk," said Flora Jean with a wink. "Always has. He's the kind of man who prefers his meat on the dark side, if you get my drift."

Chapter

11

CARMEN'S VOICE ROSE TO A CRESCENDO. "CJ, he's here. He left a message for me at my condo. My father's here in Denver."

CJ nudged the slice of sweet-potato pie and a half-eaten ham sandwich Mavis had brought him for lunch across his desktop and adjusted his cell phone from his left ear to his right ear. "Calm down, Carmen."

"Okay, okay."

"When did he leave the message?"

"About nine this morning. I would never have known he came by until this evening but I had to run home for lunch to pick up some papers I'd forgotten. Fortuitous, don't you think?"

"A little. Did he leave a phone number? Say where he was staying?"

"No. Just a message with the building concierge saying he'd come back."

"Did he say what time?"

"No." Carmen's voice trailed off.

"Did the concierge describe him to you?"

"No. I didn't ask him to. Why all the questions?"

CJ chose his words carefully. "Because we're dealing with a man who's been missing in action for over three decades, an army deserter. And in case you've forgotten, the man in command of the unit he deserted turned up dead the other day. The important thing here, Carmen, is your safety."

Carmen paused and thought for a moment. Thought about never having had a father—never having known her mother. About five-hundred-pound bombs whistling as they dropped from the sky, about the chatter of machine-gun fire and the nauseating disinfectant smell of napalm. She thought about escaping from Vietnam with Ket as part of a flotilla of boat people in 1979 and landing just south of San Francisco, seasick, half-starved, and petrified in a strange new homeland. "I'm tougher than you think, CJ," she said finally. "And I'm not really concerned with my safety. What I'm concerned about is connecting with my father."

"Do you have to go back to work?" asked CJ.

"No. I finished the experiment I was working on late this morning."

"Good. I'll be over there in twenty minutes. If he shows up before that, stall, but whatever you do, don't let him in."

"For God's sake, CJ. He's my father!"

"Stall, Carmen. I'll be there as soon as I can."

Carmen's response was halfhearted. "Okay."

"See you in a few," said CJ, shutting off his cell phone and reaching across his desk for Carmen's file. He opened the file and jotted down Carmen's phone number and address, stroked his chin thoughtfully, slipped his snub-nosed .38 out of his top drawer, and laid it on top of the file folder before finishing his sweet-potato pie.

◆ ◆ ◆

Ginny Kearnes was seated in the Palace Arms Restaurant of Denver's Brown Palace Hotel, one of President Dwight Eisenhower's favorite places to dine, enjoying a late lunch and leaning heavily on Owen Brashears for moral support. The half-empty room full of well-dressed businesspeople had a classy retro look that shouted 1950s. Staring across the table at Brashears, Kearnes twirled her fork around slowly in what was left of her apple-crumb dessert. "I've exhausted every lead, Owen. Talked to that black cop, Newburn, and the bail bondsman, Floyd, looked for dirt on the Republicans' new fair-haired boy, Alfred Reed, and I've got nothing."

Not the least bit surprised, Brashears said, "You can be certain as September snow in the Rockies that Newburn won't toss you any bones. He didn't get to be a black homicide lieutenant by stepping outside the bounds of the rule book. Just be glad he served you up the day-planner connection between Langston Blue and Cortez. That's at least something."

"But he and Floyd stonewalled me on that, too."

"Doesn't matter. Or have you forgotten I was a wet-behind-the-ears journalist during Vietnam? If Newburn or Floyd won't give us anything, I'll do some digging on my own. I'll turn up something; count on it."

Ginny smiled, aware that Owen had been a *Stars and Stripes* reporter and then a war correspondent during Vietnam. When he'd come home and begun protesting the war, some media insiders claimed that his "on-the-front-lines" war bravado and sudden antiwar switch were nothing more than a ploy for moving up the media ranks. He'd also made some mistakes and garnered more than a few enemies in high places during the war, largely because he'd played a little too fast and loose with facts and cultivated a few too many relationships with noncombatant ladies. But his troubles with stateside media people and military brass subsided over the years, and he'd settled comfortably into the editor-in-chief slot at the *Boulder Daily Camera*, where he'd been for over fifteen years.

"You lost your footing once playing advocate, and look what it got you," said Ginny.

Brashears shrugged off the inference that his career had been stifled because of his back-and-forth stance on the war. "It got me out of playing pretty boy in front of a camera and back into the print media where I belong. Or maybe you forgot."

"I'm not forgetting anything, Owen. I'm just repeating what Peter always said, that you lost your footing for a while after Vietnam."

Visibly upset, Brashears forced a smile. "And I found it. I edit the third-largest newspaper in the state, we've won five Pulitzers, and now I've lost one of my closest friends." He reached across the table and clasped Ginny's hand. "We'll find out who killed Peter, with or without the cops or that bail bondsman Floyd."

"How?"

"Simple. I'll play reporter. I've done it before."

"Do you think Peter's murder is tied to this guy Blue?"

"I don't know. But it's our only lead besides the possibility that Elliott Cole and his band of Republican cut-throats are somehow involved."

"They wouldn't kill someone to get into office."

Brashears's eyebrows shot skyward. "Ginny, you're a press secretary, for God's sake. It's politics, remember? I wouldn't put anything past them."

"You could be right," she said, shaking her head.

"When I have something I'll let you know," he said, patting her hand and watching her eyes well up with tears.

"Be careful, Owen. I don't want someone shoving you over the edge of a retaining wall, too."

"Is that what happened?"

"Yes. Newburn told me during one of his dreadful visits. You didn't know?"

"No."

"Guess they're holding back on the press."

"Don't they always? I'll start digging."

"So will I," said Ginny as a tear trickled down her cheek. "Sooner or later Peter's killer will have to answer to me."

◆ ◆ ◆

Celeste Deepstream knew about the iron lung because of her brother's illness. Frail, failing to thrive, unstable on his feet, and barely able to breathe, Bobby had been taken to a reservation infirmary when he was barely six, diagnosed with polio, courtesy of the seventy-five-year-old alcoholic doctor who attended to their Acoma Indian tribe's health needs, and placed in an iron lung.

Bobby had spent two nights confined to the iron lung on the strength of the old drunk's diagnosis before an astute visiting intern determined that Bobby was actually suffering from malnutrition and a postherpetic neuritis courtesy of a systemic infection with the herpes virus that had started out as a case of fever blisters. The two nights in the iron lung, its negative pressure pulling at his chest, suffocating his breathing, trying its best to asphyxiate him, had nearly killed Bobby. The image of Bobby trapped in a seven-foot-long cylinder on wheels with nothing protruding except his head, his eyes pleading for mercy, had remained with Celeste for the rest of her life.

After Bobby's death she'd spent most of her days and nights thinking about killing Floyd, but she'd never been able to come up with a plan that would take away his life and at the same time make him suffer the way she had over Bobby. Finding the iron lung had been her salvation. She had stumbled onto the breathing contraption at a Denver flea market six months earlier, and it had been the catalyst for her backup plan to deal with Floyd.

It had been a struggle to transport the seven-hundred-pound relic left over from the polio scourge of the 1950s almost to the top of a mountain, but she had done it by herself, with help from no one but the bearded salvage-store owner, who had sold it to her and helped her load it into the bed of her pickup.

Now, as she looked at the iron lung, unloaded with the help of a rusted winch, and watched the sunlight from the front window of the converted New Mexico line shack she had been living in off and on for the past few months dance off its polished metal skin, she smiled and thought about her prey.

First the Sundee woman. She would be easy. Then Floyd. He'd be harder, but like a bitch in heat, Mavis Sundee would serve up a trail for her hound to follow.

She hadn't determined how'd she kill them. Not yet. That would take time, patience, and thought. But she'd construct a plan to follow. A plan that would satisfy her need to avenge Bobby. One that would make him proud of his twin sister.

A strong mountain breeze kicked a knot of sagebrush against the ramshackle line shack's flimsy front door with a thud, startling Celeste. Turning her attention from the iron lung, she walked across the shack's creaky wooden floors and stepped outside onto the sagging front porch. The porch's hundred-year-old planks groaned with each step. Just to the south, a row of fifty-year-old aspen quaked in the breeze. To the southwest, a petered-out cow trail worked its way down a steep slope toward a dry wash just beyond the aspen stand's leading edge. Less than a mile away, white-capped Sangre de Cristo mountain peaks kissed the New Mexico sky. She was only 220 miles south of the Mile High City, but the abandoned line shack where she was squatting, hidden on a sweeping hogback above a high-mountain meadow, might as well have been lost to the world.

To find her—and she had made certain that he could—Floyd would have to find the valley, scale the hogback, and assault the shack. There was almost no way he could, short of climbing the mountains from the Taos side, without her being able to see him coming.

Watching the sun track west, she checked her watch and went back inside. It was almost 4 o'clock, and she wanted to be back in Denver by sunset. The nearly four-hour drive back north would do her good, give her time to think, allow her to congeal her plan.

She glanced at the iron lung. For some unexplained reason the cylinder reminded her of a life-saving airlock between two space capsules. Walking past the lung, she patted it and smiled, aware that the use she had in mind for the half-century-old breathing relic was meant to be life-ending, not life-preserving.

Chapter

12

"WE HAVE NO IDEA IF HE'LL COME BACK," said Carmen, pacing the floor of her living room, her eyes darting between CJ and Ket.

"He'll be back. The man didn't drive two-thirds of the way across the country to cut and run. Besides, he can call you. You're listed, aren't you?"

"Yes," said Carmen, recalling all the trouble she'd had packing up her cancer research laboratory at St. Mary's Hospital in Grand Junction, subleasing a condo in Denver for a half-year sabbatical, and trying to agree on a wedding date that would accommodate her busy schedule and that of her fiancé, Walker Rios. Only Ket's steady hand, a nurturing, caring force that had been there all of her life, and Walker's infectious optimism had nudged her ahead. And then out of nowhere, at home alone one night, without Rios there to hold her or Ket around to tell her no, she'd decided to send her letter to Blue. "I wonder if he likes motorcycles?"

"Flora Jean told me that you ride an Indian," said CJ, surprised by Carmen's response.

"And she's a pro," Ket proudly interjected.

"A '47 Chief. Restored it myself. But I've only ridden it a few times since I've been here in Denver. I leased a car."

"Smart. We don't have the kind of wide-open spaces you have over in Grand Junction. Besides, a vintage ride like that— you're looking at some chop shop's ultimate fantasy."

"I know, but that bike's part of me, and I couldn't leave it behind. Somehow it grounds me."

"Carmen learned to ride as a child in Vietnam," said Ket. "She had to in order to survive."

CJ knew that part of Carmen's story. Flora Jean had told him that Carmen had cleaned houses, collected garbage, driven a cyclo—the Vietnamese pedicab equivalent of a taxi—and begged on the streets of Ho Chi Minh City after the war, but unlike most of her Amerasian compatriots, who all too often ended up wallowing in the muck of discrimination in their homeland, she had been lucky. She'd had the privilege of an education and the advantage of a strict upbringing by a loving, caring aunt. By the age of ten she was a math whiz and fluent in English, French, and Vietnamese. He also knew that despite her success in her adopted homeland, Carmen was haunted by voids in her life. She knew nothing of her father except that by Ket's account he and her mother, who had died when Carmen was only two, had been star-crossed lovers. And there were other demons in her past: horrific war-linked memories that still occasionally triggered night sweats and bouts of terror. Haunted by memories of the same war, he and Carmen Nguyen had more in common than either of them could imagine.

"We've got a lot in common," said CJ, walking over to the living room's picture window. He stared west toward the Rockies.

Carmen nodded without answering, caught off guard.

"What kind of research do you do?" asked CJ, walking back toward Carmen, broaching a subject that he expected would offer no such common ground.

"Cancer research, molecular biology. Some people call it gene splicing."

Shaking his head in disbelief, CJ said, "I have a friend over at CU who does the same kinda thing. A pathologist. Name's Henry Bales. I served with him in Vietnam. He was a combat medic."

Carmen's face lit up. "You're kidding! He was one of the first people I met after I got to Denver. He helped me with a piece of equipment I was having problems with. He's delightful."

"Tell him hello for me."

"I will," said Carmen, finally taking a seat.

CJ was about to do the same when an intercom near the condo's front door erupted in a loud buzz.

Carmen flashed CJ and then Ket a look of anticipation and headed for the intercom. Her hand shook as she pushed the button below the speaker. "Yes?"

"You have a visitor, Dr. Nguyen. A Mr. Blue," came the voice on the other end.

"Send him up," she said, her voice quivering.

"Certainly."

Carmen turned back to find that CJ was standing beside her. "Hope I'm ready for this," she said, full of nervous tension.

"You'll do fine. I'll be right here next to you in case there's a problem," said CJ, uncertain of whether the man Carmen was about to let in to her home had killed a U.S. congressman.

"No. If he sees you he might bolt."

"Listen to CJ," said Ket.

"Both of you go back in the living room and sit down, please."

"But . . ."

"Please," said Carmen, motioning for CJ and Ket to move out of the hallway, watching them reluctantly head back to the living room.

Carmen reacted to the doorbell's ringing with a start. She shot Ket a final nervous glance, looked through the door's peephole, and slowly pulled open the door.

Langston Blue had changed from the clothes he'd been wearing earlier. Dressed now in loose-fitting faded khakis, a freshly laundered long-sleeved blue chambray shirt with the sleeves rolled up, and a pair of rarely worn workboots, he looked less rumpled, somehow even younger. Uncertain whether the woman calling herself his daughter might be linked to Cortez, he'd slipped a sixty-year-old .32 Smith and Wesson his father had owned into one of his pants pockets. He had no way of knowing whether the woman standing in front of him was there to end his life or to give it meaning, but he was taking a chance on the latter. Since he had nowhere and nothing to go back to, he figured it was worth the gamble.

"I'm Langston Blue," he said matter-of-factly, extending his hand as he stared at a smiling Carmen. She was a smaller woman than he'd imagined, and more beautiful. She had

Mimm's deep-set eyes and silky jet-black hair, but she shared his smile, broad forehead, and prominent cheekbones. She had the nasal flare and cocoa-colored skin of an African American, but he suspected that most white people would mistake her for either Latin or Polynesian.

Carmen inserted her hand into Blue's. "I'm Carmen."

Blue tried his best to hide his limp as he followed her toward the living room. Ignoring his limp, Carmen concentrated instead on how large a man her father was. Standing just under six feet and with massive forearms, he could have been a logger. When they reached the great room, CJ and Ket were standing. Blue froze when his eyes met Ket's. She looked so much like Mimm.

"Ket," he said, walking toward her, uncertain whether to shake hands, bow, or embrace her.

"It's been a long time, Langston." Ket stepped forward, her hand extended, her words still laden with the French accent of her youth.

Blue held her hand momentarily as if it were a highway back to the past and then let go. They stared at one another in silence, teetering at the edge of a thirty-five-year gulf, until Carmen gently tugged at Blue's arm and said, "I'd like you to meet a friend of ours. CJ Floyd. I hired him to help find you."

Blue eyed CJ suspiciously before shaking hands. "Pleasure."

"The same," said CJ.

"CJ served in Vietnam, too," said Carmen, wishing she could retract the statement as soon as she'd made it.

The look on Blue's face turned defensive.

"Forty-second River Patrol group," CJ said boldly.

"Navy," said Blue, wondering if he'd been set up. He glanced back toward the entryway, measuring the distance to the front door in his head. Slipping his hand into his pocket and thumbing the .32's hammer, he said, "I'd sure like a glass of water."

"Certainly," said Ket, sensing the sudden tension between the two war veterans. "I've prepared a snack as well. I'll go get it. Meanwhile, why doesn't everybody take a seat?"

Carmen sat down, leaving CJ and Blue standing. Silence filled the room until Ket returned with a pot of tea and a tray of Vietnamese ginger cookies. Blue recognized the fare and smiled. He'd shared it with Mimm scores of times, decades earlier.

Arranging the teacups on their delicate hand-glazed saucers, Ket filled the cups with tea, smiling briefly at Blue as she did. It was a smile that bridged three decades and seemed to finally put a damper on the tension in the room.

The teapot was empty and the dozen ginger cookies that Ket had baked were gone by the time any of the four broached the subject of Vietnam again. Instead, Blue recounted the highlights of his drive across the country, barely mentioning how he'd made it back home after the war and very little about his cabin having been torched by Cortez. They had been surprised by Blue's stories of being mesmerized by gas pumps that talked to you, puzzled by fast-food mania that he'd thought was only regional, and fascinated by the waves of hotels, motels, gadgets, theme parks, and sports stadiums that blanketed the land.

When Carmen asked him if he felt out of touch with the world, he said, "No, just not interested."

After clearing their dishes, Ket was the one to return the discussion to the war. "Why did you desert, Langston?" she asked with the straightforwardness of a child.

Unhesitatingly, Blue said, "I had to," as if he'd been preparing for the question for years. "It was that or get fragged."

"By who?" asked CJ.

"My captain."

"Peter Margolin?"

Blue reacted with a start. Ket would have known who Margolin was, but why would Floyd? Blue inched up in his chair, making certain he had easy access to the .32 in his pocket.

"We all know part of the story, Langston. We're just searching for the rest," said CJ.

Blue stood, right hand in his pants pocket, and began pacing the floor.

"We need to put an end to your hiding, shed some light on the truth," said Carmen, rising and grasping Blue's left hand in hers.

Blue stopped short, fingering the butt of the .32. "Maybe you're all in with Margolin."

Again it was Ket who restored calm. "Come on, Langston. You know better. Besides, Margolin's dead."

"I know that. It was on the news."

"That's all the more reason we need to know what happened on that mission that caused you to desert," said Ket. "If we're ever going to put an end to your running, we'll have to know the truth."

Blue's emphatic response was uttered like the denial of a child. "I didn't desert. I've got proof. A citation—an official one. It's in a lockbox in my trunk."

CJ rose from his seat. Realizing that the situation was fluid enough to escalate out of control, and concerned that Blue hadn't removed his right hand from his pants pocket since Ket had first mentioned Margolin, CJ said, "Good. Proof's a great thing to have." He nodded for Carmen to take a seat. "Maybe we should all sit back down and try and sort everything out."

Carmen slipped her hand out of Blue's and took a seat. CJ followed.

Looking confused, Blue swayed back and forth before finally slipping his hand out of his pocket and taking a seat.

There was a half minute of silence before slowly, starting at the end of a long tale as if trying to accurately piece its fragments together, Langston Blue began the story of what had happened at Song Ve. "It started with one of our team's missions. A simple one, if you looked at the kinda things we got assigned. But only three of the eight team members lived through it. Margolin, another sergeant named Lincoln Cortez, and me. Everyone else in our unit was killed. Margolin and Cortez shot 'em all."

Ket and Carmen reacted with shock, but the expression on CJ's face remained unchanged.

"Go on," said CJ, glancing at Carmen and Ket, who both looked as if they didn't want Blue to continue.

"We were a Star 1 unit, which meant we had carte blanche to do anything necessary to accomplish our mission. Kill or assassinate anyone, go anywhere, trash the rules of engagement, and cover our tracks. We started from a base camp at Duc Pho in the heat of the day and headed west. Our target was just outside a village in the Song Ve Valley south of Quang Ngai." Blue hesitated and swallowed hard before continuing. "Our mission was to take out the target and anyone within a quarter-mile perimeter. Our intelligence said we'd have no resistance."

"Big target?" asked CJ.

Ignoring CJ, Blue continued, "We reached the perimeter zone about 5:30 in the mornin'. Turned out the target was sittin' on a spit of land south of the Song Ve River in the middle of a swamp. Wasn't but one way in and one way out. A two-hundred-yard-long land bridge of mud, fallen timber, and bamboo stretched between the target and us. Captain Margolin posted two men at the end of the land bridge, and the rest of us followed him through knee-deep oatmeal muck over fallen tree limbs and through rice grass toward the target. He left two more of our guys stationed halfway up the land bridge, and four of us continued on."

CJ said, "What was the target?"

Blue looked around the room as if he expected to spot an eavesdropper. Once again he swallowed hard. The sound of the swallow could be heard across the room. "A school," he said in a near whisper.

Too stunned to respond, Carmen and Ket sat dumbfounded until CJ said, "What?"

"A school," Blue repeated as if a second response were necessary to provide him absolution. Continuing, this time talking a little faster, he said, "Captain Margolin posted me at the end of the land bridge 'bout forty yards from the thatched-roof building that was the school, and he, Cortez, and a private named Ricky Wells headed for the buildin'. The school was sittin' on a football-field-sized knot of sandy soil. The sun was comin' up when I spotted a strange-lookin' wooden contraption just ten or fifteen yards from the building's entrance that reminded me of a set of monkey bars. Pretty close to daylight a Vietnamese man, maybe twenty-five or so, and dressed in civilian clothes appeared in the school's doorway and walked out to meet Margolin. Seemed strange that someone would come walkin' outta our target to speak with our captain. Like they was about to have coffee or tea. So I spotted up on him with my binocs while he and Margolin stood talkin'. Biggest thing about him was he had a streak of silver runnin' straight down the middle of his hair. And he was dark, no more than a shade or so lighter than me. I was too far away to hear what they was sayin', but when they quit talkin' Margolin motioned for Cortez and Wells to go to opposite ends of the buildin'."

Blue took a breath. The muscles in his face stiffened and his eyes lost their focus. "All of a sudden outta nowhere I heard singin' comin' from inside the buildin'. As the singin' got louder, Margolin started walkin' toward me, and the man he'd been talkin' to disappeared into the swamp. It took me a while to realize that the singin' was all mixed up with laughter. Even longer to realize the singin' was comin' from kids. I asked Margolin what was goin' on when he got back to me. He nodded toward Wells and Cortez, who'd pulled a couple of handheld rocket launchers from the tall grass at the edges of the schoolyard.

"'We're going to torch the place,' Margolin said. He didn't look the least bit bothered.

"'But there're kids inside!' I said.

"'Orders,' was all he said.

"Next thing I knew, the buildin' was on fire and streams of kids, all of 'em screamin', come rushin' out the front door. Margolin leveled his M16 on a boy who couldn'ta been more than ten. Took his legs right out from under him."

Carmen gasped, and Ket began weeping. CJ remained silent, gnawing at the fleshy part of his lower lip.

"I reached out and pushed the nozzle of Margolin's M16 into the ground. Sand ricocheted back up into our faces from the backspray. Wells and Cortez, who'd retrieved their own weapons, were firin' at the children. By then the men Margolin had posted along the land bridge came runnin' outta the muck. 'Captain's lost it,' I screamed, grabbin' Margolin in a bear hug. He elbowed me in the gut. His M16 was wedged between us, and half a clip went whizzin' past our heads. There was gunfire everywhere. So much of it I couldn't tell who was shootin' at who. I choked Margolin 'til he was half out, then got up on one knee to see Cortez open fire on Wells and two of my best friends. All three of 'em dropped in their tracks, and Cortez took aim at me. I grabbed my weapon, began firin' back, and started crawlin' for the marsh at the edge of the schoolyard. I could hear kids cryin' and screamin' as the gunfire continued. Then I heard Margolin holler, 'Get Blue!' Toby Featherwood, a North Dakota Rosebud Sioux, and the other sentry Margolin had posted were standin' at the edge of the schoolyard when I reached it. I screamed, 'Get down!' but Featherwood took a bullet to the head. Cookie Vance, the guy with him, realized his own men were shootin' at him and tossed a grenade. I heard Cortez scream, 'Captain, I'm hit!' Margolin rose to both knees, sighted in his M16, and took Vance out. I could hear Cortez screamin', 'Captain, Captain!' as I began my run through the gumbo. Bullets was singin' through the trees and slammin' into their trunks. I continued surfin' my way through the gumbo and never looked back once until the gunfire and the voices and the cries of children comin' from behind me began to fade. To this day I still hear the cries in my sleep."

CJ's eyes misted over as Carmen and Ket sobbed uncontrollably.

The pleading look of a man seeking forgiveness engulfed Langston Blue as he slowly lowered his head. "That's it. Now you know why I ran."

Chapter

13

BY THE TIME CARMEN, KET, AND CJ had regained their composure and heard the rest of Blue's story, Carmen's condo was awash in the glow of the sun's final lingering rays. CJ and Blue had changed seats and now sat across from one another.

Still jittery from her father's account of how after the schoolyard incident he had hidden for months in shacks, tunnels, rice paddies, and huts, chaperoned and protected by other deserters, peasants, and acquaintances of Mimm's, surviving on a diet of rice milk, bamboo shoots, and rats, Carmen had left the room half a dozen times in an attempt to get a handle on her emotions. CJ and Ket had each left the room once, Ket for a bathroom break and CJ in a failed attempt to get in touch with Flora Jean.

Blue had wound down his tale, explaining that six months after making his run from the schoolyard and settling in with a small band of U.S. and South Vietnamese army deserters camped out in a subterranean dug-out near a once functional sewer plant in the central highlands, he'd gone to try and find food for the week. Noting that food and supplies were hard to come by and deserters paid the black marketeers a stiff pre-mium for both, and for their silence, Blue explained that while on his food hunt he'd been plucked from a dirt road on the outskirts of Saigon by two men, a Vietnamese man who spoke near perfect English and an American with a noticeable South-ern drawl.

Within twenty-four hours of being blindfolded, drugged, and interrogated, he'd found himself alone on a twin-engine, twelve-seat turboprop on his way to Guam. Once there, he'd been taken to a ten-by-ten-foot cinderblock bunker, given an official-looking document stamped with what looked like a U.S. State Department seal, told that he'd be living for the rest of his life in West Virginia on an allotment that would be deliv-ered annually, and warned that if he ever found it necessary to tell the story of what had happened in the schoolyard at Song Ve, he would be provided with a script that he would be required to memorize and deliver verbatim. The alternative was to be killed on the spot. He'd chosen life and the isolated backwoods cabin that days earlier, with the help of Lincoln Cortez, had gone up in flames.

The room was silent, but the despondency was less palpa-ble than when he'd finished the first part of his tale.

Rising from his chair, CJ broke the lingering silence. "And you're sure Cortez torched your place?"

Blue only nodded.

"Do you know what happened back in the schoolyard after you made your run?"

"Only what I told you earlier."

CJ shook his head. "Sounds like something out of *Tales from the Crypt*."

"It's the truth."

"I'm not doubting you. Just trying to figure out what the hell this is all about. Sounds like somebody trying to cover up something ugly."

"CIA?" asked Ket, directing the question to CJ.

CJ stroked his chin thoughtfully. "Maybe. But it still doesn't make a lot of sense. Why not just eliminate your troublesome eyewitness? No, there's more to this whole Star 1 team thing than your run-of-the-mill *New York Times* 'American Troops Shoot Unarmed Civilians and Kids' headline."

"I never saw anybody but children that day," said Blue, his tone low pitched and doleful.

Ket shuddered.

CJ said, "Bottom line is, we really don't know what happened in that schoolyard after you made your run for it or why your unit was assigned that mission in the first place."

"Right." Blue nodded in agreement. "All I know is that we were told to take out a target. I never knew the target was a school full of kids."

"But I'm betting our late would-be-senator Peter Margolin did. And that's what ratchets this whole sordid thing up another notch and probably why Margolin's dead. What we need to do is take a look up and down the chain of command," said CJ, watching Blue's eyes light up.

"I been thinkin' the same thing for years," said Blue. "But right now the buck stops with me and Cortez. Margolin's dead."

"And just when you happen to pay a visit to Denver. If I were a cop, you'd make top dog on my suspects list."

"I didn't kill him!"

"Then we need to find out who did," said CJ, delighted by Blue's forceful denial.

"How?"

"We start by taking a long, hard look into the past. We'll have to piece together the why behind what actually happened in that schoolyard and who set it up."

"And find out who had something to gain," interjected Carmen.

"That too," said CJ. "In the meantime, your father's gonna have to fade into a hole in the sky."

"He can stay here," said Carmen, looking at Ket for support.

Ket's answer was silence and a quizzical stare. She wasn't giddy over the fact that Blue had suddenly turned up, even though she'd given Carmen Blue's address. Now Carmen, normally a methodical analytical thinker, appeared momentarily blinded by finding something she'd been searching for all of her life, but Ket wasn't about to let someone Carmen had known less than two hours take up residence.

Reading the tea leaves, CJ spoke up. "Won't work. You can be certain the cops are doing their own investigation into the life of our late would-be senator, and by now they've even touched base with the army and the FBI. It's a safe bet they'll unearth information on Margolin's Vietnam service record that'll lead them back to the Star 1 team he commanded, and you."

Carmen protested, "But they don't anything about me."

"Don't be so sure," said CJ, uncertain why Carmen was lobbying so hard to keep Blue there with her. "This whole Song Ve thing has an intelligence stench smeared all over it. You can never be certain of what 'the Company' knows. Our patrol boat ferried more than a few 'Company' types up and down the Mekong during the war, and the one thing that struck me about every CIA type our skipper ever let aboard was that they were never quite what they seemed." CJ eyed Blue. "Those dregs you lived with when you went underground, did any of them know about Mimm?"

Blue stared at the ceiling, his face screwed up in thought. "Yes."

"Then you left a trail to Carmen, and that gives anyone with a nose for it a trail back to you."

"Then where do I go? I don't want nobody comin' within a hundred miles of my daughter." It was the first time he'd used the word *daughter* in front of Carmen. The word hung on his lips.

"You can stay with a couple of my friends. The accommodations aren't five star, but you'll be safe."

"Here in Denver?"

CJ nodded. "Let me make a phone call to my office and get my partner to set things up."

"What should I do?" asked Carmen, feeling left out.

"Sit tight. Do what you normally do. Cure cancer. Save lives. But whatever you do, don't say one word to anyone about your father."

Carmen nodded, still feeling excluded.

CJ headed for the kitchen, a phone, and privacy, formulating the things he needed to tell Flora Jean. First off, they'd need to find out exactly what Margolin's Star 1 team had done during Vietnam besides sacking schools, and there was no better place to start than with Flora Jean's friend General Alden Grace. She was also going to have to locate Morgan Williams and Dittier Atkins, CJ's two down-and-out friends who'd once been rodeo stars, and round up a place for Blue to stay.

As he dialed his office, he heard Blue tell Carmen that he had some of her mother's things down in his truck. Pictures, her wedding ring, a necklace.

"Things that were special to us," said Blue, his voice laden with sadness.

It was Ket's voice he heard next. A hopeful voice full of anticipation.

"We'd both love to see them," said Ket, emphasizing the word *both*.

"I'll get 'em," said Blue, his voice full of pride, happy that CJ had left and he could share his treasures with no one but Carmen and Ket.

◆◆◆

Mavis disliked having to be the one to have to close the restaurant during the summer. The long work days made her think that she'd missed out on too much of her life. It had been close to twenty years since she'd come back home to Denver with a Boston University MBA and the skills to help her father organize and recapitalize the half-dozen Five Points businesses he owned. She'd ended up running most of them, and when

Willis Sundee's diabetes had nearly overwhelmed him ten years earlier, she'd taken over the day-to-day management of Mae's Louisiana Kitchen.

The restaurant, named in honor of her deceased civil rights-pioneering, New Orleans-born and -bred mother, remained the jewel in a string of her father's successes. And though she sometimes hated to admit it, her father's entrepreneurial blood rushed through her veins. As CEO of Sundee Enterprises, she had the highest profile of any black businesswoman in Denver.

Mavis stood near the restaurant's tunnel-like entry, where there was barely room for three people to stand. Less than an arm's length away, a mahogany pulpit that had belonged to her grandfather, an itinerant Holy Roller preacher from Baton Rouge, served as a hostess station just as it had for forty years.

Mavis rubbed an emerging charley horse in her right calf and sighed. "Go on home, Thelma. It's almost 9," she called out to the restaurant's lead waitress. "I'll lock up."

Fumbling with a wad of keys, Thelma shouted back, "You got the master?"

"Don't I always? Now, hurry up and get out of here so I can set the alarm."

"I'm gone." Thelma rushed past Mavis through the front door and out onto Welton Street, keys clanging, purse swinging, her new 100 percent human-hair wig cocked slightly off kilter. "See you tomorrow—and don't forget, tell CJ I'm still in love with him."

Thelma's parting remark was the same one she'd been reciting to Mavis since their junior high days, when, six years CJ's junior, she'd announced her undying devotion to the man. Now a mother of three, with two sons who played football for Colorado State and a husband who had never appreciated the statement's humor, Thelma still ended most work days delivering the same straight line to Mavis.

Mavis's response never changed. "If I see him, I'll pass it along," sent Thelma scurrying off giggling.

Mavis was set to meet CJ at his apartment, where they had planned an evening of pizza, cabernet to wash it down, and lovemaking. On Saturday and Sunday they would make up for her hectic work week and CJ's crazy schedule by simply going with the flow. As she walked toward the back of the restaurant, adjusting tables and pushing in chairs, she felt the week's tension start to fade. Stepping outside, she threw the deadbolt of the back door, shut the burglar-proof wrought-iron outer door with a clank, set the alarm, and headed for her car in the hazy moonlight.

The parking alcove at the rear of the restaurant offered barely enough space to park two cars, and since she knew her father wasn't coming in, she had straddled both spaces. She'd pushed the button on her privacy key to unlock the car's front doors when someone grabbed her by the hair from behind, slammed her headfirst into the hood of the car, and sent her keys sailing into the night.

Fuzzy-headed, Mavis screamed. Only an adrenaline rush of fear kept her on her feet. Celeste Deepstream grabbed a second handful of hair, but Mavis took the wind out of her with a well-placed elbow to the gut.

Gasping for air, Celeste screamed, "Bitch!" and slammed Mavis's head into the car's hood a second time, and a third, then a fourth, until Mavis slid down the fender and onto the ground, barely conscious. Extracting a nearly spent roll of duct tape from her jacket pocket, Celeste tore off a piece and plastered it over Mavis's mouth. Mavis let out a muffled groan as Celeste clasped her by the ankles and dragged her the ten yards across the parking lot to her pickup.

The easy part was over, Celeste told herself. Now she had to lift 120 pounds of deadweight into the bed of a pickup and stuff the body into a dog kennel. Grunting and groaning, she struggled to lift Mavis into the truck bed, telling herself all the while that she'd once been a world-class athlete. Mavis groaned again, and Celeste slammed her head against the bed's side rail, finally knocking her out. When Mavis's legs wouldn't quite make it inside the greyhound kennel, Celeste forced them until Mavis's knees were wedged solidly against the kennel's ceiling. "Serves you right, wench." She slammed the door to the kennel, locked it, and draped a tarp covered in bird droppings over it.

She tied the tarp to the side rails with rope, checked the tautness, jumped out of the truck bed, and headed for the cab. Her heart was thumping. She hadn't felt such a rush since she'd won the NCAA 1,500-meter individual medley her senior year in college. Bobby had been there, along with her coaches, a long-forgotten lover, and a gaggle of friends. It had been her defining hour, her shining moment at the top of the heap. The feeling had been intoxicating and it was back. She checked her watch as she slid inside the cab. The whole kidnapping, which she had spent almost a week planning, had taken just under five minutes. Armed with a sense of self-satisfaction, she eyed the silver can of ether resting on the seat next to her. "Like clockwork," she said out loud. "No drugs required."

She smiled and started the truck, wondering what it might be like to be a caged greyhound. What it was like to be CJ Floyd's beaten-to-a-pulp lover, to be on your way to die. She laughed out loud as she eased the pickup onto Welton Street and pointed it south toward the central New Mexico highlands.

◆◆◆

CJ pulled into his driveway a little past 9, top down on the Bel Air, his left foot tapping to the sounds of Muddy Waters's voice booming from the car's tape deck. He rarely dropped the top on the Bel Air or cranked up that kind of volume on the stereo, but he was celebrating and anticipating the evening with Mavis. He had a second check from Carmen Nguyen in his pocket— payment this time, not for finding a man who had wandered into Denver on his own, but instead for hopefully finding Peter Margolin's killer and eliminating Langston Blue as a suspect.

He had landed a place for Blue to stay, Flora Jean had nailed down an early-morning meeting the next day with her Colorado Springs intelligence contact General Alden Grace, and Julie Madrid, his former secretary turned lawyer, had called him on his way home to inform him that her ex-husband, Pancho, a prime suspect on CJ's probable-shooters list, had died in a water-skiing accident in San Juan less than a month before. With Pancho and Bobby Two Shirts Deepstream both dead, the list of people out for his scalp had dropped to only two, and

Julie had assured him that she would have a fix on Celeste Deepstream's whereabouts first thing in the morning and Mohammad Rashaan's by early afternoon.

He turned Muddy off as the blues master was in the middle
of a gut-wrenching lament about losing his house, his woman,
and his dog to another man, stepped out of the Bel Air, and
headed up the wrought-iron fire-escape entrance to his apartment, smiling to himself as he contemplated a night of lovemaking, a weekend of decompression, and the relaxing
lighthearted pleasures he'd enjoy when he was halfway through
the forty-five-dollar bottle of cabernet he was carrying.

At first he didn't see the dark square of the envelope taped
to his door. Hoping it wasn't a demand from a collection agency,
or worse, a note from Mavis saying that something had come
up, that she had to work late or her father was ill, he teased the
envelope away from the door, opened it, and read the one-line
message printed on the piece of cardboard inside: *I've got Mavis.
505-555-1288. I'll kill her. Best you call. Celeste.*

His mind was suddenly filled with his worst memories from
the past. Being abandoned by his mother when he was barely
able to walk. His inability to fully connect with Mavis. His Uncle
Ike dying. Sitting on the back of a navy patrol boat strapped to
a machine gun and taking enemy fire from every direction. The
war, the war, especially the war. His mind began to drift. The
door to his apartment suddenly became the Mekong River bank
as he stepped through the door to the sounds of machine-gun
fire. Raising both hands to his ears to block out the noise, he
stumbled over to a chair and sat down, his eyes glazed over, his

temples throbbing. He tried to gather his thoughts, to move forward into the present and out of the past. When he realized he had crumpled the note into a ball in his left hand and that he was squeezing the neck of the wine bottle so hard that his right hand was numb, he slowly rose, walked to the kitchen phone, and dialed the number on the card.

After several rings and no answer, a message clicked on: "You've reached me. I'm in the New Mexico high country. You've got thirty-six hours. Try your garage." There was no mistaking her voice. He'd heard sound bite after sound bite of it during her manslaughter trial. He suspected she was probably sitting by the phone screening the calls, enjoying the havoc she was wreaking.

Suddenly the only thing he could think about was Mavis. Was she injured, in pain, suffering, alive? He slammed down the phone and screamed through clenched teeth, "I'll kill her!" He finally set down the wine and slammed both fists into the closest thing at hand, the aging calico fabric covering the seat back of his prized Mormon rocker. The seventy-year-old fabric ripped at one wooden seam and shredded at the other as he slammed his fist into the seat back over and over. Finally he let out a wail, a sound that recentered him in the present, signaling that it was time to move ahead.

He thought about the message: *Try your garage.* Grabbing a flashlight from a nearby kitchen drawer, he scooped up his .38 and walked back down the fire-escape steps past the Bel Air to his garage. When he saw a second envelope taped to the garage door, he ripped it off and opened it to find a detailed, hand-drawn map inside. Flashlight in hand, he studied the map carefully. Celeste had highlighted a location with a yellow pinpoint dot, 220 miles southwest of Denver, somewhere in the Sangre de Cristo Mountains miles from the nearest paved road. He'd been through that country before, fly fishing, but he didn't really know it—not the way he knew the high country in Colorado. He couldn't tell how far the dot was from the main highway, but he knew that in order to get there he'd have to trek through rugged country. Folding the map in half, he stuffed it into his pocket behind the butt of his .38 and walked back to the Bel Air. He opened the trunk, laid the flashlight down on the trunk's custom carpet, then abruptly sat down inside the trunk as he assessed his options. He could call the cops, who'd more than likely get Mavis killed. He could take off after Celeste alone and end up a casualty himself. Or he could call Flora Jean and detour her from her assignment to try to help exonerate Langston Blue.

Rising from his uncomfortable position, he closed the trunk and headed back to the house to call Flora Jean. He was halfway up the fire-escape steps when he stopped, pulled the map out of his pocket, and reexamined it, his flashlight on high beam. "Billy!" he shouted, nearly dropping the map. "Son of a bitch! I forgot about Billy!" Taking the remaining steps two at a time, he raced into the house, grabbed the leather-bound personal phone book Mavis had given him the previous Christmas, and flipped through it until he came to the boldly scripted name "Billy DeLong."

CJ walked back across the kitchen, sat down in a pressed-back chair, grabbed his cell phone from a countertop, and punched in Billy DeLong's Baggs, Wyoming, number. After eight unanswered rings he was about to hang up when a voice full of gravel and grit said, "This here's Billy."

"Billy, it's CJ. Got a problem, and I need your help."

Aware that CJ had the habit of ranking bounty-hunting jobs on a scale of 1 to 10, and suspecting that it was a bounty-hunting job that CJ needed help with, Billy asked, "Your job got a number?"

"Can't rank this one."

"That bad?"

"Worse. Somebody's snatched Mavis."

Billy let out a lengthy whistle. "How soon you need me?"

"Now."

"I'm on it this second."

"And Billy, bring two horses, trail-riding gear, and a couple of Winchesters."

"Anything else?"

CJ swallowed hard. "Yeah. The two M16s I gave you. The ones I brought home from 'Nam."

"Shit." Billy checked his watch. "I'll be there by 3 in the mornin'," he said, popping a couple of sticks of chewing gum in his mouth, gearing up for the five-and-a-half-hour drive.

"See you then." CJ flipped his cell phone closed. He looked around the room until his gaze settled on the unopened bottle of wine. He gauged his chances of ever again seeing Mavis alive at about an even five as he walked over to the table, picked up the bottle, and brought it gently to his lips. He had no idea of how things would turn out, whether he would ever again see the person he cared most about in the world alive. But he knew one thing for certain. Sadly, Vietnam had taught him what he was capable of when the stakes were high enough. And he knew that if he ever had to kill again, he could. He hoped Celeste Deepstream wouldn't force him to make the choice.

Chapter

14

SINCE MEETING FLORA JEAN when she was a freshly promoted twenty-four-year-old marine intelligence sergeant, Alden Grace had always thought that except for her larger-than-the-prototype breasts, she could have had a career as a Folies Bergere dancer. He had never mentioned it to her because she was adamantly opposed to being seen as a sex object, but she had the height, a dancer's legs, the upper-body strength, a well-tapered waist from years of working out, an upright carriage, and a showgirl's derriere. What she lacked was stamina.

"Alden, no more," said Flora Jean, easing from astride her on-again, off-again lover, clasping his still erect penis in her right hand and squeezing tightly.

"I thought you were a marine," said Alden.

"And I thought you were human."

They both laughed as Flora Jean fell onto the bed and into the comforting cradle of the former general's right arm. They lay in silence momentarily before Flora Jean spoke. "You could've retired in D.C.," she said playfully, responding to Grace's earlier lament that although they lived just seventy miles apart,

Flora Jean's visits were so irregular that he might as well be living in Afghanistan. "This ain't the service, General. I set the rules now. You agreed to it."

"But I am retired, Flora Jean." Grace slipped his arm from beneath Flora Jean and sat up.

"You know I got my reasons for keepin' my distance."

"We've been through that before, babe. So I'm an old geezer and you're a spring chick. I've just spent close to an hour showing you my youthful credentials. Need more convincing?" He slapped Flora Jean lightly on the butt.

"It ain't about age, Alden. Fifty-four and thirty-eight ain't that far apart. And it ain't about sex," she added, running her index finger up the inside of his thigh until her hand found pay dirt.

"Don't start," said Grace.

"I won't," said Flora Jean, removing her hand from his incipient erection. "This is serious. I'm not gonna let you turn me away from the issue by tryin' to turn me on."

"I've asked you to marry me before. I'm asking again."

"I said no before, and I'm sayin' it again."

Grace stared out the bedroom window directly into the 8 a.m. sunlight. When he finally spoke, the previous playfulness in his voice had been replaced by the tone of a man who was used to having things his way. "You scared?"

Flora Jean nodded.

"Of what?"

Rising until her arm was directly next to his, she said, "The difference in the color of these two appendages mean anything to you?"

Grace didn't respond. The defining issue that had kept them on-again, off-again lovers had finally fully bubbled to the surface. He had pretty much suspected it all along, despite Flora Jean's concerns about their forbidden fraternizing when she was an enlisted woman and he was an officer, or about their age, their differing levels of education, their dichotomous upbringing, even the potential problem of their markedly differing incomes. It had all been a smokescreen.

Deflated, his tone now a mere echo of its lovemaking pitch, he said, "What finally brought it to a head?"

"I don't know. This case I'm workin' on, maybe."

"The one you came here to see me about?"

"Yes."

"What's it got to do with us?"

"Maybe nothin'. Maybe a lot."

Grace leaned back against the headboard. "Might as well spell it out. I'm tired of roadblocks."

Flora Jean settled next to him, and the headboard banged into the wall. "You know that congressman that got murdered up in Denver last week?"

"Yes," said Grace, fully attentive.

"Well, CJ and I are workin' for the daughter of a possible suspect. Pretty woman. Amerasian. Beautiful, in fact. One of them war babies that got spit out during Vietnam. Her father's black. She's *my den*."

"And that's what has you so skittish? Some war baby stuck with the label of being *my den*? In case you haven't noticed, that's a problem for the Vietnamese—we're here in the States."

"That ain't the whole issue, Alden. But it started me thinkin'.
What if we had kids? Might be they'd end up in the very same
fix."

"Come on, Flora Jean. That's one hell of a stretch."

"Okay, okay. Maybe the thing about kids ain't a real issue,
but it's food for thought."

"Life's always a risk, Flora Jean. You know that. You can't live
your life looking for bogeymen." Grace's tone was insistent.

"I don't wanna argue, Alden. And sure as shit we're headed
down that road."

"Me either."

"Then let's park the issue in the garage. Save it for discussion
later."

"Fine by me, as long as there'll be a discussion."

"I said there would." Flora Jean leaned over and kissed Grace
lightly on the cheek, relieved that at least temporarily the issue
had been defused.

"And an honest one," added Grace, looking Flora Jean squarely
in the eye.

"It'll be honest."

"Good. Let's get back to your Amerasian friend."

"Okay. Here's the deal. Her daddy, a guy named Langston
Blue, served in one of the army's Star 1 units during Vietnam,
back when you were a wet-behind-the-ears captain tryin' to
buck up." Flora Jean giggled and wiggled her butt up next to
Grace's. "That congressman who got killed, Peter Margolin, was
his CO. Blue ended up desertin' right in the middle of a mission. That's what I knew before I got in my car and drove down

here from Denver last evenin'. What I didn't know came courtesy of a message on my cell phone this mornin'. Came in at 4 a.m. from CJ. He didn't sound like himself, sort of sounded lost in space, but at 4 in the morning, who wouldn't? Said he was on his way down here to Colorado Springs on somethin' urgent. Told me to meet him at 9:30 this morning at a Denny's over on Academy Boulevard."

"What's the new information?"

"He said that our client, her name's Carmen Nguyen, had her father show up unannounced in Denver late yesterday afternoon at her condo. Claimed he'd been hidin' in the West Virginia woods for more than thirty years. According to CJ, he got smoked from his hole when one of his former Star 1 team buddies dropped out of the sky and flamed the shit outta his house."

Grace slowly began shaking his head.

"I know that dance, Alden. Come on, let me in on the secret."

"What is it I've always said about the military and government?"

Flora Jean's answer was close to automatic. "That one's for killin' and one's for connin'."

"You've got it. Sounds to me like Blue's Star 1 team got caught up in some serious political shit. Governmental crossfire would be my guess."

"Ours or theirs?"

"Don't know. Maybe both. One thing for certain—those Star 1 teams were few and far between, and by the end of the war most of them ended up being labeled black sheep. No one wants to talk about them, even today. They were an off-shoot of the military's Studies and Observations Group, a cross-service bunch that was responsible for covert assignments in the deadliest, most forbidding theaters of the war."

"The SOG. Before my time. But I've heard of 'em," said Flora Jean.

"They were a handful. Subordinate to no one. Not the military assistance command or the four-star general in charge. They answered directly to the Joint Chiefs of Staff in the Pentagon and, more often than not, with White House–level input. Word has it that only four or five non-SOG officers in Saigon were ever even briefed on their top-secret doings, which involved penetrating the most heavily defended North Vietnamese military facilities, going behind enemy land lines to rescue downed U.S. pilots, holding off mass enemy attacks, engaging in sabotage and espionage, and if called upon, even overthrowing governments."

"Alden, you're preachin' to the choir."

"Well, here's what you didn't know," said Grace. "Most SOG units were made up of volunteers who were air force commandos, army Green Berets, and navy SEALs. Star 1 teams were composed of army personnel only. They were the unauthorized brainchild of an army general named Cassidy Hicks who wanted the army to have a kick-ass elite unit capable of out-shining the SOG."

"How could they have operated without authorization?"

Grace shook his head. "Come on, Flora Jean, you've been to war. Or maybe you didn't run into any nutcases like Hicks during Desert Storm."

"Oh, we had them all right," said Flora Jean. "Guess they just didn't have enough time to flower."

"Well, Hicks did. His little Star 1 band of brothers operated for six months during the summer and fall of 1971. It took that long for someone below him to get up enough nerve to turn whistle-blower."

"With only six months in the saddle, how much damage could these Star 1 units have done?" asked Flora Jean.

"Plenty. That's why nobody wants to admit they existed. The army buried their existence under miles of red tape. Hicks was discharged honorably, and he and his invention were brushed under the rug. He died about the time your war started, another whacked-out army two-star footnote."

"Hell, Alden. This thing's startin' to sound a whole lot bigger than I thought."

"Don't worry, babe. I'll point you in the right direction."

Grace slid out of bed, walked across the room naked, and retrieved a three-inch-thick leather-bound book from a nearby desk. Turning and strutting full-frontal back toward Flora Jean, he said, "See anything you like?"

"Serious—remember, Alden."

"Yeah." Frowning as he slipped back into bed next to Flora Jean, he thumbed through the book, stopping near the end. "Contacts," he said, smiling. "Here's a name. I'll start you at point A. You and CJ will have to work your way to Z."

"Hope there ain't any women's names in that book," said Flora Jean.

"Serious, remember," said Grace.

"I am."

Grace smiled. "It's not that kind of book. Here's your man," he said, tapping the page just below the name. "Le Quan, Denver . . . best I can tell you is he works out of Denver."

"Works?" asked Flora Jean, surprised at Alden's choice of words. "What does he do?"

"Don't know. I've been out of the intelligence loop for too long. My guess is that he's still doing the same thing he did during the war: double-dealing, talking out of both sides of his mouth, taking money under the table. Playing both ends against the middle. He's slick. Should've been a politician."

"What did he do in Vietnam?"

"He was a Vietcong youth organizer. Spent his time revving up nine-year-olds to swear allegiance to the Communist Party and go out and kill Americans. Quan's got an errand boy, an odd jobber of sorts, a kid named Jimmy Moc. I've got a Denver East Colfax Avenue address for Moc, not much else."

"Then I'll start with Moc and work my way up."

"Watch it, Flora Jean. Moc's a snake."

"I've dealt with them before."

"I know you have. But he's a Hydra. You never know which one of his heads is going to bite you. Keep CJ real close at hand on this one."

Flora Jean smiled. "You're still working, aren't you, Alden? That's why they moved you from D.C. out here to Colorado Springs."

"You're imagining things, Flora Jean."

Flora Jean laughed out loud. "Like I am imagining this little thing can grow," she said, cupping Grace's member in her hand, massaging it slowly.

"Don't you have a meeting with CJ?"

"This won't take long," said Flora Jean, rolling her warm, supple body on top of Grace's. "Trust me," she said, kissing him, encouraging him to maneuver his body to meet hers.

Chapter

15

TEN MINUTES LATE FOR HER MEETING WITH CJ, Flora Jean rushed across the parking lot of the Denny's at the intersection of I-25 and Academy Boulevard. The low profile of the rambling ranch-style eatery stood in sharp contrast to the expansive wooded grounds of its Colorado Springs neighbor, the U.S. Air Force Academy. She rushed into the restaurant past a startled hostess and scanned rows of booths and tables filled with customers. She spotted CJ and Billy DeLong in a booth against the west wall, regained her composure, walked over to them, and slipped into the crescent-shaped booth next to CJ.

Surprised to see Billy, she said, "Didn't expect to see you here, Billy." She reached across and shook his hand.

"You're late," said CJ, surprising her with an out-of-character admonishment.

"Sorry, I got hung up."

CJ picked up his half-full coffee cup, took a sip, and watched Billy start through a second short stack of pancakes. "You might as well have ordered a full stack, Billy."

Ignoring CJ, Billy reached for the nearby syrup. The look on his face was stoic.

Flora Jean sat back in her seat, looked at CJ, and said, "What the hell's got you so twisted in knots?"

CJ didn't answer, so she looked at Billy. When Billy, staring down at his pancakes, didn't look up, she knew something was wrong. She turned her attention back to CJ. She hadn't actually paid much attention to the man she had worked side by side with for almost six years when she'd rushed into the restaurant. She normally didn't have to. CJ was usually as predictable as a finely tuned clock. In the office by 8 each morning, working on cases, touching base with lawyers, working out a way for clients to make bail. He usually ate lunch at Mae's, worked the phones in the afternoon, and hunted antiques and Western memorabilia when times were slow. He knew the bail-bonding and bounty-hunting business like he'd written the book, and if he and Billy were on an urgent case, she couldn't imagine anything that had to do with bail bonding or bounty hunting that would have him wound so tight. But he looked different, haggard and drained.

"You okay, CJ?"

"Yeah," he said, taking a sip of coffee.

Billy looked up from his pancakes, his glass eye fixed, and gave CJ a *that's bullshit* kind of stare. "No, he ain't. Tell her the truth."

"We know who my shooter was," said CJ, his voice a low, muffled drone.

"Who?"

"Celeste Deepstream."

"How'd you find out?"

CJ looked up from his coffee directly at Flora Jean. His eyes were clouded over, and he had that foggy look that Mavis said he'd had for months after coming home from Vietnam. "Last night she snatched Mavis."

"Shit!" Flora Jean draped an arm over CJ's shoulder. At a loss for words, she asked, "Is . . . Mavis okay?"

"I don't know."

"What do the cops say?"

"Haven't called them."

"What!" Flora Jean relaxed what was now close to a bear hug and eyed CJ sternly. "CJ, come on!"

"They'll get her killed."

"It's a kidnappin', for God's sake. You've gotta call 'em." She looked at Billy for support.

Billy didn't respond.

"You're not goin' after her yourself!"

This time it was CJ's turn to be silent.

"CJ, are you crazy?" Flora Jean shook her head. "And you dragged in Billy."

CJ set his fork down beside the food he'd barely touched.

"Didn't require no draggin'," said Billy.

"Pushin', pullin', draggin', whatever. I don't care. This is a kidnappin'. You don't even know where they're at."

"Yes, we do," said CJ. "Somewhere in New Mexico. We know that for sure."

"That's across the state line. You can call in the FBI."

CJ shook his head. "I'm not calling anyone. Billy and I'll handle this."

"Then I will!" The instant she uttered it, Flora Jean knew she'd said the wrong thing. The tortured look on CJ's face turned angry. A deep-throated, one-word response rumbled up from his stomach: "Don't."

Easing her arm from around CJ's shoulder, she swallowed hard and said nothing.

"Here's what we're gonna do," he said, his tone that of a soldier on a mission. "Rescue Mavis. We have a good idea where Celeste is holding her, and we've got a real good fix on the terrain. What we don't know is what we'll run into once we're there. Armaments, booby traps, diversions, an army of her friends."

"You sound like it's a war, CJ."

"It is."

Realizing there was no way CJ was ever going to call in the cops, or for that matter anyone in law enforcement, Flora Jean said, "Slow down a minute, CJ. Look at it through her eyes for a moment. What she's after is revenge. And that makes her vulnerable. She wants you to suffer the same way she has over her brother. That's your ticket in. Do somethin' she ain't expectin'. Catch her off guard."

CJ stroked his chin as Flora Jean continued, "My bet is she's goin' it alone. Not many people want a kidnappin' charge hangin' over their head. You've got an advantage—you got Billy. And you have at least a general idea of the terrain. Get Celeste away from Mavis, have her focus on you or Billy. Unless she has help, she's gotta have Mavis subdued, drugged, or shackled. She'll leave her in a second if she figures she can deal with her later, once she settles her score with you."

Imagining Mavis bound, battered, and helpless turned CJ's face to stone. Glad that he'd heard the input of someone he trusted his life with, he asked, "Any other advice?"

"None that would help. Unless you want me to come?"

CJ smiled and looped an arm around Flora Jean's shoulders. Only then did he realize she was shaking. "It's gonna work out okay," he said, squeezing her affectionately, something he'd never done before. "You've got other business to tend to. The paying kind." CJ's tone was forced and rehearsed. "What did your friend the general say that can help us with our Langston Blue problem?"

Recognizing that the question was meant to distract her from her concerns, minimize the difficulty of the task he was facing, and send her away with a sense of purpose, she said, "He dropped a couple of pearls. Said the Star 1 team that Blue was part of was an unauthorized army copy of an official SOG model. And he gave me the names of a couple of Denver contacts. Some guy named Quan and a kid named Moc. Said they might be able to help us out with Blue."

"What's their connection?"

"Moc's, I'm not sure, but Quan was a Vietcong youth organizer during the war."

"Umph," said CJ. "Guess he found a new home. Might as well check them both out, see if they have any connection to Blue. And watch out for Newburn and that Kearnes woman. They're working the angles, too."

Flora Jean nodded, then hesitantly said, "CJ . . . Never mind."

As his eyes glazed over, CJ cupped his right hand over Flora Jean's. "Do your job, sugar. Billy and I will take care of ours. If you haven't heard from us in forty-eight hours, come looking." He slipped a photocopy of the topo map that Billy had brought out of his shirt pocket, unfolded it, and handed it to Flora Jean. "The little square highlighted in yellow, that's where we'll be. It's in the Taos Mountains about twenty-eight miles south of the Colorado and New Mexico border."·

Flora Jean glanced down at the map and then back up at CJ. "What about Willis? He's bound to ask about Mavis."

"Stall. Tell him we took a trip to Santa Fe."

"Okay, but what if he presses?"

"He won't," said CJ, checking his watch. "It's 10:15. We've gotta go. We only have thirty-six hours."

"From when?" asked Flora Jean, unaware that they were on a clock.

"From about 9 last night when I found the note Celeste left taped to my door."

"What's she gonna do if you don't show?"

"Kill Mavis."

"Better get goin'," said Flora Jean, forcefully.

"And Flora Jean, make sure Dittier and Morgan keep Blue under wraps. Newburn would have Blue for lunch if he knew he was around."

"I will," said Flora Jean, her voice trailing off to a near whisper. Turning to Billy, she said, "Make sure you both come back, Billy. And with Mavis."

"We'll be back," said Billy, watching CJ head toward the cashier. "Count on it," he added, turning and walking away with the self-assurance of a wiry, rough-cut cowboy. A tough-as-nails little black man who during his lifetime had managed $30-million ranches, honchoed fifty men at a time, lost an eye to diabetes and Old Crow, and nearly killed a tax assessor back in Ohio who'd tried to steal his family's farm. A man who always meant exactly what he said.

Chapter

16

THE ADDRESS ALDEN GRACE had given Flora Jean for Jimmy Moc turned out to be a Denver car wash that occupied the northeast corner of Colfax and Yosemite, the street that separates Denver from its neighboring stepchild, the city of Aurora. The neighborhood was a mixture of fast food eateries, laundromats, auto-body shops, secondhand stores, and tattoo parlors. But Aurora was changing. The city had recently stolen the University of Colorado's Denver-based Health Sciences Center, jumping aboard the federal government's plan to fund alternative uses for deactivated military bases such as the former Fitzsimons Army Base, one square mile of pristine Aurora land. In fine American tradition, politicians jockeying for position, entrepreneurs looking for a quick buck, and real estate developers on the prowl would eventually make the Rinse and Shine Carwash and its neighbors a historical footnote.

The noise from the car wash's massive dryers could be heard a block away, and when business was heavy, as it was today with eighty cars an hour rolling through the Rinse and Shine gates, the noise was deafening. Weary from her early-morning start, lovemaking, and the 140-mile round-trip drive to Colorado Springs and back, Flora Jean didn't feel much like staking out a car wash.

With CJ and Mavis on her mind and a tinge of guilt still nagging at her for not calling the cops in on a kidnapping case, she had strolled into the Rinse and Shine fifteen minutes earlier, asked the cashier who was sitting in a bullet-proof glass enclosure if Jimmy Moc was in, and been told that Moc didn't start work until 1. With nothing better to do while she waited, she'd queued up her seven-year-old Tahoe, one of the few sport utility vehicles with enough leg room for her, plunked down fifteen dollars for the daily wash special unabashedly called "the works," and sat down on a bench outside to drink an overpriced Coke and watch the workers dry her SUV.

When she spotted a man who fitted the description Alden Grace had given her for Jimmy Moc, she thought, *Short-term stakeout—lucky in love, lucky in love.* The man looked pretty much as Alden had described him: late thirties, early forties, short, with a mop of wiry black hair, a round, cherubic face, a broad no-question-about-it-brother-man's classic nose, skin the shade of dried tobacco, and unquestionably Amerasian.

He smiled at the cashier, who flashed him a look that said, *Jimmy, you've got a problem,* before nodding in Flora Jean's direction.

Jimmy glanced at Flora Jean, dropped the McDonald's bag he was holding, grabbed a wad of keys out of his pocket, and took off, Air Jordans screaming across Colfax.

"Damn," said Flora Jean, bursting from the bench in pursuit.

A customer waiting for his car said, "Wow!" Another simply pointed at Flora Jean. Most stared and kept quiet.

Jimmy was fast, but Flora Jean had a stride advantage. After being kissed on the shoulder by a passing RTD bus and temporarily losing her balance, Flora Jean charged north on Yosemite, noticeably winded. Jimmy maintained their half-block separation until he made the mistake of heading for his car. He jumped in the unlocked driver's door, jammed the key into the ignition, and cranked the engine. With tires squealing and his door still ajar, he was ten feet from the curb when Flora Jean reached inside, grabbed the collar of his blaze-orange Denver Broncos sweatshirt, and slammed all 140 pounds of Jimmy into the freshly paved Yosemite Street asphalt. His car, a lime-green Neon, jumped the curb on the opposite side of the street, slammed nose first into a thirty-foot-high cottonwood tree, and stopped.

"Fuck you! Fuck you! Fuck you!" Jimmy screamed at a near machine-gun clip.

"And your mother," said Flora Jean, gasping for air as she dropped to the asphalt and slammed her right knee across Jimmy's neck.

"I—can't—breathe." Jimmy's words were now muffled and slow. As he gasped for air, every part of his body but his head flapped around, gyrating as if he were a pithed frog.

Asserting control, Flora Jean demanded, "Why'd you run, Jimmy?"

"'Cause—I—didn't—want—nobody—repo'in' my car."

"I'm not the repo man." She eased the pressure on Jimmy's neck.

"Hell if you ain't—you're wearin' silver and black."

"So do the Oakland Raiders," said Flora Jean.

"You were waitin' for me at my job."

Flora Jean shook her head. "Maybe I'm from Publishers Clearing House."

"Ain't funny, bitch."

Flora Jean laid every ounce of her weight back into Jimmy's neck. "That's Ms. Benson to you, you little worm."

"Ahhhh—you're killin' me."

"Bullshit. But I might if you call me a bitch again."

"Whatta ya want?"

"Real simple. An address." Flora Jean glanced up and down the street to see if anyone was taking in the show. The last thing she needed was some overeager cop or Good Samaritan dropping by to pay their respects. She saw a woman walking her dog moving toward them and figured she had less than a minute to get what she'd come for.

"Whose address you want?"

"Le Quan's."

"No way."

"Wanna keep breathing, sugar?" Flora Jean ratcheted up the pressure on Jimmy's neck.

"He'll kill me."

Flora Jean increased the pressure.

"Aww—I."

"The address."

"He . . ."

"Go on, sugar, finish."

"He has a shoe store over on Federal Boulevard in Little Vietnam. I don't know the address."

"Does the store have a name?"

"The Shoe Tree." Jimmy gasped for air.

"You're a dear," Flora Jean said loudly, helping Jimmy to his feet just as the woman with the dog walked by.

"You don't want no part of Quan," said Jimmy, shaking his arm out of Flora Jean's grasp. The dog, a chow-husky mix, growled, but the owner, eyes straight ahead, kept walking.

"He's that tough? Well, I'll be sure to mind my p's and q's when I tell Quan you sent me to see him."

"Don't. Don't do that." Jimmy's face was a snapshot of fear. "You ain't never seen me, lady. I don't exist." Jimmy brushed himself off, eyed Flora Jean disdainfully, and headed for his car. Before stepping into the idling vehicle, he turned and said, "You're cruisin' for a cut block, bitch."

Flora Jean took a quick step toward Jimmy as he slammed the door, backed away from the tree trunk, and sped off.

As she headed back to the Rinse and Shine for her car, she couldn't help but wonder what the link between Le Quan, a former Vietcong communist youth organizer, and an obviously U.S.-bred Amerasian loudmouth like Jimmy Moc might be.

She'd almost reached Colfax when the woman with the dog, now coming back the other way, looked up and smiled at her. "Have a nice day," said the woman.

"You too," said Flora Jean.

◆◆◆

Clad in a terry cloth bathrobe and matching slippers he'd stolen from a Four Seasons in Boston, Lincoln Cortez belched out a laugh as he sat down on the edge of the bed in the South Santa Fe Drive motel room he'd rented and reread Peter Margolin's obituary. He couldn't help but think that Margolin had probably written the glowing piece himself. "Always did love himself," Cortez muttered. "Guess he just never learned to fly." Smiling, he tossed the paper aside, checked his watch, and sat back on the bed, suddenly wondering why he hadn't heard from his contact in two days.

Chapter

17

LOMBARDI AND ASSOCIATES, the Rocky Mountain region's top polling analysts, had a sterling reputation, penthouse offices in the Republic Plaza in Denver's downtown high-rise 17th Street power-broker canyon, and an unblemished record of never having called the wrong side in a Colorado senatorial election in seventy-five years.

Benjamin Lombardi, Benji to his closest friends, had taken the company's reins from his father ten years earlier and had moved the staid and proper old firm into the twentieth century, outfitting it with the finest hardware and software money could buy and hiring a gaggle of highly paid analysts who'd cut their teeth inside the Washington Beltway.

Alfred Reed, Peter Margolin's Republican opponent, and Elliott Cole, the state Republican Party chairman, were seated with Benji at one end of a long oval teakwood conference table in the Lombardi and Associates offices, engaged in conversation amid uncleared plates and glasses, remnants of their earlier power lunch.

Lombardi paused, took a sip of tepid coffee, and eyed Cole.

"From all accounts, Elliott, Margolin's death gave you a two-point blip. A week or two from now you may slip a little because of a sympathy reaction. It's common. But you're gaining. I'm certain you can carry it into November." Lombardi reached for a stack of computer printouts, slipped two five-page documents off the top of the stack, and dealt them across the table. "Our latest poll results. Take one with you. They'll go out to the rest of your people tomorrow."

Cole picked up his printout, looked at it briefly, and placed it face down on the table. "You know how I feel about these things, Benji. They're too rough to wipe your ass with and too slick for catching snot. It's people who tell you what you want to know when it comes to an election, not a bunch of hotshot Harvard-trained analysts."

Used to Cole's objections and unfazed by them, Lombardi said, "It's what you're paying for, Elliott."

"And a damn pretty penny. Now that we've settled that and you've pawned off your latest data sheets on me, here's what I really need. I want somebody walking Five Points, going door to door, making sure we get our proper share of the nigger vote. And people canvassing every tamale and taco joint in Denver so I know the Mexicans are with me, too. I want to know that every yuppie kissing the boss's ass and every unhappy housewife, hooker, and soccer mom gives Alfred their vote. I don't want to know what they think. I want to know how they'll vote. And if necessary, we'll grease a few palms."

Looking incredulous, Lombardi said, "We don't do that, Elliott, and you know it."

Cole picked up his printout and waved it in the air. "If you don't, you should. As far as I'm concerned, your exit-poll, pie-chart, bar-graph, sample-size bullshit just gets in the way. You've always said your margin of error is 4 to 5 percent. Shit, if that's the case, Alfred and whoever in the shit the Democrats end up picking to take Margolin's place are pretty much in a dead heat." Cole pounded his fist on the table for effect.

"Trust me, Elliott. There's no way. They're scrambling. They're two weeks away from even having a candidate."

"Then what you're saying is that we are pretty much dead even with a dead man!"

Tired of watching Cole and Lombardi gnaw at one another, Reed stepped in to referee. "Why don't we wait and see who the Democrats pick before we chew off each other's legs?"

Cole gave Reed a look that said, *You're out of your league, boy*, but instead of saying *Shut the fuck up*, the way he would have ten years earlier, he calmly set the printout back down on the table. "I spent ten years growing you on the vine, Alfred. Don't blow it."

"And I'm the party's candidate; take it or leave it," Reed shot back.

Cole shook his head, eyed Reed, and said, "So you are. So you are."

After a few seconds of steely silence, he turned to Lombardi. "I've shot my wad on this subject, Benji. You do your thing, and I'll do mine. As long as the Democrats stay as disorganized and as dope-headed as they normally are, we'll skate home free in November."

Lombardi nodded without answering and began straightening the stack of papers, which had gone cockeyed when Cole pounded the table. They were perfectly aligned when Cole asked, "Have the cops been by to see you yet?"

Startled by the question, Lombardi asked, "Why should they?"

"Because when it comes to the murder of a congressman, instead of some gang-banger they tend to look under a few more rocks. You're connected to the campaign, you're highly visible, and after all, you and Peter had your differences."

"So Ginny picked him over me. That's yesterday's news."

"Doesn't matter with the cops. All they'll see is a lovers' triangle."

"Horse shit."

"Maybe not," said Reed. "A homicide lieutenant named Newburn has already been by to see me."

"And me," added Cole. "And he's pretty sharp for a black man. Even dug up the fact that Peter and I didn't always see eye to eye while we were in Vietnam. My guess is Owen Brashears sicced him on both of us. He and that Boulder rag of his are good at dishing dirt."

"Well, if he comes to see me, I'll send him packing," said Lombardi.

Cole forced back a chuckle. "You do that. And while you're at it, make sure not to mention anything about being a former Penn State linebacker. Peter was shoved to his death at the construction site. Newburn as much as told me so. My guess is, you'd have to be a pretty strong person to do that."

"Don't bait me, Elliott." Lombardi rose from his chair, a signal that the meeting was over. "We all had our differences with Peter."

Cole smiled, enjoying the fact that he'd ruffled a few feathers. "Call me tomorrow. I'll have some data from Cherry Hills, the Stapleton district, and the Baker neighborhood that I'll want you to crunch. I'll need it by the first of next week."

"Just get it to me," said Lombardi, thankful that not all of his clients shared Elliott Cole's view of the polling business.

"It's been ducky," said Cole, reaching out to shake Lombardi's hand. Lombardi pumped it once and turned to Reed. "Good luck with the race." He patted Reed on the shoulder.

"We don't need luck," boomed Cole with the certainty of someone who'd been playing a game and rigging the outcome for years. "Just more black folks, Mexicans, and empty-headed vessels we can fill full of what we're selling."

He smiled at Lombardi's stunned expression and walked out the door.

◆ ◆ ◆

Federal Boulevard, one of Denver's major north-south thoroughfares, parallels the Rockies as it shoots arrow-straight across the west side of the city, piercing nearly fifteen miles of ethnic neighborhoods that haven't changed in fifty years, except for a two-mile-long stretch extending from Alameda to Florida Avenues. Over three postwar decades that stretch, now known as Little Vietnam, has burgeoned into a Far East megacenter.

Le Quan's shoe store, the Asian Shoe Tree, anchored a small shoppette at the corner of Federal Boulevard and Louisiana. The front of the store, at the far south end of the V-shaped shoppette, was all tempered glass. Its egg-yolk-yellow interior walls and open-beamed eighteen-foot ceilings, highlighted by basketball-arena-style lighting, could be seen from a block away, as could shoes stacked floor to ceiling from every imaginable state, republic, province, and island on the planet. Quan did a bustling business in everything from woven bamboo sandals to knockoff Nikes. And if he didn't have what a customer wanted, he'd guarantee to find it within a week.

The shoe business, from all outward appearances, had made him financially comfortable, although detractors both inside and outside the Vietnamese community claimed that his success had more to do with peddling illegal contraband, including tobacco products sans tax stamps, stolen French and Italian wines, and brand-name footwear knockoffs. However, Quan had managed to fend off critics, bankruptcy, and the law and had flourished since his arrival in Denver from the war-torn Vietnamese province of Quang Ngai twenty-five years earlier.

Flora Jean called the Shoe Tree on a pretense of trying to locate a pair of size 11 Gore-Tex-lined, U.S. Army–issued, World War II–style field boots. It was a shoe she was pretty certain Quan wouldn't have because all the knockoffs, popular among bikers, hunters, college kids, and Goths, came without a Gore-Tex lining. She had talked to Quan himself, who had lamented that he wasn't certain whether he had the shoe in stock, but she could come by the store to take a look. It was Quan's version of a bait and switch, since he knew he didn't have the shoe. When she'd asked how long he would be in, he said, "'Til 9," and cheerfully added, "Just ask for Le."

On the way to Quan's, Flora Jean called Julie Madrid, to find out the arraignment status of a client. She filled Julie in on the Langston Blue saga but skirted the issue of Mavis's kidnapping, knowing that Julie would call the cops. When she parked in front of the Shoe Tree it was just past 6 o'clock.

The ten-foot-high double door to the Shoe Tree was dwarfed by the store's front wall of glass. The interior lighting, a notch below blinding, assaulted Flora Jean as she walked in.

"Help you?" asked a young Asian woman who looked to be in her mid- to late twenties. She was pretty, long-boned, and pale.

"Lookin' for a boot," said Flora Jean. "I called earlier and spoke to Le."

"I can help you."

"Thanks, but Le said to ask for him."

The woman eyed Flora Jean with a hint of suspicion. "I'll get him." She headed toward the back of the store, working her way between boxes stacked high with shoes, shelves over-flowing with stock, and an array of uncomfortable-looking benches. Near the back, she glanced over her shoulder at Flora Jean and flashed the kind of smile one displays when running interference.

Moments later a thin wisp of a man appeared from behind a six-foot-high stack of shoeboxes. A foot shorter than the boxes, he was dressed in droopy khaki pants, a bold-colored Hawaiian shirt that featured violet flowers, and penny loafers. The woman who had retrieved him followed close on his heels as he walked toward Flora Jean.

"Hi," he said, stopping a few paces short of Flora Jean. "You the lady lookin' for field boot? I'm Le."

"Yes," said Flora Jean, realizing that the little man standing before her, his gaze locked on her chest, had a two-inch-wide silver streak that started at his forehead and ran Mohawk-style right through the middle of his jet black hair.

"I got plenty. But don't know if they what you want." Quan glanced toward the front of the store, turned to the woman who had summoned him, said something to her in Vietnamese, and waved her toward a group of teenagers who had just walked into the store.

"Boots in other aisle," he said, eyeing the teenagers suspiciously. "Follow me." He watched the teenagers until a stack of shoeboxes blocked his view.

"Got every style," he said when they reached a series of nine-foot-high shelves overflowing with trail boots, hiking shoes, military boots, and work shoes. "What you want boot for?"

Suspicious that Quan's question was intended to determine her true reason for the visit, she said, "Backpackin'."

"Got a better boot for that than one you asked about." Quan extracted a pair of size 11 hiking boots tied together at the laces from a shelf just in front of him and handed them to Flora Jean.

Flora Jean took a seat on one of the rock-hard benches and began untying the laces. "How long have you been in business here?" she asked, slipping her right foot into one of the boots.

"Twenty-four year this winter."

Flora Jean nodded, slipped on the other boot, and gazed around the store. There were only a few customers milling around a Nike display in addition to the teenagers, now busy with the woman who'd been Quan's escort. Flora Jean eased off one boot and rubbed her foot. Responding finally to Quan's statement, she asked, "Since you came here from Vietnam?"

Unfazed by a question he'd been asked hundreds of times, Quan simply nodded as he stared down at the rows of intricately carved African bracelets that encircled Flora Jean's arms.

"Fit?" asked Quan, looking Flora Jean squarely in the eye.

"Seems a little narrow."

"We can stretch."

"Were you a soldier in Vietnam?" asked Flora Jean, slipping off the other boot.

Le Quan frowned. This time the question Flora Jean had asked was far too personal. "No."

Flora Jean set the boots aside and stood. Smiling, she looked down at Quan. "A VC youth organizer, then?"

Quan stepped back and flashed Flora Jean a look of disdain. "What you want, lady?"

"Nothin' but some boots and a few answers. A friend of mine told me you might have some information for me. Said you knew Peter Margolin—that you might know something about his murder."

Visibly shaken, Quan stammered, "Who your friend?"

"Someone who doesn't like his name tossed around."

Quan's eyes darted in every direction until the look on his face turned into a hostile stare. Glancing toward the front of the store for the woman who'd escorted Flora Jean in, he shouted. All Flora Jean could make out was "hurry" and the name "Chi." Turning back to Flora Jean, he said, "You get out my store."

Before Flora Jean could say anything, Chi, whom she thought must be Quan's daughter, was standing directly in front of her. "Leave," she said, her tone clear and demanding.

"What about my boots?" said Flora Jean.

"Leave now or I'll call the police." Chi Quan grabbed Flora Jean by the arm.

"Take your hand off me if you want to keep it, sugar," said Flora Jean, suddenly and unmistakably a marine.

The look on Quan's face told Chi she'd better comply. She released her grip, but not before flashing Flora Jean a look that said she wasn't afraid. Determined to show the woman that she could also play the fearless game, Flora Jean sat down and, as the woman and Quan towered over her, slipped her shoes back on, placed the boots side by side back inside their box, and turned to leave.

Le Quan offered a parting shot: "Don't come back."

His daughter said nothing. The hostile look on her face said it all.

◆ ◆ ◆

Five minutes later, in a back room, Le Quan chewed on the remains of a stale Slim Jim. He was still shaking. Half of the unappetizing Slim Jim, still partially wrapped in cellophane, disappeared with the next bite.

Chi, still smarting from Flora Jean's visit, stood next to the walker her mother had been forced to use for six months before she succumbed to ovarian cancer, and eyed her father. Before

Quan could take another bite from the greasy beef stick, Chi said, "Things just never seem to change. Now we have some black Amazon threatening to disrupt our lives."

Quan ate the final piece of Slim Jim, deep in thought. The cellophane crackled. He was fifty-nine years old, resilient, and well schooled in the ways of the world. Chi was naive, sheltered, and still unsure of herself even at the age of thirty-two. He had spent his formative impoverished Vietnamese childhood outwitting French colonials in order to survive. He and his wife had learned from, outwitted, and out-thought the Americans who Ho Chi Minh had once predicted would slowly bleed to death on the soil of his homeland. Chi had been born in America on laundered sheets in a hospital in San Francisco, and as his firstborn, she'd been educated, indoctrinated, and even indulged in a way he still didn't fully understand. There were things she needed to learn that she hadn't.

"Daddy, are you listening?"

"I am."

"Why was she here?"

"I don't know."

"You know something. Why else would you have called for me to help?"

A look of acquiescence slowly worked its way across Quan's face. "Panic."

"Like you did when you read about that congressman, Margolin, dying? Like you did for more than a year and a half after Mother died? What did the woman say to you that made you call out?"

"She threaten me with my past." Quan lowered his head and eyed the floor.

Chi Quan's eyes widened and the muscles in her face went taut. "That's it! That's enough! I'm calling Robert. Whoever they are, whatever that woman's after, they won't destroy us again."

"Your brother can't help."

"I think he can." Chi slipped a cell phone out of the pocket of her jeans.

"This not his fight."

Chi didn't respond. She was too busy punching in her brother's number. Robert could help. He was a lawyer, the lethal, take-no-prisoners kind. Unlike her, he had fought his way off the streets of Denver after a youthful stint with Vietnamese gangs. Above all, he had connections. He was a New Mexico assistant attorney general.

♦♦♦

It was a few minutes before 9 p.m. when, in response to his sister's plea for help, Robert Quan made a phone call.

After detailing their father's continued meltdown since the death of their mother, his panic seemingly triggered by the death of a Colorado senatorial candidate, and the visit from the jack-booted black woman, Chi had been blunt. "I don't plan on taking a return trip to that world we grew up in, Rob. It may do wonders for your political poor-mouthing, but it doesn't suit me."

Her brother's response had been terse, calm, unruffled, and accepting, as if he'd somehow been expecting the call. "I'll handle it," was all he said before hanging up.

His phone call to a Washington, D.C., suburb was equally brief. From dial tone to dial tone, his message to the man on the other end of the line, who grunted into the phone only "This is Alex," took thirty seconds. "We've got water buffalo in the duck pond," Quan said, clearing his throat before hanging up.

Chapter

18

ALEX HOLDEN'S 8 A.M. FLIGHT from Dulles Airport to Chicago was bumpy, the flight from O'Hare to Albuquerque bumpier still. He detested choppy air; it reminded him too much of his days as a fighter pilot. And he disliked Albuquerque for the simple reason that its moistureless air and five-thousand-plus-foot elevation gave his chronically inflamed sinuses fits. But more than anything, especially when it came to the necessities of his job, he hated mopping up.

The hour-and-fifteen-minute drive north on I-25 from Albuquerque to Santa Fe, a drive that traversed high-plains piñon forest, moonscape-looking arroyos, and an endless expanse of chickweed and sage, reminded him that he was a born-and-bred creature of the East, an unabashed lover of the bean and the cod, and that despite the odds against it, he'd been forced to make more trips west in the past three weeks than his sinuses could handle.

By the time he checked into his $39.99-a-night bed-and-a-deadbolt, no-cable, no-frills, no-questions-asked Cerrillos Road motel, his sinuses, sucked dry by the altitude, had started bleeding. He took several cottonballs out of a plastic baggie he removed from his briefcase, stuffed one in each nostril, and shook his head disgustedly before taking a seat and punching in Robert Quan's number on his cell phone.

When Quan answered, he said, "Holden. We still on for 3?"

"Yes." Quan's answer was a nervous whisper. He didn't like the idea of meeting with someone who lived his life as if it were the days after World War II instead of sixty years later. But meet, they would.

◆◆◆

Owen Brashears had driven the thirty miles from Boulder to Denver in a rush of noonday traffic at Lieutenant Wendall New-burn's request. It was a summons more than a request when you split the hairs of their tense conversation. "Meet me at Cold Stone Creamery ice-cream parlor in Cherry Creek at 12:30. Wear your military history hat and try not to be late," was the way Newburn had actually put it.

Upset at having to bow out of a meeting in which the specifics of a new layout for the *Boulder Daily Camera*'s editorial page would be discussed, Brashears had acquiesced, and he now sat at an undersized bar-height glass-topped table nursing a vanilla milkshake and preparing for a second round of questions from Newburn.

He'd already told the flat-foreheaded black cop with a reced-ing hairline, who seemed as interested in being noticed in the trendy ice-cream parlor as he was in getting answers to his ques-tions, that he had indeed been a *Stars and Stripes* reporter dur-ing the Vietnam War, that his *Stars and Stripes* assignment had coincided with Margolin's tour, and that he had no idea if Peter had had enemies left over from his days in Vietnam.

"Love this place," said Newburn, continuing to put away the triple-scoop French vanilla cone he'd ordered. "Best ice cream in town," he added, surprising Brashears by taking a small bite from his ice cream instead of licking it. "Come here all the time. Gets me out of the office. A little sunshine and sweets never hurts." When Brashears didn't return his smile, Newburn said, "It's a phrase my mother used to use. Now, back to Margolin. Any familiarity with the army's Star 1 teams?"

"Yes," said Brashears, aware that the best way to respond to lawyers, commanding officers, and cops was to tell the truth.

"Have any experience with 'em during the war?"

"No."

"Full of words today, aren't we? Well, let me fill you in on what we know about the army's Star 1 teams and your friend Margolin. Were you aware that Captain Margolin commanded a Star 1 team during a portion of 1971?"

"Yes."

"But you said you didn't have any experience with them," said Newburn, trying to determine if Brashears was lying.

"I meant that I didn't serve in one. *Stars and Stripes* reporters didn't serve in fighting units."

"You're yanking my chain," said Newburn. "Funny how your service records follow you everywhere. No matter what. Like with CJ Floyd, one of our city's high profile bail bondsman. Heard of him? Maybe from Ginny Kearnes?"

"I've heard of him."

"Good." Newburn took a lick of ice cream and grinned. "When I tried to connect a few military-record dots, just for the fun of it, I started with Floyd, looking for prior service in a Star 1 team." Newburn looked down at the spiral-bound notebook lying on the tabletop. "I didn't get a match, and believe me, I was sure hoping I would. But when I tried the same kind of match with the name Cortez, bells and whistles started popping."

"And all this has what to do with me?"

"Oh, I'll get to that. Once that military-records search of mine really got rolling—and it took a couple of days for the army records folks to agree to play ball—I came up with a whole list of names and a bunch more connections."

"What's your point, Lieutenant?"

"This," said Newburn, taking a lick from his ice cream, which had started to run. "Your friend Captain Margolin was in charge of what's sounding more and more to me like an eight-man team of army misfits." Newburn referred to his notebook. "Sergeants Langston Blue and Lincoln Cortez, Private Richard Wells, and their captain, Peter Margolin. Now, that's as far as my search was able to take me before I got stonewalled, but I did pick up a little tidbit when I did an end-around the army and called up some public records on our trusty departmental computer. Drew nothing but blanks for half a morning until I somehow ran across a link that took me to our military's sterling example of covert fighting heroes in Vietnam, its so-called Studies and Observations Group." He eyed Brashears intently. "Any idea how such a fine example of a fighting man like Margolin got picked for Star 1 team duty instead of drawing an assignment with the SOG?"

"Sure. Peter got stuck with the Star 1 job because someone up there didn't like him. The whole time he was a Star 1 team commander, and it was only for about six months, he was griping, feeding me inside dope. Telling me about their missions, giving me fodder for postwar stories. We even thought about writing a book."

"What derailed your plan?"

"Peter's team went on a mission in the Song Ve Valley south of Quang Ngai. Only three of eight men in his unit came back. Seven weeks later all the teams were dismantled, gone."

"What happened to Margolin?"

"He got reassigned."

"And the other men in his unit?"

"One of the sergeants you mentioned earlier, Cortez, mustered out. Blue, the other sergeant, deserted."

"They ever find him?"

"Don't think so."

"Pretty heady stuff," said Newburn.

"War usually is, Lieutenant."

Newburn stroked his chin, took a lick of ice cream, and stared Brashears down. "You wouldn't have had any reason to kill Margolin?"

"Are you crazy?"

"Maybe Margolin kept you from winning your Pulitzer."

His eyes burning with rage, Brashears said, "If I were you, Lieutenant, I'd start with Peter's enemies, not his friends."

Newburn smiled. "You're the navigator here. Point me in the right direction."

"I'd try Elliott Cole, chairman of the Colorado Republican Party. He'd be first."

"The reason being?"

Reveling in the fact that he finally had a chance to be one up on Newburn, Brashears flashed the probing lieutenant a quick *gotcha* kind of smile. "Cole was the one who stuck Peter with that Star 1 team assignment in the first place."

Newburn caught a drip of ice cream with his left hand. "Well, well, well. I'll do that. And while I'm at it . . ." The chime of Newburn's cell phone interrupted him. Flipping the phone open, he said, "Newburn, here." He listened intently to the caller for a few seconds before saying, "I'm on it." He flipped his phone closed and glanced over at Brashears. "Guess we'll have to stop here. Got something urgent. But I'll be in touch." He bit off the shrunken head of the remaining ice cream and tossed his waffle cone in the nearby trash can.

"That urgent?" asked Brashears.

"Things are always urgent when you're a homicide cop," said Brashears. "Surprised they didn't teach you that in journalism school," he added, shooting Brashears his own version of a *gotcha* smile before making his exit.

◆◆◆

Newburn got back to the precinct a little past 2:30, set to log in another John Doe homicide. He didn't see the salmon-colored Post-It note resting on his desk until, looking as if it had floated down from outer space, the note made a perfect landing in his lap as he swiveled in his chair to get a fresh computer disk out of a side drawer.

He picked up the note, read the lightly penciled lowercase letters that read, *See me. Morris. 2 p.m.*, and said, "Shit!" Responses to e-mails from his division captain, Emery Morris, could for the most part be delayed and sometimes flat-out ignored, and Morris's phone calls could also be returned when necessary, which meant not immediately, about half the time. But a personalized *see me* note, the kind Morris delivered only when someone higher up the food chain was chewing at his ass, meant trouble. And a delivery time on the note, printed out as if it had come from some hourly worker's time card, meant there would probably be hell to pay. Newburn rose from his chair, checked his watch, and headed off to meet his captain.

When he reached Morris's office the outer office door was open. He walked into an area no bigger than an oversized dining-room table to find Morris talking to a man wearing a black pinstriped suit and a charcoal-and-cranberry tie. The man had the hint of a contrived 5 o'clock shadow, and his hair, not a single strand out of place, looked as if it were waiting for some-one to say the word, *Action!*

"I'll come back," said Newburn, watching the eyes of both men land directly on him and knowing without having to ask that the man talking to Morris had to be a lawyer.

"No, no, come in. We're discussing something that pertains to you," said Morris. "Adam Marx, Wendall Newburn," he added by way of introduction. They shared a brief handshake before Morris went on, "Adam's one of Colorado's premier assistant attorney generals. He came by to pay us a visit at the request of a friend."

Marx said, "A buddy of mine from law school asked me to drop by. Nothing official, of course. We work in different states." His tone rose as he talked, becoming higher pitched, almost effeminate.

"But it's the same street," said Morris, his tone full of butter.

"Anyway, my friend, Robert Quan, who has a job similar to mine in New Mexico, asked me to see if I couldn't get a line on where you guys are with the Peter Margolin murder."

"That's . . ."

"Let him finish, Lieutenant," said Morris, cutting Newburn off.

Marx smiled and continued, "Anyway, Robert says that yesterday a huge black woman barged into his father's shoe store over on Federal and implied that his father was a communist, when in fact he's a Vietnam War survivor, a naturalized U.S. citizen, a community leader, and a prominent businessman. On top of that insult, according to Robert, she suggested in the next breath, although she didn't actually say it, that his father might know something about Peter Margolin's murder." Marx barely took a breath before adding his high-pitched trump card: "So I'm here to share my outrage, to offer you a new lead in your investigation, and of course to pass along to Robert Quan any insights you might have—without, of course, compromising your investigation."

Aware that he was under no obligation to share anything about his investigation with anyone, especially some nasal-sounding tight-assed junior league A.G., Newburn simply smiled. But politics and peace of mind being what they are, and payment-on-demand missiles from one's captain being key to one day being either promoted or punked, Newburn asked, "Did your friend say whether the woman who confronted his father had both arms encased in bracelets?"

"In fact, he did," said Marx, surprised by the question. "Brightly colored ones, and she wanted to buy combat boots."

"Got a make on her?" asked Morris, ready to score a few points with the office of the attorney general.

"Flora Jean Benson, more than likely," Newburn said matter-of-factly. "She's a dog-sniffer for CJ Floyd."

Morris's eyes widened. "That cheroot-smoking bail bondsman?"

Newburn nodded.

"Well, we have a connection," Adam Marx said enthusiastically. "I told Robert our Denver homicide detectives were first rate. Anything else I can share with him about the case?"

"Not really," said Newburn.

"You'll deal with the Benson woman, and Floyd?" Morris said sternly.

Newburn nodded. "They're now officially part of the Margolin case."

"I told you we'd move quick to have an answer for you," said Morris, his expression now a broad, shit-eating grin.

"I'm certain my friend will appreciate that, and the fact that you'll of course put an end to any further harassment."

Morris looked at Newburn, hoping that since the Margolin case was his, he'd offer Marx a plum that would make them both look good. On most days Newburn would've kept his investigative moves and methods close to the vest, especially when it came to sharing them with an outsider and an obvious up-bucking weasel like Marx, but most days didn't afford him the chance to stick it to CJ Floyd or his insolent partner. Smiling at the thought of having the opportunity to make CJ and Flora Jean squirm, Newburn said, "I'll move the Benson woman and Floyd to the top of my docket. You and your friend can count on it."

◆ ◆ ◆

Robert Quan and Alex Holden walked slowly west along the sunny south-facing portal of Santa Fe's historical Palace of the Governors, eyeing blanket after blanket of Indian pottery, jewelry, trinkets, and assorted tourist come-ons spread casually on the uneven brick walkway at their feet, all within a quick stretch of the doleful-looking Native American people selling them.

"This place has been standing since 1610," said Quan, taking a step back from the historic building and sweeping his right hand boldly in a semicircle.

"But clearly after the Jamestown settlement," countered Holden, smugly.

"And way before America discovered Vietnam," said Quan, fed up with Holden's incessant one-upmanship, his unending references to his days as a fighter pilot and champion motocross rider, his constant griping about his nosebleeds, and his disparaging comments about Indians, the West, and Mexican food.

"You got what you came for," said Quan, eyeing the large manila envelope Holden had tucked under his right arm. "Everything on everyone involved at Song Ve, including Sergeant Blue, Margolin, and my father." It was all he could do to keep from laughing at Holden's retro crew cut, horn-rimmed glasses, rubber-soled wingtips, and all-black clothing. Instead he said, "Time's a-wastin'."

"Don't get smart with me, Quan. You came calling."

"I know, but it's hard to break a dependency," said Quan, his tone meant to be biting. "It's like drugs."

Holden smiled. "Then you shouldn't start one."

"You're right."

Holden bent to look at a turquoise squash-blossom necklace. Frowning at the stoic-looking Indian vendor, he picked it up and dangled it in front of Quan. "What do you think?"

"I'd pass and head back to Washington. It's definitely not you."

Holden put the necklace down. "You're right. Too flashy."

"And too Western," said Quan, aware that Holden, an operative who had the authority to use any means necessary to set "Company" matters straight, spent nearly every minute of his life working at that unending project. Unless the dirtiest of the "Company's" laundry was about to be aired in public, he'd never chance sticking out. Overjoyed that Holden would be gone in less than an hour, Quan said, moving away from the portal, "The Wild West Show's over. Let's go."

Chapter

19

MAVIS HAD NEVER FELT ANYTHING quite like it. The endless thumping behind her eyes, the pounding in her forehead, the stabbing achiness in her knees. Although she knew better, she couldn't help but think that she had dropped through a hole in the universe directly into the bottomless pit of hell.

She knew she'd been unconscious, but she had no idea for how long. She knew she'd been assaulted and slammed against the hood of her car and the side rail of a truck bed, that she'd been caged and driven somewhere in the blackness of night. And she'd grown to know the pain.

What she didn't know was where she was or who had taken her to a place that smelled of mildew and pine trees, creosote and rotting logs. Above all, she didn't know why. She could move most of her body and everything seemed to be intact, and she could think, turn her head, even cough. But she was forced to do all those things while lying flat on her back, her head resting on some sort of cushion, supported by a metal tray, her eyes staring skyward toward two massive hand-hewn wooden beams that spanned a ceiling of rough-cut logs high above her.

She had tried to roll onto her right side, but she couldn't, and when she tried to raise her head off the pillow support she couldn't move it more than a few inches. Frustrated, she fought the pain and forced back tears. She thought about CJ and her father, about the restaurant and getting to work on time. She knew she was confined inside some kind of cylindrical contraption, because she'd been able, after a while, to feel around its rounded walls. And she realized that her head was poking through some sort of porthole made of plastic or rubber. There were several pressure gauges and valves jutting to the right and left of her head, but she had no idea what they were for.

A surge of pain shot between her temples, exploding behind her right eye. She tried not to cry, but she was losing her stamina, and a single tear began to trickle down her right cheek.

"Hurts, doesn't it?" said someone at the foot of the cylinder. Someone she couldn't see. "It hurts to be locked up, waiting for someone to set you free."

It was a woman's voice, Mavis was certain. A cold voice with a calculating edge.

Mavis didn't answer. She was too startled, too afraid.

"Don't worry, Mavis. Your sentence won't last long. You're on borrowed time now, Ms. Sundee. The kind we all come to dread, sooner or later."

Mavis lifted her head off the pillow, struggling to see above the edge of the cylinder. Realizing for the first time that the tube had a subtle brass-like hue, she stretched her leg, bumping it against the inside of the cylinder. There was a sharp punch of laughter.

"No need to struggle, Mavis; save your energy." The woman's voice resonated from the end of the tube. "I can see you quite well from where I'm standing. It's the advantage of having an understanding of geometry. If I stood just a little bit higher, an inch, maybe two or three, the triangulation would work to your advantage and sooner or later our eyes would meet. But I won't move, and you can't. So the issue's moot." The woman snickered. The snicker lingered momentarily before trailing off to a snort.

"May I have some water?" asked Mavis, uttering her first words since the abduction.

"In due time, Ms. Sundee. All in due time."

Suddenly Mavis heard footsteps moving away from her, and then what she was certain was a door slamming, followed by what sounded like someone walking down stairs. She couldn't tell if the woman had left the room or gone upstairs, outside, or down to a basement. All she was certain of was that the woman had moved away from the foot of the cylinder.

The pain behind Mavis's eyes resurfaced. Gritting her teeth and calling on her resolve, she thought about what CJ had once told her about a mission he'd been on in Vietnam when he was only nineteen. He'd said the mission had taught him the value of patience. It had been a routine predawn search and rescue, the kind that every grunt and sailor, marine and airman needed to experience early in their tour if they wanted to stand half a chance of coming home alive. His boat, the *Cape Star*, was taking fire from the Mekong River bank, and CJ found himself blazing away with his double-barreled .50-caliber machine gun at some faceless shoreline enemy instead of waiting to take aim at whoever was trying to take out the patrol boat. His gunnery chief, sensing his greenness, made his way to the back of the boat and said, "Slow down, son. World ain't made up of ammunition." He'd taken the twenty-year navy chief's advice, and when they swung back around to take aim at the enemy position, this time it was the impatient Vietcong cherry-picker with a shoreline grenade launcher who launched one too many grenades too fast in their direction, so fast that CJ could get a bead on him, who paid the price. The mission taught CJ that when it comes to life and death, your choices are to be patient or to rush ahead. More often than not, it's patience that ultimately enables you to survive.

Mavis knew it was going to take all of her mental strength to wait out her captor and all the patience she could muster to keep from being drawn under by the pain. But patient she would be, and in the end she told herself she would somehow survive.

◆ ◆ ◆

The leading edge of a heat wave carrying 90-plus-degree temperatures had knifed its way into southern Colorado and northern New Mexico by the time CJ and Billy left Fort Garland, Colorado. They had spent the night there mapping out a strategy for rescuing Mavis and exploring the surrounding mountains to get a feel for the terrain. They rolled past the old fort, which had been commanded by Kit Carson from 1866 to 1867, horse trailer in tow, with CJ gunning Billy's pickup, foot to the floor.

"Slow the shit down, CJ," said Billy. "'Case you forgot, we're towin' a 1,500-pound trailer loaded with 2,200 pounds of horse-flesh. You wanta kill us? I knew I shoulda been the one to drive." Billy slipped his ever-present wad of Doublemint, five sticks to the wad, never less and never any other brand, from his left cheek to his right and sat up straighter in his seat.

CJ eased off the accelerator without answering, deep in thought, his mind racing over and over through their rescue plan. He had thought through a half-dozen plans before finally settling on an early-morning surprise assault. He didn't know how many people he and Billy would have to deal with, how well armed they were, where Mavis would be, or how he'd initiate the whole thing. What he did know was that once he had worked his way into the Taos Mountains to the spot Celeste had pinpointed, he had to bring Mavis back.

"You gonna drive fast or slow?" asked Billy, watching the truck's speedometer needle drop below 50.

"Oh," said CJ, realizing he'd lost his concentration. He nudged the accelerator, a thud came from the trailer hitch, and soon they were cruising along at 65.

Comfortable with the fact that CJ had regained his focus, Billy asked, "Know why I think that Celeste woman snatched Mavis?"

"We've been through all that, Billy. She wants to even the score. She thinks I'm responsible for the death of her brother."

Billy shook his head. "No. I mean really," he said, removing his boot and sock, and massaging his toes.

CJ glanced over at the wiry little man with curly black hair and tried to figure out where Billy was heading. He watched

Billy, who'd lost not only an eye but a little toe to diabetes and rum, massage the ball of his foot and thought about how Billy had once saved his life in a gun battle outside Baggs, Wyoming. A black debutante, the daughter of a federal judge, had gotten tangled up with a bunch of whacked-out ecoterrorists. Billy had ridden in on horseback to the ranch the environmental nut-cases had been leasing, roped their leader, who was about to shoot CJ, and then dragged the fruitcake kicking and scream-ing across two acres of rocky pasture land. Aware that Billy in his folksy way was trying to make a point, CJ asked, "Why?"

"Easy," said Billy. "'Cause she's crazy."

Before CJ could laugh, Billy beat him to it. "And crazy peo-ple, no matter how hard they plan somethin', got vulnerabili-ties. Now, this Celeste woman, maybe she's scared of the dark or the light or heights or loud noises. Who knows? Could be she don't like lookin' at herself in the mirror, or she hates men or goats or one-teated cows. One thing for sure, anybody who went from bein' a world-champion swimmer and one of them Rhodes Scholars to where she's at now got a screw loose some-where."

CJ pondered Billy's grassroots assessment of Celeste for the next few miles without responding. When he slowed down to cruise through San Luis, the oldest town in Colorado, its main street dotted with crumbling adobe homes and boarded-up cantinas, CJ said, "Billy, I think you've hit on our solution."

"How's that?"

"A way to get inside Celeste Deepstream's head. Is that beat-to-crap rodeo announcer's kit you pack around in the trailer?"

"Sure is." Billy looked puzzled. "I just used it at a 4-H junior jamboree outside Cheyenne last week."

"And did you bring the two M16s?"

"I told you I did back in Denver. You're thinkin' too hard, CJ."

"Could be. Anyway. We're gonna stop here in San Luis and pick up some road flares."

"For what?"

"For an early-morning party. Or a late-night one. Depends on how you look at it."

Billy shrugged and slipped his sock back on. "Glad you decided to stop. I gotta pee and get some gum."

CJ shook his head in mock protest, aware that with his supply of Doublemint restocked, Billy would be smacking gum in his ear all the way to their destination.

Ten minutes later, his stash replenished, Billy sat back in his seat, his head planted against the head rest as CJ nosed the pickup into a stiff southwesterly wind. As they closed in on a semi filled with cattle, CJ said, "We're a half hour from our turnoff. Think we need to water Maggie and Butch before we head into the mountains?"

Billy turned around in his seat and peered through the cab's rear window at the swaying horse trailer. "They'll be fine. Ain't like this is the first time they've ever been on a road trip."

"How much ammo did you bring?" CJ's tone turned edgy.

"Enough for two M16s."

"And the rifles?"

"Got plenty for them, too. Why all the questions, CJ? You all right?"

"I'm fine." CJ gripped the steering wheel tightly, clenched his teeth, and watched a blanket of steam rise from the seemingly unending asphalt. As the cattle trailer ahead of them swayed from side to side in a 30-mile-per-hour wind, CJ had the uneasy feeling he was once again on the *Cape Star*, cruising the Mekong River delta waiting for the enemy to rear its ugly head.

◆◆◆

The woman was back. Mavis could hear her moving around the cabin, or house, or lodge, whatever the rustic building with the rotting beams and sagging split-rail walls actually was. The woman stayed well out of view, shifting objects, arranging and lifting things that sounded heavy. She spent several minutes next to a source of light that had to be a window, fiddling around with something faintly aromatic. There was silence that lasted a few minutes, and then the woman was back at it, moving something made of metal. For a fraction of a second Mavis thought she smelled gas. The next instant the smell was gone.

Mavis had had time to think, to come to grips with the pain and to consider the parameters of her confinement. She knew now that she was being held in a single large room in what she thought must be some type of diving or airlock apparatus. A full cycle of sunlight had moved across the floor and faded. When she'd summoned the courage to run her hands over her exquisitely tender knees, the palm sweat had triggered a spike of agonizing pain, and she'd realized that large pieces of the flesh covering both knees were missing.

She wondered what time it was, what the woman had planned for her, and how long she'd been there. She was about to drift off to sleep when suddenly the woman appeared just to the right of her head, out of nowhere, like a bolus of light. She was holding a glass of water in one hand and two white nuggets the size of jawbreakers in the other. Mavis turned her head to get a better look at the woman. The first thought that came to mind after seeing a puffy-faced, cocoa-skinned woman with severely cropped black hair was that the woman had probably been very striking at one time. Then Mavis thought about how the woman could kill her.

"Water as you requested," said the woman, dropping the two white pellets into the glass of water. "It's evanescence," she added, erupting in laughter. "And briny. Like the ocean, Mavis. Like the ocean. You wouldn't like it," she said, pouring the water onto the floor. "Too salty." Tossing the glass aside, the woman squatted until she was at Mavis's eye level. "How do you like your accommodations? A bit confining, maybe? But aren't we all? Confined, I mean."

When Mavis didn't answer, the look on the woman's face turned hateful. "Tongue-tied? I can cut it out if it's bothering you."

"I'm fine," said Mavis.

"Oh, are you? And I'm Celeste. Pleased to meet you." Again she burst into laughter. "Deepstream, that is. Perhaps you knew my brother, Bobby."

"No."

"You're lying." The woman rose from her crouch and slapped Mavis across the face. "You're lying. You're lying."

Mavis gasped and gritted her teeth. The room turned quiet

except for Mavis's labored breathing. Finally Celeste stepped back and said, "You know CJ Floyd, of course. Better not lie to me."

"Yes."

"And you love him?"

"Yes."

"Like I loved Bobby."

When Mavis didn't answer, Celeste slapped her again. "Your lover's coming for you, Mavis." She watched Mavis's eyes widen. "No need to doubt me. We've been in touch. He's following my orders, and I'm certain he'll be here by daybreak. That's when he'll find you here in your iron lung waiting for him so faithfully, alive and well. And then I'm going to kill him. And you too, Mavis. I've mapped it all out, planned ahead for you and dear Mr. Floyd." Celeste's words seemed to swirl around the room, reverberating off the walls, the beams, the flooring. As quickly as she'd appeared, she was gone. Not like an apparition or a bolt of light this time but like the ghost of a madwoman screaming.

An iron lung, thought Mavis as the room grew darker and silent. She'd never considered that, but it made perfect sense. She turned toward the fading sunlight, knowing there was no more time for tears, or guilt, or fear. Only time for hoping, praying, and thinking—time to somehow alter the woman's game plan and disrupt whatever it was she had in mind for CJ.

◆ ◆ ◆

CJ and Billy had ridden in slowly and quietly on horseback, leaving their rig at the end of a gravel road that had turned into dirt, the dirt into tire ruts in the tall native grass, and the tire ruts eventually into a cow path that nipped its way into the Taos

Mountains. Their horses walked side by side with stately ease, nudging one another's hindquarters occasionally as if to serve notice that one or the other was ahead by a nose.

They'd watered and saddled the horses just south of Costilla, a mile west of where they'd turned off Highway 522 and less than a mile from the rushing waters of the Rio Grande. Billy had pulled out the dog-eared, leather-bound New Mexico topo map he'd been using for years, checked the distances and contours of the terrain they were about to butt heads with, patted his horse, Maggie, just below the swell of her neck, and said, "Don't want no shit outta you here today, Maggie."

They traversed arroyos and crossed cactus fields, sagebrush nobs, and marshy springs as they negotiated their way deep into the mountains. Instead of following a jeep trail into the mountains, as Celeste had probably envisioned with her carefully placed yellow dot on the map, they were approaching from the southwest and on horseback.

The terrain became steeper and rockier, and the horses labored in the heat as they worked their way south. Duel scabbards housing two over-and-under Berettas and Remington and Winchester 30.06's hung angled across the horses' hindquarters. Each horse carried a saddlebag jammed with road flares and the two M16s, which had been broken down and oiled. Billy's 4H announcer's bullhorn made a lump like a melon in one of the saddlebags.

"Whatta you think, Billy? A couple of miles farther?" asked CJ, rubbing Butch behind the ear.

"More or less," said Billy, his West Indian accent becoming

more pronounced with each new mile, as it always did when he was getting edgy. "I'm thinkin' maybe I should've brought my sawed-off shotgun," he said as they began their ascent of another rocky hillside.

"I'm hoping there won't be a need to get that close," said CJ.

"Don't count on it."

CJ didn't answer. He was too busy thinking about Mavis, wondering if she was okay, whether she was holding her own. He hadn't asked Celeste's drugged-out, slow-thinking twin brother to transport stolen art objects or unregistered guns and fireworks across state lines, and he hadn't forced Celeste to kill the man who had hired him to track down Bobby. But the game had started with Bobby, and now they were about to finish it.

As the winded horses trudged uphill, he couldn't help thinking that Mavis had been right all along. Right about the way he lived, right about the futility of the job he went to every day. And right about the bottom-feeding people who provided his living. Maybe he could be happy peddling Western memorabilia and antiques. Maybe it would give him, and now Mavis, a shot at a much longer life. He wasn't sure, but he'd reached the point where it was at least worth considering.

He didn't realize they'd reached the top of the hill until Billy drew Maggie to a halt. Butch did the same without need of a command.

"Guess we get to see the wizard's place now," said Billy, pointing down toward a structure peeking out from the tall grass in the valley below. CJ pulled a set of binoculars from his Wrangler vest and spotted in on the structure, a low-lying rectangular shack with a mud roof and walls of rotting timber. A corral made from welded oil pipe rose out of the dirt, just south of the shack. A pickup sat inside the corral.

"How the hell did she get a truck down there?" asked CJ.

"I'd put my money on that dried-up creek bed," Billy said, a set of binoculars to his eyes. "She probably followed it up from the south. Gotta know the territory to play the game, CJ. She's one up on us when it comes to that."

CJ glanced back toward the sun, now hidden beneath the edge of the Taos Mountains. "She's probably inside that line shack," he said. "With Mavis." He dropped his binoculars back around his neck. "Looks to me like it's pretty close to sunset. Time to set things up."

"You gonna set up the way we planned?" asked Billy.

"Just like we said on the way down."

"What if Mavis ain't inside?"

"Then we'll have to find her."

"Think the woman will tell us where she's stashed?"

"If she ends up still alive." The look on CJ's face turned solemn. "No more talk, Billy. Time to set up camp."

Chapter

20

CJ WAS COUNTING ON THE FACT that he was the one Celeste wanted to see dead. Mavis was only the bait, and he had a hole card: Billy. He and Billy had hobbled the horses on the west side of a hogback that sat between them and Celeste, then slipped over the hogback to set up camp in a dense clump of aspens a hundred yards from what they could now clearly see was an old line shack. They'd eaten the two ham sandwiches they'd bought in San Luis, waited for sunset, and scouted to within forty yards of the line shack before inching their way back to their base camp.

Billy had slipped close enough to the shack to see that it had four windows and a back door of warped plywood. Fear of being spotted had stopped him from moving closer, but he had seen a woman's shoe and a set of drag marks leading across the dry, grainy soil to the shack's back door.

Celeste came out of the teetering building and headed for her truck just before sunset, binoculars slung around her neck, a 30.06 in one hand. She looked chunkier, shorter, and older than CJ remembered, and she moved without any of the grace he recalled from her court appearances half a decade earlier. He thought about shooting her on the spot, but Billy reminded him that not only would it be murder, but if he missed, he'd be endangering Mavis. Putting a damper on his temper, CJ watched Celeste retrieve a folder and a pistol from the truck and quickly return to the shack.

Although they hadn't seen Mavis, just before 10:30 CJ decided to go with his plan. Over the next several hours they set everything up, caught a couple of catnaps, and never once saw the cabin lights go out.

At 4 a.m. the buzzer on CJ's watch went off. He'd been awake since 3, watching a night sky filled with stars and a bright three-quarter moon. There was an early-morning mountain chill in the air as he slipped a lightweight poncho over his shoulders and whispered, "Billy, time to move it."

"I'm on it," said Billy, already awake.

"As soon as you hear me, set off the flares."

"Gotcha."

"And Billy, remember, scream like somebody's whipping your ass."

Billy nodded and took off into the darkness.

Walking in a half crouch, CJ began his trek toward the shack, his progress hidden by a three-foot-high growth of timothy and brome. Fifteen yards from the front of the shack he stopped just short of the line of flares he and Billy had planted in the ground earlier. Giving Billy the time he needed to slip into place behind the shack, CJ crawled along the ground adjusting the twenty-five-foot wax stringer cord Billy had earlier laid across the tops of the flares, checking to make sure the cord was still in place. Relieved that it was, he slipped a match out of his pocket, struck it on the heel of his boot, and touched it to the cord. The flares dazzled to life, erupting in a bright yellow glow.

Hoping that Celeste would take the bait, uncertain whether she had cops, the FBI, CJ, or a madman outside her door, he shouted into Billy's tinny-sounding bullhorn, "Celeste Deepstream, come out! Come out now, unarmed."

The next second automatic-weapons fire erupted from behind the house, punctuated by the sounds of Billy screaming obscenities at the top of his lungs as CJ repeated into the bullhorn, "Celeste Deepstream, come out; come out now!" There was no movement from inside the house until four shots rang out from an open window. The shots took out several flares as Celeste slithered through the open window, dropped onto the ground, and broke for her pickup. CJ snatched his 30.06 out of the grass, took aim, and briefly hesitated, aware that he was about to shoot at a woman. That hesitation gave Celeste time to turn and, in the approaching light of daybreak and flare flash, squeeze off three well-aimed rounds from her GLOCK. One round caught CJ in the fleshy part of his right arm. "Fuck!" he screamed, returning fire, but Celeste had already reached her truck. The pickup's engine erupted, and the truck, pointed south toward the dry creek bed and safety, broke out of the corral. CJ fired at the fleeing pickup, realizing as he did that the bullets pinging off the metal tailgate matched the sound of small-arms fire dinging the shell of his navy patrol boat, the *Cape Star*. Two of his rounds shattered the rear cab window, and as the pickup momentarily fishtailed out of control he thought one of his shots might have struck home. But the truck continued to buck and dance its way across the rutted grassland toward the creek bed until suddenly, as if swallowed by the earth, it dropped out of sight.

"Son of a bitch!" exclaimed CJ, shaking his head, realizing only then that he'd broken into a cold sweat and his arm was bleeding badly. He was shaking, his heart racing in a rush of fear and anticipation.

When he heard Billy scream, "Clear!" CJ raced toward the house. The only thing on his mind was Mavis. Several feet from the house he thought he heard someone yelling from inside. He stopped and duck-walked his way slowly toward the front door as Billy slipped up in a half crouch beside him. The yelling became louder. As they worked their way up the rotting porch steps, the shouts became a mantra: "Don't come in! Don't come in!"

"It's Mavis," CJ said.

"The place is booby-trapped!" Billy yelled. "Shit! How the hell are we gonna get in if she wired it?"

"Stay put." CJ rushed back down the steps, breaking off the edge of a rotting timber, and raced for the window that Celeste had climbed through to get away. As he wriggled through the window, and Mavis's shouts faded to a raspy plea, CJ dropped onto the floor in a nosedive. He was on all fours when he saw the iron lung. Realizing that Mavis had to be inside, he wondered whether it too was wired.

"Mavis?" he shouted.

"CJ?"

"Yes."

Mavis's voice was barely audible. "Be careful. I think she booby-trapped the place." Dehydrated, afraid, and quivering, Mavis began to hyperventilate. CJ scanned the room, trying to determine what Celeste had planned. When he stood, he realized that blood was dripping from his fingers. He clamped his hand around his wounded arm, but the flow of blood didn't stop. He could see Mavis's head poking out from the opposite end of the iron lung. A hospital gurney holding half a dozen blazing candles sat next to the lung. Across the room, spread along the wall on either side of the front door, four perfectly aligned twenty-pound propane tanks, the kind used for backyard grilling, sat kissing one another. Four-foot lengths of rubber garden hose ran from the propane tanks across the floor, stopping just short of the gurney.

CJ walked over, blew out the candles, and shouted for Billy to come in. "She was gonna blow the place up," he said, uncertain whether he was speaking to himself, Billy, or Mavis. His thoughts drifted to the distant ghosts of war. "But she didn't have the patience," he whispered to himself.

As he moved toward Mavis he could see that her forehead was a solid patch of dark, crusted blood. His eyes widened as he realized that her face was swollen and pale as cream and that her eyes were sunken in her head. He swallowed hard, choking back his anger when he saw that her nostrils were plugged with clotted blood. "Fuck!" he shouted.

Eyeing the propane tanks, Billy came cautiously toward him. Blood trickled off CJ's fingertips and splattered into an ink blot next to his right foot. "CJ, you got hit!" said Billy, eyeing the floor.

"I'm okay," said CJ, looking down at Mavis. Teary-eyed, he whispered, "You okay?"

Her answer was barely audible. "Yes."

"I'll kill her."

Her eyes pleading *no more*, Mavis said only, "Please."

CJ kissed her softly. He stroked her hair, caressed her cheek, and tried not to cry. It was the same way he had forced back the tears the day his Uncle Ike had died, and swallowed his tears the day he came home from Vietnam.

◆◆◆

Wendall Newburn was parked, legs crossed, on the front porch of CJ's office at 7:30 a.m. He was seated in a weathered, turn-of-the-century-style bench rocker that had occupied the same spot since CJ's Uncle Ike had placed his wife's favorite piece of furniture outside, in the fresh air and sunshine, to ease the pain of his grief after she had died unexpectedly from a Labor Day heart attack when CJ was barely seven.

Flora Jean didn't see Newburn until she walked up the porch steps to the office, her arms loaded down with a caffe latte, a Danish, and a large book bag. Startled, she said, "Guess it ain't gonna be my lucky day." She set her book bag down, slipped her keys from her pocket, and opened the door.

Newburn rose from his seat. "Wouldn't count on it." As tall as Flora Jean but thinner and several shades lighter, the slightly stoop-shouldered lieutenant followed her inside.

Flora Jean wondered for the hundredth time what Mavis had ever seen in Newburn as they walked through the dimly lit foyer and into her tiny, stale-smelling office. She placed her coffee,

Danish, and book bag on her desk, punched the start button
on her computer, looked at Newburn, and said, "Why do I have
all the good fortune?"

Newburn pulled up a nearby pressed-back chair, spun it
around so the seat was facing him, sat down, leaned forward,
elbows on the chair back, and said, "Good karma, I guess."

Flora Jean considered saying *I didn't offer you a seat* but
thought better of it.

"Where's Floyd?"

"Outta town."

"Business or pleasure?"

"Don't think you're someone he'd want me to tell."

"No matter. I'm here to see you."

"And you didn't bring roses." Flora Jean batted her eyelashes.
"Damn, sugar. I'm brokenhearted."

"Cut the shit, Benson."

Flora Jean planted herself on the edge of her desk so that
instead of being at eye level with Newburn, she was towering
over him.

Looking frustrated, Newburn said, "You've been busy, Sergeant Major," calling Flora Jean by her former military rank, his
tone intentionally condescending. "Really busy—harassing
people, threatening them, disrupting their work in their place
of business."

Flora Jean flashed Newburn a well-rehearsed look of surprise.

"Can the I-don't-know-what-you're-talking-about look. I've
got a whole slew of complaints."

"About moi?" said Flora Jean.

"Don't fuck with me, Benson. I can take this whole process to another level. Make it a lot more formal."

Flora Jean had had enough of playing cat-and-mouse. "The hell you can. If you could, you wouldn't be here playing kissy-face. Say what you have to say, Lieutenant, and shove off."

Newburn thought for a moment before responding. Over the years he'd had dozens of head-butting sessions with CJ, but this was the first with Flora Jean. Certain that it was her MI background that made her such a tough nut, he decided on a more straightforward approach. "Le Quan and his daughter say you've been harassing them."

"Bullshit."

"The daughter said you threatened her."

"Don't think so."

Newburn shook his head. "She described you to a T: six-one, black, female, African bracelets on both arms."

Flora Jean eyed the chain of bracelets on her arms without responding.

"Got some advice for you, Benson. Quan's son is an assistant attorney general down in New Mexico, and he's got friends who have friends, if you know what I mean. I'd lay off the shoe salesman if I were you. The bigger question is why you were bothering the man in the first place. He says you called him a communist and asked him about Peter Margolin." Newburn looked at Flora Jean for a response. When he didn't get one, he said, "Margolin—murder—congressman—now, that's serious shit. Hope you and Floyd aren't working some kind of angle."

Sidestepping the Margolin issue, Flora Jean said, "Last I heard,

Lieutenant, it wasn't against the law to call somebody a communist."

"It's not. But like I said, it's the Margolin murder I'm concerned about. You and your boss stick your hand in that fire, and it is likely to get burned off. If you've got something I should know about, better spit it out now."

"I got nothin' for you, sugar."

"Fine," said Newburn, wondering whether or not he had enough sucker bait to get Flora Jean to spit out anything more. He had the information he had gotten from Owen Brashears about Peter Margolin's Star 1 team service. He knew that Margolin had served reluctantly at Elliott Cole's request, and now he knew that Flora Jean, probably on orders from her conveniently missing boss, had tried to connect a little shoe salesman to Margolin. No question, she was holding back something, but short of slapping her with a charge of withholding evidence, a charge that would be hell to get to stick, he had no more than when he'd arrived at 7:30. There was no way he was going to tell Flora Jean about the note that had been found in Peter Margolin's day planner, but deciding that one sucker-bait cast was worth it, he asked, "Does the name Lincoln Cortez mean anything to you?"

"Nope," said Flora Jean, poker-faced.

Unable to decide whether she was telling the truth, he said, "Hope you're not lying."

Flora Jean answered with a shrug.

Conceding that he wasn't going to get much else out of her, Newburn decided his next step would be to go see Le Quan.

Rising from his chair, he said, "Tell your boss I hated missing him. And don't go near Le Quan again. Next time he complains, there'll be paperwork."

"Don't let the door hit you in the ass, Lieutenant," said Flora Jean, watching Newburn depart.

Slipping off her desk, she walked to the door and watched Newburn move down the sidewalk and out of view. "Damn!" She headed back to her office, wondering when CJ and Billy would be back, whether they had found Mavis, and if Mavis was okay.

Taking a seat at her computer, she called up her e-mail, uncertain of whether she'd done enough to stonewall Newburn until CJ's return.

◆◆◆

The tiny New Mexico village of Questa is little more than a stoplight, a couple of cafes, two barbershops, and several gas stations at the intersection of state highways 522 and 38. The only real things the sleepy village that sits within point-blank range of the Sangre de Cristo Mountains has going for it are its proximity to the Red River state fish hatchery and the fact that it has the only regional community health center between the Colorado border and Taos. That fact, emblazoned in red on one of Billy DeLong's topo maps, was why CJ, Mavis, and Billy had showed up at the squat, mud-brown adobe health center a few minutes before 9 a.m. looking for help.

The physician's assistant on duty eyed them as if they were a cross between gypsies and war refugees when they walked in, seeing a woman who looked like she'd been battered, a disheveled, one-eyed West Indian–looking cowboy, and a big black man wobbling as they supported him, as if he were drunk. Finally recognizing that CJ wasn't drunk but in serious trouble, the physician's assistant, a petite Spanish woman with bulging green eyes, called for a nurse who was busy filling out charts to help her. By the time they reached CJ, he had collapsed.

Earlier, as the sun had risen, CJ had helped Mavis from the iron lung. With a towel wrapped tightly around his own arm, his wound continuing to ooze blood, CJ had draped her in a towel and attended as best he could to her head trauma and knee injuries. He'd finally helped her into a pair of sweatpants and an oversized T-shirt he'd found stuffed into a shopping bag next to an old army cot near the back door of the line shack.

Billy, in the meantime, had followed the snaking outline of the creek bed that Celeste had raced away in and had come back to the line shack shaking his head, announcing in confused amazement that he had followed Celeste's tire tracks for at least a mile before they had skipped out of the arroyo up a hillside and disappeared. He announced that during the trek he'd found a shortcut back to their horses and truck as well as several pieces of blood-stained shattered glass, suggesting that Celeste had more than likely been hit.

Waving off Billy's offers of help, CJ had walked a near-catatonic Mavis over to the army cot and laid her down so she could rest while Billy attended to his wounded arm. Once he'd stopped the bleeding and rewrapped the wound, Billy had gone back to where they'd hobbled the horses, ridden back over the ridge, and followed the arroyo to within fifty yards of where they'd left their pickup. He'd come back, horses in tow, to pick up CJ and Mavis, wondering how in the hell they'd ever missed Celeste's shortcut to the line shack but glad they had, because that was the way she'd obviously expected them to come in.

The seventeen-mile ride to Questa had been harder on CJ than Mavis. The fact that the physical part of her ordeal was over seemed to provide Mavis with a strange temporary sense of solace. The bright New Mexico sunshine had given her hope, and having two men she cared about squeezed next to her, asking her in between every mile marker if she were okay, gave her strength. But CJ was dealing with a two-pint blood loss, and by the time they reached the health center he was barely able to stand.

◆◆◆

Thanks to a liter of lactated Ringer's solution and two units of blood, CJ sat still light-headed but stabilized, on the edge of a gurney, squeezing Mavis's hand while Billy sat nearby flipping through a battered year-old copy of *Field and Stream*.

Looking up from the medical chart she'd been writing in, the physician's assistant paused, glanced at CJ's bandaged arm and the fresh white dressing that encircled Mavis's head, and said, "Now, tell me again how the two of you were injured."

"A couple of propane tanks we was usin' to heat up branding irons exploded out at the ranch, just like my friend told you," Billy said before CJ or Mavis could respond.

The woman shook her head. "That arm wound sure looks like a projectile wound to me," she said, eyebrows raised.

"Caught a piece of flying metal from one of the tanks," said

CJ, rubbing a bandage that extended from his elbow to just above his wrist.

"And the lady?" asked the PA, returning to her notes. "What about her injuries? They look old."

CJ squeezed Mavis's hand. "Same thing. Propane."

"Let her answer for herself if you would. Ma'am?"

Mavis nodded without answering.

Aware that if she probed any further she'd likely have paperwork to fill out from then until sunset, the woman asked, "Did you give the clerk at the front desk your insurance information?"

"Yes," said CJ, easing off the gurney, smiling at Mavis.

"Then I guess we're done," said the PA. Looking first at CJ and then at Mavis, she added, "Keep the wounds dry; don't scratch at them. And have the bandages changed and looked at by a *professional* once you are back in Denver."

"We can go, then?" asked CJ.

"Unless you want to answer more questions about that explosion."

CJ draped his arm around Mavis's shoulder, nodded for Billy to drop the *Field and Stream,* and headed for the room's exit. They were nearly out of the room when Mavis turned back to address the PA. "It's not what you're thinking, miss. No lovers' spat. I didn't shoot him, and he didn't beat me up."

The woman looked relieved. "What happened, then?"

Mavis smiled. "Like he told you—a problem with propane."

Chapter
21

WENDALL NEWBURN RETURNED to his office just before noon, disappointed that after putting in almost half a day's work, he had nothing to show for it.

He had gotten little information out of Le Quan and his daughter, and nothing to help him with the Margolin murder investigation. When he had asked Quan if he wanted to file a harassment charge against Flora Jean, Quan had said no, his response knee-jerk, as if he'd been coached. When he'd asked Quan if he had known Peter Margolin, the little man had looked at his daughter, sidestepped the question, and answered, "I know the congressman was murdered."

Disappointed at getting next to nowhere on such a high-profile crime, Newburn sighed, turned on the shirt-pocket-sized radio that sat on his desk, and tuned in KUVO, for a much needed jazz respite. He had to suffer through an NPR news rap and a book review before John Coltrane hit full stride in his indelible 1959 "Giant Steps" cut, a cut that reminded Newburn so much of the brief time he'd had Mavis Sundee's attention that he turned the radio off in frustration and went to lunch.

He was back at his desk at 1 o'clock, busily running his finger down a list of names in a notebook, stopping near the bottom of the page on a line that read, *Floyd and Friends.* Rising from his chair, he walked out of his office and down the hall to an area filled with cubicles. He stopped at a cubicle bordering the hallway, tapped a man busy at a computer on the shoulder, and said, "Joey, I need you to drop a little heat on some folks."

Not at all startled, in fact looking disappointed at having to once more pay the penalty for sitting right next to a hallway, the man looked up, flashed Newburn a look that said, *Again?* and continued typing.

"This is about the Margolin case."

When the man kept typing, Newburn said, "There's pennies from heaven in it for you."

"Shit, Wendall, my people are spread thinner than the hairs on a monkey's nuts."

"Heaven, Joey. The kind they reserve for sergeants."

Joey Greene turned his back on his computer, shrugged, and said, "What?"

"I want you to sic one of your patrol units on the associates of a bail bondsman I'm tracking. Nothing big. Drive by their jobs, their residences, maybe do a few stop-and-checks."

Greene shook his head. "I can buy trouble, Wendall, movin' my units around where they don't belong."

"Hell, Joey, I'm not talking about checking on the White House here. I just want you to move your boys past a place in Five Points, a gas station, and the digs of a couple of street bums."

"Five Points is fine. How far do I have to move my unit to check on your street people?"

"A little bit farther, but nothing serious. Just west of LoDo."

"Hell, Wendall, that's downtown. I don't want my people runnin' all the way down there."

"Come on, Joey. Who's to know? You're down there five minutes at the most. Something comes up, you say you got a disturbance call. Trust me, it'll be worth it in the end."

Greene sighed. "What am I lookin' for?"

"Not much. At the gas station, all I really want your people to do is make sure the owner's there. I don't want him out doing something on the side for my bail bondsman. As for the two street people, they're pretty much Frick and Frack—never see one without the other. And they don't let anybody else inside their little world. Pretty much keep to themselves. They've got an abandoned building in LoDo they call home."

"How long?" asked Greene.

"Two, three days at the most."

"I'll do what I can. Try and work it in. A couple of outta-bounds plays a day. That's it."

"You're the man, Joey."

"Yeah. I've heard that song." Greene turned his back on Newburn, eyes locked on his computer screen.

Newburn pivoted and headed back for his office. Back at his desk, he eyed the open spiral-bound notebook, and put check marks next to the names *Dittier Atkins*, *Morgan Williams*, and

Roosevelt Weeks. Flora Jean Benson and *CJ Floyd* had earned their check marks long ago. They were both up to their eyeballs in the Margolin case. He knew it. He just hadn't figured out how or why. Keeping tabs on the two of them was always a chore, but over the years he'd learned that whether you were a cop, a preacher, a lawyer, or a politician, it was more often than not the people around you who caused you to sink or swim. Keeping tabs on two broken-down former rodeo cowboys and a jock turned grease monkey wouldn't be so difficult.

Flipping the page, he added a check mark next to a name just beneath the heading *Friends of Margolin.* Nodding, stroking his chin, and looking satisfied, he picked up the phone and dialed information. "Can I have the number for the office of the state Republican Committee?" he said to the pleasant-sounding operator on the other end.

"Here's your number," she responded.

Newburn jotted the number down next to the name *Elliott Cole,* closed his notebook, and smiled, thinking, *Every dog has his day, and the second half of this day will be mine.*

◆◆◆

The moldy, wet-dog-smelling converted sixteen-unit Denver motel on South Santa Fe Drive where Lincoln Cortez was staying had once been a cardboard box manufacturing plant. Now painted bright kelly green and trimmed in chartreuse, every unit still reeking of damp cardboard and machine oil, the building had become a haven for transients and illegal aliens moving up from Mexico on what they hoped would be their first step toward the good life.

Cortez had settled into a first-floor unit at the far southeast corner of the building, away from everyone else, close to the always overflowing dumpsters and hopefully, to his way of thinking, out of sight and out of mind.

He hadn't heard from his contact in two days. He hadn't been paid for all the extra legwork, planning, and time he'd put into the Margolin affair, and his atrophic right leg was hurting like hell. Chalking up the pain to the dry air a mile above sea level, he'd been popping Motrin and watching rented porno flicks. To keep from being totally overwhelmed, he had taken to mid-day walks, cane in hand, along the banks of the South Platte River, his .44 Magnum strapped to his good leg.

If it weren't for Langston Blue, he'd be fishing off the Maryland coast, with a couple of women he knew from D.C. there to stroke his balls and feed him grapes. If it weren't for Blue, he'd also have two good legs. He was carrying a lot of baggage because of Blue, and usually he had no problem dealing with it. But today was different. The sky was crystal blue, and the temperature had dropped from the blistering 90s to a comfortable 78. The air was mountain fresh, and noonday joggers were running past him on their way to cardiac health. He could see kids playing Frisbee in a nearby park that hugged the river. Blue's run at Song Ve had caused Margolin to flinch and drop Cortez's cover. Blue had cost him the use of his leg. Blue had taken something from him that day in the schoolyard in Vietnam, and sometimes the thought of it made his head hurt.

He'd miscalculated in West Virginia on his first assignment, but he wouldn't make that mistake again. Once he finished his business in Denver, he'd head back east and this time, without orders coming down from Margolin, or anyone else, he'd settle up with Blue himself.

His cane made a light thump against the asphalt path with each new step, a sound that was perceptible only to him. He watched a boy in baggy shorts and a grease-stained muscle shirt race his dog to the river's edge, stop, and burst into laughter as the eighty-pound Lab went sailing out into the water. For half an hour he stood and watched a single cloud work its way over the Front Range and move toward him. He thought about the money he'd had to dole out to Blue over the years, money that Margolin had paid to someone so simple-minded he'd probably have kept his mouth shut about Song Ve forever anyway. But Margolin had never listened to him, and he'd been forced to play bagman to a slow-thinking recluse whom nobody in the world gave one shit about. Now there'd be no more bowing or scraping, no yes-sir-boss-man to Margolin. Now it would be tea time at the Ritz, and fishing, and having women from D.C. stroke his balls.

A young boy chasing a friend rushed past Cortez, shouted, "'Cuse me, mister," and continued running. The boy was nearly out of sight when Cortez began his slow trek back to the motel. Feeling momentarily refreshed, he stopped a few feet from the ugly structure, wondering why anyone would paint a building chartreuse and kelly green. Deciding it was the mark of someone trying to save money on paint rather than an artistic statement, he opened the door to his room, shaking his head. He'd taken two steps inside when the door slammed behind him and the blow from a ballpeen hammer crushed the back of his skull. He was dead before he hit the floor, well before the second blow severed his middle cerebral artery and sent blood streaming from his nostrils onto the black-and-white checkerboard tile.

"Son of a bitch is gonna bleed out," Jimmy Moc shouted to Cortez's killer, who was clutching the hammer and looking momentarily surprised.

"Do everything just like we planned," the killer said calmly.

Moc nodded. Eyeing the enlarging pool of blood, he took two steps sideways toward the room's tiny kitchen and rolled an empty five-foot-tall, ninety-weight oil drum, its insides still tacky with remnants of crude, over to the lifeless body. Following the killer's unspoken instructions, he turned the drum on its side, and together they stuffed 165 pounds of deadweight headfirst into the drum.

"What about his cane and his clothes?" asked Moc, stuffing two fifty-pound sandbags into the drum.

"Put them in there with him."

Moc rushed around the room gathering Cortez's few articles of clothing, then jammed them into the drum along with Cortez's cane. As the latex-gloved killer mopped up the serving platter–sized pool of Cortez's blood with several shop towels and swiped six square feet of surrounding tile with a towel soaked in a chemical reagent used by hospitals to deal with blood spills, Moc hurriedly adjusted the oil drum's lid, capped it with a flexible plastic rimmer, and snapped the rimmer into place.

The killer nodded, slipped the bloody towels into a heavy-duty trash bag, and, after policing the room a final time, said, "Let's move."

Moc opened the door and peered around the motel's nearly empty parking lot, looking for any movement before saying, "It's clear." He stepped back inside and helped the killer, who was struggling to roll the drum onto a hand truck. Dressed in caps and cleaning-service coveralls, complete with bib-stitched name tags, they wheeled the oil drum out of the room and loaded it onto a pickup at the rear of the building. They would head fifty-five miles southwest along the Platte to the tiny mountain outpost of Deckers and drop the drum, which they planned to weight even further, from a convenient backwoods overhang into an inaccessible, forty-foot-deep, rock-walled icy pool in the South Platte. It was there, not D.C. or the Maryland coast, that Lincoln Cortez was expected to rest forever.

Chapter

22

MAVIS LIVED IN ONE of the half-dozen Mission-Revival-style homes that lined the south side of Curtis Street, the boundary between Five Points and the neighborhood of Curtis Park. Most of the houses in Curtis Park were small restored Queen Annes and Victorians, and for almost twelve years a steady stream of yuppies had been moving in, driving up the prices and causing the value of everything in the neighborhood to nearly double. Ornate replicas of turn-of-the-century gaslight streetlamps had recently been installed along Curtis and California Streets in an effort to give Curtis Park what the mayor and city council called a return to its "turn-of-the-century grace."

CJ sat on a chaise longue in Mavis's sun room. Mavis was resting safely between his outstretched legs with her back to him, soaking up the midafternoon sun. "I'm outta here, CJ," said Billy DeLong, heading toward the front door. "Got a five-and-a-half-hour drive back to Wyoming, a couple of tired-as-hell horses, and a quiet life to get back to." He winked at Mavis.

"Billy, you're the best." Mavis slipped out of CJ's arms, walked stiff-legged across the room, and kissed Billy on the cheek.

Billy smiled, slightly embarrassed, and continued chomping on the wad of Doublemint in his mouth. "Keep Nat Love over there in line, and the two of you get them bandages changed like you was told. And call me if you need any more help."

Chuckling at Billy's reference to the West's most famous black cowboy, CJ got up from the chaise, inspected the bandage on his arm, and said, "Count on it," before calling out to the kitchen, "Flora Jean, Billy's leaving."

Flora Jean appeared from the kitchen, two fruit smoothies in hand. "Sure you don't need nothin' for the road, Billy?"

"Just backup for my wad," he said, extracting an unopened pack of Doublemint from his shirt pocket.

"Okay." Flora Jean handed one of the smoothies to Mavis as CJ draped his arm around the shoulders of the wiry old Baggs, Wyoming, cowboy.

"Plucked my ass right out of the soup as usual," said CJ. "And Mavis's."

Billy shrugged. His face slowly took on the look of someone bearing bad tidings. "She'll be back, CJ. Trust me. Sure you don't want me to stay?"

CJ glanced over his shoulder toward Mavis and continued walking Billy to the door. "I'll call you if I need you. Right now I have Mavis to worry about, and Flora Jean and I have another situation on our hands."

"You're dealin' with a madwoman, CJ," said Billy as they walked across Mavis's soggy, freshly watered front lawn toward Billy's pickup and horse trailer.

"I know that. I'll handle it," said CJ, looking frustrated.

Maggie let out a whinny and nudged one side of the horse trailer with her hindquarters as Billy opened the driver's door. He eyed CJ sternly. "Take my advice, CJ. Can everything else for right now and concentrate on Mavis."

"I hear you."

Chomping on his gum, Billy slipped into the cab. "I know you do, but I can tell I ain't comin' through clear enough. Mavis needs all of what you got right now. A lesser woman would probably need a padded room and a shrink. Better tend to her. That's all I'm gonna say to you. Take it for what it's worth." Billy started the pickup, slammed the door, and clutched the steering wheel one-handed. "Like I said, call me if you need me."

CJ waved as Billy backed his rig onto the quiet street. Billy nodded, waved back, and was gone in what seemed like the blink of an eye.

CJ took a series of deep breaths, pulled a cheroot out of his vest pocket, and lit up. He smoked the cheroot down to a nub, perplexed at how to handle everything that was swirling around him, before heading back to the house. Stubbing out the cheroot on the heel of his boot, he slowly climbed the front steps and disappeared inside.

◆ ◆ ◆

On the strength of CJ's insistence that he didn't want Mavis to end up being a target again because of him, Flora Jean agreed to spend alternate nights at Mavis's and assured him that she'd stay as long as Mavis wanted her to. She headed back to the office to wrap up things for the day, indicating that she'd return with enough clothes to stay a week, her tunes, and a 9-mm pistol. She deliberately said nothing to CJ about their Langston Blue problem, deciding to save the high points for a better time.

Mavis and CJ were finally left alone together. As a late-afternoon breeze picked up out of the west and the massive fifty-year-old cottonwoods that lined Mavis's backyard rustled in cadence with the rush of the wind, CJ sat back in the chaise, holding Mavis as he had just before Billy had left. They hadn't said a word for several minutes when Mavis finally said, "I don't see why you can't stay here, CJ."

"I've told you, Mavis. Because I'm her target. Celeste wants me, and I don't want her coming near you again, ever." CJ ran a finger in a wide circle over Mavis's stomach.

Anchored in CJ's grasp and feeling safe, Mavis said, "Maybe we should call the police."

"I did."

Startled by his response, Mavis looked up at him. She'd never known CJ to ask for help from anyone except Flora Jean, Rosie Weeks, or Billy, and of course Ike when he was alive. Julie Madrid helped him work the legal side of the street, and his two broken-down rodeo cowboy friends, Morgan Williams and Dittier Atkins, sometimes did odd jobs for him. But she'd never known him to ask for help from the cops.

Reading her surprised expression, CJ said, "This is about you, Mavis. Not me. I told the whole story to a District 3 cop during the first few hours you were sleeping after we got back."

"What will they do?"

"What cops do most of the time—nothing. They respond to crime, Mavis. They don't prevent it."

Mavis's face turned expressionless. She hurt physically and mentally, and it was all she could do just to cope. She didn't want to believe that she'd been kidnapped, beaten, and caged without any recourse. She wanted to tell CJ to fix it, to make the pain disappear and erase the memories, no matter what the cost. But she knew that if she did, she'd unleash a piece of him that she never again wanted to see. The angry, confused, hostile side of the man she loved. That dark side he had struggled with after coming home from Vietnam. If she gave him the green light she knew he'd hunt Celeste down and possibly kill her, and in the process he'd destroy his life and hers.

She glanced around the brightly lit sun room. It was a cozy, cluttered room filled with inviting overstuffed furniture. The walls were filled with family photos, including pictures of her as a Denver Owl Club debutante and Boston University debate team captain. There was a photo of Ike embracing CJ the day CJ had come back from Vietnam, with her brother, Carl, her father, and Rosie Weeks standing in front of Mae's grinning at the scene. And on an end table, along with a lamp base and shade covered with etchings of black rodeo cowboys, was a photograph of CJ and Mavis hugging sweetheart-style in the Bel Air. That photograph had always been her favorite.

Forcing back tears, she said, "She intended to kill us, CJ."

CJ brushed her hair back from her bandaged forehead. In an attempt to soothe his psyche as much as Mavis's, he said, "But she didn't."

"And we have no recourse?" Mavis asked.

"Not much. Besides, the cops'll want to hear your side of the story before they even consider getting one hair out of place looking for Celeste. If we're lucky, maybe her parole officer will do something to help, but I wouldn't count on it."

"That's ludicrous. Did they see your arm?"

"They took my statement, Mavis. It's the way the system works."

Mavis rested her head back against CJ's chest. She'd always thought she understood the origins of his passions. His rage at watching the system succumb to never-ending manipulation, his frustration and anger at having to struggle so hard to earn a living at what she until that very moment and society as a whole viewed with disdain. The cops couldn't restore what had been stolen from her, and now, for the first time in her life, she understood why people came to CJ for help. Why Newab Sha's wife had asked CJ to hunt down the man who had beaten her, stolen who she was, and laughed while he'd done it. Letting out a barely perceptible sigh, she turned until she could see his face and asked, "Can we do anything?"

CJ lowered his eyes to the floor. It was a telltale look she knew too well. Having navigated CJ through mountaintop highs and rock-bottom lows, she knew that when he wouldn't look her in the eye it was usually because he was debating whether to tell her the truth.

"CJ! We can't just wait for her to come back."

CJ squeezed her hand. "Mavis, we're on our own."

The noise of the refrigerator compressor clicking on in the kitchen caused Mavis to jerk an arm across her face. She suddenly began to shiver. CJ wrapped his arms around her tightly and rocked her slowly from side to side, realizing that it would be a long time before the woman he loved overcame her psychological pain. Continuing to rock her, he said, "Remember when I first met you and you rang me out on that old cash register that used to sit next to the pulpit at Mae's?"

"Yes," said Mavis.

"Remember what I bought?"

"What else? A whole sweet-potato pie."

"Remember how I made you wrap it in tinfoil and put it in a box inside a box?"

"Yes."

"Know why?"

"Not really."

"Because that pie was special. My reward for days of gathering soda-pop bottles and collecting two- and three-cent store return deposits for my efforts. Guess I'm still a little paranoid about protecting things of mine that are special. Like my woman, for instance. I don't have a special box to put you in to protect you, and I don't have a magic wand to make your pain go away. But I can spend more time with you, quit thinking that no matter what, you'll always be there, and stop surfing for dollars from the bottom-feeders and lowlifes of the world who don't really count."

Mavis looked CJ squarely in the eye. "Do you think you're really up to changing the way you live?"

"I can try." He kissed her on her bandaged forehead.

"Then try. See what happens."

"I will. But with two small catches. Flora Jean stays here with you like I said. And if necessary, she stays until all the noises fade into the background where they've always been."

"Okay. What's the other catch?"

"I have to wrap up the thing with Carmen Nguyen's father. I can't leave it hanging."

"I see," Mavis said hesitantly. "And after that you'll call it a day? Cut back? Turn over things to Flora Jean?"

This time it was CJ who hesitated before finally saying, "Yes."

"It'll work, CJ. I know it." Mavis smiled for the first time since she'd been liberated from the iron lung. As she turned to kiss him she brushed his bandaged arm and banged her left knee against his. They both let out pained groans as she hugged him tightly.

"You'll hurt your knees," said CJ as Mavis tried to squeeze closer.

"Doesn't matter," she said, wrapping both hands around his neck and pulling him toward her until their lips met. "Doesn't really matter at all," she said, kissing him over and over again.

◆ ◆ ◆

CJ got back to his office a few minutes before 6 just as a conga line of commuter traffic made its daily jail break for the suburbs. Flora Jean was on the phone when he came in, looking like she had a powerful story to tell. Before he could get out a word, she said, "We need to go check on Blue. Morgan says he's gone way past antsy over being cooped up at their place, and Dittier's promised him he'll take him out after dark for a transient's view of the city. Dittier said he'd even outfit him with a shopping cart full of aluminum cans and a bedroll, just so things look kosher while they're out cruisin'. Morgan claims that with

Dittier being a deaf mute and Blue seemin' kinda slow, they've sorta connected."

"Damn," said CJ. "We don't need Blue getting picked up by the cops while he's out sightseeing."

"That's what I told Morgan. Said we'd be down to their place as soon as you came in. I told Carmen to meet us there, too."

"Okay. Just let me get a few things out of the Bel Air. On the way over to Morgan and Dittier's you can fill me in on what went down with that character General Grace had you dogging."

"Two characters."

"Two?"

Flora Jean shook her head. She almost said, *You need to start listening* until she realized that when she'd mentioned Le Quan and Jimmy Moc to CJ earlier, he'd been road weary, still woozy from losing two pints of blood, and concerned about only one thing—Mavis.

"Two seconds and I'm all yours," said CJ. He headed outside for the Bel Air.

"I'll drive," Flora Jean called out after him, aware that CJ was still frazzled. "I'm parked out front."

CJ trotted across the lawn to the Bel Air, opened the trunk, and slipped out one of the M16s Billy had left. He rushed back up the driveway, opened the garage door, and walked to the back of the garage toward the navy footlocker he'd brought back from Vietnam. The name *Floyd, Calvin J.* was stenciled below the edge of the lid. He ran the lock combination, flipped back the lid, and set the M16 down on top of a neatly folded pea-coat. As he stared down at the footlocker's contents, he thought about Mavis and his promise to chart a new course. Knowing how difficult it had always been for him to sever ties to the past, he closed the footlocker, spun the combination, pivoted, and headed back toward the street. The glare from the sun hit him squarely as he came out of the dark, mildew-smelling garage, forcing him to shield his eyes as he began the first leg of his journey into a bright new day.

◆◆◆

Morgan Williams and Dittier Atkins lived in an abandoned Platte River Valley building just west of Denver's lower downtown shopping, business, and sports arena district. The building, scheduled for demolition in the fall to make room for business pods and condos, had always reminded CJ of a gigantic chicken coop, and the cluttered yard behind it filled with junk, overflowing with firewood, commodes, sinks, pipes, electrical wiring, and mammoth wooden spools, triggered images of the aftermath of war.

Morgan Williams, a cigar stump of a black man with a shaved head and skin as smooth as a carnival Nubian's, was sitting on a World War II–vintage army cot nursing a Coke when CJ and Flora Jean arrived. Morgan had jury-rigged the place with salvaged wiring, light fixtures, and lamps that he and Dittier had scrounged from the trash of a society with too much time and money on its hands. They had furnished their six hundred square feet of living space with cots, chairs, tables, and even Oriental rugs they had picked up during their years on the street, ultimately setting up shop in the low-profile cinderblock building that had once been a warehouse. They had been in the building three years, and it was the longest they had stayed in any one place since their rodeo days. Now they were upset that the mayor, normally an advocate for the homeless, had finally sided with developers and downtown businesspeople in their efforts to have the building demolished and turned into high-rise residences for upwardly mobile all-about-me's.

Carmen had arrived a half hour ahead of CJ and Flora Jean, and she'd spent what was her fourth visit talking to Blue about her life, listening to him tell her about his, learning about living isolated from the world, and most of all trying to bond with her father. They'd made inroads, but she and Langston Blue were still generations, cultures, and life experiences apart. As Carmen regaled Blue with her knowledge of motorcycles, Morgan pulled a beer out of a minirefrigerator that he and Dittier had bought at a garage sale for a dollar, popped the cap with a church key hanging from the refrigerator door handle, and said, "Sure you don't want nothin', CJ, Flora Jean, Dr. Nguyen?"

"It's Carmen. And no, thanks."

"Got more beer if you want it, don't we, Dittier?" Morgan signed as quickly as he spoke. Dittier nodded dolefully toward a paneless window covered in plastic and at the case of Miller Lite below.

"Nothin' for me," said Flora Jean.

"Me either," said CJ, looking at a clearly disappointed Dittier. "So now that we're all clear on why Langston can't go traipsing around the city, maybe we can get back to pinning a tail on Margolin's killer." CJ eyed Blue. "Flora Jean has a couple of leads. Go ahead, Flora Jean, fill us in."

"Here's what I got. Ain't a lot, but at least it's somethin'. I turned up a little Amerasian street worm named Jimmy Moc a couple days ago. He's thirty-five or so, five-foot-four, skinny, bug-eyed, and the color of underdone toast. Ever heard of him?" she said, looking at Blue.

Blue shook his head.

"What about the name Le Quan? Ring a bell?"

"Is he Amerasian, too?" asked Carmen.

"No," said Flora Jean. "A long way from it. He's a hundred percent Vietnamese, drawn lookin', thin as a rail, about fifty-five, and strange enough, he has a silver streak runnin' down the middle of a mop of jet-black hair."

"What?" CJ and Carmen responded almost in unison.

"A silver streak in his hair," repeated Flora Jean.

"You didn't say that on the way over here," said CJ. He and Carmen both eyed Blue.

"You didn't ask me for no description," said Flora Jean, looking perplexed.

"It's gotta be him," said Blue. "Silver streak, skinny as a beanpole. Gotta be him."

"Would somebody clue me the hell in?" said Flora Jean.

"In a minute." CJ turned his attention to Blue. "Do you remember anything else about him? Your man at the school?"

"Not really. Been thirty-five years. He was just there. In that schoolyard, talkin' to Margolin outta the blue."

"No matter," said CJ. "Now at least, we've got a reason to light a fire under Quan's butt. Here's the scoop," he said, turning back to Flora Jean. "The day Blue made his run, a man matching Quan's description showed up at a school full of children that Blue's Star 1 team boys wiped out. I'll tell you about it later."

"Damn," said Flora Jean. "You mean Blue turned out to be the only human being?"

"You pegged it," said CJ.

Blue spoke up, almost as if he were afraid. "About that mission. I've been thinkin' about it more and more. And the thing I've been thinkin' 'bout most is how our team ended up drawin' the short straw. Now I think I know why."

"Might as well spit it out," said CJ, watching Dittier, to whom Morgan had been signing the entire time, inch forward onto the edge of his chair.

"Go ahead," said Carmen. "It might be the key."

"Okay," said Blue. "We got picked for that mission 'cause of Elliott Cole, our battalion's buck-up light colonel and XO. He was in charge of Star 1 team mission assignments, and since Margolin had complained about not wantin' to command no Star 1 team from the beginnin', we was dealin' with somebody who was already pissed off."

"So you think that's why Cole stuck you with the schoolyard assignment?" said CJ, frowning, trying to place a name he knew he'd heard before.

"Think so," said Blue.

CJ stroked his chin, walked over to the refrigerator, and took out a beer. "Two leads, better than none. Le Quan and his stand at the schoolhouse door and a ticked off lightweight colonel. It gives us somewhere to go." CJ popped the beer cap. "I'll run down Cole. Flora Jean, you're back with your buddy Quan. Think you can handle him and that little roadrunner of his, Moc?"

Flora Jean laughed, headed for the refrigerator, and pulled out a Miller Lite. "Do eagles have wings?"

Chapter

23

AFTER THREE FAILED PHONE ATTEMPTS to get in touch with Elliott Cole and ask him about being Peter Margolin's Star 1 team commander, Wendall Newburn had decided to call it a day. He was having an early dinner and taking in some live jazz at the Dazzle Restaurant and Lounge on the northern edge of downtown, a weekly custom, when his pager went off in a middle of a delicious Houston Person saxophone riff. If it had been his cell phone ringing he would have ignored it and continued drinking in the melodic, tender sax sounds, but the pager was his direct link to Sergeant Joey Greene, and the intrusion meant that something serious was up.

Leaving his salmon dinner half eaten, he left the restaurant area, walked through the lounge, perched on a stool just inside the club's doorway, and punched the number flashing on his pager into his cell phone.

Greene's answer was mechanical. "Sergeant Greene, Third Precinct."

"It's Newburn. Whatta ya got, Joey?"

"I'm not sure."

"Speak up; it's hard to hear you. I'm at Dazzle, taking in a set."

"Said I'm not sure. But it may be something. Didn't you say those two street bums I've got my people tagging after pretty much kept to themselves?"

"Yeah."

"Well, they've turned real sociable tonight. The word I'm getting is there's at least six people at the dump they live in. Your two streeties and a friend have been there all the time. Half an hour ago, they got visitors. Your street boys came out to greet them. An Asian chick with a rump on her that won't quit, a black woman who looks like she's been on steroids, and a huge black guy dressed in a black leather vest and cowboy boots and smoking a cheroot."

Newburn's voice quivered with excitement. "Don't let any of them leave," he said, wondering only who the third street person and the Asian woman could be. "I'm on my way."

"Okay, but what do we hold them on?"

"Shit! Loitering, breaking and entering, trespassing, a fire-code violation, I don't care. Just make sure they stay put. I'm ten minutes away—twelve at the most."

"I'll relay it to my people," said Greene.

"You're the man, Joey."

"Looks like I am tonight," said Greene, shrugging and cradling the phone.

◆ ◆ ◆

Dittier was the first to see the headlights of a car dance off the plastic window covering. The light appeared so suddenly, rising out of the surrounding twilight, that he barely had time to rush over to Morgan and point toward the window before the entire front of the building was awash in the glare of police-car spotlights. "We got company," said Morgan, nodding toward the front of the building.

"Damn!" said CJ.

"No problem. All sorts of folks come around here from time to time, includin' the cops. Everybody just sit tight."

Aware that there were just two ways out of the place, through the only window or out the front door, CJ scanned the room looking for somewhere for Blue to hide. "Blue, get over in the corner out of the light and on the cot next to Dittier. And don't budge."

Blue quickly followed CJ's command.

"You, inside there, you're trespassing. Get out here where we can see you," came a sudden order from a bullhorn.

"I'd say we've got cops," said Flora Jean.

"Everyone stay put," said Morgan. "I'll try and send 'em packin'."

Morgan walked outside, his arms extended well out in front of him. His mouth went dry when he saw the two uniforms. "Problem, officer?"

"You're trespassing, buddy."

"But the place is abandoned."

"I don't make the rules, friend," said the taller of the two cops, each stationed to one side of a police cruiser just beyond the glare of the car-mounted spotlights.

"Everybody inside there, outside now," said his shorter, much thicker partner through the bullhorn.

One by one, Dittier, Carmen, and Flora Jean filed slowly out of the building.

"There're two more inside," said the short cop. "I saw them all go in."

Flora Jean flashed Carmen a look that said, *Stay calm*, just as another set of headlights came bouncing across the rutted vacant lot toward them. The unmarked car wound its way through a maze of junk and stopped a few feet behind the cruiser. Wendall Newburn hopped out from behind the wheel and walked up to the tall cop.

"Got two more inside, Lieutenant," said the short cop. "Started out with six."

Newburn eyed the lineup before him, counted noses, and smiled. He reached for the bullhorn the short cop was holding. "Come on out, Floyd, and bring whoever's in there with you," he shouted into the bullhorn.

When there was no response, he said, "Everything's been friendly up to now, Floyd. I don't know who you've got in there with you, but I know there were six of you to start. I've only got four people standing out here under the party lights; better move it. You've got one minute to get out here with your friend before I call for backup and turn this thing from a tea party into a real mess."

Moments later CJ appeared in the doorway, cupping a hand over his eyes to shield them from the spotlight glare. He walked through the doorway, followed closely by Langston Blue.

"My, my," said Newburn. "Time to recount noses." He pointed to a weathered cable spool and motioned for Morgan and Dittier to queue up next to it. Looking at Carmen, he said, "And you are?"

"Carmen Nguyen."

"I see. You can join your friends over there. You, too, Benson." He watched Flora Jean move toward the cable spool and smiled. "And then there were two." He stared at CJ. "Okay, Floyd, you over there with the others." Newburn stepped forward until he was eye to eye with Blue. "And you are? Let me guess. The owner of this building? A developer, maybe? The mayor?"

Blue remained silent, doing exactly what CJ had told him to do when they were inside.

"Guess not. Got any ID?"

"No."

"Okay. I can make this hard or easy. I can detain you for loitering, trespassing, and probable fire-code violations while I run your prints, or you can tell me your name, call your lawyer, and get a running start. Either way, it'll all come out in the wash. Now, you got a name?"

Blue looked at Carmen, standing at parade rest, her outline becoming less discernible in the approaching darkness. She gave him a quick wink. He turned his attention to CJ, who gave him a subtle nod. "Langston Blue," he said finally, relieved that although the circumstances weren't anywhere close to what he'd imagined they'd be, he'd finally come in from his own unique version of the cold. He looked at a suddenly slack-jawed Wendall Newburn, who took a half step backward and said, "Well, I'll be damned. The fish I've been waiting for. Guess I'll toss the rest of you back."

◆◆◆

Celeste Deepstream stood beside a small brook that ran through the base of a sheer rock canyon in the New Mexico Carson Forest wilderness. She looked skyward, searching for stars. There hadn't been but a few in the sky all night, and she was bothered by their absence. Starlit skies had always brought her good luck.

The brook gurgled past, slipping through rocks and tree limbs, knifing and squeezing its way downhill toward the Rio Grande. Deciding that it was time to take a break from stargazing, she took a seat on a nearby boulder and gingerly rubbed her right shoulder. Thanks to a quarter bottle of Motrin and a heat pack, the shoulder pain had subsided, but the numbness in her right arm was still there. She'd been injured, a lot more seriously than she had originally thought, as she'd fled from Floyd.

After hiding in the Taos Mountains for most of the day afterward, nursing her wounds and psyche, she had ventured into Taos that night, found a Wal-Mart, and told a pharmacist who she hoped could help her that she'd been riding fence line at her ranch, checking for barbed-wire breaks, when something had spooked her horse. She'd taken a spill onto a rusty barbed-wire strand and injured her neck and shoulder. What did he know? He wasn't a doctor. The lacerations caused by flying glass from a truck window that had just taken a couple of rounds from an M16 and those caused by an encounter with a rusty strand of barbed wire probably looked pretty much the same to him. The pharmacist had bought her story and even taken a look at her neck lacerations, some still caked with blood. He'd given her a brief lesson in wound cleansing and given her enough gauze to last for a month, several tubes of Neosporin ointment, a vial of Betadine, two bottles of hydrogen peroxide, and a heat pack. She'd taken his advice, bought the first-aid supplies with what was very close to the last money she had left from selling the dump she and Bobby had grown up in, and hurried from the store.

As with prison life, she could learn to deal with the pain. She knew it was temporary. But the numbness in her arm was a different story. She'd never been able to cope with things that weren't transitory. That was why she wanted so badly to settle up with Floyd.

Uncertain what to do next, she'd been searching the sky for stars and at least temporary solace. She could seek medical attention or wait things out and hope that her arm would eventually get better. She thought about Bobby—his innocence, his bad luck, the price he had paid for being her unlucky twin. She knew she couldn't afford another mistake. She should've killed the Sundee woman. Let her starve or die of thirst, trapped in the iron lung in the middle of the wilderness, or at least blown up the line shack, like she'd planned. But she'd been too intent on killing Floyd. This time she'd have to be smarter, more thoughtful, more methodical and patient when it came to carrying out a plan. First, she'd stop hiding in the hills, sleeping in her truck, and dodging every police car she saw. Then she'd find somewhere to reenergize and mend. Floyd had come at her with plenty of firepower, but from what she could tell, there had been only one other person with him, someone who certainly wasn't a cop, which meant they were still fighting their personal war outside the bounds of the law. She wasn't worried about finding Floyd again, and she suspected he wasn't about to change his MO.

She ran her options through her head one last time. "Time to mend," she said, so loudly that it startled her, as she flipped on her flashlight and swung the beam around in a circle.

"Bobby, are you there?" she called out into the darkness.

"Are you there? Are you there?" echoed off the walls of the canyon.

When the echoing stopped, she aimed the beam skyward and headed for her pickup, still scanning the sky, thinking about Floyd, Mavis Sundee, and Bobby, and hoping to find at least one lucky guiding star.

◆ ◆ ◆

Julie Madrid, a petite green-eyed Puerto Rican, had left CJ's employ six years earlier to make way for Flora Jean and begin her career as a lawyer. Three years out of law school, she had been plucked out of a solo nickel-and-dime divorce practice by one of Denver's big three law firms, where she had honed her criminal defense leanings and spent three years with a caseload that had turned her into a top-rung criminal defense lawyer.

Julie was solidly anchored in twilight sleep in her recently remodeled West Denver Highlands neighborhood home when CJ's call awakened her.

"Julie? It's CJ."

She groggily rubbed her eyes and tried to focus on a nearby clock as she forced the sleep demons from her head. Still eyeing the clock, its digital signal locked at 2:21 a.m., she said, "Early start, don't you think, Mr. Floyd?"

CJ smiled, aware that Julie's *Mr. Floyd* reference meant that she was truly irked and that her nose was probably twitching and her facial muscles tight as a drum.

"Got a problem, and I need help."

"Surprise, surprise." Julie sat up in bed and flipped on the switch near her headboard.

"A client of mine's being held downtown; just got booked."

"Couldn't it wait until morning?"

"Would I call you if it could?"

This time it was Julie's turn to smile. The man who had extracted her from a physically abusive marriage, given her a job, taught her son to dribble a basketball, fed her clients when she was starving, and schooled her on the finer points of Western antique collecting—now her favorite passion—had a penchant for being direct. "Guess not. Shoot."

"It's big."

"So am I," said Julie, the look on her face suddenly courtroom serious.

"You up to speed on the Margolin murder?"

"I've been following it. Hope your client isn't in on that."

"It's sure gonna look like he was."

"And you sure he's not in on the murder?"

"As sure as I am that those eyes of yours are green. He wasn't even in the state."

"How long have the police been holding him?"

"Just over four hours. On a trespassing charge."

"Have they got anything to link him to the murder?"

"Nope."

"Then they've got nothing. They'll waltz him in to a magistrate tomorrow morning and plead a non-evidence-based case for holding him on a possible Margolin connection, the judge'll toss it and slap him with a fifty-dollar fine for trespassing, and he'll walk."

"It's not that simple."

"Okay," Julie sighed. "What else have they got?"

"He's a deserter. Took a powder from the army during Vietnam. Name's Langston Blue."

"Uh-oh. That spins the wheel. The cops will plug his name into the national crime reporting service computer, and trust me, if he's a deserter, his name'll pop up."

"How soon can you get on it?"

Julie ran her schedule for the day through her head. "I've got a trial all afternoon. I can meet you at the office at 8. You can bring me up to speed, I'll clock in as his lawyer and go visit him downtown."

"That'll work. And Julie, there'll probably be a lot of legwork on this."

"Isn't there always? I'll see you tomorrow at 8," she added, realizing only after hanging up that she had uttered the sentence exactly the same way she had when she'd left work every day during her five years as CJ's secretary.

Chapter

24

THE DAY BROKE OVERCAST AND GRAY, a rare summer occurrence for the Mile High City but a refreshing change from the mid-90s temperatures that had been scalding Denver and the Front Range for the past week.

Julie Madrid arrived at CJ's office a little past 7:30, let herself in with the master key she'd had for nearly a decade, brewed a pot of the Honolulu Coffee Company Kona blend that she'd brought with her, and plopped down at CJ's desk. She was there, enjoying her coffee, just before CJ arrived a few minutes past 8.

"Flora Jean?" he said, nudging the door open with the toe of his boot, clasping a box of LaMar's glazed donuts in one hand and the realty section from the *Denver Post* in the other.

Smiling, Kona brew in hand, Julie approached CJ from the back side of the center hall stairway that led up to his apartment, a means of access that he rarely used. "She's not here yet," said Julie, startling him.

"Julie!" Breaking into a wide grin, CJ wrapped all five foot four inches of his former secretary in a bear hug that sent a splash of coffee spiraling down onto the floor.

They laughed and stepped back from the spill. "You're wasting the good stuff. I brought some real Hawaiian brew to replace that foul-tasting poison you and Flora Jean pass off as coffee." Julie held up her coffee cup Statue of Liberty style.

"You're living too large, Ms. Madrid."

"And I'm liking it." Julie eyed the box in CJ's hand. "See you're still starting the day on a sugar high."

"Gotta. It's that or lose my edge."

Spotting the bandage on CJ's arm, she frowned, recalling the always dangerous bounty-hunting side of CJ's business. A side she had never been comfortable with and one that, to no avail, she and Mavis had pleaded with CJ to give up the entire time she had worked for him. "What's with the arm?"

The look on CJ's face turned solemn. "Got into a skirmish in the mountains outside Taos with Celeste Deepstream. She's out of prison."

"I thought she got twelve years," said Julie, aware that Celeste had once tried to kill CJ during the time that Julie had worked for him.

"Guess she sweet-talked the parole board."

"What happened?" asked Julie, still concentrating on CJ's arm.

"She snatched Mavis."

"Is Mavis okay?" Julie's voice rose three octaves.

CJ nodded.

Aware that the nod meant CJ was too choked up to speak, Julie said, "What about Celeste?"

"She sidestepped us. Billy was with me."

"Thank God!" said Julie, grateful that Billy DeLong had been along, certain that with Mavis as bait, had he been alone, CJ might well have killed Celeste.

"Is Mavis at home?"

"Yes."

"I'll go by and see her this evening."

"Thanks," said CJ, lowering his head.

The room fell silent. CJ set the box of donuts down and topped off his coffee cup as Flora Jean walked in with Carmen in tow. Spotting Julie, Flora Jean rushed across the room. "Hey, sugar," she boomed, giving Julie a hug.

"That's attorney sugar to you," Julie said, returning the hug.

"Hope you're here to lend a hand," said Flora Jean. "We sure as hell need one."

"I know. CJ called me this morning at 2:21!"

"Ain't that always the way?" Flora Jean glanced at Carmen. "Want you to meet somebody, Julie. This here's Carmen Nguyen. The sexy-looking Puerto Rican lady standin' here callin' herself a lawyer is Julie Madrid. And she can deal. All 104 pounds of her. You don't wanna be on the opposite side of her in court."

Carmen smiled and shook Julie's hand. "Pleased to meet you."

"Did CJ fill you in?" asked Flora Jean.

"A little," said Julie. "I know you've got a client the cops are trying to stick with Peter Margolin's murder."

"Turns out our client's Carmen's daddy. Name's Langston Blue."

Carmen nodded, her eyes full of sorrow. She'd known her father for less than a week, and now he was lost to her again.

"How much else did you tell Julie, CJ?" asked Flora Jean.

"That Blue was an army deserter. That's about it."

"There's more," said Flora Jean. "A whole lot more." Spotting the bag of Honolulu Coffee Company, Kona blend, that Julie had brought in, she said, "Let me brew some more of that high-priced barrister's blend you ship to us poor folks every Christmas, and I'll dial you in." Flora Jean walked over to the coffee alcove, poured herself the last of what was in the pot, and started a new one. Doctoring her coffee with two teaspoons of sugar, she glanced at Julie. "Did CJ tell you about Mavis?"

"Yes."

Flora Jean shook her head. "That Deepstream woman's like a cat. She's got nine lives. And on top of it she's psychotic, sugar. I told Carmen about her, and she agrees with me." Flora Jean winked at Julie. "And that's sayin' somethin', 'cause the girl's a doctor."

"You get no argument from me," said Julie.

Seizing the opening, CJ said, "Now that Flora Jean's psychoanalyzed the situation, can we get back to Langston Blue?"

"Where do we start?" asked Julie as CJ took a seat across from her and slipped a cheroot out of his pocket.

Lighting up the cheroot, he paused and blew a smoke ring into the air. "Where else? With Vietnam, at the beginning."

◆◆◆

The dozen donuts CJ had brought in were gone and so was most of the coffee when Julie checked her watch and realized that they'd been discussing the Langston Blue case for more than an hour. She'd taken a lengthy set of notes, highlighted a few points with bold underlining, and assured everyone, especially Carmen, that she would represent Blue at his arraignment, which she expected would involve a minor trespassing charge and a possible fire-code violation and more than likely conclude with Blue being held to be remanded to the army, which would deal with the issue of his desertion.

"It's not cut in stone," said Julie. "But you can pretty much bet that's the way things'll shake out."

"What will the army do?" asked Carmen.

"He'll be court-martialed," said Julie.

"And go to prison?"

Julie thought for a moment, rolling her tongue around her lower lip, a habit she'd had since childhood whenever she was forced to ponder a difficult question. "Unless we can prove the desertion was somehow related to his being in fear of his life for having to obey an unlawful order, probably. But there's always the chance the army will show a little mercy. It's been over thirty years. I'll find out more. There're people at my firm who'll know a whole lot more than me."

"Good," said CJ. "We'll deal with it when we have to. For right now, let's figure out who did kill Margolin before some overeager prosecutor on a mission to build his rep decides that Blue gets the nod. The clock's ticking, so we'd better dole out assignments. I'll start with the Margolin connections and hook up with Ginny Kearnes, that girlfriend of his. Since she tried to squeeze information about Blue out of me the other day, I think it's time I return the favor. Who knows, she might be able to shed some light on how Le Quan and Margolin and even Cortez were connected."

"If she knows, she probably won't tell you," said Carmen.

CJ gave Carmen a wink. "Sometimes the way you deny things speaks volumes. We'll see how much she's willing to give up." He looked at Julie. "Why don't you look into putting a better face on Elliott Cole, and while you're at it, see if there's any dirt circulating about Margolin."

"No problem," said Julie.

Feeling left out, Flora Jean said, "And what do I do? Plant potatoes?"

"Nope. You get to dig up everything you can on the Quan family, father, son, and daughter. And while you're at it, find out what you can about Jimmy Moc."

"That'll be a chore," said Flora Jean. "Federal Boulevard, Little Vietnam, I'll stand out like a sore thumb."

"I can help," Carmen said eagerly.

Flora Jean flashed CJ one of her patented *I don't need no help* looks. Ignoring the look, CJ said, "Good. Having the right ethnic profile can't hurt." He hoped Carmen had a streak of toughness that belied her charming demeanor and delicate looks.

"I've gotta run," said Julie, packing up her things. "I don't think I'll get an arraignment until tomorrow morning. Let's hope I get a judge who'll deal with the charges on his desk and not one who's looking to help some prosecutor build his rep."

"And that the army drags their feet," Carmen added.

Julie smiled. "That, too." She moved to leave. "Great donuts, Mr. Floyd."

"Wonderful coffee, Ms. Madrid," said CJ. "I'll get everybody back together when we have something." He draped an arm over Julie's shoulders and walked her to the door, leaving Flora Jean and Carmen staring at one another.

Carmen finally spoke up. "Ever ride on the back of a motorcycle, Flora Jean?"

"No," said Flora Jean, looking puzzled. "Why?"

"Just wondering," said Carmen. "It just might be our ticket to fitting in over on Federal Boulevard," she added, leaving Flora Jean to ponder what it would be like to straddle the back of a motorcycle.

◆◆◆

CJ had no problem getting an appointment to see Ginny Kearnes. He suspected that her eagerness to meet with him was tied to a desire to wrangle information out of him that would sink Langston Blue's ship for good. It wasn't likely that she'd invite him to her home in one of Boulder's most exclusive neighborhoods so he could skunk her again. He'd had the luxury of being the one in charge during their earlier meeting, but this time he'd be on her turf, and he suspected that he'd have to play it by ear. He didn't think Newburn had had time to tell her they had collared Langston Blue, but he couldn't be certain. And it was likely that once Kearnes knew about the collar, she'd have little or no use for him.

The twenty-minute drive north from Denver on the Boulder Turnpike had become an excursion through land-use idiocy. Pristine farmland that five years earlier had been a pastoral gateway to the University of Colorado with its breathtaking view of the Rockies and Boulder's Flatirons had become a twenty-five-mile stretch of cookie-cutter shoulder-to-shoulder ticky-tacky houses, strip malls, hotels, motels, fast-food eateries, second-tier, high-tech Silicon Valley wannabes, and the shopping mall behemoth known as Flatiron Crossing.

Kearnes lived in a sprawling ranch home on a windswept hillside overlooking Boulder Reservoir and the face of the Rockies. The home's entire west-facing wall was floor-to-ceiling glass that on most days accentuated the view, but clouds and 40-mile-per-hour winds had kicked up just past noon, and today the quivering glass seemed more appropriate as a protective barrier than as a window to the world.

CJ arrived on time and was whisked into the living room, where Kearnes apologized for the view. "It's normally not this windy," she said. "And I wouldn't usually be home at this time of day. I'll get right to the point. First off, I know all about Langston Blue. Owen Brashears, the man I was with when you first met me, got Blue's story from one of his beat reporters, who got it from a Boulder cop—that the Denver police were holding a suspect in the Margolin killing. Sounds like Blue could have had a reason to kill Peter, since he was an army deserter, and I hear he deserted during a mission where Peter was in command."

"Heavy info you're dispensing. Did that filter up from a beat reporter, too?" said CJ, suspecting that Owen Brashears with his contacts was a more likely source.

"I can't say," said Kearnes. "But I'm certain it's fact. Let's forget about sources and who said what to whom for the moment. After all, what I'm interested in is finding Peter's killer. I've asked you to come here for several reasons. First, I want the lowdown on Langston Blue. And don't tell me you're not working for him; word is you were there when the police arrested him. Now, since neither you nor I is a cop or an officer of the court, we're not bound by their rules. I've spent years spinning information, Mr. Floyd, tightroping the rules of the American criminal justice and political systems, and I know the way both systems work very well. I don't want our judicial system grinding Langston Blue through the courts only to find out a year from now that because of politics, media hype, prosecutorial overzealousness, or plain incompetence, the system has made sausage out of the wrong wiener and Peter's real killer is long gone. Quite frankly, I don't care about Langston Blue. What I care about is finding Peter's murderer. So here's what I know about your Mr. Blue. He's a deserter whom no one's seen for over thirty years. He showed up in Denver out of nowhere, and there's little more than circumstantial evidence to link him to Peter's murder."

"Are you suggesting that we share information?" said CJ, looking puzzled.

"That's one way to put it," said Kearnes. "Whatever's necessary to find justice."

"Or vengeance," said CJ, homing in on the fact that Kearnes's face was red and the muscles in her jaw were cast-iron taut. "What do I have to gain?"

"Nothing. But your client certainly does. He might not end up having to spend the rest of his life in jail, or worse, dead."

CJ stroked his chin thoughtfully. Celeste Deepstream had taught him a lesson about revenge that he understood very well.

But he couldn't put his finger on why Ginny Kearnes was so intent on fingering Peter Margolin's real killer. For most people, Blue would've been enough. He was a flesh-and-blood human being with all the right links to Margolin. He had apparently been in Denver when Margolin was murdered, he was a deserter, and the cops had him locked up. That should have sufficed. But it didn't. Kearnes seemed not only to want revenge but to be able to wrap herself up in it.

"Okay, what have you got for me?" he said, deciding to play along.

Wagging her finger at him, Kearnes said, "No, no, Mr. Floyd. I just tossed you a bone. The question is, what have you got for me?"

"Okay," said CJ. "Blue came to Denver to see family. He didn't kill your boyfriend, and when you net it all out, technically he may not even be a deserter."

"That's a lot of didn'ts and nots, Mr. Floyd. How about some dids?"

"Fine. Here's a straight-out fact. I'm having a profile run on the congressman, the kind that'll surface every wart."

"You won't find much. Peter's congressional record was sterling. He wasn't a womanizer—I should know—or a special-interest sop, a drunk, or an ass-kisser. He was on the right side of every issue that counted, at the forefront of civil and women's rights struggles, and believe it or not he was revered by his colleagues."

"In this life," CJ said coldly. "The one after Vietnam."

Kearnes shook her head. "If you're referring to Song Ve, I know about that."

Surprised that Kearnes would react so nonchalantly to what Blue had described in vivid detail as a slaughter, CJ said, "I am."

Kearnes flashed CJ an incisive stare. "So some of Peter's men got killed during a mission. It was a war."

"That's all Margolin told you? That some of his men got killed?"

"What do you mean, told me? There are official military records."

"He never said anything to you about a firefight in a school-yard?"

"No."

"And he never mentioned a school full of children being killed?"

"No." Kearnes eyed CJ quizzically. "Why? Is that Blue's story?"

"Sure is, and it's as different from Margolin's as night and day."

"What does Blue claim happened?"

"That the men in his unit opened up on a bunch of kids."

"And that's why Blue says he deserted? Because the men in his unit killed a bunch of children?"

CJ nodded.

"Far-fetched."

"Not if you're trying to keep from getting killed by the same men."

Kearnes looked startled.

Hoping to capitalize on the effect, CJ said, "Tell me, does the name Le Quan ring a bell?"

"No."

"What about Elliott Cole?"

"Yes. He was the colonel in charge of Peter's team."

"Know where I can find him?"

"He's easy to locate. He's chairman of the state Republican Party, and he lives in Denver."

"Ummm," CJ said, suddenly thinking ahead.

"What about this Le Quan person?" asked Kearnes.

Suspecting that he'd shared enough, CJ chose his words carefully. "Blue says he was there in the schoolyard at Song Ve."

"Maybe Blue's lying or confused," said Kearnes. "We're talking about something that happened more than thirty years ago."

"Don't think so," said CJ. "Besides, someone else was there," he added, smiling. "The guy in that note the cops found in Margolin's day planner. A sergeant named Lincoln Cortez. Military service has a way of tracking you all the way to the grave. A little reserve duty after you've been on active, VFW membership, military funerals, VA loans—they all add up to following you everywhere you go. Count on it, Cortez'll turn up sooner or later."

"What makes you so certain?"

"The .50-caliber machine gun I babysat during my two tours of Vietnam and the sweet little bureaucratic love letters the navy sends me from time to time."

"And Le Quan?" said Kearnes, unwilling to drop the issue.

"I've got somebody on that," said CJ.

"Then in the future we can compare notes?" said Kearnes.

"We can, but like you mentioned during our earlier meeting, I'm not exactly bosom buddies with the law."

"I'm not interested in law. I'm interested in finding Peter's killer."

"They've got Blue. Most people would let them run with that."

"And we've got a dozen unanswered questions. There're just too many dangling participles here. Let's do what we can to get rid of them."

"Fine by me," said CJ, marveling at Kearnes's tenacity and wondering whether he had spent the past forty minutes trading information with an enemy, an ally, or a grieving lover who was simply a loose cannon.

Chapter

25

CJ HEADED BACK TO DENVER in pre-rush-hour traffic that had already started to back up in the northwest suburbs near the junction of the Boulder Turnpike and I-25. Still puzzled by why Margolin's grieving girlfriend would want to seek out an alternative killer when Langston Blue had been delivered to her on a platter, ready to be garnished by some ambitious DA with the moxie to build a case on circumstantial evidence, he decided that the reasonable thing to do was to dig up all he could on Ginny Kearnes. It was possible she was trying to hand him a little bit of misdirection, hoping to get everyone involved in the investigation to look everywhere but in the right place for Margolin's killer. And especially not at her.

Making a mental note to have Julie profile Kearnes for him, he swerved to miss a partially smashed windblown cardboard box that was heading directly toward him, muttered, "Damn," eyed the morbid-looking gray skies, and wondered if the weather front that had knifed into the Front Range would bring rain. Two I-25 exits later he took the 23rd Street viaduct into the city, cruised past the northern edge of Coors Field, where the Rockies were preparing for a rare 3:05 p.m. start, skirted the central Denver hospital traffic, and headed for Dave Johnson's Realty Company, a few blocks from the center of Five Points on 28th and Downing. Johnson, a longtime friend and contemporary of Mavis's father and CJ's Uncle Ike, had managed to keep his all-black realty company afloat in an age of big-broker mania by playing the corner-drugstore and mom-and-pop game, catering to the black community, and hustling like hell.

CJ angled the Bel Air into a space in the oversized driveway that passed for Dave's parking lot, grabbed the realty section of the *Post* that he'd been carrying with him all day, and headed for the squat blond brick converted bungalow's front door. Oletha Simmons, the middle-aged daughter of a bunco artist he'd bonded out of jail more times than he could remember, greeted him before he was three steps into the sour-smelling reception area.

"CJ, hey there."

"How you doin', Oletha?"

"Doin' just fine. Daddy's out, ya know."

"Heard it over at Rosie's. What's he doing?"

"Workin' for King Soopers, unloadin' trucks. He's straight as an arrow these days. Guess it takes diabetes and a little mileage on you to make you change your ways."

"Tell him I said hello."

"Sure will."

"Dave in?"

"Sure is. I'll get him for you. He ain't doin' nothin' but readin' girlie magazines. Business has been pretty slow." Oletha smiled and picked up the phone. "Mr. Johnson, CJ Floyd's here to see you." She squeaked, "Okay," into the phone's mouthpiece, then hung up. "Go on in, CJ. You know the way."

CJ nodded and said, "Great seeing you," before stepping across the room and walking into Dave Johnson's office.

Johnson placed the *Hustler* magazine he'd been reading on top of a bin full of papers near the edge of his desk, smiled, and rose to greet CJ. "CJ, my man, what's the word?"

"It's your word, Mr. J. I'm just rentin'." CJ eyed the room as they shook hands. Nothing had changed in the dingy little space except for what looked like new carpeting since his last visit three years earlier.

"Take a load off, son," said Johnson, nodding for CJ to take a seat in one of two uncomfortable-looking barrel-shaped imitation-leather chairs that faced his desk. "And tell me what I can help you with."

CJ slipped the neatly folded section of the *Post* from under his arm and opened it up. On the first page, he'd circled several property listings. "I've been watching the market. Prices seem to be pretty good."

Salesman that he was, Johnson tried his best not to salivate. "Thinkin' of buyin'?"

"Nope. Selling."

Johnson's face went slack, and the fatty pouch that hung beneath his chin wiggled. "Not Ike's place?"

CJ nodded. "Don't have anything else to sell."

"Damn, CJ! I spent the best years of my life hangin' out there, drinkin', playin' poker." Johnson's eyes lit up. "Havin' fun with the girls. You ain't havin' hard times, are you?"

"No harder than normal."

"Then why you wanna sell? That's prime property down there off of 13th, all them old Victorians lined up in a row, kissing the edge of downtown, waiting for the next big realty boom."

"I'm about burned out, Mr. J. Too many years of doing the same thing I was when I was twenty-one."

"Don't mean you gotta sell Ike's, your building."

"It does if I'm gonna start another business. I'm thinking about peddling antiques."

Aware of CJ's passion for collecting, and equally aware of his take-no-shit reputation as the most savvy bail bondsman on Bondsman's Row, black, white, green, or purple, Johnson said, "Hell of a leap from what you're doin' now."

"Sometimes you gotta move before you lose."

"Mavis got anything to do with this?" asked Johnson, cognizant of CJ's relationship with the daughter of one of his oldest friends.

"She's been pushing me to do something else for a long time."

Instead of saying, *I know,* Johnson bit his tongue. "Got a buyer in mind?"

"My partner, Flora Jean Benson."

Johnson broke into a lecherous grin. "That built-like-a-brick-shithouse ex-marine? I thought she just worked for you. Hell, I didn't know the two of you were partners."

"We're not really. But selling the building to her will give me a chance to make it official."

Johnson looked confused. "I thought you wanted out of the

business. How you gonna sell her the building and still be a partner?"

"I said I was *about* burned out, Mr. J. Can't dig a hole and bury everything, you know. There's no question I need to cash in on the equity in the building if I plan to buy another place, and sell antiques. But like Ike always said, *A rabbit's gotta have more than one hole.*"

"Ain't that the truth." Johnson relaxed back in his seat, knowing that sooner or later the payday he was looking for would be his. "Well, whattaya need from me?"

"I need you to do some building comps for me, give me something to pass on to Flora Jean so I can let her know what I'm thinking pricewise. I haven't really said anything to her about it yet."

"Okay. I'll work up a market-value survey for you and a broker agreement. But you're gonna need a lawyer when it comes to that partnership agreement."

"Got one."

"Who you usin'? Adolfus Moore?"

"No. Julie Madrid."

Johnson thought for a moment before breaking into the same lecherous grin he'd flashed when CJ had mentioned Flora Jean. "That little Puerto Rican sexpot who used to be your secretary?"

"Watch what you say, Mr. J. She's a lawyer now. Talk like that'll get your shorts sued off."

Johnson laughed. "I'll try and remember that the next time I'm sniffin' panties. It'll take me a day or two to work up those comps, but you can count on havin' somethin' by the end of the week."

"Sounds fine."

Johnson shook his head. "Damn! Ike's place. I'd never've figured you'd ever sell it."

"A man's gotta move ahead, Mr. J.," said CJ, trying to picture Mavis's reaction when he broke the news to her.

"Ain't that the truth? I'll call you when I've got somethin'. Meanwhile, give my best to Mavis."

"I'll do that," said CJ, motioning as he turned for Johnson to keep his seat. "No need to get up, Mr. J. I know my way out."

"Okay. I'll be talkin' with ya."

Before he reached the door, CJ could hear the rustling of papers, and he knew that Johnson had his *Hustler* back open.

It had started to sprinkle as CJ slipped back into the Bel Air. The layer of dust covering the parking area was barely even dimpled, but he never drove the Bel Air in the rain. Eyeing the position of the storm clouds overhead, he figured he still had time to make it to the office before the Bel Air had to take a street bath. He'd then log in with Flora Jean and tell her about his meeting with Kearnes, switch to his fifteen-year-old Jeep that Rosie Weeks somehow kept running, and drop by to check on Mavis.

He'd just turned onto 13th Avenue, a straight shot to his office, when the rain picked up. He hated driving the Bel Air in the rain. It caused him and the forty-eight-year-old vintage drop-top too much distress, and like Ike always used to say, *Distress breeds anger, and anger breeds hate.* When he caught a stoplight at 13th and Grant, the rain began coming down in sheets. Suddenly he found himself grinding his teeth. It wasn't until the light changed that he realized he'd been thinking about Celeste. Recalling his uncle's wisdom, he accelerated, aware that it was time to get the Bel Air home.

◆◆◆

Elliott Cole lived in a thirteen-story high-rise condo in the recently developed neighborhood just west of downtown and east of the South Platte River known as Riverfront Park. Billed as Denver's "downtown neighborhood," the area's ten-year development master plan called for a variety of top-end residences, neighborhood shops, and assorted recreation. Commons Park, in truth no more than a greenbelt along the South Platte River, fronted Cole's building, Riverfront Tower. The building's west-facing tenants were afforded a view of the Rockies that only Hollywood could imagine. Cole, a sports fanatic, had chosen the location not because of that view but because Coors Field and the Pepsi Center were close at hand to the north and south, and a six-block walk in either direction put him in the center of either the Boys of Summer or Roundball and Hoops action nearly year-round. And since his job as state Republican Party chairman called for him to keep an ear close to the body politic, he could walk across the Millennium Bridge that connected Riverfront Park to Denver's 16th Street pedestrian shopping mall, hop a free mall shuttle bus, and be at the State Capitol, lobbyists' eateries surrounding it, or committee headquarters in a matter of minutes.

Cole was pacing his penthouse apartment's study on a remilled wide-planked floor that had risen from the ashes of a 150-year-old Pennsylvania farmhouse, sipping a gin and tonic and watching a C-line light-rail train slice through the rain toward the Pepsi Center along tracks just east of his building. The Millennium Bridge blocked his view of the train until it reached 15th Street, where three sharp blasts from the warning bell let its riders know that the Pepsi Center stop was imminent.

He'd spent most of the afternoon and now into early evening watching the rain, waiting for a phone call, and staring intermittently at the bone-white two-hundred-foot-high tapered steel mast that Riverfront Park developers had built just to the south of the Millennium Bridge on its 16th Street side in an effort to make a landmark statement that would impressively and forever define the eastern entrance to the Riverfront Park neighborhood. They had succeeded beyond their dreams, since photos, paintings, stylized designs, and any number of convention bureau renderings statewide and nationally more often than not now captured the Millennium Bridge mast in any rendering of the Denver skyline.

Cole was heading for the bar to mix another gin and tonic when one of three phones in his bedroom rang. Sensing that it was the call he'd been waiting for, he set his glass aside and headed for the bedroom. The flashing light on the phone, a privacy phone with an access code and a security lock, told him it was indeed the call. He picked up the receiver, punched in 6-1-4, and said, "Cole here."

"Quan," came the one-word response on the other end of the line.

"You home?"

"At the store. We close at 7."

Cole checked his watch. It was five past 6. "I'll be there by 7."

"What the problem?"

"Blue. He's in Denver." Cole cradled the phone without saying another word, walked back out to the bar, made himself a fresh gin and tonic, and strolled back to his study. The mast, rising majestically out of the rain and highlighted with floodlights and a bank of lights above nearby Union Station, had the look of a needle-nosed rocket ship awaiting blast-off, tethered to the ground only by cables.

Cole sat down in a well-used chair, nursed his drink, and listened to the clang of another train passing below. He savored his gin, thinking that privilege had its perks and that if he were a little late for his meeting with Quan, what did it matter? After all, Quan had kept him waiting all afternoon, and regardless of the dicey circumstances necessitating the meeting, it was only with an over-the-hill Vietcong gook.

◆ ◆ ◆

Federal Boulevard was flooded just south of 6th Avenue, the power was out, and Cole was forced to run a gauntlet of four-way stops all the way to Le Quan's shoe store. He walked through puddles to the store's front door, his feet squishing inside his shoes, and pounded on the door until Chi Quan appeared, swung the door open, a candle in her right hand, and said, "We're in back."

Without responding, Cole followed her through a ghostly canyon of shoe boxes and benches to the store's back storeroom, where Le Quan was busy gluing Nike swoosh labels onto knockoff running shoes. Methodical in his approach, he never failed to get the logo properly positioned as he ran through a series of a dozen pairs of size tens.

Cole stomped his water-logged shoes on the cold concrete several times and removed the Aussie bush hat he was wearing. Scented candles sat on tables in all four corners of the room, and the dimly lit storage area, amid the smell of Vietnamese spices and rubber adhesive, seemed to flicker like an old celluloid movie.

Cole pushed his thinning hair off his forehead, slipped out of his raincoat, and said, "It's wet."

Quan nodded and continued with his labeling. "No foot traffic all afternoon. Business poor." He finished two more sets of shoes, handing them to Chi to rebox and price, before looking back up. "Now, what about Blue? How you know he here?"

"The police arrested him the other night, and today the cop who busted him, a detective named Newburn, paid me a visit at work! He said the DA's office was looking to stick Blue with Margolin's murder but admitted when I pushed him that it would be hard to get the charge to stick."

Chi glanced at her father, nodded, rose from her chair, and began stacking shoe boxes against the wall.

Watching her, Cole asked, "Are you sure she should hear all this?"

Quan frowned. "She my daughter. How much this detective know?"

"Just about everything. The history of Margolin's Star 1 team, the name of the men who served in it, the fact that Blue deserted, and that I was the colonel in charge."

"How he get information?"

"It could've only come from one of three places. Maybe Margolin kept records, and the cops found them. Or Newburn got the war records from the army or pulled information off the Internet, or it came from Owen Brashears."

Quan eyed Chi and spoke sharply in Vietnamese. He watched as Chi rearranged the boxes into two tiers, to a height he found acceptable. "Okay," he said, turning his attention back to Cole. "Problem easy to solve. We talk to Brashears."

"And what if he's working for the cops?"

"We deal with him. He don't know about Margolin and us."

"I'm glad you're so calm about the whole thing," said Cole, irritated that their problem barely caused a ripple in Quan.

"Always calm," said Quan.

"Yeah," said Cole, seething. "Because you're not walking point. I'm in the middle of an election with a candidate who's a notch above paint-dry interesting. Every day I have to rein in a gaggle of overpaid pollsters who don't know their ass from a hole in the ground. I'm dealing with an opponent's murder, and now there's this thing with Blue." Cole took a half step toward Quan and slammed his fist into his palm. "If you commies hadn't been such fucking racists, we wouldn't have this problem."

He'd barely finished his rant when Le Quan spoke again to Chi. A split second later Chi was eyeball to eyeball with Cole. The shiny blade of the Qing Dy elephant bone knife she was holding kissed the loose, rubbery flesh of Cole's upper neck.

Quan gave another order in Vietnamese. The tip of the blade nicked Cole's skin, and three drops of blood fell onto his shirt collar.

"Shit," said Cole as Chi stepped back. He rubbed his neck, then eyed his fingertips for signs of blood. There was none. Chi backed away toward the shoe boxes.

During Vietnam, Cole had seen enough bodies with their heads completely severed and enough legless and armless torsos to know the capabilities of this kind of knife. He moved out of the candlelight to hide the fact that he was shaking. "You're crazy, Quan." He glanced at Chi. "So's she."

Quan smiled. It was the self-satisfied smile of a man in control. "You not curse in front of my daughter, and don't call me racist. You, America, are the racists. You the ones who contaminated us."

Regaining a measure of composure, Cole said, "And you're the one who asked for help fixing the problem."

"It was mistake." Quan's face turned serene. "We need to handle current problem."

"And how do we do that?" asked Cole, still uncomfortable, his eyes darting back and forth between Quan and Chi.

"Eliminate Blue. He only outsider who can piece together what happened at Song Ve."

"He's in jail."

"He get out. Your American justice system weak. In Vietnam we kill him—long ago."

Not wanting things to get out of hand again, Cole said, "Strange that Blue would show up now."

"And strange that Margolin dead," said Quan with a hint of a snicker.

They exchanged accusatory stares until Cole said, "Then you'll handle the problem?"

Le Quan nodded.

"Good." Cole watched Chi slip the knife between two shoe boxes. "Let me know if there're problems."

Quan nodded again and smiled at the pasty-faced white man who was barking orders at him as if he were the one in control.

Sensing that his allotted time was up, Cole turned to leave. He'd taken a step toward the storeroom door when the room's lights flickered on. He looked back and realized that Chi Quan was at his heels and that her father had a fresh pair of fake Nikes in front of him. Continuing what he'd been doing as if Cole had never been there, Quan reached for his glue bottle. Cole walked away with Chi following him silently toward the now well-lit building's front door. Afraid to look back, he stepped outside into what was now a drizzle before finally glancing over his shoulder. There was no Chi, the door was shut, and the building was completely dark.

Squishing his way toward his car in rain-soaked shoes, he thought about the day that had changed his life. The day he had given the captain of a Star 1 team the go-ahead to erase what had become an ethnic stain on Vietnamese culture; to remove, in the words of Ho Chi Minh, *the Con Lai, half-breeds who are the recruits, malcontents, and rabble-rousers, the dust of life who would disrupt the pure soul of a nation.*

Chapter

26

THE RAIN HAD STOPPED, but the sound of water gurgling through the downspouts and past the slate-roofed dormer window of Mavis's bedroom served to punctuate the storm's intensity.

"Can't believe it's cold enough for a fire," said CJ, eyeing the antique barn thermometer he'd bought at a garage sale five years earlier. A thermometer he had, at the risk of breaking his neck, nailed to the dormer's soffit so Mavis could look outside each morning and see the temperature before her feet ever hit the floor. "It's 43 degrees."

Seated across the room in an overstuffed wingback chair, Mavis said, "It's supposed to warm up tomorrow, get back into the 70s. It's Colorado, you know." She watched as CJ stoked a fire that he couldn't seem to get to burn evenly. She was in love with a predictable man, she told herself, and smiled.

Looking frustrated, he said, "I think something's wrong with the damper." CJ tugged at the damper. "The thing's never worked right since you had the house remodeled."

"The house was built in 1918, CJ. You have the same problem

every time you try to start a fire. I don't think they were expecting the kind of homecoming bonfires you prefer back in 1918. Take out one of the logs."

"Can't now. All the wood's caught."

Mavis got up from her chair, walked over to where CJ was kneeling, and wrapped both arms around his neck. "You're an impatient man sometimes, CJ Floyd." Taking the poker out of his hand, she leaned over his back, pulled one of the bottom logs forward so it no longer kissed its neighbor, allowing space for an updraft, and said, "Now, wait."

Moments later the cusp of a flame danced through the opening. Within minutes there was a roaring fire. Smiling and with her left fist balled tightly, she tapped CJ lightly on the top of his head. "See?" she said, placing the poker back in its rack. "Let's watch it from bed."

They walked over to the wrought-iron bed that had belonged to Mavis's grandparents. Barefoot, both dressed only in sweatpants and T-shirts, they slipped onto the bed, and CJ pulled the comforter up just beyond their knees.

"It's the middle of July, not December," said Mavis, slipping the comforter off them. "I know what you're up to," she said with a smile, "but I'm not ready, CJ. The pain's too fresh. Sex would just be too raw. Just hold me."

Sensing that CJ was embarrassed, she said, "My head's the problem, baby, not my body." She guided CJ's hand gently to the warm spot between her legs. "I'll be fine; just give me a little time." Relaxing back into CJ's arms, she added, "I'm still all yours."

Unwilling to push the fragile envelope of intimacy any further, CJ sat back against a bank of pillows, pulled Mavis into the crook of his uninjured left arm until she rested comfortably against him, and stared at the fire.

They watched the sawtoothed flames in silence until Mavis spoke up. "Henry came by this afternoon to look at my injuries." Mavis rested her head on a pillow at the edge of CJ's chest.

CJ nodded. "I know." He had sent his longtime friend and physician, Henry Bales, to check on Mavis's injuries after dropping by Henry's cancer research lab at the University of Colorado to have Henry take a look at his injured arm. After he explained what had happened in New Mexico, his friend had checked CJ's arm, scurried to a hospital outpatient clinic, and returned with tape, a spool of fresh gauze, and antibiotic ointment.

"Damn, it's like old times," Henry had said, shaking his head as he rebandaged the wound, recalling his days as a combat corpsman with their 42nd River Patrol group during Vietnam. "Haven't done this in years," he'd added as he thought about the hundreds of men he'd treated for everything from shrapnel wounds to organ eviscerations during the war.

Sensing that CJ's attention had drifted, Mavis lifted her head. "You okay?"

"Yeah, yeah. Just thinking about Henry and that damn war."

"The war's been over for a long, long time," said Mavis, watching what she called CJ's "foggy look" creep across his face. It was a look that she dreaded. A look that meant that CJ had, at least momentarily, been swept back to the killing fields of war. Sitting up in bed, she gently massaged CJ's neck, hoping to get the look to fade.

"Henry said my knees will be fine, other than a little scarring," she said, continuing the massage.

"What about your forehead?" asked CJ, his thoughts still drifting.

Mavis swallowed hard before answering. "He said I may need what he called a little cosmetic recon." Mavis tried to smile but couldn't. Tears pooled at the corners of her eyes. Her voice cracked as she continued. "He said that it was way out of his league and he gave me the name of a plastic surgeon he works with at CU."

CJ gently removed her hands from his neck and turned to meet her gaze. Eyeing her bandaged forehead, he thought about who the woman he'd been in love with for most of his life really was. She'd always been beautiful in the dark-haired Nubian princess sense of the word. And smart. And driven. He'd never thought of her as being the least bit vain. And she'd always worn her good looks as if they were a mandatory component of one of the things he admired most about her—her class.

He knew it wasn't vanity that had Mavis teary-eyed over some minor cosmetic surgical procedure down the road. He suspected that what had her really upset was that fact that she had discovered that she was vulnerable in ways she'd never known, and more fragile than she'd ever expected.

Squeezing her hand, he said, "The hurt's going to linger for a while, Mavis." He kissed her, barely pressing his lips to hers. He could taste the salt from her tears. "We'll make it through this. We will."

Shivering, Mavis said, "I'm not like you or Flora Jean, CJ."

She fought back the urge to sob. "I'm not a war hero or a combat marine."

"But you're just as tough. Think about it. Look at what you do. You run a successful business and two more of your father's on the side. You're a civic leader whose opinion everyone in Denver seeks out and respects. You're educated and beautiful, and nothing but class. Flora Jean and I couldn't climb that mountain in a thousand years. Your only real problem is you're stuck with me." CJ forced a smile.

Mavis remained silent, choking back tears.

CJ gently lifted her chin until their eyes met. "I started working on something today that will help." When Mavis didn't answer, he said, "Mavis?"

"Yes."

"I went by to see Dave Johnson this afternoon. Talked to him about selling the building. Told him I'm packing it in."

Thinking that she'd somehow heard CJ wrong, Mavis sat back and stared at him blankly.

"I said, I'm getting out of the bail-bonding business."

At a loss for words and unable to fully comprehend what CJ was saying, Mavis asked, "Have you said anything to Flora Jean?"

"No, but that'll get handled. I'm going to ask Julie to draw up a partnership agreement."

"Partnership? You just said you were getting out." There was a tinge of disappointment in Mavis's voice.

"I am, but I have to do it my way." Recognizing that Mavis was seeing the glass half-empty instead of half-full, he said, "I brought you something to take a look at." He rose, walked over to where he had draped his jacket over the back of a chair, and returned with the limp, slightly damp section of the *Denver Post* he'd been carrying around all day. "I circled it, page 8." He handed the paper to Mavis.

Mavis slowly read the real estate ad that CJ had circled. *For Lease, antique row section of South Broadway. 800 square feet. Perfect location to start your business. Call Lou Biggs, 303-555-3551.*

"What do you think?" said CJ, a sense of urgency in his voice. "Worth looking into?"

Mavis nodded, eyes on the floor.

"What's wrong?"

Her words came out slowly, as if she'd been storing them up for a long, long time. "This has to be something you want, CJ. Not something you're doing because you feel sorry for me."

Recognizing that he'd just bombarded someone he loved, someone who'd been through the most traumatic episode she'd likely ever face, with too many issues at once, CJ said, "Think about it. There's no hurry." He squeezed her hand. "You'll have a part in it too. You can teach me the ins and outs of running a business. How to market and advertise, all the dos and don'ts. Sound like a plan?"

Mavis smiled, aware of how hard it must have been for CJ to decide not only to shift gears at this stage of his life but to sell the only home he'd ever known.

"Sounds like a plan," she said softly, forgetting her own problems for the moment, snuggling comfortably into the crook of CJ's arm.

CJ ran his finger in loose circles along the nape of her neck, the way he usually did as a prelude to their lovemaking. Instead of continuing the rituals of passion, he squeezed her closer to him and said, "Love you," as they listened to the satisfying crackle of the fire.

◆ ◆ ◆

The day broke crystal-blue Rocky Mountain clear, leaving Denver awash in sunshine. The 8 a.m. view of the Rockies from Julie Madrid's twenty-second-story 17th Street law office was glossy-brochure convention-bureau perfect, and the temperature, a notch above 60, was slated to rise into the 70s by midafternoon. Flora Jean had arrived at the law offices of Thorne, Hawkes, Slater, and Madrid just before 8. Per Julie's instructions, she'd been immediately whisked into Julie's office by a tiny young secretary, who, gawking at Flora Jean's size and fixated on her African bracelets, had nearly walked into the door.

Julie had walked in moments later, a briefcase in each hand, with CJ on her heels. "Frick and Frack," said Flora Jean, admiring the view from a nearby window. "Glad you could make it," she added, looking directly at snow-capped Long's Peak. "Snow in July. Hard to believe."

"Unless you live here," said CJ, taking a seat.

Julie placed both briefcases next to her desk and, looking harried and hurried, said, "Be right back; I have to photocopy something."

She returned a few moments later with several papers in her hand. "I've got an arraignment at 9," she said, checking her watch and handing the photocopies to CJ. "Where was I? Oh, yes," she said, continuing a conversation she'd started with CJ earlier in the elevator. "Bad news, bad news. The bad news is, Blue's still in jail. I called Carmen and told her earlier. Because her father's a deserter, even setting aside his minor trespassing charge, the army still has dibs on him. And the cops know that. Even though they'll have to let him out on the trespassing charge once he's arraigned and pays the fine, they can drag their bureaucratic feet while they look for a connection to Margolin's murder and delay the arraignment, in cop language, *just a wee tad*. You know the game, CJ. By then the MPs will have shown up to cart Blue away, and the cops will still have him under lock and key."

Nodding, CJ asked, "How long do you think the cops will stall?"

"No more than twenty-four hours, at the most thirty-six."

"Then what's next?"

"We can't do much about Blue. He's going to have to cool his heels for a while. If I were you, I'd try to find Margolin's killer. I can deal with the desertion charges later."

CJ stroked his chin and slipped a cheroot out of his vest pocket. "Got a mess."

"And a bigger one if you light that thing," said Julie. "You know there's no smoking in here."

CJ put the cheroot away. "Thought chewing on it might help me think."

Julie checked her watch. "Better think real fast. I'm due in court in forty minutes."

"Okay, let's start with what's new since yesterday. I met with Ginny Kearnes. I'm surprised she didn't have her guard dog with her, that *Boulder Camera* editor, Owen Brashears."

Julie whistled. "Brashears. Now, there's a heavy left-winger from way back."

"How do you know him?" asked CJ.

"You've gotta know editors of newspapers in this business," said Julie.

"Well, in addition to being a newspaper editor, he was one of Margolin's longtime friends."

"Makes sense," said Julie. "They mugged around the political circuit together for years, supporting all the right political causes. Word is, he was Margolin's Fourth Estate lapdog."

"Ummm. Anyway, Kearnes did drop one pearl. She told me that a colonel named Elliott Cole gave Margolin's Star 1 team their marching orders."

"Elliott Cole! He's head of the state Republican Party."

CJ nodded, surprised at Julie's political savvy. "You're sure in the know."

Julie smiled. "Have to be. Knowing the political landscape means money for the firm. As for Cole, he's a real wheeler-dealer, and a card-carrying right-winger. Comes from an old-time Colorado cattle-ranching family on the Eastern Slope. I hear they made a lot more money brokering water rights and selling land than they ever made running cattle."

CJ thought for a moment and stroked his chin. "Take away their politics and Brashears and Mr. Republican Party Cole have two things in common: Peter Margolin and Vietnam."

"What did Brashears do during Vietnam?" asked Julie.

"He was a *Stars and Stripes* reporter, according to Kearnes."

Flora Jean, who had been strangely quiet, looked at CJ pensively. "Hey, folks, wanna get back to Blue? I been thinkin', could be Blue's Star 1 team went all-out rogue. We had a few of those during Desert Storm. Killin' just to be killin', wild dogs instead of men."

"Maybe. But I don't think that's the whole problem here," said CJ. "From what I've heard, Margolin was a soldier's soldier. And so was Blue. Any bad apples had to be either above or beneath them in the chain of command."

"Or fightin' on the other side," said Flora Jean.

"Le Quan?" asked CJ, giving Flora Jean a thumbs-up for the timely assist.

"Why not? He was there, accordin' to Blue, silver streak in his hair and all. And he was a communist youth organizer, accordin' to what Alden told me. Could be Margolin and them Star 1 boys got sent on a mission to wipe out a bunch of budding Vietcong communist youth-camp guerrillas."

"Then why all the fuss?" asked CJ. "Firefights with Vietcong guerrillas who were no more than kids happened all the time. Sending a special unit to eradicate a group of guerrillas, regardless of whether or not they'd just started to shave, wouldn't be big news. Guerrillas were guerrillas. Nobody asked them their age. Nope, there's something else bubbling up from below the surface here, and we're all missing it. Something that runs deeper than the plain old everyday savagery of war."

"What could be worse?" Julie asked.

"I'm not sure, but my guess is that whatever it was, or is, got Peter Margolin killed."

"Well, we need to find out pretty quick because more than

likely thirty-six hours from now Blue will be in the hands of MPs and under the jurisdiction of the U.S. Army, and it will be a heck of a lot harder for me to try to help." Julie looked at her watch. "I'm going to have to run."

"Two more minutes, Julie, and that's it. Promise."

"As long as you understand the meaning of the word *contempt*."

"First off, did you find any dirt on Margolin?"

"Nothing yet. I've got a law clerk working up a detailed profile on him. The only thing I got so far is that over the past twenty years, Margolin made a lot of money. I'll have more for you before the day's out."

"Good," said CJ. "And while you're at it, add Ginny Kearnes to your list."

"What about Le Quan and that kid you mentioned on the way up to the office, Jimmy Moc?"

"No need," said Flora Jean. "Carmen and I have plans for Moc this evening. I've got a call in to Alden about Quan."

Julie picked up one of the briefcases she had brought in. "Gotta go."

"Go," said CJ, watching Julie rush out the door.

"Talk to you this evening," she called back.

CJ grinned as he watched the only high-priced trial lawyer he could ever say he had affection for rush through the door. It was the grin of a proud older sibling.

"She's somethin'," said Flora Jean, shaking her head.

"I know," said CJ, thinking as he watched Flora Jean head authoritatively toward the exit as if she owned the building, *and so are you.*

Chapter

27

IT WAS MIDMORNING, and Flora Jean had just hung up after talking to Alden Grace when CJ walked up to her desk carrying a photo album under one arm. She looked up, excited, jotting a note at the bottom of a Post-It. "Got another lead in the Blue case. Alden says to keep hammering at Jimmy Moc and Quan. He doesn't know what really happened at Song Ve, but he did find out from another old-time SOG operative that during the weeks leading up to that Star 1 team mission, a man fitting Le Quan's description, right down to the silver streak in his hair, was rounding up kids from all over Quang Ngai province and arming them. Sounds like Margolin and his men walked into somethin' they didn't expect."

CJ looked unconvinced. "Except that Blue claims that whoever was in the school building when they arrived never opened fire on them. Most of the action was between Blue and the men in his unit. Sounds screwy to me. The little VC river rats we ran up against wouldn't have thought one second about coming up out of the bottom of a sampan and blowing your head off, or lobbing grenades at you from the tall grass at the edge of the Mekong River and turning you into sausage."

"Does seem strange, sugar, but it is what it is."

"'Til we find out something different," said CJ.

"Trust me. We'll crack the nut," said Flora Jean, salivating over the fact that she was as close to once again being a marine intelligence sergeant as she'd been in years. Watching CJ take a seat, she said, "Me and Carmen got a date with Jimmy Moc tonight." Puzzled by the look arching across CJ's face, she added, "Nothin' big. Just your basic surveillance and meet-and-mingle kinda evening."

"I'd be careful, Flora Jean, especially if Carmen's tagging along. This is probably way out of her league."

"I don't think it is, CJ. Her fiancé, that MI captain I served with during Desert Storm, says the good doctor's a lot more than eye candy. Claims she's got Freon runnin' through her veins and she can flat-out ride a motorcycle like Evel Knievel. Besides, I need somebody who looks Vietnamese along with me."

"Your call. But remember you're partnered up with an MD, not a daredevil." CJ rolled his tongue around the inside of his mouth, the way he did when he'd been pondering something for a while. He shot a quick glance at the photo album he was holding and placed it on Flora Jean's desk.

"What's that?"

"Pictures."

"Somethin' to do with the case?"

"No. Take a look."

Flora Jean opened the album and started scanning the pages.

"Damn, sugar. Never knew you were actually young." She snickered. "And look at this one of you decked out in your uniform. Shit, sugar, you wasn't much more than a baby."

"Nineteen and . . ."

Flora Jean cut him off. "On your way to Vietnam." She turned to the next page. A page filled with photos of a much lankier CJ standing on the aft deck of a 125-foot navy patrol boat. He was wrapped in a flak jacket, his helmet shading his eyes, hammering away at the Mekong River shoreline with a .50-caliber machine gun.

"The next page is the one I really want you to see. Check out the photo in the bottom right-hand corner."

"Ain't that your Uncle Ike on a ladder?"

"Yep, he's putting up that little hand-carved sign that still hangs out front over the door. The one that says *Floyds Bail Bonds*."

Flora Jean chuckled. With the array of the neon signs now on the street, signs that screamed *Bail Bonds Anytime; Bonds; OPEN 24 HOURS*, the tiny sign above the door had all but been lost.

"Notice anything special about the sign?" CJ asked.

"Not really."

"Do you see an apostrophe in the word *Floyds*?"

Realizing what CJ was getting at, Flora Jean said, "Well, I'll be damned, sugar, there sure ain't none."

"You're right; the word's plural. Ike bought me the blank piece of wood the week I came back home from 'Nam. Had me carve the sign myself. Told me that when two people become partners, the 'baby' partner always gets the job of making up the business sign."

CJ walked over to the coffee island. The bitter, acidic smell of overbrewed coffee wafted up his nostrils. Bending, he teased a three-foot-long, one-foot-high piece of smooth-surfaced Philippine mahogany from behind the coffee island, walked back over to Flora Jean with it swinging from his hand, placed it on her desk, and said, "Floyd & Benson will do just fine."

◆ ◆ ◆

Twenty minutes later, Flora Jean was still floating on an adrenaline rush that had her thinking she was in a dream. She'd been pushing CJ for three years to make her a partner, and now that he'd said he would, the strongest emotion she felt was disbelief. She'd never owned much of anything in her life except a car. And the only thing she'd ever totally vested herself in was the U.S. Marine Corps. She'd been pinching pennies, denying herself, stashing every cent she had earned for more than four years, hoping that one day CJ would ask her to become a partner.

When she called Alden Grace to tell him that CJ had just handed her what, except for her promotion to sergeant major in the marines, was the highlight of her life, she'd sounded flatout giddy. They'd talked about the fact that she'd have to buy CJ out and take half ownership in the building, and Grace had told her that if necessary, he would float her a loan. Near the end of the conversation he'd asked her once again to marry him.

Surprising herself, she'd said, "Let me think about it." Her response had left a man who'd been a combatant in both the Vietnam and the Persian Gulf wars, a career soldier who'd slipped in and out of the shadows of espionage and marine counterintelligence for years, a man who'd provided security for kings and presidents, speechless.

They'd ended their conversation with Flora Jean finally asking Grace what new insight he might have about their Langston Blue problem. He'd lamented that the only angle he'd come up with worth pursuing was the fact that Blue's Star 1 team's botched mission had never hit the intelligence community's front burner, or for that matter the front pages of any major newspaper. This fact suggested to him that someone with enough political or intelligence clout had been able to bury what sounded to him like a possible war crime or even collaboration with the enemy. Grace had ended the call with the words, "You think long; you think wrong," sounding like a schoolboy as he hung up.

◆◆◆

Julie called CJ just before noon, her cell phone in one hand, a hot dog in the other. Shouting to be heard above the traffic noise and the clanging of a light-rail train in the background, she said, "I'm down the street from the courthouse getting a hot dog. Gotta be back in court at 1:30, but I've got something for you concerning the Blue case."

CJ laughed. Aware of Julie's weakness for junk food, he said, "Better watch out. Too many dogs and burgers and you'll lose that *West Side Story* figure."

"But I'll still have the looks," Julie countered.

Smiling and thinking that no matter which way he turned he was surrounded by take-charge women, CJ said, "Okay, what've you got?"

"A money trail you need to follow."

"No riddles, Julie," said CJ. His mood was uneven because he had been dealing all day with a powerful case of seller's remorse.

"Here's the skinny," she said, sensing that something was off kilter. "My law clerk snooped out Margolin's shorts. Turns out that in the past thirty years, Colorado's would-be senator made himself a lot of money."

"No news there. He came from money."

"It's news if you started out before Vietnam plain old rich and ended up afterward flat-out blueblood wealthy. Seems like all of Margolin's real wealth came rolling in after Vietnam."

"Maybe he just built himself a big fat political war chest?"

"Come on, CJ. I'm talking about his personal money, not nickel-and-dime campaign contributions. That construction site he got killed at—turns out the building was a partnership deal with Margolin as the general partner. The building was worth seventy-five million."

CJ whistled into the phone. "Now you're talking real money."

"It's real money all right, but here's the kicker. Guess who his partners were on the high-rise deal?"

"Got me."

"How about Ginny Kearnes and Elliott Cole?"

"What?"

"Like they say. Politics makes strange bedfellows."

"Hell, those two are at lunar opposite poles."

"I'll say. My law clerk's still digging, working up Internet sources, newspaper stories, microfiche files, the whole works, to see if he can ferret out a few more of the good congressman's financial connections. But so far, his post-Vietnam windfall and the building deal are our best angles."

"Gives us plenty to start with," said CJ, listening to the clang of a light-rail train in the background on Julie's end.

"I'll keep on it," said Julie.

"Good," he said, pausing to take a long breath. "I've got something else for you to deal with. But it's not about the Blue case."

"I'm listening," said Julie, noting a hint of hesitation in CJ's voice.

"I need you to draw up some papers for me."

"What kind?" said Julie, pressing the cell phone tightly to her ear and putting her hot dog down.

"Partnership papers. And a lease-to-buy agreement. I'm gonna sell half the business to Flora Jean."

Stunned, Julie looked for somewhere to sit. "Are you serious?"

"As a heart attack."

Making her way over to an unoccupied 16th Street pedestrian mall bench, Julie sat down and stared at the ground. During the time she had worked for CJ, his job had consumed his life. She had watched him almost singlehandedly rid Five Points of a late-1990s gang stench that had threatened to tear the community apart. She'd seen him track down scores of petty criminals, arsonists, and even murderers and been there with him as he butted heads with unscrupulous bail bondsmen, insipid lawyers, and out-of-control cops. Aware that except for his passion for collecting Western memorabilia and antiques, the bail-bonding business was all CJ knew, Julie was at a loss for words.

"What will you do?" she asked finally, her gaze fixed on the sea of mall pedestrians.

"Take some time off. Make sure my fly-fishing arm heals up, peddle a few antiques, and give Mavis the time she deserves."

"Makes sense. How's Flora Jean with it?"

"She's ready." CJ's voice trailed off as if the rash of recent decisions somehow had him winded.

"I'll need more specifics, but I can do the papers for you," said Julie, sensing his fatigue and thinking that as a criminal defense attorney she hadn't tackled anything as mundane as a partnership agreement in years. "I'll come by the office after work. We can talk over things then."

"Fine. I'll make sure Flora Jean's there."

A 16th Street mall shuttle bus lumbered by. Its pedestrian warning bell clanged as Julie rose, tossed her unfinished hot dog into a nearby trash container, and headed back to the courthouse.

"And remember to bring whatever else your law clerk can dig up to help with the Blue case," said CJ.

"Will do," said Julie, picking up her pace, wondering as the courthouse steps came into view what she would do if she ever had to give up practicing law.

◆◆◆

Flora Jean's voice was churning with frustration. Looking up from her computer screen, she said, "Ever tried to dig up anything on a war crime that nobody ever heard of? I've Googled, Yahooed, MSNed, and AOLed everything from Auschwitz to Sherman's march through Georgia. Ain't nothin' nowhere about a U.S. Army Star 1 team committin' no atrocity during Vietnam. I knew I was gonna end up havin' to go classified when I started lookin'."

"Meaning?"

"Meaning, I'm gonna have to rely on Alden or somebody he knows to scrounge up somethin'."

"Might as well. I'm not convinced after what Julie told me about Margolin's finances that that's why he was murdered anyway."

Flora Jean gave CJ one of her *this is my territory, sugar,* looks. "Maybe not, but Margolin's team was involved in a killin'; maybe it just wasn't the kind you was gettin' paid to do."

CJ nodded. Still only partly convinced that Flora Jean's take was accurate, he looked around her cramped quarters nostalgically. "Julie's coming over after work. She wants to talk to us about the partnership agreement."

"Works for me."

CJ eyed the toaster-sized recess behind Flora Jean's desk, a niche in the plaster that housed a West African figurine. Recalling that the niche had started as a plaster crack that his Uncle Ike had repaired half a dozen times with auto-body Bondo, he thought about how Julie and now Flora Jean had transformed the cramped little space into a place where each could be comfortable working every day. Staring at the hand-carved teakwood replica of an African queen that now filled the niche, CJ said, "I'm gonna run by and check on Mavis real quick before I try and locate that Republican Party chairman, Elliott Cole." He headed for the door, trying to push a lifetime of memories to the back of his mind.

"You haven't said anything to Willis about what happened to Mavis, have you?"

"No. Mavis told him she's staying in because she has a cold. But she can't hold that line much longer. Thelma's been running things at Mae's, but she starts vacation next week."

"I checked on Mavis at noon. She don't look too bad for what she's been through. Probably because you're the one who stayed with her after that rainstorm last night instead of me. Look's like she's tryin' to heal."

"The scars are all on the inside."

"Then you need to spend all the time you can helpin' her get better."

"I am," said CJ, thinking as he walked out the door, *That's why I'm about to entrust you with the better part of what's been my whole damn life.*

◆ ◆ ◆

CJ and Flora Jean's 5:30 meeting with Julie was a step above the somberness of a funeral. Julie laid out preliminary plans for a partnership agreement, told each of them to give the issue at least two days of serious thought before acting, and said she'd handle things on the real estate end with Dave   Johnson.

Sitting in CJ's office in a reupholstered chair that had been Ike's favorite, Julie pushed aside the sample legal forms she'd brought for Flora Jean and CJ to have a look at and said, "Now that that's done, I've got a piece of information on Le Quan that my law clerk dug up. Seems that during the late 1970s, Quan was a broker for the hordes of Vietnamese boat people like Carmen and Ket who fled their homeland for the United States. He wasn't a biggie; lots of people brokered deals for refugees, taking their money, property deeds, artifacts, and anything of value in return for safe passage to the United States. But it turns out that Quan was also brokering safe-passage deals for U.S. military deserters. Whether it was Quan or someone else who gave Blue a free trip home, it might explain how Blue got back to the States and ultimately to West Virginia."

"Makes sense, but why would Quan, Margolin, or anyone else want Langston Blue back on U.S. soil? If they were trying to bury something that had happened in Vietnam, they sure wouldn't want him stuck under their noses," said CJ.

"No. But they might want him under their thumb," Julie countered. "It's always important to have a way of controlling a loose cannon. Especially if what happened at the Song Ve schoolyard had international war-crime implications. And Blue, after all, is a little slow. If whoever brought him back from Vietnam sold him on the idea that they were protecting him, keeping him out of military prison, they'd have their cake and be able to eat it too. Blue would be there if necessary to tell his story and theirs to the whole world, and they'd also have someone who was beholden to them and willing to keep his mouth shut for fear of going to prison."

"That's one way of looking at it."

"Have you got a better scenario?"

"No."

"Then chew on that one for a while. I'll talk to Blue about it tomorrow when Carmen and I go by to see him before his arraignment. And one last thing. It's not about Blue, the partnership, or the building. Just food for thought."

"Yes?" said CJ, looking perplexed.

"Sooner or later you're going to have to let the police deal with Celeste Deepstream. You can't keep waging your own private war with her. I talked to Mavis for twenty minutes before I came here. She's fragile. More fragile than you think. You can't ever let her get caught up in the middle of one of your messes again."

"I know," CJ said softly.

"Then talk to the police again. Who knows? It might help."

CJ looked up to see Flora Jean nodding. Swallowing hard, he locked eyes with Julie and said in the most peaceful voice she'd ever heard come out of his mouth, "I will."

Chapter

28

CJ TOOK A LONG DRAG on his next-to-last cheroot, looked up at Elliott Cole's building, and told himself that sooner or later even the most elusive politicos had to come home. He'd had no luck trying to get Cole to return his phone calls, so he'd pulled a photograph of Cole with the Republican senatorial candidate, Alfred Reed, off the state Republican Party's website, dug up Cole's surprisingly accessible Riverfront Park condominium address, and planted himself on a bench in front of the Japanese restaurant across the street. Morgan Williams, cell phone and color photo of Cole in hand, was staking out the building's back garage entry with instructions for Dittier to tip over his aluminum-can-filled shopping cart in front of Cole's car and block the entrance until CJ could get there if Cole showed at the back entry.

CJ planned to watch the building until 10 o'clock. If Cole didn't show by then, they'd regroup in the morning. It was now five past 7. The smell of deep-fried seafood wafted from the restaurant behind him, and his thoughts turned from Cole to the signature deep-fried catfish served at Mae's. He scanned the block-long, eighty-foot-wide courtyard square, taking in the lay of the land. The northern boundary included the restaurant and the Riverfront development showroom, with its full-scale window model of the entire planned development. Three stories of lofts rose above the showroom and restaurant. Across the courtyard from where he sat, an assortment of shops took up the first floor of Cole's Riverfront Tower building. Little Raven Street bordered the building to the west. A dry cleaner and bank occupied the first floor of the Promenade Lofts building that sat just east of Cole's building, and the Millennium Bridge anchored the courtyard's eastern edge, completing the square.

During the hour that he'd been there, foot traffic in the square had been minimal. Most of the people he'd seen had been restaurant goers. As they'd leave, at least half of them would gravitate to the Millennium Bridge, where they'd climb its three tiers of steps to view the towering masthead or have their photos taken in front of it.

Thirty minutes into the stakeout, a city public works crew had shown up with jackhammers, two giant air compressors, and stacks of blaze-orange construction zone cones and parked on Little Raven Street, the street that paralleled the courtyard square to the west. Several minutes later a flatbed semi loaded with ten-inch pipe and carrying an offloader pulled up and blocked the entire street. Aware that the best development planning in the world had to accommodate the occasional retrofit, CJ suspected that by the next morning the idyllic Tuscany-style setting would be a zone of clanging sewer pipe, roaring jackhammers, air compressors, and heavy machinery.

He might have missed spotting Cole walking down the Millennium Bridge steps toward him if Cole hadn't moved briskly past his own building and walked over to several of the construction workers.

Five-foot-ten, fit-looking, and outfitted in a Stetson and cowboy boots, Cole shook hands with the crew's white-hatted foreman. They chatted for a couple of minutes until Cole slapped the man on the back, grinning, then pivoted and headed for his building. He was halfway across the courtyard when CJ intercepted him.

"Construction's a bitch, ain't it?" said CJ, smiling, blocking Cole's path.

"Sure is," said Cole, trying his best to place CJ. "Looks like they'll be here for a couple of months. New sewers."

"Drag. By the way, I'm CJ Floyd. Been trying to connect with you all day, Mr. Cole."

The look on Cole's face turned defensive. "Can't talk to you now." He sidestepped CJ and headed for his building.

CJ continued with him stride for stride. "Doesn't matter to me. Sooner or later you're gonna have to talk to me about Star 1 teams, Langston Blue, and Peter Margolin's murder. It's talk to me now or talk to the cops later."

Cole stopped and stared straight at CJ. "What do you want, Floyd?"

"Not much. Just an answer or two."

"Like what?"

"Like what happened at Song Ve?"

"Fuck you, asshole." Cole took off again.

"Ginny Kearnes told me you were Peter Margolin's commander when that Star 1 team of his went berserk."

Cole stopped again. His face had turned bright pink when he turned to face CJ, and his jaw muscles were twitching. "Captain Margolin was in command of his own fucking men. As for Kearnes, tell her to mind her own business." There was a look of disappointment on Cole's face, as if someone had let him down. "Now, get the shit out of my face." Cole brushed past CJ and pushed open the front door of his building. Turning back to CJ, he said, "You bother me again, Shine, and you'll get a chance to find out what I did in Vietnam."

"You call me Shine again and I'll kick your fucking ass, old man."

Cole drank in the defiant look on CJ's face and hurriedly disappeared into the building.

CJ stepped away, seething. He turned, stared up at the Millennium Bridge's mast, and tried to calm himself. Cole had surprised him by coming home from the downtown side of the bridge, more than likely arriving by light-rail. He had been even more surprised by Cole's belligerence. Telling himself that Cole wouldn't surprise him again, he walked away. The encounter hadn't produced much beyond the fact that Kearnes needed a much closer look.

As he headed across the empty courtyard toward the rear of the building to hook up with Dittier and Morgan, he had the sudden feeling that someone was watching him. He stopped and did a 360-degree sweep of the courtyard, now awash in the glow of twilight, but saw nothing. He continued walking, this time a little more briskly, unable to get the sense that he was being followed or the image of Celeste Deepstream out of his head.

◆ ◆ ◆

Trying her best to get comfortable on the back of Carmen's 1947 Indian Chief motorcycle, Flora Jean shifted her weight to the right as Carmen turned left off Alameda Avenue onto Federal Boulevard. "Sit still, Flora Jean," Carmen yelled, leaning into the turn and gunning the vintage machine to keep them from taking a spill.

They sped several blocks through light late-evening traffic, made a right turn on Kentucky Avenue, and followed the street west for several blocks until Carmen shut down the engine, doused the bike's headlight, and let the Indian coast to a stop behind a towering Colorado blue spruce, several car lengths from a shabby six-unit apartment building on the corner of Kentucky and Patton Court.

"Thank God," said Flora Jean.

Carmen slipped off her helmet and turned to face Flora Jean. "You're not meant for motorcycles."

"You're tellin' me?" Flora Jean backed off the uncomfortable jumpseat and rubbed her butt. "Too much metal for these sweet buns, sugar."

Carmen smiled. "I told you the Indian was mint, Flora Jean. No convenience packages—and that means no padded rumble seat."

Flora Jean shook her head. "Next time we take my vehicle. Vietnamese or not, sugar, you're gonna stand out like the icing on a cake if we follow Moc around on this thing."

"Maybe, maybe not," said Carmen, unconvinced. "One thing for certain, it'll get us out of a tight spot a lot faster than a car if it comes down to it. Besides, we're in Little Vietnam; there're motorcycles everywhere."

"Hope so. Just like I'm hopin' that tailin' Moc turns out to be more than just a joy ride. It cost me fifty bucks to get one of his car-wash buddies to tell me where he lived and another hundred to get him to tell me about that club Moc supposedly frequents." Flora Jean eyed the apartment building. "Looks like he was right about one thing. Moc's place is just as funky as he described it." She glanced across the street. "That Neon, the one with the dent in the nose. It's Moc's. Now, if the little worm does spend all his nights at that China Bay club like his buddy claims, my money was well spent."

"What do you expect to find there?"

"Information, and maybe a few contacts, sugar. People who'll be willin' to give us inside dope on Moc and maybe even Le Quan and that ice-queen daughter of his. Just remember, I do the trollin', you do the throttlin'."

"I will, but . . ."

"Surf's up," whispered Flora Jean, watching a lone figure saunter toward the Neon.

"Is that him?"

"Yes."

"Not much to him," said Carmen, taking in Moc's wispy five-foot-four-inch build.

"Maybe not. But I betcha he's packin'."

"What makes you think so?"

Flora Jean smiled. "Intuition, sugar. And them baggy pants he's wearin' with the ten different pockets. Now, let's see where he'll take us."

Moc slipped into the Neon, turned on the engine, made a U-turn, and headed west on Kentucky.

"Hop on." Carmen cranked the Indian as Flora Jean grimaced and reseated herself. "He sure ain't headed back for Federal," said Flora Jean.

"Maybe he's got a pit stop to make before he hits that club."

"Hope it's a short drive," said Flora Jean, her arms wrapped tightly around Carmen's waist.

"Me too." Carmen nosed the Indian away from the curb, her eyes locked on the taillights of Jimmy Moc's Neon.

◆ ◆ ◆

With a carton of cigarettes swinging from his left hand, Jimmy Moc made a cell-phone call outside a 7-11 fifteen blocks from his apartment, grinning and spitting love bouquets into the phone's mouthpiece. His voice became louder as he walked toward his car.

"He's high," said Carmen, whispering to Flora Jean from their vantage point across the 7-11's parking lot, where a pop-up camper obstructed Moc's view of them.

"What makes you say that?" asked Flora Jean.

"He's unsteady, slurring his words, and loud. I spent two years as an ER doc, remember?"

"Can you make out what he's sayin'?"

"Only the words *baby* and *fuck*."

"Horny little toad."

"He's in the car!"

Flora Jean waited for Moc to start the engine. As he pulled away, she said, "We'll follow him 'til we're sure he's goin' to that China Bay place, then pull in a few minutes later if he does." Flora Jean was all business. "We go in the place and come out together. No potty breaks, and no movin' away from me for drinks or food. You stick to me like glue, got it?"

Carmen nodded.

"And just so you know, Moc ain't the only one packin'."

◆ ◆ ◆

Ten minutes later Jimmy Moc disappeared inside the corrugated-steel, single-story China Bay club, a square box that had been retrofitted with a facade to give it the look of a 1960s Saigon bar and nightclub. The low-hung ceilings, grass-cloth walls, bamboo furniture, smoked-glass-topped tables, and strobe lights gave the club the dark, eerie feel of one of the Vietnam war pleasure palaces frequented by American GIs. A small dance floor barely large enough for three couples flanked a fifteen-foot-long mahogany bar with a floor-to-ceiling mirror behind it. Both ran almost the entire length of the mildly acidic, Pine-Sol-smelling room. Piped-in Hawaiian music played in the background as Flora Jean and Carmen walked in.

"They call this a nightclub?" said Flora Jean, shaking her head as they headed for an empty table a few steps from the dance floor. "Shit, it ain't nothin' but a grimy-assed bar."

As they took seats at a wobbly table, Flora Jean scanned the room, her eyes still adjusting to the darkness. A sign taped to the mirror above the bar read, *Capacity 60 people.* Noting that

Jimmy Moc was nowhere to be found in the half-empty room, she scooted her chair up to the table and nodded for Carmen to do the same. Moments later, a waitress dressed in jeans and a gravy-stained pink blouse appeared. "Something to drink, ladies?"

"I'll have a Seven and Seven," said Flora Jean.

"A Coke," said Carmen, smiling at the waitress and carefully studying her features before picking up a menu from the table. She opened the menu but continued eyeing the waitress as the woman retreated. "She's Amerasian," Carmen said, looking around the room. "So's the tall guy over behind the bar and the man and woman three tables over." She paused in disbelief. "And the two guys at the table next to the blacked-out window."

"Still don't see Moc," said Flora Jean, nodding.

"Did you hear me, Flora Jean? Almost everybody in here's Amerasian."

"I heard you," Flora Jean said, recalling the old Southern adage that one black person could spot another one anywhere in the world. "Maybe Moc's more comfortable hangin' out with his own."

"They're all *my den*, Flora Jean, half-breeds just like Moc and me. Everybody in the place."

"Ain't against the law."

"But it's noticeable and damn shit different."

"Heady language," said Flora Jean, arching her neck, unaccustomed to hearing Carmen curse. "I get your drift, sugar. Now we got ourselves some information we didn't have before we came." Glancing at a restroom sign above a doorway draped with a curtain, she nodded and said, "Moc's back."

Moc angled across the dance floor and took a seat at a table with a petite Amerasian woman.

"What do we do now?" asked Carmen as their waitress appeared with drinks.

"Keep an eye on our mark. He'll spot me sooner or later. Everybody else in the room has. We'll see what he does." Flora Jean took a sip of her drink, sat back in her chair, and listened to the final melodic strains of "Blue Hawaii."

A half-dozen more Hawaiian tunes had played and the woman he was talking to had left when Moc spotted Flora Jean. There was as much surprise as terror on his face. He quickly finished the drink he'd been nursing, walked over to another table, spoke to a muscular man with a tattoo of a snake encircling his neck, and returned to his table. A few moments later Snake Neck rose and walked over to Flora Jean and Carmen's table. "You ladies don't seem to be havin' no fun," he said, looking squarely at Carmen. "Maybe you're in need of a man."

"We're doin' just fine," said Flora Jean.

Still looking at Carmen, the man said, "What do you say to that, sweetie?"

"The same as my sister," said Carmen.

Looking astonished, the man leaned back and slapped his forehead. "You two are sisters? Wouldn't have expected it. Guess the old man did a lot of wick-dippin'."

"Just like yours," said Carmen, staring at the man's almond-shaped eyes, broad-based nose, light olive skin, and straight jet-black hair.

The man laughed. His breath had the rancid smell of stale liquor.

"Jimmy Moc a friend of yours?" asked Flora Jean.

"We know each other."

"And Le Quan? Do you know him, too?"

The man eyed Carmen. "The shoe guy? Who don't? He has one hell of a good-lookin' daughter, but she can't hold a candle to you. Can I get a name, sweetness?"

"Carmen."

"Ummm, that's different. Thought I knew every mixed-breed from here to the Utah border. Where're you from?"

"Now you know one more," Flora Jean interjected.

"What's the story behind Amerasian City here?" asked Carmen.

The man broke into a full-gauge laugh. "It's a tropical paradise for half-breeds. Can't you hear the music in the background?" The man reached across the table and put his hand over Carmen's. "Wanna dance?"

Carmen pulled her hand away. "Don't think so."

"Oh, I see. One of our uppity *my den*s."

"Think you should probably move on," said Flora Jean.

"Think I'll stay," Snake Neck said defiantly.

"Okay," said Flora Jean, glancing across the room, noticing that Jimmy Moc was preparing to leave. "But you're on your own." She slipped a ten-dollar bill out of her pocket, slapped it on the table, and looked at Carmen. Nodding toward Moc, she said, "Let's go." Looking back at Snake Neck, she said, "Shame we didn't really get to know one another," as she and Carmen rose and headed toward the exit.

As they made their way across the China Bay club's parking lot, Flora Jean took note of a couple of motorcycles parked at the lot's edge that hadn't been there when they'd arrived. Moc was standing next to one of the bikes. As they continued walking across the dimly lit lot toward the Indian, Moc called out, "Hey, ladies, want you to meet a couple of friends." Seconds later Moc and two engineer-booted Amerasian men who looked to be in their early twenties had stepped in front of the Indian, blocking Carmen and Flora Jean's way.

"Hell of a ride," said one of the men, eyeing the bike.

"Bet you're even better," said his stocky friend, grinning at Carmen, who began edging around him toward the rear of the Indian.

"Move out of my way, sugar," Flora Jean said to the stockier man, who now stood directly in front of her. She eyed Moc. "Better tell your friend I mean what I say, Jimmy."

"Never really been able to get him to listen to me. Besides, I owe you for the other day." Moc slipped a six-inch hunting knife out of one of the three pockets that stair-stepped down one side of his baggy khakis, unsheathed it, and moved toward Flora Jean. "Don't know whether I should mark you on the right or left," Moc laughed.

Stern-faced, with a look of intensity in her eyes that Carmen had never seen before, Flora Jean said, "You gonna get yourself killed, you don't watch out, son."

Moc inched the hunting knife toward Flora Jean's face. He was halfway into a broad, toothy grin when the toe of Flora Jean's boot caught him solidly in the groin. He spun backward, arms spread, and dropped screaming to the asphalt. The knife skated handle first into the Indian's rear tire and stopped.

"Get on the bike, Carmen," Flora Jean said calmly.

The chunky man moved toward her as the other man stooped to help Moc. "Take another step and I'll blow off your nuts." Flora Jean aimed the Walther .25-caliber pistol she'd pulled out of her pocket squarely at the man's crotch. The Indian's throaty roar punctuated fifteen seconds of stand-off silence. With the Walther still trained on him, Flora Jean sidestepped the man, took two steps backward, and straddled the uncomfortable jumpseat. Glaring at Moc, who was still on the ground, writhing in pain, she retrieved the hunting knife and said, "Think I'll keep it." Wrapping her arms around Carmen's waist, she barked, "Let's roll."

Carmen throttled up, whizzed past a still dazed Jimmy Moc, the Indian's rear tire screaming, and blasted onto Federal. As the Indian gained speed and she wove in and out of traffic, she could feel her heart pounding. But strangely, as tightly as Flora Jean was hugging her, she couldn't feel Flora Jean's heart racing one bit.

Chapter
29

ELLIOTT COLE SAT AT THE EDGE of a floor-hugging frame-less bed, naked except for his socks. The look of pleasure on his face broadened. Close to fulfillment, he glanced at Le Quan, who was seated across the room, and said, "There's no other way to deal with Floyd and his partner," as the nude, doe-eyed Vietnamese woman down on her knees in front of Cole lubri-cated his fully erect penis with a sandalwood-scented gel and returned to stroking it.

Le Quan looked out the second-floor bedroom window of the clapboard-sided farmhouse into the night, oblivious to Cole and the woman, wishing he were still at his shoe store making sales. Hours earlier following his encounter with CJ, Cole had demanded that Quan make the drive to the eighty-acre farm that had been in the Cole family for three-quarters of a century. The farm, eighty-five miles northeast of Denver, was surrounded by other farms and thousands of acres of corn, wheat, and milo.

Uninterested in the sex game being played out behind him, Quan asked, "How did Floyd end up in the way?"

Near climax, his buttocks now barely touching the mattress, his back fully arched, Cole said in a low rumble, "I don't know."

He then screamed, "Yes, yes, finish it!" as the woman brought him to a tumultuous climax. She quickly wiped away his semen and draped a large, moist, heated towel over him. Waving her off as if she'd never been there, Cole looked at her and smiled. "Get dressed and go downstairs."

The woman nodded and quickly disappeared.

Cole rested back onto his elbows. Matter-of-factly, as if he'd never been aroused, he said, "Somehow Floyd's tied to Blue."

"Should've killed Blue at Song Ve," said Quan.

"But we didn't."

"Now we pay."

"I never pay," said Cole. "I get paid, or have you forgotten?"

Quan gritted his teeth. "How we deal with Floyd, then?"

"We'll use Chi," said Cole.

"No!"

"She's a woman. It'll be easier for her to get close to him."

"Won't use her!"

"Then who?" asked Cole.

"Moc."

Cole shook his head. "We can't trust him. The little fucker spends too much of his time trying to figure out how to play both ends against the middle."

"He's family," said Quan.

"And I'm the fucking king of Siam. Goddamn half-breeds like Moc are the reason our balls are in the fire in the first place."

"And the reason you got all this," Quan admonished, licking his right thumb, slamming it into his left palm, pretending to count out money.

Ignoring Quan, Cole said, "You're awfully loyal to a *my den* lowlife like Moc."

"He the son of my sister."

Cole shook his head. "You're a trip, Quan. A fucking trip. Today he's the son of your sister. Thirty-five years ago you wanted every Jimmy Moc in the world's head on a stick."

"Times change."

"That they do." Cole raised himself off his elbows. "We'll use Moc. But the little half-breed better not fuck up. I'll keep an eye on him myself. Family, my ass. That cocksucker would sell you out for a dime."

Quan was silent, having dealt with Cole's arrogant outbursts for years. During the war he'd supplied Cole with women, which he continued to do. He'd catered to his wishes and listened to him whine. He'd made money because of Cole, a small fortune, in fact, but the Margolin thing had pushed him to his limit, and this time, when all the loose strings were knotted, he and the brash, over-the-edge former colonel whom he'd met on a rainy day in Quang Ngai province while at the zenith of his communist youth-organizing days would have to part ways. Eyeing Cole with disdain, he said, "I'll contact Jimmy."

Cole, who'd seen the same look on Quan's face scores of times before, simply smiled. "Still don't like taking orders, do you, Quan? Well, here's one more. Have Chi send Do Thi back up here to finish her business. And have her bring a gin and tonic with her." Cole reached beneath the towel, cupped his penis, and laughed. "Don't think too hard about things, Le, my boy. It might hurt your brain."

Gritting his teeth, Le Quan turned and left.

◆◆◆

Chi Quan was pacing back and forth in front of the farmhouse's draped living room picture window when her father appeared at the foot of the stairway. The floors of the half-century-old farmhouse creaked as he walked toward her. He nodded for Do Thi, who was wrapped in a white floor-length terry-cloth robe, to go back upstairs. "And take his gin." Quan whisked a half-empty bottle of gin from a nearby table and handed it to the nervous-looking woman as she left the room.

Angry at herself for not having put Cole in his place years earlier, Chi said, "What does he want us to do?"

"Have Jimmy take care of things."

Chi stopped pacing. "Is he crazy? Jimmy can barely take care of himself. That black woman who came to see you will eat him for lunch."

Quan frowned. "Only two choice—you or Jimmy."

Chi thought about how far she'd come from the moldy bug-infested rat trap of a triplex she'd lived in for the first six years of her life. She thought back to having to share a building that should've been condemned with twenty other Vietnamese boat people, about years later losing her mother to cancer, about crying and nightmares and urinating in her bed. And Cole was the man who'd put them there. The man who had made her and Robert and her mother and father wait and suffer and struggle.

Cole and Margolin, two men without conscience, men who'd helped destroy her homeland.

She had never known why it had taken so many years for Margolin and Cole to settle up with her father, only that it had. But she knew about Song Ve and what had happened there, painfully aware that her father had been a middleman between Vietnamese men without conscience and Americans in search of cash. Frustrated and boiling with anger, aware that she could never go back to being the equivalent of a boat person again, she asked, "What does he want you to do about the black woman and Floyd?"

"What you think?"

Chi thought for a moment as she listened to the grunts and groans coming from upstairs. She wondered what could happen if Floyd or the woman were able to squeeze the truth out of a story that had been buried for over thirty years.

Looking at her father, she said meekly, "Let me talk to Jimmy."

Quan shook his head. "Don't get involved. Leave to Jimmy."

"This time I can't," she said, shaking her head as she pulled back the drapes and stared out into the surrounding 2 a.m. darkness. She'd spent too much time living the American dream, and she knew it. She could never go backward.

◆ ◆ ◆

Carmen, Flora Jean, and Mavis, who'd spent half the night up talking, were seated in the breakfast nook just off Mavis's kitchen, enjoying the bright morning sunshine. They were sipping orange juice and finishing the last of four fresh gourmet raisin rolls that Mavis had brought home from the Left Bank Bakery and Café in LoDo the previous evening.

"CJ's gonna have a fit," said Mavis, puffy-eyed from lack of sleep. "Next to sweet-potato pie, raisin rolls are his favorite. He's expecting to have them for dessert this evening."

"Go get him a refill," said Flora Jean, polishing off the last of her roll.

"Can't. They only bake them on Tuesdays and Thursdays."

Pouting her lips and trying to sound as nasal as possible, Carmen said, "C'est une chose Française," aware from their late-hour conversation that they were all fluent enough in French to translate "It's a French thing." She had learned the language from Ket and by way of her early-childhood schooling in Vietnam, Mavis via a college language requirement and a year abroad in Paris, and Flora Jean as the result of a marine corps directive that required all sergeant-major-level intelligence types to be fluent in a second language. They erupted in laughter as Carmen, still pouting, stood and stuck out her derriere can-can style.

Mavis was aware that in one night Flora Jean and Carmen had returned something to her that Celeste had stolen, something that regardless of the depth of his love for her, or his overprotective hour-by-hour perimeter checks of the house as she slept at night, CJ couldn't possibly provide: a woman's sensibility.

"You better get your man some sweet-potato pie, then," said Flora Jean, forcing back a final giggle.

"I'll call Thelma and ask her to drop one by on her way home from Mae's," said Mavis.

"Fast thinkin', sugar. But not as fast as Carmen peeled that Indian of hers outta harm's way last night." Reenacting their getaway from the parking lot of the China Bay club for the fourth time, her knees bent, Flora Jean mimicked straddling the Indian, then burst from her chair and raced from the breakfast nook through the kitchen, weaving between stools, plants, and a three-foot-tall copper vase before returning to stop on a dime just short of Carmen. "For a sawbones, you're somethin', sugar," she said, laughing. "Hell, I thought you was gonna kill us weaving in and outta that traffic on Federal. I'm tellin' ya, Mavis, the girl could've been a marine."

"No way," countered Carmen. "Flora Jean's the one. The way she drop-kicked Jimmy Moc and sent him sprawling. I thought she was a Hollywood stuntwoman."

"Nope," said Flora Jean. "Just your basic out-of-work East St. Louis sista who Uncle Sam plucked off the street one day and taught how to drop-kick. Ask that fiancé of yours, Rios, how long it took the staff at Quantico to teach somebody with legs as long as mine that move. Sugar, I'm a legend."

"I'll ask Mr. Daredevil as soon as he gets back from that whitewater shoot of his in Bolivia. Men!"

Carmen's comment rekindled a sudden sense of vulnerability in Mavis. She eyed the floor sheepishly. Sensing the mood swing, Flora Jean said, "Told you last night, you can't take away what makes a man tick, Mavis. CJ's gonna cut back, let me handle the lion's share of the business, but trust me, he ain't the kind that can spend the rest of his life peddlin' antiques. You're comin' off a bad time right now, sugar, but it won't stay that way forever. You got me and Carmen here to ease the hurt, and you got your man. And although you may not think so right now, you gonna pretty much need him the way he's always been."

"I'll work at it," Mavis said softly. "But once he's out of the bail-bonding business, I don't want him ever going back again."

"Then point the man in a new direction. But whatever you do, don't let your experience with that Deepstream woman be the thing that breaks his will. Hear me?"

"Loud and clear."

Eyeing an antique wall-mounted kitchen clock, Flora Jean said, "Damn! I gotta get out of here and head for work."

"CJ'll want to know about last night," Mavis said, trying her best to sound vested in her man.

Flora Jean grinned. "Don't worry—he'll get the unedited version." Rubbing her butt, she eyed Carmen. "Almost forgot, sugar; I don't have a car. I'm gonna need a ride."

As Carmen rose from her chair, Flora Jean added, "And this time, try not to make it the ride of my life."

◆◆◆

CJ eased the gas nozzle into the Bel Air's gas tank, squeezed down on the handle, and set the automatic shut-off. Rosie's Garage was flush with business. All three of the auto service bays had cars up on hydraulic lifts, and five of the six stately 1940s-style gas pumps were in use. "You're hummin' this morning," said CJ, looking up at Rosie, who, shop rag in hand, was busily wiping away fingerprints from the Bel Air's doorjamb.

"Gas prices just went down, that's the reason. Don't mean nothin'. They'll go up again next week." Eying the Bel Air's coral-red lacquer paint job, he said, "No more prints," slipped the shop rag into his back pocket, and took a step back to admire his handiwork. "How's Mavis doin'?" he asked, having gotten a blow-by-blow about the kidnapping from CJ a couple of days earlier.

"Fine. Flora Jean and I have been taking turns staying with her at night. Last night was Flora Jean's turn." CJ thought about telling Rosie that he was planning to sell his building and business but decided to wait for a time when they both had beers in their hands.

The gas nozzle clicked off with a thump at $19.39. CJ nursed the pump to an even $20.00 as Rosie said, "You ain't seen no more of that Deepstream woman, have you?"

"No."

"You will. She ain't the kind that's gonna drop the issue."

"So I've been told," said CJ, his jaw muscles tightening as he thought about what she'd done to Mavis.

Sensing that CJ was about to continue a battle that might end up getting him killed, Rosie said, "Call the cops, CJ."

CJ eyed his old friend quizzically. "Have you been talking to Julie?"

"No."

CJ teased his wallet out of his back pocket, slipped out a twenty, and handed it to Rosie. "You sure?" he said, still perplexed.

Rosie shrugged. "Come on, CJ."

CJ shook his head and housed the gas nozzle. "I'll be talking to you," he said, slipping into the Bel Air.

"Later." As Rosie waved his old friend off, he realized that he was perspiring, his stomach was undulating, and he felt a sudden heavy dose of guilt. During all the years they'd known one another, he couldn't remember ever lying to CJ before then. He had in fact talked to Julie because he was concerned about CJ and about Mavis's safety. And, whether CJ liked it or not, if CJ didn't follow up some more with the cops, he'd call them himself.

◆◆◆

CJ took the long way from Rosie's to his office, top down on the Bel Air, hoping the ride would give him time to think over the Langston Blue case. He eased down tree-lined Monaco Parkway, the Bel Air's speedometer pegged just below 30, thinking that there were plenty of people who had reason to kill Peter Margolin. At the moment, Elliott Cole and Le Quan topped his list. He was certain that Cole, Quan, and Margolin had been involved during Vietnam in something so horrific that the long arm of international war-crimes law could probably still reach out and touch them. What he wasn't certain of was that Cole or Quan had killed anyone. They could easily have hired Jimmy Moc to do their bidding, or Lincoln Cortez, the invisible man with the cane who'd set Langston Blue on his cross-country run in the first place. It wasn't a stretch to make Cortez the killer. Shaking his head and thinking, *Hell of a mess,* CJ pulled to a stop at the corner of Monaco and 6th Avenue Parkway as a partially restored, recently primed '65 Mustang convertible filled with teenagers cruised up alongside him. The girl riding shotgun eyed the Bel Air lovingly and called out, "Sweet!"

"That your car, mister?" said the boy behind the wheel.

"Yeah."

"You must be rich," giggled a pimple-faced girl in the backseat.

"Not hardly."

"Looks like it to me." The girl was on her knees, pointing back at the Bel Air as the light changed and the Mustang sped off.

Laughing at the thought of being rich, he continued down 6th Avenue Parkway, partially shaded from the intense morning sun by the overhang of eighty-year-old elm trees. Thinking about what Julie and now a pimple-faced teen had said, he told himself it was time to forget about war atrocities and start following the money. That was at least one place where, except for the dead man, he'd met all the players. And since Ginny Kearnes, Margolin, and Cole had been involved in a $75 million building project, it was time to start looking forward instead of backward.

Nosing the Bel Air toward the office and home, he thought about following the money, wondering as he did what it was really like to be rich.

◆◆◆

Elliott Cole sat in his office, fuming. The Owen Brashears editorial in the *Boulder Daily Camera* as much as said that the Republican Party leadership, and worse, by inference, their candidate Alfred Reed, might somehow be behind Peter Margolin's murder. There were innuendos suggesting that friction between Cole and Margolin had started thirty years earlier in Vietnam, when he'd been Margolin's battalion commander. What irked him most about the article was that there had been nothing but bouquets, love pats, and love-ins for Peter Margolin.

There was nothing in the piece about Song Ve, Star 1 teams,

or Langston Blue's defection. Brashears had been more subtle. He understood the editorial's purpose, the world of politics, and the mark it needed to strike. Cole was certain that Brashears was using the editorial page of his newspaper not simply to eulogize a friend but to sway the electorate. He was shaking when his secretary stuck her head in the door and said, "I have Mr. Brashears on line three."

"Thank you." Cole's voice trembled as he punched up Brashears on the line. "Brashears?"

"Yes."

"I'll sue the fuck out of you and your paper if you drop another shit-stain on me like you did today."

"Maybe you should read the big type at the top of the page, Elliott. I think it says, *Editorial*."

"I don't care what it says, you fucking weasel. We're talking libel."

Brashears laughed. "You're my tenth call today threatening libel. Had one earlier this morning from somebody claimin' we made him look bad because he got caught in a police prostitution sting. Comes with the territory."

"Listen, you prick. I know you've got problems with never being any more than a second-rate gossip-monger, but you're fuckin' with something here that's bigger than your need to be paperboy of the month. Keep pushing the envelope and you'll lose the blood supply to your testicles."

"My, my, my, Mr. Party Chairman. Our judicial system may have a lot of problems defining libel, but it sure as hell can recognize a threat."

"Call it what you like, you fucking loser. You're the same manipulative kiss-ass lying shit you were thirty years ago. I can still smell you in my nose hairs."

"I love you, too, Elliott. Remember, the smell of shit wafts both ways." Brashears laughed. "Looks like it's going to be one hell of an election."

"Have it your way, you asshole wannabe. But like they say, don't look back. Something might be gaining on you." Cole slammed down the phone, sat back in his chair, and briefly stared out of the window of his office before punching in Quan's number.

Chi Quan answered, "The Shoe Tree."

"It's Cole. Let me talk to your father."

Moments later Le Quan answered in a rush. "Busy. What you want?"

"We've got a new problem," said Cole, his voice seething with anger.

"What that?"

"We've got an editor who needs to learn some respect."

"Who that?"

"Margolin's friend, Owen Brashears."

"What we do?"

"I'll come by your place," said Cole. "I need to get off this line. How's noon?"

"Okay, I'll have Jimmy here."

"Good." Cole cradled the phone, stroked his chin, and walked to a nearby liquor cabinet. He didn't normally drink before lunch, but Brashears had pushed a button. He poured himself a stiff drink, stared out at the Denver skyline, and thought as the gin tickled the back of his throat that sometimes in the heat of battle you had to alter your course.

Chapter

30

GINNY KEARNES WAS SURPRISED by CJ's request to meet her at his favorite Mexican eatery, La Cueva, in the heart of old downtown Aurora. She had declined at first, but when CJ had intimated that he was homing in on Peter Margolin's killer, she had reluctantly agreed.

As they sat eating just-made tortilla chips and spicy salsa, Kearnes wasn't at all sure that she should've dropped what she was doing to come meet someone who, during the first few minutes of their conversation, had had nothing but disparaging things to say about the man she had planned to marry.

"You make Peter sound like a mercenary. He was fighting a war, in case you've forgotten," said Kearnes, accepting a steaming plate of tacos and refritos from Lorita Prado, daughter of the restaurant's owner.

"You're eating light today, CJ," Lorita said, handing CJ a small plate with a single taco.

CJ smiled. "Watching my weight." He'd ballooned up to just over 240 pounds, as he did nearly every summer, but at forty-nine, the extra weight he'd been carrying off and on for the past ten years had started to look like what it was, fifteen pounds of excess baggage. "Besides, I've got raisin rolls and ice cream waiting for me this evening."

Lorita smiled back. "Sounds like a reason."

Turning to Kearnes as Lorita walked away, CJ said, "Right now I don't know if Margolin was a mercenary, a fall guy, a traitor, or a hero." He took a bite of taco. "All I know is that he came back from Vietnam a whole lot richer than when he left."

Kearnes added a dollop of guacamole to her taco. "His family had money," she said in protest.

"Not the kind of money it would take to finance a seventy-five-million-dollar building." Deciding it was time to drop the bomb that he'd been saving, he added, "Maybe he only had a small interest in the project. Maybe you and Elliott Cole put up the lion's share of that seventy-five million."

Trying not to look surprised, Kearnes set her taco down on her plate, but her hand shook and the look on her face announced that she was. "Where did you get that information?"

"We may work different sides of the street, but I've got friends who occasionally stroll down yours. The real question is, why the secret?"

"It's not a secret. Look how easily your people found out. It's just that you don't go around broadcasting to the world that you're sleeping with the enemy. Politics is a messy business, Mr. Floyd. Word gets out that a high-profile Democrat like Peter, his press secretary, and the state Republican Party chairman are involved in a seventy-five-million-dollar business deal, and the public's eyebrows shoot skyward. Especially in the middle of an election."

"And the press starts digging?"

"That, too."

"Then why do it?"

Kearnes laughed. "You go where the money is or find out how to get it. Peter had part of the money for the investment, and Cole knew where to get the rest."

"And you?"

"They took me along for the ride."

"I see." CJ took another bite of his taco. "How much money did you put up?"

"I mortgaged my house, my car, and a small apartment building my mother left me, and I drained my retirement savings."

"How much?"

"$750,000."

"Out of my league," said CJ, his eyes ballooning.

"What about Margolin and Cole?"

"Peter put up seven million. Cole's ante was five."

"That's just under thirteen million," said CJ, adding the numbers. "Guess you don't need 20 percent down on your humble abode like us common folk when you're dealing with numbers that big."

"Yes, you do," said Ginny, scooping up a dollop of guacamole. "Sometimes more."

"If you do, my math says your cartel was still short a couple of million."

"Unless you've got connections," countered Kearnes.

"And Cole and Margolin had them?"

"They had something. Peter never told me what or who the connection was, but the construction loan papers and the promissory note I got back from the lawyer who handled the closing for us showed a down payment of fifteen million even."

"You were two and a quarter million dollars short, and out of the blue up pops that money. It had to come from somewhere," said CJ, rubbing his right temple.

"Well, I don't know where it came from!"

CJ picked up the slightly tepid Coke he'd ordered when they first arrived and took a sip. Eyeing Kearnes as if he wanted to slip inside her head, he asked, "How close were you to Margolin, really?"

"Have you lost your place in this book? We were engaged to be married."

"I understand that. I'm not talking about that kind of closeness. I'm talking about the kind that says *I know everything there is to know about this man.* How bad he snores, how many pairs of his drawers have holes in them, what brand of gum he chews when he's out of his favorite, how much money he makes, where he keeps his most prized possessions, who he owes money to, the names of every one of his former girlfriends, his sister's day of the month . . ."

"Stop!" said Kearnes, visibly offended. "Peter wore boxers, never briefs. His underclothes never had holes, and he didn't chew gum, ever. He made $158,100 a year, not counting speaking engagements that netted him another ten, and he kept all the most important things in his life, including letters we'd written to one another over the years, in a strongbox in the unfinished second-floor attic of his home."

It wasn't until CJ began smiling that she realized she'd been baited. Trying her best to maintain her composure, she said, "Oh, you're smart, Mr. Floyd. And your question tells me you've been in love. Who would've ever guessed it!"

"Which one?" said CJ. "That I'm smart or that I've been in love?"

"Both," said Kearnes, her tone meant to be biting. "What is it that you want, besides trying to prove that I didn't really know Peter?"

CJ looked at her intently. "Have you got the key to his house?"

"Of course," said Kearnes, as it dawned on her what CJ was really after. "But the police have been there a half-dozen times. They've probably already found what you're looking for."

"I'm betting they haven't."

"Why's that?"

"It's simple. Because they weren't in love with Peter Margolin."

Ginny shook her head. "You're a complex man, Mr. Floyd."

"And you're a loyal woman."

"Then you've run into my kind before."

"Once," said CJ, finishing off his taco. "Just once."

"She got a name?"

"Mavis," said CJ, looking Kearnes squarely in the eye.

◆◆◆

CJ followed Kearnes to Peter Margolin's Washington Park home, a brick two-story Tudor directly across the street from Denver's second-largest public park, and pulled up behind her in the driveway.

Ginny Kearnes glanced back nostalgically at the scores of joggers, walkers, and rollerbladers moving around the walkway that circled the park as she and CJ mounted Margolin's front steps. "Peter and I used to sit on this front porch for hours and watch the people traffic," said Kearnes wistfully. "Seems like so long ago." Looking at CJ, she said, "Have you ever had to grieve, Mr. Floyd?"

CJ thought about his Uncle Ike, looked skyward, and said, "Yes."

"Then you know it's a place you don't want to be for too long." She swung the front door open and they stepped inside a musty-smelling foyer. "That's if you want to keep your sanity," she added. "Let's get some light." She flipped a wall switch and the entryway was awash in light. "These old Tudors. There's never enough light. I never understood why Peter loved them so much." She glanced back at the mail slot in the door and down at the entryway's Spanish-tiled floor. "No mail. Looks like Peter's lawyer's been by. He's handling the estate."

"Did Margolin have any relatives?"

"A great-uncle in a nursing home in Montana. That's it. Why? Are you looking for an heir or a murder motive?"

"Just don't want to overlook anything."

"I've done some thinking myself, and some overlooking and underlooking, too," she said. "I've thought long and hard about who might have wanted to see Peter dead. And the surviving men from his Star 1 team always end up topping the list. There's nothing to connect either Blue or Cortez directly to the murder. No physical evidence, no phone calls, no threats. But there's still Peter's day planner note. The one where he reminds himself to ask someone named Cortez about Langston Blue. Since the police are, at least for the moment, saying Blue isn't Peter's murderer, I'd put my money on Cortez."

"Logical reasoning," said CJ, following Kearnes up a circular stairway that led to the second floor. "Except that no one has seen Cortez since Blue claims Cortez torched his cabin back in West Virginia."

"Cortez burned down the man's home? I'd say that's even more telling." She flipped on the lights as they walked down a short center hall. "The master bedroom's at the back of the house." She hesitated before entering the bedroom. "Coming here hurts," she said, opening the door.

The room inside was exquisitely furnished, filled with dark oak campaign-style furniture and antique accents. Seascape art adorned the stark white walls. The king-sized bed with its massive brass headboard had been stripped to the mattress cover.

Looking surprised, Kearnes said, "I wonder who stripped the bed? It wasn't stripped two days ago."

CJ shrugged, still drinking in the room. "Anything else look out of place?"

Kearnes slowly scanned the room. "No." She faced the wall to her left and said, very businesslike as if she wanted to get what they had come for and quickly leave, "The attic entry is behind that armoire." As she stared at the armoire, her eyes filled with tears. "It's still full of Peter's clothes."

CJ eyed her sympathetically. "Looks heavy."

"It is, but two people can move it. Peter and I have moved it lots of times."

CJ looked down at the carpet for signs that the armoire had been moved recently. There were no carpet tracks and no indentations. "Okay, whenever you're ready."

"Can I ask you something first? It's tied to my question about grieving."

CJ looked at the sad-faced, teary-eyed woman. "Fine."

"Was the person you were grieving for a woman?"

"No. My uncle."

"Then maybe it's not the same."

"Oh, it's the same."

"Does it ever go away? The pain, I mean?"

"In time it fades."

"You didn't answer my question."

Inching one side of the armoire away from the wall, CJ thought of those ice-clear days of winter when his office was drenched in sunlight and the ninety-year-old wooden floors suddenly began to expand and creak, when memories of Ike never failed to find him. "No," he said finally.

"At least you're honest," said Kearnes, easing her end of the armoire away from the wall.

They had moved the bulky piece of furniture three feet into the room before Kearnes said, "That's enough," and CJ spotted the three-by-four-foot door it had been hiding. "It lifts up like a garage door," she said. "The strongbox is somewhere about mid-attic, resting on a sheet of plywood. You'll have to tightrope the headers. It's tricky, so watch yourself. If you make a misstep there's nothing beneath you but insulation and the first-floor ceiling."

CJ shook his head. "You watched Margolin do this?"

"Several times. There's a light switch on the inside wall, on your left."

"Here goes." CJ raised the door, climbed into the attic, fumbled for the light switch, and flipped it. The attic was larger and seemed more forbidding than he'd expected. The toaster-oven-sized lockbox rested on a four-by-six-foot piece of plywood supported by headers. He tightroped his way down a header, dusty with insulation, steadying himself by grasping a rafter. He reached the box easily enough, hefted it, turned around, and started back. He was halfway to the door when he lost his balance. The lockbox dropped safely onto a three-foot cushion of insulation, but CJ's right leg punched through the clingy foam; his foot and a quarter of his leg slammed through the first-floor ceiling. "Shit!"

"What happened?" screamed Ginny.

"Lost my balance."

"You okay?"

"Yeah, but there's a hole in the ceiling below." Embarrassed, he wiggled his foot and leg back through the drywall hole and insulation, retrieved the strongbox, tucking it under his left arm, and followed the header back to the wall opening.

He handed the lockbox to Kearnes and crawled through the opening, insulation clinging to his clothes. "Won't try that again," he said, brushing himself off. "Hope the trip was worth it."

"You're gonna itch," she said, setting the lockbox down.

CJ brushed a prickly piece of the insulation off his neck. "Already do. Let's see what we've got," he said, nodding at the strongbox.

"Might as well." There was a hint of trepidation in her voice as Kearnes reached beneath one of the armoire's chunky legs and retrieved a key. She tossed it to CJ. "You open it."

CJ slipped the key into the lock and raised the lid. "It's full of papers." He pulled a two-inch-thick stack of rubber-banded 8.5-by-11-inch papers out of the lockbox and placed them on the bed. "And bigger papers," he said, thumbing through several legal-sized sheets. "Property deeds, one to this house." He placed one deed on the bed next to the first pile and read through a second deed quickly. "One to the high-rise. Your name's on the second one along with Cole's. And cash," said CJ, thumbing through three stacks of banded twenty-dollar bills. "Three or four thousand here at least." He set the bills aside.

"And the letters I told you about," said Kearnes, retrieving a stack of letters from the bottom of the lockbox.

"Not so fast. There're a few more things in here," he said, extracting four blank sheets of 11.5-by-13-inch paper from the strongbox. "Know what this stuff is?"

"First time I've ever seen it."

"Got something else. A bunch of faded newspaper clippings." He placed the blank sheets in a pile and began reading one of the newspaper clippings aloud. Before he'd finished the first paragraph his eyes were half-dollar sized.

Vietnamese Amerasians, the children of US citizens, primarily GIs and Vietnamese women who are uniformly viewed with disdain by their Vietnamese countryman, are the living unpopular legacy of America's longest war. Afflicted by poverty, lack of education, and unemployment and often abandoned, these children, referred to by their countryman as the dust of life, an expression used in Vietnam to define the poorest of the poor, are being resettled in cluster sites throughout the United States.

He placed the clipping face down on the bed, pressed out the folds, and opened a second one. "This one's about Amerasians, too."

He handed a couple of clippings to Kearnes, who quickly read them. "These too."

"Any dates on them?" asked CJ.

"No," said Kearnes, her eyes darting from one clipping to the other. "And no bylines, either. I'm guessing they're wire service stories. Wait a minute." She picked up one of the clippings and reread the last two paragraphs. "This one's about a family who resettled here in Denver. A woman and her son."

"Any names?" asked CJ.

"The mother's. Nam Kim Moc, age forty-one."

"I'll be damned." CJ's eyebrows arched skyward.

"You know her?"

"No, but I know a little about the man who's probably her son."

"Could he be Peter's killer?"

"Possibly."

"Why?"

"That I don't know," said CJ, teasing another legal-sized sheet of paper out of the lockbox. "Well, I'll be double damned," he said, reading down the page.

"What now?"

"Looks like you've got yourself a silent partner in that high-rise."

"What?"

He handed the document to Kearnes. The heading at the top of the page read, *Quit Claim Deed: Commercial.* Kearnes slowly read the deed's authoritative simple language.

*THIS DEED, Made this day of June 12, 2005, between Grantor Peter S. Margolin and Grantee Le Thi Quan, for the consideration of ***TEN DOLLARS AND OTHER GOOD AND VALUABLE CONSIDERATION*** IN HAND PAID, hereby sells and quit-claims to LE THI QUAN, Grantee, whose street address is 1388 South Federal Boulevard, City of Denver, County of Denver, State of Colorado, the following real property in Denver, County of Denver, and State of Colorado, to wit: ownership in the amount of 3% of the AIA appraised value in the below listed property. See attached legal description. Exhibit A. Also known as street and number 931 Cherry Creek Drive, South, TOGETHER with all its appurtenances. The singular number shall include the plural, the plural the singular, and the use of any gender shall be applicable to all genders. Signed as of the day and year first above written.*

"*Damn's* the right word," said Kearnes.

CJ turned over the lockbox and shook it. "This thing's a regular horn o' plenty. Don't wanna miss anything else. Guess maybe you didn't know your man as well as you thought."

Looking as if she'd just been kicked in the belly, Kearnes frowned and said, "Guess not."

◆◆◆

Two white helmeted army MPs out of Fort Carson, each one the size of an NFL nose guard, showed up at Denver's overcrowded concrete bunker of a jail to take Langston Blue into custody at precisely 4 p.m. It was clear but windy, and two tractor-trailers and a half-dozen RVs had been blown off I-25 at the exit just north of Monument Hill and the Palmer Divide twenty miles from Colorado Springs. The MPs, who didn't want to suffer the same fate in a soft-topped Humvee, were in a hurry to get back to Colorado Springs, but paperwork had slowed them down.

Julie Madrid and Carmen waited with Blue in a prisoner counseling holding area as Julie laid out her strategy for dealing with Blue's case, informing both father and daughter that there were precedents for his release.

Blue, seeming stupefied, sat handcuffed and shackled, eyes to the floor, in the drafty, cinderblock-walled room, a bunker that reeked of sweat, stale smoke, and urine.

Carmen, with an arm draped over her father's shoulders, forced back tears as, addressing Blue, Julie continued. "There'll be a court-martial, and you'll have to have an army-appointed lawyer, but I'll prepare the case and run all the traps."

"What about your fee?" Carmen asked.

"We'll deal with that later. Besides, a cheroot-smoking street cowboy I owe said I had to make my services affordable. Right now we need to look through those papers you brought."

Carmen hugged Blue, who barely responded. "The papers were right where you said. In a jewel case inside a lockbox under the front seat of your pickup. The case was beautiful. Was it my mother's?"

Blue nodded without answering.

Carmen handed Julie several sheets of paper. "The important one's on the bottom."

Julie thumbed through Blue's promotion papers to sergeant, two Bronze Star citations, and his marriage certificate before hitting paydirt, an official-looking citation that in three lengthy paragraphs exonerated Blue of desertion. "Never seen anything like this before," said Julie. "How did you get it? In fact, how did you get any of these things after Song Ve?"

"Wasn't easy," Blue said in a soft monotone. "Two months after Song Ve I gave a half-blind South Vietnamese army tunnel runner who'd deserted a couple of months before me the last five hundred dollars I had in the world, along with my weddin' band, watch, and dog tags, to take back to Mimm to show her I was still alive. The tunnel runner was gonna help us hook back up. He brought me the jewel box as proof that he'd met with Mimm. Two weeks later he told me Mimm was dead. It was a lie. I stayed on the run until those guys I told you about dropped out of the sky and picked me up."

"And this?" Julie held up the citation exonerating Blue.

"I got it after they parked me back in the West Virginia hills."

The strain of years of running and hiding was apparent in Langston Blue's eyes. He had the confused look of an animal who'd finally been trapped and overwhelmed. It was the same lost-soul look Julie so often saw in the eyes of the violent offenders she represented, three-quarters of whom had been abused as children. Blue was slower than normal, no question, but thankfully he was a world apart from those damaged souls, and he at least had Carmen. "They who?" she asked finally.

"Cortez and Margolin, I guess. I never saw Margolin after Song Ve, but Cortez gave me the citation, and for the first five years after I was back, he brought me the money I lived on—delivered it himself, once a year. After that, I picked the money up every six months at a post office box outside Baltimore."

"Why did you stay back in those hills?"

"Afraid, I guess. Afraid of showin' my face. Afraid of lettin' folks know I was a deserter. Afraid of goin' to prison."

"And afraid of Cortez and Margolin?"

For the first time since the conversation had started, Blue looked Julie square in the eye. "No. Them two never scared me." The look on his face reflected the fact that he meant exactly what he said.

"Who do you think killed Margolin?"

"Cortez, probably."

"What about Le Quan, that man you mentioned during our pre-arraignment conference, the one with the silver streak in his hair?"

Blue thought for a moment. "Don't know nothin' about him except he was at Song Ve. He could've killed the captain, I guess." Looking exhausted, Blue eyed Carmen. "You takin' care of my truck, baby?"

Caught off guard by the question, Carmen said, "It's safe in the garage below my condo."

"And you and Ket? How you two doin'?"

"Ket went home to Palisade this morning." Carmen squeezed her father's hand. "I'm fine."

The simple straightforwardness of Blue's questions and his concern for what in his mind mattered most gave Carmen new insight into a man she'd known for barely a week. It comforted her to know that the uncomplicated rule book in his head favored desertion, dishonor, and a life of exile over the commission of an atrocity and that concern for a dilapidated truck and a sister-in-law who'd cursed his memory for more than three decades outweighed self-concern. She was about to ask Blue if there was anything he needed when the sour-faced cop standing outside the room cracked the door, poked his head in, and said to Julie, "Time's up. Your boy's army escorts are here."

Blue, dressed in a baggy orange jumpsuit, followed Julie's lead and stood.

Carmen rose and gave him a hug and a kiss on the cheek. "Stay strong."

"You, too," said Blue.

"I'll be in touch as soon as you're processed at Fort Carson," said Julie.

Blue shook Julie's hand. "Thanks. And thank CJ and his people for me, too."

"I will."

The two MPs walked briskly into the room as the cop ushered Julie and Carmen out.

"Sergeant Langston F. Blue?" said one of the MPs, who now stood directly in front of Blue.

"Yes."

"You are now under the control of the U.S. Army."

Chapter

31

CARMEN STOOD IN CJ'S OFFICE, looking fascinated as Flora Jean pointed toward the last row of a photo gallery of the more than ninety bond jumpers CJ had delivered to justice during his years as a bail bondsman and reluctant bounty hunter. The gallery included a few photographs of him.

Unaware that CJ had walked in, Flora Jean said, "Hard to believe that CJ's hair was once black."

CJ, dressed in Levi's, a blue chambray shirt, and his trademark riverboat gambler's vest, rolled an unlit cheroot from side to side in his mouth. Tossing a large manila envelope onto his desk, he said, "Maybe I should start with the temples, get rid of the gray, fit in with the girls."

Startled, Carmen took a step backward, but Flora Jean remained unperturbed. "And while you're at it, why don't you get yourself a tutu?"

"Because my partner saved them all for herself."

The banter continued until smiling, Flora Jean said, "Have you been to check on Mavis?"

"Yes." CJ's tone was edgy. "Right after I met with Ginny Kearnes. But Mavis wasn't home. I checked the restaurant, logged in with Willis, and even went by Rosie's to see if she'd been by there. Nothing."

Flora Jean looked at Carmen. "What time did you leave Mavis's, sugar?"

"About 11."

"How was she doin'?" CJ asked.

"Fine."

Eyeing the new bandage on CJ's arm, Flora Jean said, "She's a big girl; she ain't gone far. See you got yourself a fresh wrap. Henry Bales do you up?"

"Who else? Says I'm healing just fine."

"You're too ornery not to. But you're a step behind Mavis. She got rid of that head wrap of hers last night. Her forehead's still a little swollen and her left eye's still puffy, but she's way past where she was three days ago."

"Sounds like she's on her way back to being a beauty queen," said CJ, feeling a bit less on edge. "Did you turn up anything during your motorcycle excursion last night?"

Flora Jean winked at Carmen. "We danced the two-step with Jimmy Moc."

"Who led?"

"Who else?"

"Get anything to connect Moc to the Margolin killing?"

"No. But we did find out somethin'. Go ahead, sugar," said Flora Jean, nodding at Carmen. "Paint CJ the picture."

"Okay. That place we followed Moc to—the China Bay club—

turned out to be a hangout for Vietnamese Amerasians. Every-body in the place looked like me. Seemed eerie."

"No different from being down on the Points any night of the week. Black folks everywhere. Like the lady in New York Har-bor says, give me your tired, your poor, your whatever," said CJ.

"There's more," said Flora Jean. "I ran a few things by Alden just before you came in. Also let him know that a couple of MPs from Fort Carson were truckin' Carmen's daddy down to Colorado Springs."

"And what did your general say?"

"Plenty! Enough to tell me we may'a been workin' the wrong angle on this Song Ve thing. We been workin' on the assumption that Blue's Star 1 team ran across a school full of pint-sized Viet-cong freedom fighters when all hell broke lose."

"That's been the take."

"But what if them kids weren't Vietcong trainees at all?" Flora Jean glanced at Carmen. "What did I say Alden called 'em?" She eyed Carmen for help.

"The dust of life," Carmen said hesitantly. Her eyes welled up. "Half-breed *my den* trash. People like me."

Flora Jean nodded and continued. "Alden said that in March 1968, the official communist newspaper, *Nhân Dân*, announced a new security decree. One that included the death penalty for a bushel-basket full of counter-revolutionary offenses. Twenty-one in all, includin' everythin' from your standard aidin' and abettin' the enemy, to failin' to faithfully honor party doctrine. Now, here's the kicker. Alden says that U.S. intelligence sources always claimed there was a twenty-second offense. One that was never published but still an offense that everybody on both sides knew about. The crime of bein' a half-breed."

"The offense of being *my den*," Carmen said softly.

"Heavy stuff," said CJ, shaking his head and lighting the cheroot.

"Alden says the North Vietnamese spent half the war tryin' to find ways to get rid of their ethnic-minority problems. Everybody knows about the Khmer Rouge and the Hmong, but the *my den* issue never surfaced. Eliminatin' an embarrassin' population of South Vietnamese American-sired *my den* children would've been right up their alley."

"Sounds plausible, but where does Blue's Star 1 team fit in?"

"That's the part Alden couldn't nail down, but you can bet a month's pay on this. The commies couldn't have started their ethnic cleansin' operation, without nailin' down two important things: a way to assemble a bunch of *my den* kids in one place and—now, here's the hairy part—either American political or military compliance."

CJ shook his head in disbelief. "Le Quan and Margolin's team."

"We're on the same page, sugar. And I'm bettin' if them two cooked up some kind of ethnic cleansin' deal, there was somethin' else involved—money."

"But do you think Margolin would risk treason?" asked Carmen.

"Bigger fish than him have risked it," said Flora Jean. "Why not?"

CJ nodded. "It fits."

"So, that's my story," said Flora Jean, with a grin. "Whatta you got?"

"Just like you, plenty. Turns out that seventy-five-million-dollar high-rise project Margolin was honchoing had financial backing from Ginny Kearnes, the squirrelly state Republican Party chairman Elliott Cole, and guess who else—our friend and former Vietnamese communist youth organizer Le Quan."

"Strange threesome," said Carmen.

"Yeah," said Flora Jean. "Kearnes I get, but Quan and Cole?"

"Turns out Cole was Margolin's Star 1 team commander. In fact, he's the one who stuck Margolin with the Song Ve assignment."

Flora Jean shook her head and took a seat. "Birds of a feather. Looks like we've got a hell of a lot more here than some thirty-five-year-old commando mission goin' south. Maybe I should get back to Alden—tell him what we've got. If he knows anything else and it ain't classified, he'll ante up. Meantime, what's next?"

"I'm going on a paper chase," said CJ.

Flora Jean frowned. "What?"

"I'm headed to see Mario Satoni, that old Italian guy in North Denver. The one who keeps his eye out for antique license plates for me."

"The one everybody in Five Points claims used to be a mobster?"

CJ smiled. "Hearsay, Flora Jean. Hearsay." A sly grin crept across CJ's face.

"How's he gonna help us?"

CJ retrieved the envelope he'd tossed on his desk and opened it. "I ran across something else of Margolin's." He slipped two of the newspaper clippings and two of the blank sheets of paper that he'd found at Margolin's out of the envelope. "Found them in a strongbox in his attic. Kearnes has a matching set." He handed the press clippings to Carmen, the blank sheets to Flora Jean. "Take a good look, Carmen, and start with the paper-clipped ones."

Halfway through the article about Vietnamese boat people settling in the United States, Carmen said, "It's pretty much on target."

"Keep reading."

Seconds later, Carmen shouted, "Moc!" and handed the press clipping to Flora Jean.

"Hell, if it ain't a story about sweet young Jimmy Moc and his mother. So what's the kicker?" Flora Jean asked.

"This. Kearnes and I found the press clippings, the blank sheets of paper, and a quit claim deed giving Le Quan what amounts to more than a two-million-dollar stake in Margolin's building tucked in that strongbox."

"Serious money," said Flora Jean, examining one of the blank sheets under CJ's desk lamp. "Find any of these with printin' on 'em?"

"Nope. Just four blank sheets."

A look of recognition spread across Carmen's face as she watched Flora Jean scrutinize the paper. "Hold on while I go get something from the Indian." She raced from the office, returning moments later with the citation exonerating her father. Out of breath she handed it to CJ and said, "Take a look."

CJ placed the document on his desk and read it before sliding one of the blank sheets next to it. "Same size. Same weight," he said, hefting the sheets separately. "I'd say they're at least kissing cousins."

"What are you thinkin'?" Flora Jean asked.

"Originally I thought that maybe I'd stumbled onto a counterfeiting scam. There was close to four thousand dollars, all in new twenties, in that strongbox. That's why I was going to see Mario." CJ extracted three crisp twenty-dollar bills from his vest pocket and laid them on the desk. "Now I'm not so sure. Why would anyone running a counterfeiting scam waste good paper stock printing up citations?"

"You would if it was the only thing handy," said Flora Jean. "Besides, who says they had to be counterfeitin' American money?"

CJ looked unconvinced. "Maybe. How'd your father get that citation?" he asked Carmen.

"He told Julie and me that it came from Cortez. Margolin and Cortez probably used it to convince him that if their backwoods relocation plan ever went sour, he'd have something tangible to prove he wasn't really a deserter."

"The thing's worthless."

"I know that, and you know that," Carmen said defensively. "But in case you missed it, my father's a little slow."

Looking embarrassed, CJ said, "Sorry."

"What matters is the damn thing's important," Flora Jean interjected. "Even so, I wouldn't scrub the counterfeitin' angle, not yet."

"So, I'll still go see Mario," said CJ. "And you go back to tailing Moc, Le Quan, and that dragon-lady daughter of his. See if you can't sniff out the truth behind Moc's Amerasian connection."

"Fine, but it'll have to wait 'til tomorrow. Got somethin' planned for tonight."

CJ smiled. "And when you see the general, make sure to ask him if we're missing something."

"I'll do that," said Flora Jean. "Whatta you got goin', sugar?" she asked Carmen.

"You wouldn't like it."

"Try me."

"I'm going dirt-bike riding. I need a diversion."

"You're right. Now I see why you and Rios connected. You're both daredevils."

"Gotta do something," said CJ. "Or else you'll wilt."

A woman's voice rose from the doorway behind him. "That's right!"

Suddenly all eyes were on Mavis. She was dressed in a stylish hunter-green pantsuit, with a hand-painted silk scarf wrapped strategically around her injured forehead. Walking across the room, she smiled at Carmen and gave Flora Jean a wink before her gaze stopped on CJ. "Brought you something," she said, placing the cake dish she was carrying on CJ's desk.

"What is it?" asked CJ.

"Take the lid off and see."

CJ raised the frosted lid slowly to find a still warm sweet-potato pie.

"Like you said, gotta do somethin'," said Mavis, touching two fingers to her lips and then to CJ's.

Realizing that Mavis was on the mend, Flora Jean burst into a wheezy snicker, winked at her, and said, "Sugar, ain't it the truth!"

Chapter

32

CJ'S ONLY CONNECTION to what remained of Denver's once powerful organized crime family was eighty-year-old curmudgeon Mario Satoni who ran a secondhand furniture store in North Denver and smoked the foulest-smelling cheap cigars CJ had ever run up against. Satoni lived in a mustard-colored bungalow in the middle of an industrial park, where, over the years, he'd managed to stash a cellar full of Western collectibles, including boxes of mint-condition license plates that made a collector like CJ drool.

The drive from his office to Satoni's took CJ fifteen minutes. He'd called ahead to make sure Satoni was home, though he knew the call really wasn't needed since the Colorado Rockies were playing the Dodgers, a night game, and Dodgers fanatic that he was, Mario would be parked in front of his big-screen TV giving the Rockies hell.

It was nearly dark when CJ pulled into Satoni's driveway, got out of the Bel Air, and headed for the old man's back entrance. "I don't like people lookin' at who or what I've got comin' and goin'—always use the back," Satoni had told CJ after their first business transaction.

Manila envelope in hand, CJ knocked lightly four times on the back door, then knocked twice, waited a few seconds, and gave the door three solid raps.

Close to a minute later, Satoni, after eyeing CJ through a peephole, swung the door open. Shoeless, he was dressed in what he always wore in the summer, faded khaki Bermuda shorts, a muscle T-shirt, and a Dodgers baseball cap. Adjusting his glasses and bringing CJ into focus, he smiled and said, "Calvin."

No one but Ike and Mavis had ever called CJ by his given name—Ike when he'd been either mad or drunk and Mavis when she had a point to make. But Satoni, who'd demanded to know CJ's full name the first time they'd met, stuck to Calvin, saying to CJ's chagrin, "It's the name you'll have to give at the pearly gates, so get used to it."

CJ said, "How's it goin', Mario?" He eyed Satoni's ghostly-white spindly legs.

"About half, but it's goin', and at eighty, that's all that matters. Come on in and watch your Rockies get their asses kicked. While you're at it, you can tell me a bit more about what brings a huntin' dog like you out on a night like this."

CJ followed Satoni through a spotlessly clean kitchen, down a hallway filled with photographs of mobsters and Colorado movers and shakers from another era, and into a dingy little room that was all refrigerator and TV.

"Score's 9 to 7, Dodgers, top of the eighth." Satoni eased into his favorite russet-colored La-Z-Boy, puckered with age. Switching glasses, he nodded for CJ to take a seat as he zeroed in on the TV screen. "Get you a beer?"

"Nope, I'm good," said CJ, taking a seat in a matching avocado green La-Z-Boy.

Satoni edged forward in his seat at the loud crack of a bat. "Son of a bitch! And with two men on," he barked at the screen as the Rockies player who'd just parked the ball in the center-field upper deck touched first base on his round trip home. "Fuckin' Rockies ain't shit. It's the goddamn ownership. They're too damn cheap. But they're about to win this one." Satoni reached for the remote, turned down the sound, and looked at CJ. "I need a break from this bullshit. Good thing you came by. Wanna have a look at some license plates?"

CJ shook his head. "I'm here on different business than usual, Mario."

Satoni's eyes narrowed. "Hope it ain't got nothin' to do with the kind of business that asshole nephew of mine swears I was once in."

"Afraid so."

"Damn, Calvin. You know the rules. I don't speak ill of the dead or talk about what I did in the past."

"I know the rules, Mario. I just need a little guidance."

Satoni eyed CJ from head to toe, ultimately focusing on the bandage on CJ's arm.

"Got anything to do with that bandage you got wrapped around your biceps?"

"No. That's a whole different problem."

Satoni smiled, aware that CJ also had rules, which included never complaining and treating him with dignity. "You're a complex man, Calvin Floyd. Complex indeed. So tell me about this guidance you need and I'll give you some straight up, or let you know if you're pushin' a little too close to the edge."

Getting straight to the point, CJ said, "I need to know a little about counterfeiting, Mario."

"That's pressin' it, Calvin."

CJ laid the envelope he'd been holding on the coffee table between them. "No particulars, Mario, just a little something about the paper counterfeiters use."

Satoni frowned and peered over his glasses. "And what makes you think I'd know a damn thing about that?"

CJ smiled, "You wouldn't, of course. Why would someone in the furniture business know anything about counterfeiting? But it's always possible for a businessperson to know someone who knows someone."

Mario stared at the envelope. "It's possible."

CJ retrieved the envelope, opened it, and took out the two blank sheets of paper and one of the twenties from Margolin's along with Langston Blue's citation. Handing them to Satoni, he said, "I need to know two things about the papers and the bill. Are they all the same kind of stock? And is there any chance that the paper could've been used for counterfeiting?"

Satoni whistled. It was a loud, long whistle, the kind he reserved for amazing Dodgers comebacks and game-winning grand slams. "That's a tall task, Calvin, and one that assumes that I'd know people in the paper-hanging business."

"Nope, it just assumes, like we said before, that you might know someone who knows someone."

Satoni flexed the papers one by one. "They seem a little heavy for currency stock to me. The twenty looks real." He switched glasses and read the citation. "This Langston Blue fellow your client?"

"Yes."

Satoni stroked his chin. "Could be the answer to Mr. Blue's problem lies with this citation."

"That's the same thing I've been thinking, but I've got to close the door on the counterfeit angle."

Satoni nodded and cast an eye toward the TV screen. "Dodgers got two on," he said, his voice full of anticipation.

"Might be their day."

"Yours too, Calvin. Tell you what I'll do. First thing in the morning I'll go see a friend of a friend. Find out what this paper of yours is good for." Satoni slipped one of the sheets of paper back into the manila envelope, eyes glued to the screen.

"Thanks."

"I'll have something for you tomorrow, but I can tell you one thing right now. That paper probably didn't come cheap. It feels a lot like the kind of high-end stock we use for our full-color sale flyers at the store." Satoni hunched forward, elbows on his knees, his nose inches from the TV screen.

"Do what you can. I've got something else I need to run by you," said CJ, as the Dodgers second baseman went down swinging, ending the game.

Satoni shook his head, pulled a cigar out of his shirt pocket, wetted it, and slipped it into the corner of his mouth. "Sons of bitches lost. Sometimes I don't know why I even bother to watch 'em. Sorry, Calvin, run that by me again."

"Need to ask you something."

"Shoot."

"I'm thinking about getting out of the bail-bonding business."

Satoni clicked off the TV. "And do what?"

CJ shrugged. "Take advantage of some down time, relax, set up a business selling Western collectibles and antiques."

"Big switch, Calvin. How can I help?"

"Give me some of your business insight and, if you've got a mind to, sell me some of that stuff you've spent a lifetime collecting."

Satoni removed his glasses, set them aside, and stared directly at CJ. "You're serious?"

"As a heart attack."

"Well, I'll be damned!" said Satoni, surprised that anyone would consider his passion for collecting anything but a fetish and an excuse to stockpile junk. "I'll help you if peddling antiques is what you want to do. But let me give you a piece of advice. And take it to heart."

"I'm listening."

"Think long and hard before you make your move. Because— and you'll have to trust me on this—I've been there, and once you make your move, you can't ever go back."

"I understand."

"Good."

Satoni rolled his cigar to the other side of his mouth and lit it. The pungent odor of the cheap cigar soon filled the room. "Now, let me work on that other problem you brought me. I'll talk to you tomorrow." Rising slowly from his chair, he retrieved a third set of glasses from a hallway table as he walked CJ to the door.

◆ ◆ ◆

CJ thought about Satoni's advice during most of the twenty-minute drive to Five Points, but when he turned onto Welton Street his thoughts turned to Mavis. She was moving in the right direction, he told himself, as he parked the Bel Air four blocks from her house at Rosie's Garage, left the key in the ignition, got out, and waved to Rosie, who was in his office. Rosie, engaged in a conversation, waved back.

CJ headed across Welton Street toward Curtis Park, knowing that Rosie would garage the Bel Air in a back bay, as he had on alternate nights since CJ had returned from New Mexico. They'd both agreed there was no need to broadcast his whereabouts to Celeste Deepstream by parking the Bel Air at Mavis's.

As he turned onto Curtis Street with its gaslight replica street-lamps, uneven sidewalks, and stately seventy-year-old trees, he heard what sounded like a truck's engine revving behind him. When he realized the sound was getting closer, he turned to find himself staring into the headlight glare of a van that was bearing down on him at 60 miles an hour. The van hopped the curb and took him on point blank. He dove out of range several feet beyond a concrete-mounted four-by-four-foot traffic control box just before the van's bumper slammed into the box, dis-lodging it from its moorings and sending it bumping end over end down the street. With two of its tires on pavement and two on the sidewalk, the van sped away, nearly missing a mailbox, uprooting two newly planted elm trees, and clipping a stop sign at the end of the block before it spun into a hedge, turned north onto 28th Street, and disappeared into the night.

CJ crawled behind the mailbox, uncertain whether there would be a second assault. He waited a few seconds, then duck-walked his way across the street, leaped over a scraggly privet hedge into the yard of one of Mavis's Champa Street neighbors, and made his way toward the alley. He zigzagged his way down one side of the alley from trash dumpster to trash can to utility pole until he reached Mavis's.

As he scanned Mavis's backyard, brightly lit by two outside security lights, he tried to remember something about the van— a license-plate number, the color, the year—but all he could remember was that the van had looked like an Econoline and had white-wall tires. The only other things he was certain of were that the van had to have sustained severe front-end damage and that he'd get no help from the cops.

He hadn't seen the driver, and for all he knew the person behind the wheel could've been any one of the scores of enemies he'd made in more than thirty years as a bail bondsman. But it made sense that Celeste Deepstream was a likely suspect.

Checking his clothes for dirt, grass stains, and tears, he dusted himself off, ran a hand perfunctorily through his hair, and headed for the house, hoping that he looked like anything but someone who'd just nearly been run over by a van.

Within moments of the back doorbell ringing, Mavis was at

the door. She opened it, smiled, leaned forward, and kissed him on the lips softly. CJ swept her square-dance-style out of the doorway before reaching back to close the door.

"What was that all about?"

"Just checking to see if you're limber enough for what I've got in mind," he said, hoping the boldness of his entrance had served its real purpose.

Mavis draped her arms around his neck and squeezed her body tightly to his. "I'm limber enough to deal with a broken-down street cowboy like you," she said in the sultriest voice she could muster.

"We'll see," said CJ, kissing her passionately, sweeping her off her feet, and carrying her kicking in mock protest from the back entryway into the house.

Chapter

33

ELLIOTT COLE, GIN AND TONIC IN ONE HAND, paced the floor of his office at the state Republican headquarters. A rolled-up copy of the *Boulder Daily Camera* was clasped tightly in his other hand, and he was beside himself with anger. He thought he'd nailed everything down. He and Le Quan had Jimmy Moc dealing with the bail bondsman, Alfred Reed had a comfortable, if not commanding, five-point lead in the polls, and he'd spent the previous evening having two amazingly talented women fulfill his sexual fantasies until 1:30 in the morning. Then he'd read Owen Brashears's half-baked power-of-the-pen follow-up to his earlier editorial. A pile-of-shit piece claiming that the state Republican Party chairman had come home from Vietnam with something more than a few medals pinned to his chest—that in fact he'd returned from the war amid rumors that he'd been involved in an atrocity that had been hushed up. That he could handle. But what had him wanting to grab Brashears by the throat and cut off his air was the inference that Alfred Reed was cut from the same cloth as Cole, his mentor and handler.

Cole slammed the tightly coiled paper against the edge of his desk. "Fucker! That ass-kissing pissant of a *Stars and Stripes* scribe. Shit!" He opened the newspaper and reread the editorial. This time Brashears had named names, and he'd laid out Margolin's chain of command, fingering Cole as the man at the top.

Brashears had ended the piece with the promise that there would be more to follow, and since there were still four months until the election, that meant the Republican Party and Alfred Reed had a problem. Cole knew well that when it came to politics perception always trumped truth, and it was an even bet that Brashears could sling enough mud in the next 120 days to destroy Reed's five-point lead.

Tossing the paper onto a nearby chair, he walked to his desk, sat down, and flipped through a Rolodex until he came to the card with Owen Brashears's phone number. Deciding that for the moment Reed's input didn't matter, he punched in Brashears's phone number and took a liberal sip of gin and tonic.

Cole endured thirty seconds of elevator music before the woman who'd answered came back on the line. "I have Mr. Brashears for you."

"Elliott? You're up and at it early," said Brashears.

"That makes two of us."

"What can I do for you?"

"Don't play Eagle Scout with me, you piece of shit. You know what you can do."

Brashears forced back a snicker. "And that is?"

"Lay off the Star 1 team shit. You're trying to paint a picture that just ain't there."

"I'm running a newspaper."

"And you're doing one hell of a job fucking it up. If you wanna make me into some kind of monster in order to pump up your dead buddy, fine. Just don't try and connect any of the dots to Alfred Reed."

"I call 'em the way I see 'em, Elliott."

"Can it, Brashears. You're in over your head."

"No. You're the one taking on water. I'm just being loyal."

"My ass. You're playing king of the hill and loving it, you little twerp. This is the best thing to happen to you since somebody was dumb enough to stick you in front of a camera."

"At least my paycheck came from the U.S. Treasury."

Dumbfounded, Cole sat back in his seat. "I wouldn't go where you're headed."

Brashears laughed. "I'm the press, remember?"

Cole took a sip of his drink and eyed his elegant surroundings. He'd come a long way from being an eastern Colorado farm boy. And pushing all the wrong buttons, Brashears was testing his limits. He considered the pros and cons of what he was about to say. "We need to meet."

"Fine by me."

"What about this evening?"

"I'm out of the office by 6," said Brashears.

"How about my place? Eight o'clock?"

"Eight's fine."

"Riverfront Tower, in Riverfront Park, number 1350."

"I know where it is," said Brashears. "I'll see you then."

"Count on it." Cole hung up, finished his drink, and flipped through his Rolodex until he came to the Q's. He took several deep breaths before he dialed Le Quan's number, the way he always had before beginning a mission during his two tours of duty in Vietnam.

◆◆◆

Freshly showered, with a towel draped over one shoulder and clad in a pair of gray boxers, CJ called out to Mavis from the corner of her large walk-in closet. "I thought I left a bunch of shirts in here."

"You gave one to Morgan Williams that time he and Dittier were here for a barbecue. I don't know about the other ones." Wrapped in an oversized towel, Mavis stepped into the closet. She shook her head as she viewed the carnage. "CJ, what are you doing?"

"Looking for a shirt."

"And destroying my closet in the process. Let me look."

She placed three of her favorite blouses back where they belonged, refolded two of her scarves, and scanned the shelf next to CJ. Spotting a blue chambray shirt near the back of the shelf, she picked it up and handed it to him. "If it had been a snake . . ."

Before she could finish, CJ hooked a finger beneath the top edge of her towel and pulled. The towel dropped to the floor. "Think I'll have some more of that," he said, eyeing Mavis's well-proportioned body and winking.

"CJ Floyd!"

"That's my name." He pulled Mavis to him and embraced her tightly. "I'll worry about my shirt later."

"CJ!" Mavis's protests ended as their lips met and he guided her to the closet floor.

"Not in here," she said.

"Seems like as good a place as any."

Mavis smiled, responding with a sweeping roll of her pelvis into his.

◆ ◆ ◆

When CJ finally got to his office, Flora Jean was wrapping up a phone conversation with Alden Grace. "Thought you were lookin' at bein' an antique dealer, sugar, not a banker," she said, wagging a finger at CJ.

"Had some unfinished business to deal with over at Mavis's."

"Hope you got it settled."

"Sure did."

"Good. Because that was Alden on the phone. He didn't have much for us, but he did serve up somethin'. After I told him about me and Carmen stumblin' into Amerasianville at that China Bay club the other night, he called a few of his old intelligence contacts to check on the ethnic-cleansing angle. Nothin', but he did find out that a few years back the army investigated the whole Star 1 team thing. Nothin' that would make the front pages. It wasn't that kind of probe, and the only reason they took a look in the first place was because the army's criminal investigation command was already lookin' into war-crime allegations against U.S. Tiger Force commandos."

"Yeah," said CJ. "I remember. Didn't that probe go all the way up to the secretary of the army?"

"Sure did. And Alden thinks that's why Margolin's shit got

buried. The government didn't want both their hands full of poop."

"So he thinks Margolin may have skated because there were people out there doing worse things than him."

"Or because he knew somebody."

CJ shrugged. "Who?"

"What about that guy Cole? Isn't he some kind of Republican Party muckety-muck?"

"He is now, but he was just a know-nothing colonel back in Vietnam." CJ took a seat. "What did Alden think about the Amerasian angle?"

"Same as us. Said there were always rumors about how the North Vietnamese planned to deal with their *my den* issue. But nothin' concrete."

CJ leaned forward, elbows resting on his knees. "There's something we're missing here, Flora Jean. The key to the whole damn thing. We've got an army special-ops team assigned to kill a school full of Amerasian children. The team's captain ends up a postwar fat-in-the-wallet congressman who's eventually murdered. Turns out a Republican Party boss was the dead man's commander, and a little Vietnamese man with a silver streak in his hair seems to have somehow kicked the whole thing off. What we don't have is Margolin's killer."

"That's the tale in a nutshell, sugar."

CJ laughed. "Seems like everybody's got their story, and they're sticking to it." CJ sat up in his chair suddenly, looking as if he'd just been handed the answers to the final exam. "Or maybe we don't have the whole story. What if we're still missing a piece?"

"What could we be missin'?"

"I'm not sure, but I have a feeling that if we don't do something pretty quick to prove that Langston Blue was the fall guy in all of this, he's gonna spend a few more years out of circulation."

◆◆◆

Wendall Newburn was enjoying an early lunch break and three scoops of strawberry ice cream at the Cold Stone Creamery, thinking about a regional cooperative homicide bulletin that had hit his e-mail that morning. The bulletin reported that a dead man had been found jammed inside a metal oil drum that had floated up from the depths of the South Platte River near the mountain town of Deckers.

He wouldn't have paid much attention to the communication had it not been for the fact that the dead man was described as Hispanic, forty to fifty years of age, with a badly withered right leg and a dramatic underbite.

Since he now had photos, albeit some of them more than thirty years old, and partial army medical records on the three members of Peter Margolin's Star 1 team who had survived Song Ve, he had called the Douglas County sheriff's office and asked to speak to the officer in charge of the Deckers homicide, on the off-chance that the body in the drum might be that of Lincoln Cortez. He'd asked for a briefing and the chance to view the body that afternoon. The deputy had been happy to oblige, informing him that the body had been found along with clothing and a cane they were dusting for prints.

Deep in thought, Newburn didn't see Ginny Kearnes walk

into the ice-cream parlor. She was at his table, already pulling up a stool, when he realized she was there.

"Your office told me I might catch you here, Lieutenant."

"Ms. Kearnes," he said, looking up surprised.

"You look as if you've just been stung by a bee, Lieutenant."

Newburn spooned up a bite of ice cream and said sarcastically, "My time's your time."

"I'll be brief." Kearnes extracted two twenty-dollar bills from her purse and laid them on the table. "I found these the other day in a strongbox in Peter's attic."

"Look like twenties," said Newburn.

"And this." She placed one of the blank sheets of paper she and CJ had found on the table.

Newburn fingered the bottom edge of the paper. "And?"

"Any chance the twenties could be counterfeit?"

"They look perfectly real to me," said Newburn, picking up one of the bills. "Mind telling me where you're headed with this?"

"I hope I'm on the road to finding Peter's killer."

"Are you the executor of his estate?"

"No, his lawyer is."

"Then if I were you, I'd stay away from his house. I'm surprised a patrol car didn't spot you."

Kearnes shook her head disgustedly. "You're full of advice, Lieutenant, and as usual, just about as much help as I expected." She slipped the bills and the folded sheet of paper back in her purse.

"Sorry I can't be your own private security force, Ms. Kearnes, but the fact is, other people help pay my salary. Anything else pop up during your scavenger hunt?"

"If it did, I wouldn't tell you."

Newburn's eyes narrowed and his brow muscles tightened. "Listen, lady, whether you get it or not, I'm dealing with a real high-profile murder. Here's some advice. Sneaking into a murder victim's home, rummaging through his things, helping yourself to his money, and interfering with a criminal investigation will buy you some jail time, no matter how good your connections are. Now, while I'm still in a good mood, why don't you take the twenties and the paper back out of your purse, give them to me, and tell me why you think your boyfriend was involved in counterfeiting?"

"It's fiancé. And I never said Peter was involved in anything. What I asked was whether you thought the twenties were real."

Newburn took a final spoonful of his ice cream and tossed his empty cup into a nearby trash can. "Have it your way, Ms. Kearnes. You can keep playing the faithful fiancée and press secretary if you want to. It suits you. But don't go back in Margolin's house. Quit playing detective, and stay out of the way of my investigation. If you don't, trust me, it'll cost you more than a parking ticket."

"I'm listening," said Kearnes.

"Great. I enjoy leaving a lasting impression." He rose and stepped back from the table. "Afraid I have to leave. Oh, almost forgot." Slipping a spiral-bound notebook from his shirt pocket, he ripped out a page, placed it on the table, and wrote, *Received from G. Kearnes: Evidence: Margolin murder case. Two $20 bills;*

one sheet of paper approximately 11 x 13. "Initial this for me, please." He smiled, handed her a pen, and watched her print GK near the bottom of the paper.

"Appreciate your help." Gathering up the twenties and the sheet of paper, he turned and walked away.

Disappointed, Ginny Kearnes scanned the bill of fare printed high on a chalkboard behind the counter. She hadn't gotten much out of Newburn, but she'd played him skillfully, and he had no idea that both she and Floyd had duplicates of everything she'd been forced to surrender.

Deciding to go whole hog and order a triple-decker waffle cone, she walked up to the counter, placed her order, paid the overeager teenaged cashier, and walked back to the table. What she needed to do at this point, she told herself, was count on another of her connections. A connection that neither Floyd nor Newburn could possibly envision. One that had turned her stomach when she'd first considered it: her card-carrying-journalist link to a balding, egocentric man with periodontal disease and bad breath—the bottom-feeding investigative reporter Paul Grimes.

She had thought about using Owen Brashears but decided against it because Grimes had two distinct advantages. He was untainted by anything resembling ethics, and he always seemed to know where to look for the dirty laundry.

She'd given Grimes copies of the press clippings the previous afternoon during their brief meeting in the Western History room of Denver's central library and asked him to dig up everything he could on the woman named Moc and her son, even meet with them. As she'd expected, Grimes had asked for money, so she had given him five crisp fifties. He had promised to have something for her within forty-eight hours, which meant that her $250 investment should produce dividends by the next day.

Relaxing back in her chair, she bit off a good-sized chunk of chocolate from her triple-decker and smiled. She'd never understood or appreciated the concept of licking ice cream. Like Newburn, she preferred diving right in with her teeth, the same way she was laying the groundwork to find out who had murdered the man she loved.

◆ ◆ ◆

Wendall Newburn was cruising south on Santa Fe Drive on his way to Deckers to take a look at the John Doe from the oil drum when he called in a cell-phone request to Donny Levine, the detective who was helping him work the Margolin murder case. "I want somebody on Ginny Kearnes for the next twenty-four hours, day and night," he said authoritatively. "Stay with her at home and work. She's got something she's not telling us, there's no question. And Donny, keep your distance. She's a sly little fox. If she sniffs you out, she'll do an end around you like nobody's business."

Newburn flipped off his cell phone the instant Levine said, "Gotcha!" and continued to barrel southwest toward Deckers.

Chapter

34

CJ WAS SEATED IN HIS OFFICE beneath his gallery of bond-skippers. Fifteen minutes earlier, Alden Grace had dropped by to take Flora Jean to lunch. CJ had shown Grace the newspaper clippings and the papers he'd taken from Margolin's, hoping the former general might shed some light on their significance, but except for recognizing Jimmy Moc's name, Grace had drawn a blank.

Moments earlier the nicotine monkey had grabbed him, and the pungent, semisweet smell of cigar smoke now filled the room. He ran a hand down the thigh of his slightly too-snug jeans, thinking that maybe he needed to cut back to a single slice of sweet-potato pie a week. He slipped both feet up on the edge of his desk, noticing that the heel of his right boot had split from the sole, and thought that nothing was permanent— not love or friendships, not the good life, not even a career. As he sat in the midday glow blowing smoke rings skyward, he wondered how he could continue to justify getting paid by Carmen Nguyen when he hadn't delivered anything to her but guaranteed jail time for her father.

Pondering his decision to sell the building and get out from under a life filled with daily uncertainty, his thoughts were interrupted by the high-pitched, incisive ring of the 1920s-style Bakelite telephone on his desk. Debating whether to pick up, he listened to five more lengthy rings before answering, "Floyds Bail Bonds."

"CJ, it's Flora Jean."

"I thought you were at lunch."

"We are, but it just hit Alden where he might've seen a match for that paper you showed him in the office. The one Blue's citation was printed on." Flora Jean handed her cell phone to Grace.

"Just had a flash on where I'd seen that paper you showed me," Grace said amid the clanging of silverware. "The paper's a lot more yellowed, but it was the same size, and it had the same feel as the paper the army used to print their missing and killed-in-action notices on during Vietnam. The ones that went to battalion commanders on a weekly basis."

"I'll be damned!" said CJ, sounding as if he'd somehow been derelict.

"Don't be so hard on yourself. I missed it, too. Got something else for you. I made a call to a friend of mine who's still in the business."

CJ smiled, aware that it was next to a certainty that Grace still had his hands in the intelligence game, despite his claim that he had retired. "What did you find out out?"

"That woman in your newspaper clipping, Jimmy Moc's mother. She was connected. A distant cousin to Ho Chi Minh."

"Whewww. A chicken with lips," said CJ, rekindling a phrase

his Uncle Ike had liked to use to describe an improbability turning into a reality.

"Yeah. And when you're dealing with scheming at the level we're talking about, you never know. Could be she got paid to set up housekeeping in the U.S. on the strength of a favor or two she did for us back in Vietnam. Ratting out a relative wouldn't be far-fetched. Still doesn't prove she had anything to do with your Langston Blue problem, but it's a thought."

"Sure is. But if she was some kinda Mata Hari with a blood-line straight to Uncle Ho, why cry poverty once she was in the U.S.? You know that if she was ratting out the North Vietnamese, she got very well paid."

"Cover, CJ, cover. And that gets us pretty close to the end of what I'm able to tell you."

"It helps," said CJ.

"No problem." Grace squeezed Flora Jean's hand. "Just remember a couple of things. The lady sitting next to me had me take things a whole lot further than I really should have, and until you show me otherwise, Langston Blue's still a deserter."

"I understand. We'll set things straight in the end."

"I'll hold you to it. Good-bye."

CJ couldn't miss the fact that there'd been something unspoken in Grace's closing remark, almost as if he'd substituted the word *good-bye* for something else. It took him a few seconds to recognize what it was, a few moments more to put what Grace had said into perspective. But it was crystal clear to him now. The general's closing remark had pretty much been an order.

◆◆◆

There could be no missing the badly damaged front end of the Econoline van that sat in the middle of a quarter-acre vacant lot in Commerce City just a few miles north of Denver. Jimmy Moc had parked the van in the midst of the acreage in order to replace its timing chain, radiator, and right headlight. He had worked through the heat of the day cloaked in obscurity by an expanse of slough grass and cattails, and he'd just finished applying a final piece of duct tape to the headlamp. He tested the headlamp's stability, walked back and slipped behind the wheel of the van, and flipped on the headlights. Both flashed on, but the right one, barely visible in the daylight, beamed cockeyed toward the ground. "Good enough," he said, sounding weary.

He stepped out of the van, walked to the front of the vehicle, and smiled. The van's grill was missing, a casualty to his late-night encounter with CJ Floyd, but the replacement headlamp worked just fine. He picked up a crowbar from the dirt and worked the van's dented right fender away from the tire it had been gnawing on. Grabbing a nearby wrench, he dropped to his knees and removed the last bolt that secured the dangling bumper to its frame. The bumper dropped to the ground with a thud. That was it, done, he told himself. The van was a lot worse for wear, but it was still running, and he was back in business.

The van, a gas-guzzling relic from the 1980s, had been his mother's. Dead ten years now, she'd been his guiding star. Without her he'd become no more than a piece of trash. He had known little of his mother's life in Vietnam except that she had been a political activist and Communist Party leader from the northern province of Bac Ninh and that she had a weakness for men, including his father, a French North African he had never known. According to Le Quan, soon after Jimmy's birth she had been moved from a position of power in the party to an outcast with a *my den* child. He'd only briefly known what it was like to be a child of mixed race in Vietnam because his mother had immigrated with him to the United States when he was only three. But he had heard stories, mostly in the China Bay club, about what it was like to be *my den* trash in your homeland, and he knew firsthand what it was like to be a nigger in the U.S.A.

Counseling, alternative schools, street life, and finally jail had taught him that what mattered most in life was survival, getting a leg up on the next guy, always hitting the food bank first, and doing whatever was necessary to keep on breathing air. He had no use for revolutions, patriotism, ideologies, or a missing father. For him and the thousands of other throwaway children like him who'd survived the Vietnam War, the measure of a man would always be the number of dollars in his pocket. Loyalty, family, causes, and character were for fools.

Admiring his handiwork, Moc patted the van's hood affectionately. He then walked to the back of the van, swung open the rear doors, retrieved his toolbox from the ground, and slid it inside. The box clanged to a stop against a floor-to-ceiling metal barrier. Shaking his head, he crawled inside, laid the aluminum barrier down flat, and eyed the empty oil drum in front of him. A wooden case the size of a milk crate sat next to the oil drum. Lifting the top from the case, he stared down at the .45-caliber pistol and sledgehammer inside. Now that the van was running, he'd swing by an East Denver storage locker and pick up the final items he needed.

He replaced the top on the box, crawled out of the van, and closed the doors. Cranking the engine, he scanned the isolated marshland, thinking that after his current job was finished, he'd like to disappear into a background of cattails and weeds just as he and his van had done today.

◆◆◆

After a bumpy ride over the Rockies, Alex Holden's flight from Los Angeles arrived at Denver International Airport five minutes ahead of schedule. All he could think of as he hiked his horn-rimmed glasses up on his nose was that he was on the final leg of his nosebleed tour of the West.

Foot traffic inside the main DIA terminal was light as he made his way toward a sign that read *Ground Transportation*. He'd barely reached curbside, briefcase in hand, when a spotlessly clean yellow cab pulled to a stop. The driver, a gaunt Hispanic man, nodded, got out, walked toward Holden, and asked, "Where to?"

"The Starlighter Motel on Federal. How far's that from downtown?"

"Fifteen minutes," said the cabbie, placing Holden's briefcase in the trunk. "You're a good way south. Gonna need a ride later?" he asked, trolling for a second fare.

"No. I'll rent myself something."

The cabbie shrugged and closed the trunk lid, aware that his fare with the oversized horn-rims would have a hard time finding a car-rental outlet on South Federal Boulevard, in the heart of Little Vietnam.

◆ ◆ ◆

When Paul Grimes asked Ginny Kearnes to meet him at 3 p.m. in the Western History room of the central Denver library once again, he snickered into the phone, "You won't like what I found."

Now, as they stood at the center of the room beneath its massive stylized two-story wooden replica of an oil derrick, Grimes had the self-satisfied look of someone who'd just found a gold nugget in the dry wash.

"Your boyfriend wasn't quite as squeaky clean as he projected—or as liberal." Grimes handed Kearnes copies of several *Denver Post* and *Rocky Mountain News* stories from the early 1980s. "Check 'em out. Margolin was leading the band when it came to protesting the resettlement of Vietnamese boat people here in Colorado."

Kearnes eyed a *Denver Post* headline—*Refugees Displace Americans*—and scanned the story below. A second headline screamed, *Boat People to Cost Coloradoans Jobs;* a third, *Economy to Feel Pinch from Resettlement.* Each story quoted Peter Margolin as being strongly opposed to any further influx of Vietnamese boat people into the United States, and Colorado in particular. Frowning, she handed the copies back to Grimes.

"There's more," Grimes said gleefully. "Some folks claim Margolin was being paid to parrot what labor-protective lobbyists were telling him to say."

Kearnes shook her head. "There's no way."

"It's all down in black and white."

"Then Peter had a reason," Kearnes said defensively.

"Yeah. He had a bunch of lobbyists lining his pocket."

"No. There's something else here. Something we're missing."

"Well, if there is, unless you wanna ante up another two hundred and fifty bucks, you're on your own trying to find it."

"What about that Moc woman's story?"

"Couldn't find much beyond what you gave me. Just this AP wire piece." He handed Kearnes an Associated Press clipping. She read through it quickly.

"Somebody wrote this AP piece. Someone talked to Moc's mother."

"Could've been anybody. Back in those days the AP and UPI boys were pretty loosey-goosey with other people's work. That AP story on the Moc woman was probably a compilation from ten other original pieces, including the ones you gave me. I couldn't dig up any more on her. Seems like as soon as those resettlement stories were done, the woman vanished."

"I'll dig deeper." Kearnes smiled. "We've got one advantage over the early '80s—the Internet. Besides, we know from this AP story that the Moc woman came from San Francisco to Fort Collins to Denver."

"What the heck are you looking for?" Grimes shook his head.

"The truth. And something that points to why Peter was murdered. There's a thread of it here," she said, holding up the AP clipping. "I simply have to ferret it out."

"Good luck," said Grimes, staggered by Kearnes's tenacity. "Here's a tip. Start with the *Fort Collins Coloradoan*. When those wire service boys lifted stuff, they tended to stay local."

"I'll do that," said Kearnes, surprised by Grimes's willingness to offer uncompensated advice.

"Don't look so surprised," said Grimes. "Believe it or not, I bleed real blood. Besides, we're dealing with the murder of a congressman. People want to know what happened. You find an acorn, I'll eventually find a tree. It's how I earn my living."

Aware that Grimes wasn't just blowing smoke, she said, "I'll keep that in mind."

"Do that. And thanks for the payday. When you find that acorn, call me. You never know, we might grow it into a Pulitzer."

Grimes pivoted and walked away, leaving Kearnes wondering, as she headed for a library computer to begin her search of Colorado boat people archives, why it was that murder, voyeurism, and misery made the journalistic world tick.

◆ ◆ ◆

Mario Satoni showed up at CJ's office precisely at 4 o'clock, just as he'd told CJ he would during their midafternoon phone conversation. He was dressed in an expensive tailored black suit and a white spread-collar shirt, accented by a $150 silk tie. CJ had never seen the spindly-legged old man who had been selling him antique license plates and Western collectibles for nearly a decade wearing anything but a T-shirt and baggy shorts. Caught off guard as Mario stood in his doorway, CJ's jaw nearly dropped.

"So this is where you work," said Mario. "Always wondered. Nice."

"Thanks! Come on in and take a load off," said CJ, trying earnestly to mask his surprise.

Mario walked into the room, drank in the surroundings, and nodded his approval. Cupping both hands chest high in front of him, Mario said, "That lady who showed me in has a set on her."

"I wouldn't say that too loud. She's an ex-marine."

"Marine, Seabee, swabbie, whatever, she's built like a brick shithouse."

CJ smiled and shook his head. "What've you got for me, Mario?"

"Got plenty, Calvin. Plenty." Mario slid the now grease-stained envelope with the twenties and the special paper across CJ's desktop and took a seat. "Bottom line is, your boy Margolin wasn't counterfeitin'. Those twenties are coin of the realm."

"So what's the plenty?"

"I'll get to that, Calvin. Give me a minute. You got any water?"

"Sure." CJ walked out to the coffee-break area and returned with a bottle of water.

"Shit," said Mario, taking the bottle and unscrewing the cap. "You're runnin' first class. Bottled water, no less. Now, where was I?"

"You were about to tell me what you had for me."

"Oh yeah." Mario took a sip of water. "Here's the bottom line on that paper. I shoulda known. It's the same kinda stuff we use to do newspaper ad inserts and weekend flyers for the furniture store. My source is golden on it."

CJ nodded.

"That particular kind ain't been around since the 1970s. Here's more. It's got some kinda seal on it that keeps the ink from runnin'. My source says it was made for use in high-humidity climates like Seattle or Miami."

Deep in thought, CJ's eyes narrowed. "Or Vietnam," he said, aware that only three people involved in the Margolin murder would potentially have that kind of knowledge about the paper—Kearnes, Brashears, and Cole. "Tell your friend I owe him," said CJ.

"Already did."

Drinking in the look of concentration on CJ's face, Mario said, "Think my info'll help you find your killer?"

"If I play my cards right."

Mario looked relieved. "Then I did the right thing." Glancing at his watch, he added, "Gotta get movin'; got a funeral to attend."

Realizing finally why Mario was dressed so exquisitely, CJ said, "Sorry."

"Thanks. You can't ever look too proper when you're payin' your respects."

"Who'd you lose?"

"You wouldn't know him. He's real old school."

"I might. Try me."

"Coco Pasquali. Died of a heart attack a few days back. Same age as me."

Recognizing the name of one of Colorado's most notorious 1950s crime bosses, CJ nodded, then shook his head. "I didn't know him, but I knew who he was. He used to do a little gambling with my Uncle Ike."

Mario looked puzzled. "Ike Floyd?"

"Yes."

"Well, I'll be damned! Never knew you was related to Ike. Ike Floyd—your uncle. Ain't that a gas?" Mario turned to leave. As he crossed the threshold, he turned back and smiled. "Ike

Floyd," he said and shook his head. "Guess you're a little more connected than I ever thought."

♦♦♦

CJ spent the next half hour trying to piece together all the parts of a murder trail and unsuccessfully attempting to reach Ginny Kearnes, hoping for an update on the newspaper clippings they'd found. He was certain that he had most of the story he needed to peg Margolin's killer, but he needed Kearnes's information to seal the deal. By the time he had filled Flora Jean in on what he had found out from Satoni, tried to reach Kearnes several more times, leaving a final urgent message, and talked to Julie and Carmen about how Blue was holding up, it was 5:30.

Flora Jean was looking through the yellow pages trying to find a phone number when CJ, looking frustrated, interrupted her. "I can't get Kearnes. Makes me think she may have found a link between what happened at Song Ve, Jimmy Moc, or his mother, and our killer. Looks like one of us is gonna have to tag along after Moc."

"And I just got picked," said Flora Jean, looking up from the phone book.

"It's that, revisit Quan and that daughter of his, or follow Cole."

"I'll stick with Moc." Flora Jean smiled. "We know one another."

"Fine. I'll start with Cole and work my way down the list from there."

The look on Flora Jean's face turned pensive. "Whatta ya think Margolin's murder really hinges on?"

"Money. What else? Somebody got paid to kill off a bunch

of Amerasians at Song Ve—lost souls, half-breeds the North Vietnamese didn't want on their postwar plate. And I'm guessing it
was someone high enough up on the North Vietnamese provin-
cial government totem pole to be able to dole out cash. The way
I see it, Le Quan probably got a bundle to wrap his arms around
the problem. He works out a plan to assemble his group of
throwaway half-breeds in a school, negotiates a price for eliminating them, and lines up Margolin. Margolin and his Star 1
team end up being the cure."

Flora Jean shook her head. "The money I understand. But
how in the hell would the North Vietnamese government know
about Margolin or his Star 1 team?"

"Le Quan again, would be my guess. He had to know that
Margolin was susceptible to a little money under the table. And
Quan was probably working both sides of the street," said CJ.

"Well, if he was, he sure did one hell of a job avoidin' tickin'
off Uncle Sam. He orchestrates a genocide hit, then gets to set
up housekeepin' right here. Shit!"

"Sure did." CJ stroked his chin thoughtfully. "So, here's what
we end up with the way I see it. Le Quan who's for sure some
kind of operative, or Margolin's battalion commander, Elliott
Cole, set up the killing mission. That gives us the who, the what,
and the why—even tells us who probably got paid for the job.
Problem is, it doesn't tell us who set the whole thing up, who
started the ball rolling, who came up with the idea." CJ found
himself staring at the wall.

"You thinkin' what I'm thinkin'?" asked Flora Jean. "That
somehow 'the Company' was involved?"

"Sure am. This whole thing has a CIA smell all over it. Who else besides those assholes, who don't give a shit about who the hell gets killed as long as the game's afoot, would okay a genocide mission?"

"Could be. Most of 'the Company' types I've known have been flat-out nuts."

CJ nodded knowingly. "And nuts make mistakes. Big ones!" His face suddenly lit up.

"Like?"

"Like getting their asses played like a fiddle by the North Vietnamese. Happens a lot when you're an arrogant SOB. Damn! I should've thought about this long before now."

"Mind lettin' me in on the news flash, sugar?"

"I didn't think about it until you started taking about nuts. I should've paid more attention to what you first told me about what Le Quan's job was with the Vietcong."

"You mean about Quan trainin' communist youth?"

"Yeah. And that's why Margolin could go on a mission to line his pocket and call it legit. If the men in his team thought they were really going after a bunch of youthful communist guerrillas instead of being used by the North Vietnamese to eliminate their growing cesspool of youthful *my den,* nobody would think twice about it."

"Damn, sugar! I think you might be right."

CJ reached in his vest pocket for a cheroot. "Now we've only got one thing left to pin down. Who's 'the Company' man that set everything up? And why did he finally have to eliminate Margolin?"

"Or woman?" said Flora Jean.

CJ struck a match against the back of his boot, eyed Flora Jean thoughtfully, and said, "Or offspring—and you're right!"

Chapter

35

AFTER FOLLOWING JIMMY MOC from his apartment building to a Wal-Mart, Le Quan's Shoe Tree, and finally the China Bay club, where he'd spent almost half an hour, Flora Jean now watched Moc at his latest stop, Riverfront Park, from the backseat of her SUV. She had slipped into the construction maze on Little Raven Street in the wake of flatbed tractor-trailers loaded down with thirty-six-inch sewer conduit. Now parked in the shadow of an eighteen-wheeler, she had a perfect view of the Riverfront Tower courtyard.

Moments earlier, Moc, dressed in drab gray repairman's coveralls complete with a nametag and sporting a matching gray cap, had slipped back behind the wheel of a white Econoline van parked near the rear entrance to Elliott Cole's Riverfront Tower building. Unaware of Flora Jean, Moc had gotten in and out of the van a couple of times. This trip, he'd made a point of rolling up the van's windows before getting on his cell phone.

Deciding it was time to apprise CJ of Moc's movements, Flora Jean made a cell-phone call of her own. Unable to reach CJ on his cell or at the office, she placed a call to Mavis.

Mavis answered, sounding as close to her old self as she had since being kidnapped.

"How ya doin', sugar? It's Flora Jean."

Mavis smiled. There was no way on earth she could possibly mistake Flora Jean's voice for anyone else's. "Pretty good. And you?"

"Fine for a broken-down marine."

Mavis chuckled, aware that Flora Jean, who still worked out three nights a week, was as fit as she'd been during her days in the corps.

"Any chance that street cowboy you're strung out over might be there?"

"He's sitting right here next to me." Handing CJ the phone, Mavis said, "Flora Jean."

Gripping a Negra Modelo and a taco chip pregnant with guacamole in one hand, CJ pressed the phone to the opposite ear. "What's up?"

"I'm workin', remember? Glommin' Jimmy Moc."

"Anything interesting?"

"The little worm likes to burn gas. He zigzagged his way across most of Little Vietnam. Stopped at Quan's place, and that China Bay club, before headin' downtown. Right now he's sittin' in a van just off the back entrance of one of them high-priced Riverfront Park buildings, talkin' on his cell phone."

Eyebrows arching, CJ set his beer down. "Is there a bunch of construction going on?"

"You bet. Eighteen-wheelers and sewer pipe everywhere."

"Damn! That little sucker's down at Elliott Cole's place—

Margolin's CO. He lives in the brick thirteen-story just off Little Raven Street. Wonder what Moc's doing there?"

"Beats me. But that's sure as hell the buildin' Moc's parked behind." Flora Jean inched down in her seat and eased the business end of her Bausch and Lomb field binocs just above the ledge of the window. "He's still in the van yappin' on the phone. Damn van looks like it's been in a war. One headlight's taped in with duct tape, the thing's missin' a grill, and one of the front fenders looks like somebody took a hammer to it."

"What color is it?" CJ asked excitedly.

"White."

"Fucker," said CJ, startling Mavis. "That little rodent tried to run me down the other night." CJ shot Mavis a reassuring glance. "Any sign of Cole?"

"Couldn't tell ya. Don't know what he looks like."

"Forgot. Hold on a second." There was a hint of guilt on his face. Cupping the phone's mouthpiece with one hand, CJ eyed Mavis. "Flora Jean's got a problem—I'm probably gonna have to run."

Recalling what Flora Jean and Carmen had said to her about relationships requiring give and take, Mavis squeezed CJ's hand, trying her best not to look judgmental. "Then you better go help her with it."

Caught off guard by the response, CJ said, "Yeah," before responding to Flora Jean. "I'll be there in ten minutes."

"I'll stay put, but you better hurry. I don't know where our worm will turn next."

Still holding his hand, Mavis squeezed as close to CJ as she could. "You didn't tell me somebody tried to run you down the other night."

"I didn't want you to worry. I thought it might have been Celeste."

"Please don't keep things like that from me, CJ. I'm doing okay."

CJ rose, pulled Mavis to him, and planted a kiss on her forehead. "I'll do better."

Returning the kiss, she ran a finger down CJ's cheek. "Flora Jean's waiting. You'd better go."

◆◆◆

Hoping to avoid a construction-site parking nightmare, CJ parked the Bel Air at Union Station, deciding that the fastest way to Riverfront Park was to walk the last two blocks of the 16th Street pedestrian mall and cross the Millennium Bridge. He'd just gotten out of the Bel Air when his cell phone went off. "Flora Jean?"

"No, it's Ginny Kearnes. Thought maybe we needed to share some information."

"Make it fast. I'm in the middle of something." He locked the Bel Air and headed toward the pedestrian mall walkway.

"I found out who did those stories on Jimmy Moc and his mother."

"Who?" said CJ, picking up his pace.

"It was Owen. Owen Brashears. That AP story from the *Denver Post*, the one we found in Peter's lockbox, is almost word for word from pieces he originally bylined in the *Fort Collins Coloradoan*. That means Owen has to know Jimmy Moc and his mother. Strange. Why would Peter save Owen's stories?"

"I don't know, but Brashears is in this thing up to his ear-lobes. Either he or Cole had Langston Blue's phony deserter citation printed up, and since Brashears had the easiest access to printing facilities, I'm putting my money on him."

"What are you talking about?"

Realizing suddenly that Kearnes knew only about the paper they'd found at Margolin's and not about the Langston Blue citation, he said, "I'll tell you later."

"Okay. Where are you?"

"I'm heading up the stairs on the downtown side of the Millennium Bridge."

"I'm five minutes away at the central library. Can you stay put?"

Realizing that in his rush to back up Flora Jean, he'd just told Kearnes something he shouldn't have, CJ said, "Hey, don't." But before he could finish, Kearnes hung up.

"Shit!" CJ pocketed his cell phone and gritted his teeth, hoping that Kearnes wasn't on her way to try and find him. Easing his right hand into the pocket of his windbreaker, he patted the Beretta 9-mm he'd slipped there, prepared for the worst. He wasn't sure whether Brashears or Cole had killed Peter Margolin, but everything was weighing heavily in favor of Brashears. What didn't make sense was why Margolin had kept the paper and the clippings all these years.

As he reached the west end of the bridge's broad cantilevered deck, he glanced over his shoulder toward the sparkling twilight downtown skyline before beginning the descent into Riverfront Park. He was halfway down the parkside steps when the answer to the lockbox question hit him. He smiled, recognizing that the bridge between the old and the new Denver had been the catalyst. All along his thinking had incorrectly been mired in the 1970s, when Peter Margolin had been another Johnny-comes-marching-home, lost-war nobody just like him. Now, close to thirty-five years later, Margolin had been on the threshold of becoming Colorado's next senator. A senator who needed an insurance policy against a war crime he'd spearheaded coming back to bite him.

It made sense, CJ told himself, still smiling. Margolin had had a game plan all along. That was why he'd stashed Blue all those years, why he'd rat-holed a slightly slow-on-the-uptake, vulnerable, and malleable West Virginian country boy who would, with a little coaching, be there for him if Margolin ever needed a tincture of exoneration. And why he'd kept newspaper clippings and the paper that Blue's phony citation had been printed on. They were all insurance policies against a compliant Owen Brashears coming back on him. It made sense all right; now he just had to prove it.

◆◆◆

Elliott Cole handed Owen Brashears the whiskey sour he'd requested as they gazed out of Cole's great-room window toward the downtown Denver skyline, enjoying the full breadth of the queen city's presunset beauty.

"Got a bull by the horns here now," said Cole, soaking up the grandeur. "Cow town one day, metropolis the next. Problem is, you never know where it'll end. Sooner or later we'll just be another LA." He eyed Brashears. "But hell, I don't need to tell a newspaperman that, do I? Take a load off." He patted the seat cushion of a nearby chair, nodded for Brashears to be seated, and sat down facing him in the chair's twin.

"Big city, big problems." Brashears sat down, took a sip of his drink, and nudged the briefcase he'd come in with next to the chair. "Construction everywhere. I had to park on the downtown side of the bridge and walk over."

Cole nodded. "Like I said, big problems, big stakes. A lot like in elections. There's a ton involved if you expect to win—having a strategy, working the issues, or dodging them, and of course pressing the flesh."

"And money."

Cole smiled and took a sip of his gin and tonic. "No argument there, and that pretty much brings me full circle and back to the question I've been asking myself all day. Why on earth does Owen Brashears have a hard-on for us Republicans? And you do, sticking it to us with those *Boulder Daily Camera* pieces of yours. I know you're carrying a torch for your buddy Margolin, but he's out of the race. Think you'd be better off just reporting the news."

Sounding as if he'd saved up what he was about to say for a long time, Brashears responded, "Then I'd miss out on being an insider again, and believe me, I can't afford that."

"Am I missing something here?"

"Nope. Just stating fact."

"Mind telling me what you missed out on, son?"

"Missed out on getting what was due to me more than thirty years ago at Song Ve."

"You're talking in circles. Song Ve doesn't have a damn thing to do with this election."

"Afraid it does. You'd know that if you spent more time talking to your partners."

"Get to the point, Brashears."

"Glad to. You and Peter earned a lot of money for your role in that little scrimmage at Song Ve. And you eventually parlayed it into the war chest he needed for a Senate run and a healthy down payment on a seventy-five-million-dollar building."

"You're delirious."

"Not even close."

Cole sat up in his chair, all pretense of stonewalling gone. "Listen, you mud-slinging piece of shit. You got your chance to look into what happened at Song Ve thirty-five years ago. *Stars and Stripes* sent you digging and you came up with nothing. You're selling yesterday's news. And ain't nobody listening."

Brashears laughed. "You're a blockhead, Cole. Peter always said you had tunnel vision."

"You're testing my limits, and trust me, you don't want to do that."

"No. I was the one who got tested, or should I say screwed. Ten thousand paltry dollars and a pat on the back for running my puff *it didn't happen* piece in *Stars and Stripes* thirty-five years ago. What did you and Peter get? Bet it was closer to a million. Had to be. You had two stupid-ass governments chipping in to the kitty. A pack of North Vietnamese racists believing they were eliminating their ethnic contamination problem, and Uncle Sam thinking he was nipping communism in the bud by paying off a Vietcong bullshitter named Le Quan to finger a school full of innocent kids. I bet all Quan got was ten thousand too."

"So what's your point, asshole? That you were too stupid to get more money? That was then and this is now. Print whatever the hell you want about me or Song Ve. History doesn't mean one goddamn thing to anybody but the people who lived it, and most of today's voters don't give a shit about Vietnam. Run your fucking editorials. We'll still win."

"You myopic fool. I don't care what happened at Song Ve, or what the hell happens with this election. I want my share of what I should've gotten three decades ago. I ran those pieces in the *Camera* to try and get your attention. Looks like they grabbed the wrong side of your brain."

Cole burst into laughter. "So sue me, but if you think you're gonna strong-arm me, you're crazy."

"You better start seeing things my way, Mr. Party Chairman. That *Stars and Stripes* piece I did wasn't an accident."

"Meaning?"

"Meaning you're in over your head, friend. That piece I did was part of mop-up duty."

"What the fuck are you talking about?"

The hint of a smile formed at the corner of Brashears's lips. "You really don't get it, do you, Colonel? Guess I'll draw it for you in the sand. Who do you think set the whole Song Ve thing up? Negotiated with Le Quan, came up with the money, designed the mission? It certainly wasn't the U.S. Army, and God knows it wasn't you."

Looking puzzled, Cole said, "Get to the point."

"'The Company,' as in CIA, you idiot. And their conduit was me."

Cole shook his head. "You were CIA? Bullshit."

"Funny, about a year ago I got the same response from Peter. Just after I learned from a local informant I'd known for years that Le Quan was involved in a seventy-five-million-dollar building project in the Golden Triangle. In fact, during the war the informant's mother was my North Vietnamese intermediary to Quan. You and Peter knew Quan, of course, and I'm guessing the two of you had to let him in on your Golden Triangle deal or else no Senate seat. In fact, I bet that's why Peter was so opposed to the Vietnamese boat people resettlement in the 1980s. Nobody with something to hide wants a bad penny like Quan showing up on their doorstep."

"So what the shit do you want?"

"I want to be cut in. Paid what I should've gotten thirty-five years ago."

Cole laughed and pulled his pants pockets inside out. "Sounds to me like you got took."

Brashears nodded. "Back then, I was dumb enough to believe Peter when he told me that the payday for everyone involved was a flat ten thousand. Nobody plays the fool better than a friend. I was twenty-one, straight out of college, fluent in Chinese, Vietnamese, and French, and naive. 'The Company' gave me a glamour job. I got to mug in front of the camera, write fictitious stories, and spend weeks in Saigon on R&R. And I was stupid enough to believe in just causes, God, and country."

"But you took the ten thousand," said Cole, his tone unsympathetic.

Brashears's response was incisive. "I don't know what Quan's share in that building is, but one equal to his seems fair enough."

"Can't help you there. Afraid you'll have to take that up with the people handling Margolin's estate."

"I think you can. Carve it out of your percentage, or you can give me cash."

"And what if I refuse?"

Steely-eyed, Brashears stared Cole down. "I'm no longer twenty-one, stupid, or naive. And for what it's worth, the CIA likes to see a return on every investment. After Vietnam 'the Company' spent a lot of time honing my skills. Try squeezing me out again and you'll end up taking the same one-way trip that I helped Peter and his worthless flunky Lincoln Cortez take."

"You're nuts."

"No. Just trained to eliminate problems and out to get what's rightfully mine."

"Try the office of Social Services. Now get the hell outta here, you double-dealing fucker."

Brashears smiled. "I'd think the offer over, Colonel. It's the best one you'll get. The price goes up from here. Consider yourself lucky that tonight I had a change of heart. I decided it would be unfair of me to make demands of you without giving you time for consideration. I called that informant I mentioned, a man who does freelance work for me, and told him there'd be no need to kill you tonight, that I was giving you time to think my offer over." Brashears stood, hefted the heavily weighted briefcase, and headed toward the door, leaving Cole looking mystified. As he stepped out into the hallway, he looked back and smiled. "I'll give you a couple of days to make your decision. I'm sure it'll be one that's in both our best interests," he said, turning and heading down the hall.

◆◆◆

Except for a lone teenaged skateboarder who was peering into a shop window on the opposite side of the Riverfront Park plaza from CJ, it was too early for the youthful want-to-be-seen crowd that frequented the plaza's trendy Japanese restaurant to be out. The plaza shops had closed, and the high-rise condos and lofts above them had swallowed their owners for the evening. CJ scanned the plaza thoroughly before moving beneath the protective overhang of the Riverfront Park property sales office to call Flora Jean. "I'm on the north side of the plaza in front of the property sales office," he whispered into his cell phone. Looking west toward Little Raven Street and the construction, he added, "I can see the nose of your SUV. Whatta ya got?"

"Got movement. Moc's out of his van. Wait. Some guy just came out of the building's back entrance. Moc waved him to the van. He's gettin' in."

"What's he look like?"

"Plain vanilla. White, blond, forty-five plus. He's wearin' a blazer, dark slacks, and he's carryin' a briefcase."

CJ shrugged. "Could be anybody."

"He and Moc are still in the van. Wait a minute—they both got out." Flora Jean paused. "Moc's got the rear doors to the van open. The other guy's lookin' around inside. Shit! He's lookin' straight in my direction. Didn't see me. He took some-thin' out of the van and slipped it into his jacket pocket."

"The right or left one?" asked CJ.

"Left. He's shakin' Moc's hand. He's movin'. He's headed your way, straight for the plaza."

"Keep Moc there, no matter what. I'll check out your brief-case guy."

"Gotcha," said Flora Jean, storing her cell phone. She flipped open the leather-bound day planner on the seat next to her, eyed the 9-mm Walther inside, flipped the planner closed, and, clutching it, got out of the SUV.

When he saw Owen Brashears round the northwest corner of the Riverfront Tower building, CJ thought he was hallucinat-ing. He didn't know why he had expected to see someone else, especially since he had spent the last fifteen minutes convincing himself that Brashears was Peter Margolin's killer. Quelling the urge to second-guess himself, he intercepted the briskly walking Brashears just before he reached the Millennium Bridge's park-side steps.

"Beautiful day, don't you think?" asked CJ, startling Brash-ears as he approached from behind.

Caught off guard, all Brashears said was, "Yes."

CJ eyed Brashears's briefcase, "Down here in the Platte Valley on business?"

"Yes."

"With Elliott Cole, I take it." CJ nodded toward Cole's building.

Brashears started up the bridge's forty-seven west-facing steps. "Don't think my business is any of yours, Mr. Floyd."

Following him, CJ feigned disappointment. "But we're Vietnam comrades. Why not? You were a *Stars and Stripes* reporter during the war, right?"

Brashears responded with a grunt.

"Ever do any stories about what happened at Song Ve?"

They were halfway up the bridge steps. The tapered steel mast came fully into view. "Get out of my face, Floyd."

"You must've done some Pulitzer Prize–level writing in order to keep Song Ve out of the news, and of course to save everybody's bacon: yours, Margolin's, Cole's."

"Don't know what the hell you're talking about."

"Let me connect the dots for you. The ones that go from you to Jimmy Moc, to Margolin, to Cole, and more than likely from you to the CIA."

A quarter of a stride ahead of CJ, Brashears flinched, just barely but perceptibly as they started across the bridge deck. "Crawl back in your hole, Floyd. You've got your nose where it doesn't belong." Brashears rubbed three fingers of his left hand together as if in anticipation.

His eyes glued on Brashears, CJ slipped a hand into the pocket of his windbreaker as two kids carrying skateboards raced by. "Tell you what. Reach for what's in the left pocket of your jacket and you'll be the one they'll be measuring for a hole." CJ fingered the 9-mm's trigger.

Brashears said, "You're either brave as hell or flat-out stupid, Floyd," as they reached the halfway point of the bridge. "And you just stepped in a pile of shit you're never gonna be able to clean off."

Neither of them heard the sound of the motorcycle rev to a start behind them nor saw it burst from the shadow of an eighteen-wheeler. But they both heard the roar of the Red Special AMC sport cycle as it fireballed its way up the Millennium Bridge steps toward them. Within seconds the bike was on top of them. The helmeted rider raced past, firing two shots. One bullet pierced CJ's left calf as the bike bounded down the bridge's city-side staircase, leaving CJ yelling and clutching his leg, 9-mm in hand. He tried to draw a bead on their assailant, but to no avail.

Brashears raced for the safety of the elevator that buttressed the towering mast at the east end of the bridge as the bike's rider, now a half block down the 16th Street pedestrian mall, spun around and headed back toward them.

Safely inside the elevator, Brashears collected his thoughts and worked out a game plan in his head for dealing with the cycle rider. He pulled Moc's .45 out of his briefcase and pushed the button for the ground floor. In a crouch, briefcase shielding him, gun at the ready, he watched people racing down the mall toward Union Station as the elevator doors opened. The riderless bike was lying in the middle of the pedestrian mall less than twenty feet from him. The sounds of people screaming and the high-pitched screech of a police siren masked the sound of a light-rail train approaching Union Station.

Squinting into the twilight as he duck-walked his way out of the elevator at street level, Brashears never saw the sport-cycle rider leap from behind the elevator shaft. He didn't have time to aim the .45. All he felt as he lost his balance was the weight of someone shoving him from behind as he fell forward into the path of the oncoming commuter train. A single shot from Moc's .45 sailed skyward. Brashears's body slammed into the lead car and the crunch of his bones echoed up from the rails as the train's wheels ground over him.

The braking train wheels screeched in synchrony with the roar of the sport cycle restarting. Within seconds the rider was streaming up the stairs of the bridge, zooming past CJ, who had crawled to the safety of the elevator at the mastless parkside end of the bridge. The sport cycle sliced past him at 50 mph and the three shots that CJ got off just before the rider bounded down the Millennium Bridge steps and sped into the lengthening shadows of night all missed their mark.

Chapter

36

ONE OF TWO PARAMEDICS attending to CJ, a slender black man with a goatee, adjusted the IV in CJ's left arm while his partner, a rotund, freckle-faced man wearing wrinkled scrubs, bifocals, and a Chicago Cubs baseball cap, worked on CJ's left leg. The man in the baseball cap slipped a tissue retractor out of the crash bag at his feet and used it to elevate the bacon-strip-sized piece of loose flesh dangling from CJ's upper calf.

"You're lucky, buddy. A few inches higher and we're into your popliteal artery."

"Bad?" asked CJ, quivering, two points on the good side of turning shocky and fading.

The paramedic nodded. "Bad." He glanced at his partner. "Whatta ya got pulse and pressure wise, Terry?"

"Ninety over fifty and thready."

"I'll have him plugged up good enough for the ride to Denver Health in a couple of seconds." He looked at CJ. "You doin' okay, buddy?"

CJ nodded without answering. His head felt swollen, his stomach woozy.

"Better pop the collapsible and get ready to ball it," said the man in the baseball cap. "I don't wanna risk popping a line when we do our transfer and move him down that elevator."

The goateed paramedic stepped away briefly, returning within seconds with the collapsible stretcher he'd brought up the elevator with him earlier. "Ready to roll him."

As the paramedic in the baseball cap rose to a squat, Wendall Newburn was suddenly at his side. He flashed his badge, eyed the east and west ends of the bridge deck, where uniformed patrolmen now blocked access to the bridge, and said, "Need to ask your injury here a couple of questions."

The paramedic eyed the lieutenant's bar that was pinned to the bottom of the wallet just beneath Newburn's badge. "You'll have to make it quick, Lieutenant. We need to roll."

Newburn nodded and took a knee. "What happened, Floyd?"

Puzzled by Newburn's appearance, CJ shook his head. "Some guy on a motorcycle didn't like my looks."

"Did you get a look at him?"

"No way; he was moving too fast. Both times. Funny thing, though. On his second pass his tires couldn't have been more than a few feet from my nose. The only thing I'm certain is, he was haulin' ass, he was dressed in black, and believe it or not, he was wearing wingtips. Go ask Brashears. He might've gotten a better look."

"Could be he did, but he won't be talkin'. Motorcycle man shoved him in front of a train. Got a skateboarder who saw the whole thing."

The paramedic in the baseball cap held up his hand to stop the questioning. "We gotta roll, Lieutenant."

"Okay." Newburn eyed CJ suspiciously. "This got anything to do with Margolin or Langston Blue?"

CJ nodded.

"Figures."

The paramedics were seconds from rolling CJ to the bridge's west-end elevator when Flora Jean raced up. Rolling her eyes at Newburn, she said, "You better tell them fraternity brothers of yours down there doin' crowd control to learn some respect. The next time one of 'em puts their hands on me, when I ain't said shit to 'em or even looked like I wanted to move this way, I'll deck the SOB. If it hadn't been for me knowin' somebody, they wouldn't've let me by." She grabbed CJ's hand and squeezed it. "You okay, sugar?"

"Wouldn't want to try and walk a straight line right now, but I'm hanging in."

"You're pushin' it, Benson. This is a crime scene."

Ignoring Newburn, Flora Jean said, "I'll call Mavis."

CJ nodded as everything around him suddenly began to spin. Finally able to recall why Flora Jean was there, he said, "What about Moc?"

She smiled. "Got him tied up with bungee cords and stashed in the back of his van." Looking at Newburn as if he were a garden pest, she asked, "By the way, Newburn, how the hell did you get here so fast?"

Newburn looked past her without answering, toward his partner, Donny Levine, and a beefy patrolman who had pulled perimeter duty at the west end of the bridge. Ginny Kearnes stood a few feet away from them, looking dazed and confused, unaware that for the last half day she'd had a Denver plainclothes patrol unit watching her every move.

"Who the hell have you got tied up, Benson?"

Flora Jean said, stretching the truth, "A possible witness. Didn't want him to run away." Smiling, she added, "A citizen has to help our men in blue any way they can."

The goateed paramedic shouted, "Hey, both of you, can it! I've got an injured man here." He started rolling CJ away.

Flora Jean planted a kiss on CJ's cheek. "See you later."

"Later, yeah," said CJ, feeling as if he'd been kicked in the head.

Flora Jean and Newburn watched the paramedics roll CJ into the elevator and come out at street level on the pedestrian mall extension. They slipped him into a waiting ambulance and, moments later, ambulance lights flashing, sirens blaring, they sped off into the fading light.

Relieved that CJ was okay, Flora Jean slipped out her cell phone to call Mavis. She had dialed half the number when Newburn said, "Time for you to move outside my crime-scene perimeter, Benson. Make your call when you're off this bridge."

"You're an angel, Lieutenant," Flora Jean said sarcastically.

Reminding her that he was in charge, Newburn asked, "Where's your hostage?"

"He ain't no hostage, and he's parked behind Riverfront Tower in his van."

"Better hope this guy shares your story, Benson. Otherwise, you'll have a hell of a lot of explaining to do."

"Oh, he will." She walked away, certain that Moc would say

whatever it took to keep from being tied to a shooting and a murder.

Newburn watched Flora Jean start down the steps of the bridge and slip out of sight before he turned to go back to continue the conversation he had been having earlier with his partner, Donny Levine, and Ginny Kearnes. "It won't be hard to keep tabs on Floyd," said Newburn, walking up to them. "He'll be pullin' hospital duty for a while."

"Who was the woman?" asked Levine.

"Floyd's partner, Flora Jean Benson," said Newburn.

"How much does she know?"

"Guaranteed, at least as much as him."

Newburn turned his attention to Kearnes. "You were saying that Floyd knows as much about Brashears's involvement in the Margolin murder as you?"

"More, probably."

"I see. One thing for sure, we'll have plenty of time to find out. And we'll talk to Cole, of course. Guess for right now that's about it."

"Do you need me for anything else, Lieutenant?" asked Kearnes.

Newburn shook his head. "Nope. For the time being I need to concentrate on a man on a motorcycle."

"Then can I go?"

"Yes, but count on it, we'll be in touch."

Still shaking as she had been for the past twenty minutes, Kearnes turned and walked away.

"I'm going back down to take a look at where Brashears met

his maker," Newburn announced to Levine as Kearnes headed for Little Raven Street and disappeared into the near darkness.

Newburn took the stairs down to street level, where Owen Brashears's body lay covered by a tarp. The light-rail car that had hit him, its headlights dimmed, sat looking forlorn a few feet away. A few yards away from Newburn, the plainclothes officer who'd been talking to the train's visibly shaken engineer knelt to take a look at Brashears's mutilated body, which was jack-knifed into an awkward "V." Brashears's spine had been severed, his neck broken, and the skin on his forehead sheared to the bone.

"Tough way to buy it," said Newburn.

The other officer nodded without answering.

Newburn stood and eyed the light-rail tracks as they curved their way north and into Union Station. He and the plainclothes man followed the tracks east as they paralleled the pedestrian mall to the spot where the teenaged skateboarder had said the man on the motorcycle had dismounted. After shoving Brashears into the path of the train, the killer would have had a ten-yard sprint back to the bike, an easy enough task if he had known the train was coming, tougher if he had been leaving things to chance.

Newburn turned, stared back toward the light-rail car, its headlights aimed straight at him, and said to the silent plainclothesman, "Looks like the killer got lucky. He was probably planning on a little target practice from his bike but saw the train coming and decided to send Brashears to his reward another way."

"Worked," said the plainclothesman.

"Like a charm," said Newburn, his eyes focused once again on the headlight of the train's lead car. "Like a charm."

Chapter

37

Epilogue

THE SWEET AROMA of late-August Colorado Western Slope tree-ripe peaches filled the afternoon air as CJ, Mavis, and Flora Jean made their way across the grassy half-acre stretch of land that separated Ket Tran's Palisade, Colorado, farmhouse from the twenty-acre Colorado River Valley peach orchard that spread out behind it.

Wearing two-inch heels and a dark tailored pantsuit, Flora Jean stood nearly as tall as CJ. With the hint of a limp, and buttered to the nines in a black linen suit, CJ was locked arm in arm with Mavis, who was having far less trouble negotiating the soft grass than Flora Jean. "You're lookin' mighty fine, Ms. Sundee," he said, eyeing Mavis, who was dressed in a figure-flattering silk dress that seemed to float with each stride.

"The same to you, Mr. Floyd," she said, laughing.

In front of them, ten rows of white lacquered chairs flanked a red carpeted aisle that led to the flower-draped altar where

Carmen Nguyen and Walker Rios would be married. Half of the seventy-five guests who'd been invited to the outdoor wedding were already seated. The baby-faced man greeting guests smiled at Flora Jean, who towered over him by a head. "Friends of the bride or groom?"

"Both, sugar."

"Guess you can sit anywhere, then," he said, looking startled.

For CJ, Mavis, and Flora Jean, the last of July and most of August had been a blur. After spending two days in the hospital with a gunshot wound and a nicked popliteal artery, CJ had spiked a fever and had spent another week in the hospital in bad spirits, battling an infection and jousting daily with Wendall Newburn. Newburn had finally backed off, satisfied that Owen Brashears had killed Peter Margolin and assured by both Flora Jean and Alden Grace that the CIA had probably eliminated Brashears as a potential high-risk problem, but CJ still wasn't sure. What he did know was that, as his Uncle Ike used to say, "The truth behind a story ain't whether it's factual but whether anybody listenin' is buyin' what you say." And there weren't many people buying the idea that the U.S. intelligence community hadn't somehow been involved in the murder of Owen Brashears. The idea of a disgruntled motorcycle gang member, gang-bangers, or a transient, floated by Beltway intelligence control early on in the Owen Brashears murder investigation, had gone the way of the dodo bird after the news media had picked the suppositions apart and public opinion had weighed in with a verdict that the government explanations were bullshit. Even Wendall Newburn now discounted those stories.

As they walked to their seats, a half-dozen heads turned to greet them. Thanks to Paul Grimes's four-part Vietnam War investigative series in the *Rocky Mountain News*, "Buried Secrets: A Story of American and North Vietnamese Assisted Genocide During Vietnam," the story of Carmen, Ket, and Langston Blue had been on the front pages of every major newspaper in the country, along with their photographs and sidebars on CJ, Flora Jean, Owen Brashears, Peter Margolin, Le Quan, and the entire Star 1 team.

Blue's story hadn't been lost on the tiny peach-growing village of Palisade or its larger neighbor ten miles to the west, Grand Junction. A week earlier the *Grand Junction Daily Sentinel* had run a three-page story featuring peach orchard owner Ket Tran, her brother-in-law, Langston Blue, and her niece, local St. Mary's Hospital oncologist Carmen Nguyen. A barrage of local and regional TV coverage had made the three of them, people who had prided themselves on enjoying a low-profile life, stand out like swollen appendages.

After a few whispers and nods, the curious returned to their conversations.

"Heels are death in grass," Flora Jean complained, slipping off her shoes as she, CJ, and Mavis took their seats.

They had just gotten comfortable when a balding man in front of Mavis turned and said, "I'm Wally Fears. Grow peaches just down the road here. Aren't you the lawyer that represented Carmen's father?"

"No," said Mavis. "That would be Julie Madrid."

"Sorry, but you sure look like her to me. Anyway, she must be one heck of a lawyer gettin' Blue off so quick like that."

"She sure is." Mavis winked at CJ, aware that desertion charges against Blue had been dropped partly on the strength of Julie's legal skills, but they'd also evaporated because of potential high-level political fallout. The Pentagon brass were so interested in quelling a groundswell of charges from Congress and the media that centered on the army's involvement in a massacre-for-pay scheme at Song Ve that they couldn't move fast enough to exonerate the only man who'd been there who was still alive. A man who was not only one of their own, and a decorated sergeant who'd refused to obey an unlawful order, but also a man who could point his finger at a bona fide bogeyman: the CIA.

CJ shook his head and smiled, thinking that after a month and a half of front-page coverage, Mavis was nearly as adept at fielding a question about Langston Blue as he and Flora Jean.

CJ adjusted himself in a seat that was sinking rapidly into the soft grass. "What's the problem?" asked Flora Jean, smiling. "Weddings make you nervous?" She glanced at the engagement ring CJ had given Mavis six days earlier and broke into a snicker. "If I was you, sugar, I'd be watchin' this show for pointers." Flora Jean winked at Mavis.

Ket Tran moved up the row to greet them. Dressed in traditional Vietnamese marriage-ceremony red and yellow, she looked younger than CJ remembered, and her eyes were just as penetrating.

"See about everyone's made it." She hugged them one by one.

"Except Julie and Alden." Flora Jean looked disappointed that only she was missing her man. "They're both back east."

Ket slipped into the chair next to CJ. "I saw you walk in. It looks like you're moving pretty good."

"Better than I was five weeks ago. Body's on the mend, but my mind's pretty much mush from all the media hype. Hear you've had the same thing over here."

"Pretty much," Ket said hesitantly. "Do you mind if I ask you something?"

"Ask away."

"What do you think will happen to Jimmy Moc?"

"It won't be good. From what I hear, Newburn, the cop who initially wanted Blue's hide, found Moc's fingerprints on a cane inside the oil drum Lincoln Cortez's body was found in. They found the same kind of drum in the back of his van the night I got shot. The cops think he and Brashears were planning on supplying Elliott Cole with a new home inside the drum, the same way they had for Cortez. Moc hasn't admitted to anything, but Julie says that in the end he will. Claims that in the long run he'll be glad to exchange the death penalty for fifty or sixty years."

There was sadness in Ket's eyes. "All those unfortunate children at Song Ve. Moc or Carmen could've been one of them. Vietnamese is such a beautiful language and *my den* is such an ugly word. It's hard to believe what people are capable of during war."

"Money and politics, they twist things backward inside us human beings," said CJ.

"Ain't no question about it," Flora Jean chimed in. "Cost Margolin and Brashears their lives—Moc the rest of what would've been his. Outed Cole and Quan, and nearly got Cole killed. It'll cost him an election and damn sure end his career. Seems to me like the only folks left standin' are that motorcycle-ridin' 'Company' man who tried to take you out—and Blue."

"And Ginny Kearnes," said CJ, sympathetically. "It must be hell to pay knowing that Margolin's best friend killed him."

Ket nodded, looking worried. "Any chance they'll come after Blue?"

Flora Jean's answer was quick. "Nope. 'The Company's' got too many skeletons in too many closets in this one. And one just might come clankin' out on somebody at the top. Trust me, I been there—the CIA prefers anonymity; they don't never wanna be the lead story on the nightly news." She looked at CJ. "And that means you ain't gonna find out who your shooter was or who pushed Brashears in front of that train. I worked that street, sugar. You might as well tell folks you got shot by a ghost. No question, some CIA operative wearin' wingtips got the okay to pop your ass. If he got you, fine, if he didn't, okay. Brashears was the real target, and as far as 'the Company's' concerned the business is finished."

CJ wanted to believe Flora Jean; after all, she knew the lay of the land. But he had the feeling that in spite of all the media hype, the Paul Grimes *Rocky Mountain News* exposé, endless interviews and interrogations, the army's sudden change of heart about Blue, and the very convenient death of the man who'd killed Cortez and Margolin, he still really didn't know which way was up when it came to Song Ve. And it haunted him. But what haunted him more was the uneasy feeling that the man on the motorcycle, the man wearing wingtips and dressed in black, didn't care one bit about the truth. What had happened at Song Ve might have partially been the result of Margolin's and Cole's greed, coalescing with the agenda of a bunch of nut-ball racists from North Vietnam, but they weren't the ones who were trying to make history disappear. It was the U.S. intelligence community that was at the heart of that disappearing act. And unfortunately, like cancer, in the thirty-five years since Song Ve, the ugliness of that crime had metastasized instead of becoming an endangered species.

"He won't be getting shot at anymore," Mavis said emphatically. "As of next week, CJ Floyd is out of the bail-bonding business."

Ket looked surprised, aware of what it was that made men like CJ Floyd tick. "Big change."

"I'm up for it. So's Flora Jean. Three days from now she's the big cheese."

"You'll do great," said Ket.

"Hope so, but I've never run my own business before," said Flora Jean.

"You'll do fine," said CJ. "Besides, I'll be there a day a week for the first six months."

Ket smiled. "It'll be sort of like Langston learning how to live outside a West Virginia hollow," she said, watching the tuxedo-garbed Langston Blue limp toward them.

Beaming as he made his way down the row of chairs, he looked every bit the proud father of the bride. "Glad you're all here to help us pull the trigger on this thing." He draped an arm over Ket's shoulder. "Just wish Mimm could see it."

"She will—through Carmen's eyes," said Ket.

Blue looped his other arm over CJ's shoulder. "Got my daughter, got Ket, even got a life to live. I owe you and Flora Jean big time, CJ."

CJ smiled. "Remember that the next time you need that special Western antique."

"Or a bail-bonding service," Flora Jean chimed in.

Blue grinned. "I'll do that."

Ket eyed her watch. "You better head back up to the house, Langston. It's almost time to walk your daughter down the aisle."

"See you in a few," said Blue, barely limping as he walked away, looking as if he'd been practicing disguising the limp for one last important trip.

Realizing that nearly every seat around them had been taken, CJ asked, "Where's Rios?"

"Up there in front." Flora Jean pointed toward a line of peach trees. "Behind that first peach tree. See his head pokin' out?"

CJ nodded.

"It's a wedding, you know. The groom ain't allowed to see the bride until she does her thing." Flora Jean flashed her former captain the high sign. Rios responded by blowing her a kiss as the minister moved front and center to start the ceremony.

By the time the pianist was three notes into "Here Comes the Bride," everyone was standing. CJ caught his first glimpse of Carmen before she was two steps down the aisle. She was dressed in white silk pants, a *khan dong* adorned in an elegant gold pattern, and an ankle-length gold silk cloak embroidered with gold chrysanthemums and red accents. She looked to CJ as if she belonged in some imperial palace.

Mavis squeezed CJ's hand tightly as Carmen walked by.

Thinking to himself that he and Mavis would be next, he looked past Carmen toward the surrounding cliffs and into the ice-blue Colorado sky, oblivious to the fact that perched above the property on the surrounding desolate cliffs, a woman was watching the wedding ceremony unfold through binoculars. An Acoma Indian woman with a slim swimmer's figure who was dressed in loose-fitting pants and a matching gunmetal gray blouse. A once-again youthful-looking, exquisitely beautiful woman named Celeste Deepstream who had a score to settle with Denver antique dealer CJ Floyd.

About the Author

Photo by Elizabeth Gorman

ROBERT GREER lives in Denver where he is a practicing surgical pathologist, research scientist, and professor of pathology and medicine at the University of Colorado Health Sciences Center. He edits *The High Plains Literary Review* and reviews books for KUVO, a Denver NPR affiliate. Learn more about Robert Greer at www.robertgreerbooks.com.